Linda Jaivin is a novelist, playwright, essayist, a writer on Chinese society and culture, and a literary translator (from Chinese). She lives in Sydney.

a most immoral woman

A NOVEL

LINDA JAIVIN

FOURTH ESTATE • *London, New York, Sydney* and *Auckland*

Fourth Estate

An imprint of HarperCollins*Publishers*

First published in Australia in 2009
by HarperCollins*Publishers* Australia Pty Limited
ABN 36 009 913 517
www.harpercollins.com.au

HarperCollins*Publishers*

25 Ryde Road, Pymble, Sydney, NSW 2073, Australia
31 View Road, Glenfield, Auckland 0627, New Zealand
1–A, Hamilton House, Connaught Place, New Delhi – 110 001, India
77–85 Fulham Palace Road, London, W6 8JB, United Kingdom
2 Bloor Street East, 20th floor, Toronto, Ontario M4W 1A8, Canada
10 East 53rd Street, New York NY 10022, USA

National Library of Australia Cataloguing-in-Publication data:

Jaivin, Linda –
  A most immoral woman / Linda Jaivin.
  Pymble, NSW: HarperCollins, 2009.
  ISBN 978 0 7322 8276 9 (pbk.)
A823.3

Cover design by Nada Backovic Designs
Cover images: photograph of Mae Ruth Perkins © California Historical Society, FN-36610;
flower and butterfly © Fine Art Photographic Library/CORBIS; pear tree © Keren Su/CORBIS
Author photograph © Andrzej Liguz/moreimages.net
Internal design by Alicia Freile
Typeset in 11/18 Galliard by Kirby Jones
Printed and bound in Australia by Griffin Press
70gsm Bulky Book Ivory used by HarperCollins*Publishers* is a natural, recyclable product made
from wood grown in sustainable forests. The manufacturing processes conform to the
environmental regulations in the country of origin, New Zealand.

5 4 3 2 1   09 10 11 12

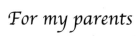

For my parents

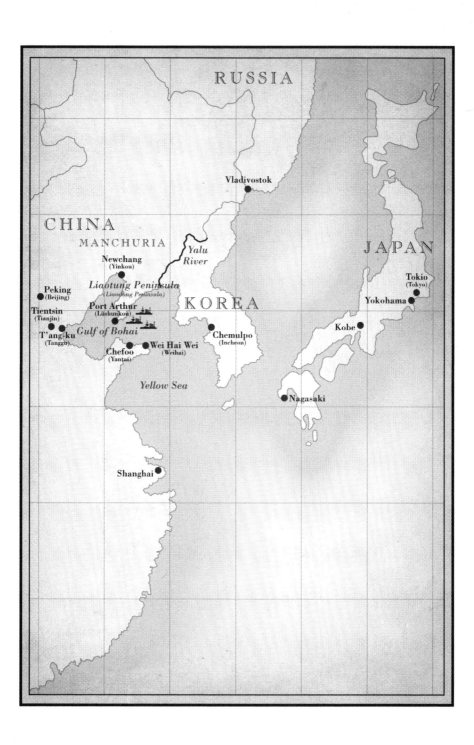

a most
immoral woman

In Which, Following a Useless Day, Our Hero Finds Himself Irresistibly Drawn to Trouble

The ravishing Miss Perkins, eyes luminous, unfurled her sultry smile. 'The famous Dr Morrison,' she purred. 'We meet at last.'

The day had not begun with so much promise. George Ernest Morrison had awoken in a second-rate hotel in the Manchurian town of Newchang, oppressed by a thick, cotton-wadded quilt and a sense of futility. The whistle and crack of whip birds in a sun-drenched dream of the Antipodes resolved into the hard smack of a crop on a horse's flank, and the crunch of eucalyptus bark underfoot gave way to the clatter of cart wheels on cobblestones. Morrison blinked open his eyes. His rheumatism frisked in the cold; he scissored his aching legs under the covers. Through the window he saw that the sky lay low and gunmetal grey. It was the last day of February, 1904.

A donkey brayed. A child cried. A man swore softly. Morrison lifted his head, still heavy with sleep, and listened. Even after seven years of living in China, his Mandarin was not perfect. But it did not take linguistic genius to comprehend profanity or despair. The first refugees, he guessed, of the war.

The Russo-Japanese War had broken out three weeks earlier when Japan's navy staged a surprise attack on the Russian fleet at Port Arthur, the deep-water port on the tip of Manchuria's Liaotung Peninsula. The news had delighted Morrison. As the China correspondent for *The Times* of London and a loyal colonial, George Ernest Morrison was convinced that it was in Britannia's interests to see its ally Japan chase the Russians out of northern China. In his telegrams for *The Times* he had agitated at length to sway world opinion in favour of the Japanese cause.

Since the war had taken off, however, Morrison's life had unexpectedly ground into stasis. Months before, he had written to his editor in London, Moberly Bell, to say he was thinking of leaving China on account of poor health. His complaints, which he did not hesitate to enumerate, included arthritis, a persistent catarrh, and occasional nasal haemorrhages due to a spear wound that had nearly killed him when he had attempted to tramp across Papua New Guinea as a young man. So when the war — *his* war — had finally broken out, Bell assigned other men to cover the conflict and ordered Morrison to remain in Peking. There he could help the other correspondents and cover the big picture without further endangering his health — or employment. How Morrison regretted the querulous moment of nose-bleeding, joint-aching weakness that had prompted his complaint to Bell.

Bored, Morrison had broken away from Peking to come to Newchang, a neutral port on the northwestern corner of the contested peninsula, hoping to find information and excitement. After two days he'd found little of either, only too many Russian soldiers and the perfidious British profiteers who supplied them with coal and arms.

Morrison threw off the fusty quilt and stretched. His long legs were cramped from the effort of sleeping in a bed made for a much shorter man. It was a familiar problem and one he considered a metaphor for his life of late.

He cleared his throat and called out for his Boy.

Even at this hour, Morrison's voice rang resonant and muscular. Pepita, Spanish señorita and his lover when he had worked as a surgeon in the mines of Rio Tinto, once told him that it was the voice of a matador. The description pleased him. For several years after Morrison left Spain, Pepita had proclaimed her undying love in purple ink on perfumed paper. He only ever answered the first letter. He hadn't thought about Pepita in recent times but in his mind's eye he now saw black, fragrant hair swinging over a supple waist; slender forearms; brown, eager nipples. As much as he tried, he could not remember her face except in parts: a flash of smile, an arched eyebrow.

At forty-two, Morrison was old enough to know how quickly red-hot passion could turn to ash, but still young enough to find it astonishing. Pepita had captured his affection not long after he recovered it from Noelle, a Parisian grisette who had escaped not only with his heart but his money and pride as well. There had been women before them, of course, and many since. His most recent affair, with the wife of a British customs official from Wei Hai Wei, had been of a relatively calm and cynical nature. He had not experienced feral attachment in a long while.

Pepita. Sweet Pepita.

The door squeaked open. It was not the time to think about Pepita.

Morrison watched Kuan, his Boy, move about the room, stoking the fire and refreshing the wash basin with hot water. Kuan laid out his master's clothes and gave them a quick brush, his movements an economical blend of grace and efficiency. Morrison took comfort in the familiar sound of Kuan's felt-soled shoes padding over the carpets, and the swish and rustle of his quilted robes. He liked his servant; Kuan was clever, curious and resourceful, his English more than competent. Morrison wondered sometimes where Kuan's life might have led if he had not been a foundling raised by missionaries to serve in foreign homes. He marvelled, not for the first time, at the young man's inborn poise and dignity. Sometimes he felt like a clumsy giant in comparison.

'Kuan. Go outside and learn what you can from the refugees, especially those from Port Arthur. What they've seen — number of Russian and Japanese ships, type of guns, how many supply wagons, how many dead. Whatever they can tell you.'

'*Ming pai.* I understand.' Kuan quickly finished setting out his master's razor, strop and flannel. His long plait had been coiled around his neck for warmth and convenience whilst he performed his chores. Now that he was going out, Kuan unwound it so that it hung straight and proper down the back of his long robe. 'Oh,' he added, 'Colonel Dumas is already at breakfast.'

Morrison acknowledged this with a nod. Charles Merewether Dumas, a British military attaché whose job, not unlike his own, was to gather intelligence, was Morrison's friend and travelling companion. 'Tell him I'll be down shortly.'

Scraping the light ginger stubble from his chin, Morrison noticed that the once proud lines of his jaw were softening. Though his complexion was still the colour of the sun and sand of his native land, grey was starting to pepper his beard and temples. Less than a month had passed since his forty-second birthday, yet his neck, like his waist, was already beginning to thicken. Morrison caught his own gaze in the looking glass. It was pale and merciless.

'You're looking chipper this morning,' Dumas observed as Morrison joined his table in the breakfast room.

'I don't feel chipper,' Morrison replied, 'so it's quite remarkable that you should say so. In truth, I was feeling rather downspirited. As I regarded my figure in the looking glass, I concluded that although I remain a bachelor, I'm fast acquiring the body of a married man.'

Dumas laughed.

Morrison narrowed his eyes reproachfully. 'I'm pleased to have so amused you — even if it is at the expense of my own pride.' He surveyed the menu, feigning annoyance.

'I wasn't laughing at you. In fact, I'd assumed that my own rather teapot-like physique was the basis for your observation about married men. I'm only two years your senior and wedded but ten, yet I'm an exemplar in this regard.' Dumas twirled the tip of his moustache around his finger; he had magnificently luxuriant whiskers and a habit of playing with them as though they were a small and attention-starved pet. 'You ought to know that my wife says that of all the Western men in China, you are still the most handsome. She is not promiscuous with her compliments, either. Handsome is certainly not a word she has ever used in relation to my good self. You really do need to find yourself a wife.'

'Now you sound like Kuan. He insists that 1904, being the Year of the Dragon, is propitious for marriage. But you both forget one crucial detail. I have no prospects. Your own wife appears to be my only admirer, and she is taken.'

'That is a matter for debate,' Dumas replied with a doleful expression. 'But seriously, I cannot credit for a moment that you would have any difficulty finding a wife if you really wanted one. *The* Dr Morrison. Hero of the Siege of Peking. Renowned overlander, author, medical doctor, eminent China correspondent of *The Times* of London. Respected, influential, etcetera, etcetera.'

'You're mocking me.'

'Not at all. I should think eligible maidens would be queuing up.'

'Piffle. I'm a man of restricted means and poor health. The only maidens who ever show any fondness for me are elderly rejects with yearnings and false teeth — the sort who suffer from indigestion and clammy hands and feet.'

Dumas chortled. 'That is not what I hear, and you do not believe a word of it, either. On the basis of the stories you've told me yourself, I believe that you have made more conquests than Britannia. Were you not relating a most amusing story about a Brunhilde to me just a few months ago?'

'I have never gone with a woman called Brunhilde.'

'Yet there was a German actress whose private performances you enjoyed with astonishing frequency over a period of two days whilst her dunderhead of a husband conducted his business in the same city. Melbourne, wasn't it?'

'Her name was Agneth. And it was Sydney. But your power of recall is otherwise frightening. Remind me never to tell you anything I do not myself wish to remember. The point is, of all these women, not one still shares my bed. Those whom I found most amusing always returned to their husbands in the end. The others turned out to be boring and spiritless — a pity, for they were the only ones guaranteed not to turn into faithless neurotics after marriage. To be perfectly honest, I would not mind a steady supply of affection and sympathy in my life. It does not, however, appear to be forthcoming from available sources.'

'Oscar Wilde once said — and nothing in my own experience would disprove it — that marriage is the triumph of imagination over intelligence. Maybe you just need to apply less intelligence and more imagination to your prospects.'

Morrison regarded the plate that the waiter placed before him. 'Do you think these are duck eggs?'

'No, just the eggs of very small chickens. It's wartime.'

'The war only broke out two weeks ago. Hardly enough time to affect the growth of chickens.' He pushed aside his plate. The subject of marriage pained him more than he let on. He extracted his fob chain from the pocket of his waistcoat and checked the time. 'We'd better hurry. We are nearly late for our first useless appointments of the day.'

'Remind me,' the soldier-diplomat sighed. 'My excellent memory does not extend quite as well to our shared professional concerns.'

'I am to see a Japanese who will treat me with the utmost courtesy but who will tell me nothing. You will call on an uncivil Russian who will share with you all manner of intelligence as interesting as it is mendacious. Following that, we will both meet a Chinese who will, with great anxiety, ask *us* what is going on in the war being fought by the other two over the northern portion of his own country. Then Kuan will convey to us the unreliable testimony of excitable refugees. Finally, having been denied permission to go to the front by our Japanese friends, we will catch a train back to China proper, stopping at Mountain-Sea Pass for the night. Along the way, we will exchange notes and ruminate on the futility of it all. I shall wonder what I can possibly write in my telegram for *The Times* and you will contemplate, with equal despair, your report to the Foreign Office.'

The morning's activities transpired as Morrison had predicted. By early afternoon, the correspondent, the military attaché and the servant stood on the platform at Newchang Station. Morrison's nose burned with cold and his toes ached numbly inside his thick woollen socks and leather boots. The saturnine sky began to dissolve into snow just as a whistle announced the train's arrival.

The journey took most of the afternoon. The men read aloud from their notebooks: missionaries were withdrawing their womenfolk from the peninsula; Russian troops had threatened to torch an entire town if the Chinese army, which had arrived to protect the frightened residents, did not leave immediately; two hundred and ninety-eight mines set by Russians and Japanese to blow up one another's armadas were adrift in open water, threatening shipping.

'A stupid day,' Morrison summed up, 'spent in the accumulation of petty detail.'

Dumas grimaced. 'What will you focus on in your telegram?'

'It hardly matters. Whatever I write, those peace lovers in Printing House Square will indubitably temper it before publication.' Morrison knew that it was not just out of consideration for his health that Bell had given the task of reporting on the war to other correspondents. His editor was wary of his partisanship. Japan might be an ally of Britain, but Britain's official stance was neutral and Bell was determined to see *The Times*'s coverage reflect that.

By the time the train pulled into the old garrison town of Mountain-Sea Pass at the eastern terminus of the Great Wall, the men were fatigued into companionable silence and the sun had set on an undulating white landscape.

Outside the station, a row of flickering lanterns indicated the presence of ricksha men. As the train disgorged its passengers, the runners jumped to their feet, shaking out their legs and shouting for custom. A Japanese invention, the ricksha had taken off in China where the press of more than four hundred million people in a parlous economy made men cheaper than horses. Now Kuan was trying to procure three of them for even less still.

At last the three men were bouncing along on the thinly padded seats towards their hotel outside the walls of the Chinese town, rough blankets tucked around their knees for warmth. Morrison glanced over at his companions. The lanterns swinging at their feet illuminated their faces from below like characters from a ghost story and captured his runner's breath as a long, thin cloud. The runners' felt boots, bound with rope for traction, slapped the frozen ground. Icicles hung from the curlicue limbs of a scholar tree and a dog barked beside a gloomy farmhouse. Ahead, the full moon was rising over the crenellated parapets of the Great Wall. If Morrison were a different sort of person, he might have remarked that the night seemed full of poetry, mystery and magic. But his mind was filled with more prosaic thoughts of war, dinner and the prospect of a good night's sleep.

The runners came to a balletic halt on bent knees at the entrance to the Six Kingdoms Hotel, a neat, relatively new, two-storey brick building with a front veranda gaudily painted green, blue, red and gold in the Chinese style.

Dumas raised one eyebrow as he surveyed the façade. 'Like a marriage of military barracks and Chinese temple.'

'What I like about it,' said Morrison, clambering out of the ricksha, 'is that the exterior exclaims, "You are in the Extreme Orient," whilst the interior whispers, "You can still relax like a European." And I, for one, am most assuredly looking forward to that.'

Once they'd checked in, Morrison threw his swag on the bed and made a note of his reluctant tip to the hotel boy as well as the money spent on rickshas. (As the son of a Scottish schoolmaster who'd gone to the Antipodes after what he called 'a run of bad luck in the mother country', Morrison had inherited a seemingly unshakeable sense of financial insecurity and the habit of counting pennies.) He then quickly sponged off the dust of the journey and changed into fresh clothes. Collecting Dumas from his room, he strolled with him down to the modest dining room.

As the maître d' busied himself accommodating a large and fussy party of German engineers, Morrison looked around with mild curiosity and low expectations. The room hummed with polyglot conversation punctuated by the clink of silver on porcelain. A warm fug of wood fire with notes of roast meat and port filled his nostrils. At linen-covered tables set in the Western manner were seated missionaries, military attachés, railway men, traders in arms and supplies, dull men and their bony wives — the usual crowd, with one heart-stopping exception. *Now here,* Morrison thought, *is excitement!*

Seated at one of the tables was a young woman of exceptional allure, whose eyes flashed with both mischief and promise, and whose style suggested that she had just stepped off Fifth Avenue or the Champs-Elysées, not some dusty street in north China. Morrison did not know enough of couture to recognise that her outfit was a confection of Worth's of Paris. But it did not take a student of the fashion plate to observe how stylish were the lines of her dress, how rich were its fabrics and how eloquently they hugged her curvaceous body. Similarly, Morrison was mesmerised by the glitter and grace of her lively hands despite it being lost on him that her rings were fabricated by Lalique. She radiated sex and money. He was drawn, sailor to siren, moth to flame.

Tearing his eyes off her, he turned to Dumas. 'Who is this?' he whispered, each syllable a compendium of wonder.

Dumas stroked his moustache and bit his lip. 'This,' he stated, 'is Trouble.'

'I fear I am much drawn to Trouble.'

'I think Trouble has noticed. She was just looking at you. Ah, she has looked away again. Perhaps Trouble is not drawn to you, after all.'

'Trouble is always drawn to me. Women are another thing. Do you know her?'

'Actually I do.' Dumas's answer was slow, cautious. 'She stays in Tientsin.'

'Tell me all.'

'Her name is Miss Mae Ruth Perkins. She's had all of Tientsin aflutter since her arrival some weeks ago. She is the daughter of the self-made millionaire, shipping magnate and US senator from California, George Clement Perkins, previously governor of that Wild Western State.'

Millionaire? Senator? Be still my beating heart! 'Pray tell, what is such a precious gem doing so far from its setting?'

'One rumour is that she has come to China to escape scandal. Others say she has come to create it. The missionaries are hiding their daughters. Young Faith Biddle has reportedly already thrown over the Kingdom of God for the worship of Miss Perkins, causing her parents no end of consternation.'

'Where does she stay?'

'With the American consul.'

'Ragsdale?' Morrison made a face. 'That's like a brass mount for a diamond.'

'Indeed. But I'm sure you've heard that as the publisher of the Sonoma County *Daily Republican*, Ragsdale obtained his post, and his escape from a howling pack of creditors stretching from Iowa to the west coast, thanks to a Party connection. That connection was apparently Miss Perkins's father. And so Mrs Ragsdale has the interesting duty of acting as the young lady's chaperone. That is her now at Miss Perkins's table.'

'So it is.' Morrison had not registered Mrs Ragsdale's presence. Although not quite fifty, Mrs Ragsdale had the unsexed appearance of a woman who had been married and thence neglected for a span of centuries. Whilst some women would have struggled against such a fate, Effie Ragsdale appeared to embrace it as Destiny.

'Will you introduce me?'

'To Mrs Ragsdale? With pleasure,' Dumas replied dryly.

At their approach, Miss Perkins looked up. 'The famous Dr Morrison. We meet at last.'

In Which Is Noted the Difficulty of Overheating a Room in North China in Winter

Morrison was still fumbling for a reply to Miss Perkins's greeting when Mrs Ragsdale, laying plump hand on ample bosom, effused in a voice notably less burdened by gravity than either her chin or chest that it was a great, no, the greatest, honour to encounter the esteemed Dr Morrison at such an outpost. Morrison, she informed Miss Perkins, was the most brilliant, the most famous, the most respectable of men. As she spoke, Mrs Ragsdale inflated with nervous excitement, as though with a noble gas. Morrison grew mildly concerned that she might burst.

Mrs Ragsdale flapped on in this manner until Morrison, sinking into his boots, began to wish she really *would* burst. A vision from a London dinner party once held in his honour came suddenly into his head. His hosts had been so mindful of the esteem in which he was held that, as he later recorded in his journal: *they seated me next to a grim old duchess long past the climacteric whilst a beautifully bosomed woman of lax morality languished at the other end of the table*. Respectability was well and good, but it had its place. He would not have endured Mrs Ragsdale's ballyhoo were it not for the ravishing creature with the chatoyant eyes seated at her side. 'You are too kind,' he insisted over and over, as if his words, stacked high enough, might dam the flow of her own.

Finally Miss Perkins spoke up in a voice like warm chocolate. 'I have heard much about you, Dr Morrison, even before tonight. You are a most celebrated man. Many have spoken to me of your great heroism four years ago during the Siege of Peking by the Boxer rebels. They say you rescued Mrs Squiers and Polly Condit Smith from the Western Hills and saved many hundreds of Christian converts when the Boxers laid siege to the cathedral. They say you were the bravest of all the men there.'

'It's true I did go to check on the American minister's wife and her guest in the Western Hills. I was trying to figure out how to convey them, three children and some forty servants back to the city and into the Legation Quarter, or at least fortify the balcony of their holiday home, when Mr Squiers arrived with a Cossack loaned to him by the Russian minister. So I cannot take sole credit. Were we not between us heavily armed, I may not have accomplished my mission. As for the converts, had I abandoned them I'd have been ashamed to call myself a white man.'

Miss Perkins's eyes sparkled. Mrs Ragsdale clasped her hands to her breast. Her own husband had distinguished himself during the Boxers' xenophobic and murderous rampage by writing a maudlin letter to the besieged in Peking telling them that he'd had a dream in which they'd all perished. The letter and Ragsdale himself were roundly maligned. News of a dispatch of US Marines was what they craved, not an outpouring of sentiment. Morrison had heard that Mrs Ragsdale was mortified when she learned that her husband had managed, once again, to become a laughingstock.

'What an extraordinary experience it must have been,' murmured Miss Perkins.

'As we should probably only meet with one siege in a lifetime,' Morrison replied, his eyes glued to her own, 'it was just as well to have a good one whilst we were about it.'

Miss Perkins laughed merrily. Mrs Ragsdale looked askance at her.

'The Boxers were very fierce,' reproved the older woman. 'They killed many people. It was no joke at the time.'

'True,' Morrison said. 'But they were little more than rabble, coolies and laundrymen. They'd been whipped into a frenzy by rumours that Christian missionaries were feeding on Chinese orphans' blood and that the foreign churches had caused drought by bottling up the rain in the sky. Old Napoleon could have settled them before lunch with a whiff of grapeshot. It was the soldiers of the Imperial Court standing behind them who worried us more. You might say the Empress Dowager was the Boxers' true leader. Which occasionally worked to our advantage.'

'Really?' Miss Perkins leaned forward and rested her chin on her hand in a most fetching manner. 'How so?'

'For instance, when they started shelling the cathedral, the Old Buddha — that's what she's called — was picnicking at the North Lake behind the Forbidden City, not far from there. The gunfire was giving her a headache. So she ordered a halt to the firing. As much as it proved her connection to the whole business, we were grateful for the respite. It gave us our chance to rescue the converts.'

Miss Perkins shook her head. 'How complex these politics are! It's no wonder that all the world relies on your reports to understand the Chinese situation, Dr Morrison. I don't know how many times I've said to my friends Mr Egan and Mr Holdsworth that if they failed to introduce us at the earliest possible opportunity I should be most horribly cross with them. Martin —

Mr Egan — lent me the book you wrote about your overland journey from Shanghai to Burma. It was wonderful. So I feel like I know you already. I do admire your wit and courage. Not another man I have met here would undertake such a journey alone. And I've heard it was this book that led to *The Times* appointing you as their China correspondent.'

Morrison felt a blush, that congenital curse of the fair-skinned, spread across his cheeks. He'd always envied the American readiness to catch a compliment and keep it. Personally, he was hardly averse to flattering remarks. But there was something deep in his Australian soul that caused him to squirm under their impact. Besides, to hear such blandishments coming from a mouth as kissable as Miss Perkins's was disconcerting. It was he who ought to be complimenting her, but he couldn't do so now without seeming reflexive or disingenuous.

'And so it was,' she continued, 'that when I was in Peking a few weeks back, I asked Mr Jameson to invite you to a luncheon he hosted for me. I was crestfallen when you sent word that you could not attend.' Her eyelashes batted a Morse code of disappointment.

Morrison was filled with horror. C.D. Jameson, a tedious, rum-soaked old duffer and long-term resident of Peking who dabbled in commerce, mining and journalism, was forever inviting him around. Morrison routinely sent his regrets. He had a few more of those now. 'If he had only informed me of your presence and told me of your request,' he said, 'I could hardly have refused.'

'Mr Jameson assured me he told you.' She widened her eyes.

'I am so terribly sorry. I do not recall ...' *That confirmed masturbator*, Morrison thought, certain that Jameson had never

16

mentioned anything about a Miss Perkins. But he knew that it wasn't the time to go into Jameson's perfidies, which were myriad.

'Mr Jameson explained what a very busy man you are, Dr Morrison, so please don't trouble yourself about it. Oh, goodness!' A look of sweet concern came over her face. 'You've gone quite red. Perhaps the dining room is a trifle overheated.'

It was impossible to overheat any room in north China in winter. Morrison could feel the maddening blush spreading to his ears. He extracted his handkerchief from his pocket and patted his forehead.

'Mae, dear,' Mrs Ragsdale admonished, 'Dr Morrison has more important things on his mind than meeting young ladies.'

'No, no, not at all,' Morrison rushed to say, plunging himself back into a sea of awkwardness.

Mrs Ragsdale, oblivious to both his discomfort and the fact the conversation had moved forward, took up her panegyric afresh. 'Mae, dear, you may not know this but when it was believed that Dr Morrison had died in the siege, *The Times* published a most beautiful obituary. A magnificent tribute.' Her eyes misted over.

'And what was even better, he was alive to enjoy it,' Dumas chortled.

Miss Perkins giggled. 'What did it say?'

'Oh, I can't recall the exact words,' Morrison demurred. In truth, he could have recited then by heart. *No newspaper ... has ever had a more devoted, a more fearless, and a more able servant than Dr Morrison ... he was characteristic of the best type of Colonial Englishman ...* 'It did rather distress my parents, and I understand the good citizens in my hometown of Geelong lowered their flags to half mast. But, just as your Mark Twain once more famously remarked, the report of my death had been greatly exaggerated.

Like him, I am apparently still enjoying ruddy good health in the afterlife, if this be it.'

Miss Perkins's laughter was musical.

Perhaps this is the afterlife. Heaven would have such angels.

The maître d', masking impatience under an equable smile, took advantage of the pause in conversation to inform the gentlemen that their table was ready.

Reluctantly, Morrison followed Dumas and the maître d' into what already felt like a kind of exile.

He had only just taken his chair, however, when he jumped up again. He rushed back over to the ladies' table and stammered out a suggestion that they all take coffee together in the drawing room after dinner.

'That would be most agreeable,' Miss Perkins said with the kind of smile that showed she saw straight through him.

In Which the Number of Courses in a Western Meal Passes Without Remark and Miss Perkins Demonstrates One Way to Eat a Boiled Pheasant

Once they had given their orders to the waiter, Dumas leaned in towards Morrison. 'Eminently squeezable that one. And not a false tooth or clammy hand in sight.'

'She thinks me self-important,' Morrison replied gloomily. 'And so I acted. I could kick myself for mentioning the flags of Geelong flying at half mast. All that Hero of the Siege business doesn't help either. I might as well go a-courting with the medals I received from Queen Victoria.'

'Young men woo with charm, energy and looks. Older ones woo with their wealth or, if that is lacking, their accomplishments.'

'I don't find that very reassuring.'

Dumas shrugged. 'I believe she likes you. Perhaps you have prospects for the Year of the Dragon after all.'

'Tosh. Even if that were true, I could hardly afford to keep an heiress.'

'That's the good thing about heiresses. They keep themselves. If you will not have her, perhaps I will. Not that she noticed me. When I spoke up just then, she looked over as though trying to remember who I was.' Dumas made mournful eyes at his champagne and then tipped it down his throat.

'I thought you learned your lesson. Your wife, if I recall correctly, has only just agreed to return to you.'

Dumas grimaced. 'I must watch my step. I am rarely allowed to forget the high position my father-in-law holds in the Foreign Office. My wife is currently threatening to have him return us to India, despite being well aware that I am in the toils of the native money-lenders there. But with regards to the tasty Miss Perkins, a man can dream, can he not?'

'Feel free,' replied Morrison, affecting indifference. 'I myself am neither a dreamer nor a poet.'

'Though,' Dumas pointed out, 'you dress like one. With your soft collars and all.'

'This conversation has degenerated from gossip to fashion. Before we mutate into a pair of old hens, I move that we discuss something of more pressing import. The number of Japanese troops surging up the Korean peninsula towards the Yalu River, for example.'

'Granger says —'

'Granger?' Morrison exclaimed, so piqued he forgot entirely about the ravishing young lady at the other table. 'That little dwarf's a deuced fool. He has managed to get closer to the action than any of my newspaper's other correspondents and yet every sentence he writes is of dubious veracity. He admitted that the information about troop movements conveyed in his last telegram was gleaned from a Chinese carter. Next he will be reporting the gossip of ricksha pullers. What's more, he echoes whatever the Russians tell him; he will swallow any wild claim so long as it is washed down with enough vodka. I have had to field complaints from the Japanese Legation. They know I am *The Times*'s senior correspondent and so they blame me for his telegrams.'

'And yet,' Dumas noted, 'as we saw again this morning, our Japanese friends are not entirely forthcoming either.'

'Indeed. They have obliged us with a war but not with any worthwhile information about its progress.'

'The Japanese tell *you* more than they tell anyone else; of that, at least, I am certain.'

'Sparse comfort.'

Dumas snapped his fingers. 'I forgot to mention that the Japanese consul in Tientsin claimed to me that his army had already sunk fifty Russian ships off Port Arthur.'

Morrison shook his head. 'I doubt it. The entire Russian fleet consists of only seventeen vessels.'

'Surely not.'

'The part that is not tied up in the Baltic Sea awaiting the thaw, most assuredly so.'

Dumas popped a sugared almond into his mouth and chewed. 'Granger. Is he really a dwarf?'

Morrison shrugged. 'He's short.'

Dumas barked with laughter. 'And you're tall. Henceforth I will call you a giant.' Reading his companion's expression, he added hastily, 'Which, of course, you are.'

'Making sense of this war requires background and experience,' Morrison grumbled. 'The motley collection of roustabouts whom my editor has hired as war correspondents have neither. They have spent most of their time, as far as I can see, re-creating naval battles in bars up and down the China coast, sinking a battleship with every beer. Those who've actually made it to Port Arthur spend most of their time investigating the syphilitic marvels of

Maud's Brothel. The rest are still in a complete cloud as to where Port Arthur even is. One old veteran, Tulloch, recently landed in Chefoo, on the Shantung Peninsula, armed to the teeth and mistaking the treaty port for the front! We're lucky he didn't fire on the British officers' mess. And yet *The Times* has made the decision to anchor me to Peking to act as an exchange clerk for these incompetents and their dispatches. It is incomprehensible.' Morrison neglected to mention that his employer's decision had been, at least partly, in response to his own belly-aching on the subject of his health. 'I have told Bell that I really must see some action myself, and not to send any more men.'

'You are most severe in your judgment of others. It makes me quite fear to leave the room. You may have wondered why you find me sticking so doggedly by your side.'

'Clever chap, Dumas. I have never thought otherwise. But you of all people should know that I reserve my harshest judgment for myself.'

'Don't we all?' Dumas's expression grew serious. 'I did wish to ask your opinion on something. I know that in all your telegrams and public statements you are sanguine about an early victory for Japan. But aren't you worried that if the war drags on, Britain, as an ally of Japan, might be dragged into the conflict? As you know, the Boer War depleted our military resources. My superiors fear that should the Russians be defeated in Manchuria —'

'Which they will be …'

'— the Tsar may invade Afghanistan and upset the balance of power on the subcontinent.'

'Balderdash. You might as well say that if the Japanese succeed in displacing the Russian sphere of influence in Manchuria, they will go on to occupy all of north China.'

'Perhaps not. But surely, following victory, Japan could possibly grow to rival Britain in commerce. People are saying —'

'People will say anything.'

Dumas bowed his head to the pigeon-egg soup.

Morrison regretted his brusqueness. 'I don't need to tell you that of course. You are no fool.'

Dumas, heartened, drew his hand over his beard, which rained crumbs.

Morrison grew aware of a sensation on his cheek like the tickle of sunshine. Out of the corner of his eye, he looked towards the ladies' table. With a prick of disappointment, he allowed that he might have been mistaken. Miss Perkins appeared absorbed in her conversation with her chaperone.

The waiters removed the men's soup bowls and placed before them anchovy on toast, broiled chicken and salad *à la Russe*.

Over at the ladies' table, Miss Perkins rearranged her skirts. One fashionably narrow boot peeped out from under her hem. Whether it had been revealed by accident or design was a question that taxed Morrison. He imagined a pale foot, smooth toes, a delicate but firm arch, finely turned ankles.

He wrenched his attention back to Dumas. 'I am glad that we came,' he insisted in a tone that implied his companion had suggested otherwise. 'It is poor work sitting in a drawing room in Peking whilst battles are raging in the neighbourhood.'

'Indeed,' Dumas concurred, patting his mouth with his napkin. 'Though I don't think you need to fear being accused of poor work as far as this war is concerned. You have done so much to advance the Japanese cause in the public mind that I've heard a number of people referring to the conflict as "Morrison's War".'

Morrison pretended to be surprised. 'Is that so?'

23

'You can't fool me.' Dumas watched the waiter top up their glasses before turning back to his friend. 'You're flattered.'

'It is not every man who has a war of his own,' Morrison conceded with a quicksilver smile.

Just then, Miss Perkins erupted in laughter. Morrison was stabbed by anguish. Had she overheard? *As if she does not already think me self-important enough.* But if she had been the least bit cognisant of the men's conversation, she gave no sign of it. He was torn between disappointment and consolation.

The waiter placed before the gentlemen a platter of cold baked ham with an accompaniment of tomatoes and candied yams. Across the room, the ladies were partaking of boiled pheasant.

Morrison's eyes met those of Miss Perkins. Holding his gaze, she speared a morsel of pheasant with her fork and conveyed it to her mouth. Fluttering her lashes and pursing her lips with a burlesque air, she inhaled the gamy scent of the meat, her bosom swelling over the line of her corset. As she exhaled, her throat, encircled in black ribbon, seemed to vibrate with pleasure. 'Mmm.'

She did not so much nibble as seduce the meat off the tines. Chewing slowly, she tipped her head back to let it slide down her throat. Her lovely round cheeks flushed and perspiration beaded her top lip.

Mrs Ragsdale observed her charge with palpable unease. 'Mae, dear, people are looking.' Her voice rang into the hush that had fallen over the room. Morrison, clearly, had not been her only audience.

Miss Perkins's astonishing reply, made after she had patted her glistening lips with her napkin, was thus heard by all. 'Yes. I suppose they are. I am so very glad I made an effort with my toilette.'

Dumas let out a squeak of laughter, which he parlayed into a cough.

'Mae!' gasped Mrs Ragsdale. She opened her mouth to say something else and then closed it, as though realising it was no use. Morrison felt he could almost see a homily wilting on her tongue.

'Quite a performance,' Dumas whispered.

Morrison was too lost in inner turmoil to reply.

The men's pudding arrived.

Not long after, the women finished their meal and passed out of the room, Miss Perkins with the air of an actress taking leave of her fans.

Swallowing down a final spoonful of tapioca and cream, Dumas patted the swollen mound of his stomach. 'If I lie down on the floor right now, I'd look like the Fourteenth Ming Tomb.'

'Raise the dead,' said Morrison. 'It is time to join the ladies.'

Dumas studied his companion for a moment. 'Is the great G.E. Morrison falling in love?' he asked.

'Love does not come into the equation, my dear Dumas.'

Morrison could be powerfully persuasive. He almost believed himself.

In Which We Find That Miss Perkins Shares Morrison's Missionary Position and, Following Talk of War, Geishas and Small Feet, a Form of Exercise Is Proposed

As they seated themselves by the hearth with their coffees, Dumas accidentally set Mrs Ragsdale off on an exposition on her health, alarming in its thoroughness. Her constitution was evidently more delicate than her sturdy architecture suggested. Miss Perkins, plainly familiar with the topic, nodded sympathetically but distantly, playing all the while with the ribbons on her skirt. She managed to appear both bored and charming.

The Victorian in Morrison found Mrs Ragsdale's catalogue of complaints vulgar. If he was also wont to dwell on his own indispositions, at least he did so in private — most of the time, anyway. But his focus was elsewhere. Much attracted to the maiden preening on the chaise before him, he feared that she considered him but some vainglorious and avuncular figure. To presume more might lead to the sort of humiliation that he did not need on a day that had begun with rheumatic pains and the discovery of incipient jowls. And yet there was that most interesting business with the pheasant. He could not help but wonder if there was a message there for him.

Just as Mrs Ragsdale blessedly ran out of steam on the subject of her maladies, an American missionary couple entered the drawing room and made a beeline for their party. Morrison's heart sank. He had taken tea in Reverend Nisbet's grim parlour soon after settling in Peking seven years earlier. He would never forget his first sight of the anaemic Mrs Nisbet, perched on a comfortless armchair underneath an engraving of *The Soul's Awakening* by James Sant. With an expression eerily parallel to that of Sant's rapture-stricken subject, and in a voice as thin as her own neck, she avowed that she had never felt the Lord so near to her as in China. She had urged Morrison to join their prayer meetings. Though he came from a God-fearing family and carried with him a thumbnail-sized book of psalms his sister had given him, Morrison was not enamoured of the Church. He had avoided the Nisbets ever since.

'We've been in the Philippines,' Mrs Nisbet announced in a flat, Midwestern voice. 'Awful place. Hot and pestilent. I don't know why we had to go acquiring it from Spain.'

Her husband concurred, reciting a litany of horrors. Amongst these was a lack of natural modesty and innocence in the native women, which, from his observation, was a common problem across the Extreme Orient.

The Nisbets found a sympathetic listener in Mrs Ragsdale. Back in California, Mr Ragsdale had been active in the anti-coolie movement. When an unsolved murder, in which a Chinese laundryman was a suspect, inflamed racial tensions in Sonoma County, he editorialised in *The Daily Republican* that the Chinese were a race that possessed 'neither conscience, mercy or human feeling', and was composed of 'monsters in human form, cunning and educated, therefore more dangerous and vile'. It had come as something of a shock to both Mr and Mrs Ragsdale to find that the road out of scandal and financial ruin in the US led them to China itself. To the Nisbets, Mrs Ragsdale now confessed that her experience of China had only deepened her natural suspicion not just of Chinese but of native cultures generally.

'They are so very, very far from Christendom and civilisation,' Reverend Nisbet agreed.

'Not to mention soap and carbolic,' interjected Mrs Nisbet. 'Despite all our efforts. You've been in China for years now, Dr Morrison, and have travelled widely in this region. Have you not also found it difficult living in heathen society for as long as you have?'

'I can't say that I have, Mrs Nisbet. I, myself, found Manila a highly civilised city. And whilst I confess I came to China possessed of the strong racial antipathy towards the Chinese common to my countrymen, that feeling has long since given way to one of lively sympathy, even gratitude. In spite of the Boxers. For the most part, I have experienced uniform kindness and hospitality from the Chinese, not to mention the most charming courtesy.'

Mrs Nisbet looked as though she was trying to smile through a mouthful of lemon juice. Reverend Nisbet studiously fumbled lumps of sugar into his coffee.

Miss Perkins, who had scarcely uttered a word in all this time, caught Morrison's eye. A complicit twinkle passed between them. Turning to the others, she said, 'I find what you say quite fascinating, Mrs Nisbet.'

Mrs Nisbet's eyes filled with dewy gratitude. Both Nisbets glowed devotionally at Miss Perkins. Like many who laboured in voluble service for the poor, the Nisbets lived in tacit awe of the rich.

'I, for one, *adore* native cultures,' Miss Perkins continued. 'They can be so clever. I think the Chinese are perfectly marvellous for inventing silk and gunpowder and printing, and for those lovely scrolls they do. In fact,' she said, pausing for effect, 'sometimes I think it would be wonderfully instructive to take a native husband.'

Reverend Nisbet had been sipping his coffee as Miss Perkins spoke. The quantity he did not instantly expel, he sucked down the wrong set of pipes. It took some muscular back-thumping on the part of the surprisingly strong Mrs Nisbet before he fully recovered.

Dumas let out another squeak, and both he and Morrison found themselves beset by minor fits of throat-clearing.

'Oh, Miss Perkins has such a sense of humour,' Mrs Ragsdale rushed to say, her smile tight. It was clear that, entrusted as she was with Miss Perkins's moral as well as material welfare, Mrs Ragsdale was near palpitations at the thought it could all end in miscegenation.

Morrison would have found such an outcome equally scandalous. But he believed that which Mrs Ragsdale only willed to be true: the maiden was having a joke. He told himself that he should never fear boredom in the company of one so audacious.

'Dr Morrison,' Miss Perkins said. 'You are so very knowledgeable about this fascinating country. I have many questions I would like to ask you. We two shall go sit over there by the window. That way, we will not bother the others, who, not being as interested in the topic, might find our conversation tedious.'

Moments later, her heels were clicking over the parquet in the direction of the window seat. Morrison, bowing a half-hearted apology to the others, followed post-haste.

As they seated themselves, he said, 'I fear I'm not that much of an expert, Miss Perkins. But what would you like to know?'

She leaned forward, smiling mischievously. 'Nothing really. I just wanted to escape that dull conversation and have you to myself. Goodness, but don't the missionaries speak badly of the natives!'

'You should hear how the natives speak of the missionaries.'

She laughed. 'You are not fond of missionaries either?'

She has a naughty giggle. 'It has been my observation that the primary effect of civilising by the missionaries is to make the natives of any country lying, fawning, cringing, deceitful and as bad as possible. The only time I ever found myself in agreement with the Empress Dowager was when she asked why missionaries didn't stay in their own countries and be useful to their own people.'

Miss Perkins's eyes filled with horror. 'Oh, but dear God, no! Then we should never be free of them. I don't think I would be able to take it. You know,' she said, glancing back at the Nisbets, 'Mrs Nisbet's irritation with the Philippines may stem from disappointment at not being sent somewhere like Africa, where she at least would have had the chance of seeing Reverend Nisbet boiled and eaten.'

Morrison chuckled. He had not expected such a wicked wit in one already so blessed with beauty and sensuality.

She leaned towards him, breasts straining against her bodice. 'Dullness is a terrible crime against society, don't you agree, Dr Morrison?'

'Certainly. And please, call me Ernest.'

'Then you must call me Mae.' She studied him for a moment and smiled wistfully. 'You remind me of someone, Ernest. Someone back home.'

'I hope it is someone you care for and not the opposite,' he said, awkward as a lad.

A cloud passed briefly over her eyes. 'I shall tell you about him another time.' She looked up again, her expression impenetrable.

Morrison simultaneously darkened at the thought of this mysterious other and brightened at the promise held out by her use of the future tense. He recalled Dumas mentioning something about a scandal. His imagination threw up several florid scenarios. All involved some version of a passionate deflowering and its aftermath. He concluded that this would not be a bad antecedent. To the contrary, it was ideal. The consequences of seducing the virgin daughter of an upstanding, wealthy and prominent family were not worth thinking about. *Oh pray God, do not let her be a virgin.* In the next instant, he berated himself for his presumption.

'A penny for your thoughts.'

Her eyes, he felt, were already unwrapping them. 'Oh, I was … I was just reflecting on the latest developments in the war.' *Pompous! Stupid!*

'I did not expect you to say that. But Martin — Mr Egan — has told me that you are a great booster of the Japanese cause.'

'That I am. The Japs won the Liaotung Peninsula fair and square in the Sino-Japanese War eight years ago. It was wrong for the Chinese to lease Port Arthur to the Russians.'

'Is it not their port to lease to whomever they like?' She shook her head. One curl came loose, momentarily mesmerising Morrison with its languid sway. 'I don't know much about it but I can't help feeling that war is rarely a good thing. If I hear of a ship sunk in battle, all I can think about are the poor sailors who sank with it.'

'Women are natural pacifists. But sometimes there's good reason for war. Your own President Roosevelt once said he's not

31

sensitive about killing, as long as the reason is adequate.' Her ears, he noticed, were exquisite — delicate shells the colour of cream.

'I know you are a brave and proven man, Dr Morrison — Ernest — so I don't mean this personally. But it has been my experience that it is normally men not themselves called to battle who maintain the most zealous appetite for war. I have known good, brave boys from the Mount Tamalpais Academy who burned with desire to serve their country as officers and gentlemen. Those who had the chance rarely returned with the same lustre about them. My own dear brother Fred nearly didn't come home at all from the Spanish-American War — and for what? For people like the Nisbets to go tormenting our new subjects with their dreary pieties?'

Here was a lively one! Morrison's last lover, the customs official's wife, had proven insufferably insipid when they finally got around to talking. It had not been an isolated experience, and went some way towards explaining his enduring bachelorhood. 'I admire the moral sentiment that drives your argument,' he said. 'Yet some wars are just and necessary. Your own Civil War, whilst brutal, did end slavery and maintain the unity of the nation.'

'True,' she said, her tone conciliatory. 'So the Russo-Japanese War would, in your opinion, be a righteous war?'

'Most definitely,' he answered with gusto. 'The British Empire has brought good governance and peace to backwards and downtrodden peoples wherever it has touched them. Japan's constitutional monarchy, which subscribes to the values of the Enlightenment, has similar ambitions.'

'You are very passionate about this.'

'Truth be told, if there had been no war, I would repine that my whole work in China had been a failure.' What had begun as a flirtatious conversation was in danger of turning into a political discourse, Morrison realised. In as jaunty a tone as he could muster, he added, 'Besides, if war failed to break out, I should hardly have known how to pass the winter.'

'Is that so?' she responded playfully, twirling the errant curl around one finger. 'I would have thought a man of your resources, and passion, could have found other diversions easily enough.'

Her expression, Morrison couldn't help but feel, suggested one or two. Yet perhaps he only hoped that was the case. He proceeded with care. 'So, what brings you to China, Miss ... Mae?'

'It's a long story. But I do adore travel for its own sake. It's most broadening. I know that you are a great traveller, too.'

'It's in my blood, actually. My family hails from Scotland's Outer Hebrides. Our clan badge is a piece of driftwood.'

She laughed. 'Travel is in my blood, as well. My papa made his first voyage as a twelve-year-old stowaway. Now, of course, he owns a shipping company. Our home in Oakland is full of maritime portraits. When I was little, I used to stare at the paintings of boats and imagine where I might go. I had the most darling little sailor suit. So I was very cross to learn that a girl couldn't be a sailor. It seemed terribly unfair. I am twenty-six now and have only just got over the injustice of it all.'

'So why China?' he asked, picturing her in her sailor suit.

'Well, I'd been to Europe.'

'That's it?' he teased. 'You'd been to Europe?'

The mysterious shadow passed over her features once more. Though it piqued his curiosity, she quickly recovered her natural ebullience.

'One cannot deny the allure of the Orient. I am quite mad for Japan, too. I've seen the *Mikado* three times. Yet I hadn't thought Japan to be such a popular destination until I sailed from Honolulu on the SS *Siberia* and Captain Tremaine Smith —'

'I know Tremaine Smith. Fine figure of a man.'

'Indeed.' She dimpled. 'Well, Tremaine … Captain Smith told me his ship is always packed to the gunwales with people who are crazy for Japan. All the men are in love with geishas, or at least the idea of them, and all the women want to become them, or so it seems. Captain Smith said to me,' and here she adopted the accent of a Liverpudlian, '"They all think they're about to disembark in the Town of Titipu!"'

She is very entertaining. 'I don't understand the frenzy over the geisha myself. Amongst other things, I find their habit of blackening their teeth with dye of powdered gall-nut and iron quite repellent.'

'And yet the idea of the geisha, who turns every aspect of being a woman into art and who may love freely, with neither limitation nor compunction, is so romantic. We have nothing like that in the West. It seems one can only be a good woman or a prostitute. I admit that I, too, have been in love with geishas since seeing the sublime Sada Yacco perform in San Francisco a few years ago.'

'I've heard of Sada Yacco. But I still think the Chinese woman is more fair to look at. And her lot is certainly better than that of her sisters in many other heathen countries.'

'Even taking into consideration those awful little bound feet of theirs?' Miss Perkins sounded incredulous.

'Most certainly.'

'Why, truly, do they do that? Bind their feet, I mean.'

It was a sexual thing, as far as Morrison knew. Feminists like Mrs Little of the Anti-Footbinding Society carried on about how the custom was intended to limit and control women's mobility. Morrison had heard more engaging stories from Confucian gentlemen about how the swaying walk of the bound-footed woman had the effect of multiplying the folds in their vaginas. He knew that Chinese men loved to play with 'three-inch golden lotuses', kissing, squeezing, licking and sucking on them. They even drank from wine cups placed in the little shoes. But it was hardly the sort of topic to raise with a young lady of recent acquaintance. 'It dates back to the Tang Dynasty, about a thousand years ago. There was a dancer beloved of the Emperor whose feet were naturally small. It became a fashion and then a custom. To have bound feet is considered evidence that a woman is respectable.'

'That's most intriguing,' replied Miss Perkins, putting a finger to her lips, which were beautifully shaped and impossibly rosy. 'And I'd always heard there was a sexual motivation.'

Morrison's heart stopped at the sound of the word 'sexual' coming from those lips. He felt himself colour. He convinced himself that he had misheard her. So tangled in thought was he that he failed to comment at all.

She shrugged. 'I would dearly love to have a pair of the little shoes as a souvenir, but I understand they are hard to come by.' She turned and lifted the heavy velvet curtain at the window. 'Oh my,' she said, standing. 'Look at this!'

Morrison hastened to her side. He felt both the chill of the night air through the glass and the heat of her body, so close to his own that they were almost touching. They gazed together at the new snow glittering like white jade in the moonlight. It was almost as bright as day. The ancient stones of the Great Wall glowed softly in the distance.

'That moonlight is enchanting.' Her eyes shone. 'Let's climb the Great Wall!'

'Now?'

'Why not?'

The heavy meal had excited his gout, and dyspepsia threatened. Thanks to his old spear wound, cold, dry air always put Morrison in danger of nosebleeds. The sensible part of him yearned for an early night and a warm bed. The sensible part of him was not in the ascendant. 'Marvellous idea,' Morrison said. 'Splendid.'

By then, the Reverend and Mrs Nisbet, needing a lie-down after the near-fatal choking incident brought on by Miss Perkins's shocking suggestion, had scuttled off to bed. Dumas, lulled by the combined exertions of digestion and conversation, was scratching at his beard and suppressing yawns. When Miss Perkins revealed the plan, Mrs Ragsdale drew a sharp breath. 'It's terribly late, dear. The ground will be most treacherous.'

'Oh, please, Mrs R.!' Mae pouted, squeezing her chaperone's hand and pecking at her cheek.

The sight of those innocent kisses made Morrison feel weak. He plied his friend with a gaze both meaningful and apologetic. 'Dumas?'

Dumas, Morrison was pleased to see, saw his use. 'A postprandial would be grand.' Morrison would owe him one.

Dumas placed Mrs Ragsdale's hand in the crook of his arm. 'Mrs Ragsdale, would you do me the honour?'

In Which Morrison and Miss Perkins Arrive at the First Pass Under Heaven

Rugged up in scarves, hats and furs, the ladies' gloved hands tucked into rabbit-fur muffs, the party set off down a road leading eastwards from the hotel towards the Wall. It was a short stroll, only a quarter of a mile. Kuan and Mrs Ragsdale's Boy, Ah Long, summoned from the conviviality of the servants' quarters, walked ahead, dangling paper lanterns from sticks. Animated by a sense of shared adventure, they tramped through the soft white landscape towards the ancient battlements, their boots crunching through the snow, their noses shocked crimson by the cold. Morrison stole a sideways look at Mae and felt his blood thrill.

The Great Wall divided the world between known and unknown, domestic and wild, civilised and barbarian. It was less a coherent wall than a confusion of fortifications scattered across the north of China like a game of pick-up sticks across a carpet. It hadn't served any real function since 1644. That year, the Ming General Wu San-kui opened the gates at Mountain-Sea Pass to a powerful army led by Manchus, the very people this section of the Wall had been designed to keep out. General Wu had asked the Manchus to help quell a rebellion against the Ming Dynasty. He hadn't foreseen that, having done so, they would enthrone their own dynasty, the Ch'ing. Once thrown open, gates in even the most carefully defended walls could be difficult to close. Morrison, relating this history to Mae and Mrs Ragsdale, never considered there might be a lesson there for himself.

Upon arriving at the Wall, Mrs Ragsdale panted and patted her chest. 'I fear I am not up for such a climb. You young folks go on ahead.'

'I shall keep Mrs Ragsdale company,' offered the faithful Dumas.

'You want me to come?' Kuan asked Morrison, looking unsurprised by the answer.

Morrison clasped Mae's small gloved hand as they negotiated the stone steps, slippery with snow. When the heel of her boot caught in a crack and she stumbled, he caught and held her for a moment, his heart banging in his chest like a schoolboy's.

Atop the summit, they surveyed the glittering landscape. The full moon had sown the snowy fields with diamonds and silvered the rippling corrugations of the Gulf of Bohai where, not far from where they stood, the Wall finished its discontinuous journey of thousands of miles, abutting into the sea.

The path along the Great Wall became less treacherous as they approached the old garrison town of Mountain-Sea Pass, nestled against the magnificent watchtower of the First Pass Under Heaven. The snowfall had laid an ermine stole over the Wall's towers and parapets and the undulating roofs of the town dwellings. Below, on deserted streets ragged with moonshadow, a nightwatchman, plump in padded robes, swung his painted lantern, calling out the Hour of the Rat and, in a gesture as self-defeating as it was traditional, banging together wooden clappers to warn thieves of his advance. Beyond the

Great Wall, a caravan of shaggy, two-humped Bactrian camels, bells jingling from their necks, loped ahead of a Mongolian herdsman on a pony. A thin breeze tinkled the chimes hanging from the eaves of a Buddhist temple inside the town. In the distance, the Great Wall, leaving the town, snaked over serrated mountain ridges.

Morrison felt as though he had never been so alive to wonder and possibility. He spread out his cloak and they sat down side by side on it, enveloped in the magic of the night. Though every part of him was yearning to touch Mae, Morrison found himself beset by an accursed shyness that might have surprised acquaintances who thought of him as the most confident of men. He took a deep breath to calm himself, but the cold air seared his lungs and he had to stifle a cough.

Mae looked up at him with a playful expression. 'How long must I wait before you kiss me?' she demanded.

Mae Ruth Perkins's soft mouth tasted of minted chocolate and black coffee, with a hint of meat and onions. She did not — *thanks ye gods!* — kiss like a virgin. Surprise quickly gave way to gratitude, and gratitude to sensuality. After some minutes, he pulled away to look at her, placing an ungloved hand on her cold cheek. She grasped it in both her own and, locking her eyes on to his, kissed it in such a silky manner that he felt dizzy. More revelations followed. Layers of clothing — not to mention freezing temperatures and a bed of ancient stone — proved no obstacle to her ability to deliver and command pleasure; her hands were as cunning as her kisses.

By the time they were ready to turn back, Morrison's senses were aflame and his legs atremble; he felt as though his bones had been reduced to gelatine. She, on the other hand, had grown irrepressibly gay and was humming American show tunes as though nothing out of the ordinary had transpired.

'Do you know "Good Old Summertime"? No? Blanche Ring sings it in the musical play *The Defender*. I saw it in New York's Herald Square. She was wonderful.' Mae launched into the song in a voice as husky, warm and throaty as that of Ethel Barrymore. 'Come on. Your turn. What songs do you know? Court me with something.'

He hemmed and hawed.

'You must know this one. "Daisy, Daisy, give me your answer do …"'

'Maysie, Maysie …'

'I like that.'

'Oh, look,' called Morrison, as they came upon the others, 'here we are. Hello.'

It was hard to say whether Mrs Ragsdale, Dumas or the two servants were more relieved at their return. All were too frozen to complain. As the little group straggled back to the Six Kingdoms, only Mae appeared as fresh as if the evening had just begun.

Morrison, head still spinning, had just changed into his nightshirt when he heard a soft, insistent rapping on his door.

George Ernest Morrison had had considerable experience of forward young women in his two and two score years. Saucy Pepita, devastating Noelle, naughty Agneth. Three nameless Scottish tarts who allowed him to sprinkle their bodies with brandy and soda one memorable night whilst he was studying medicine in Edinburgh. The harlots, grisettes, bad girls and worse wives of a dozen countries. But nothing had prepared him for Miss Mae Ruth Perkins, who looked like a lady, was every bit a woman, but took her pleasure like a man. And whose charms, he already sensed, would prove more addictive than opium.

In Which the Sun Comes Up on a New Era in Morrison's Life, a Scandalous Conversation Ensues and Our Hero Accepts an Invitation to Ride

Morrison gazed upon the sleeping form by his side. The room was dark, the moon having set. He listened to the rhythm of her breathing and watched the slow dance of her curves under the satin quilt. Her head was tilted to one side, her chin doubling slightly in repose, her long hair fanning out over the pillow. Under heavy, tasselled lids her eyes rested, guarded by the thick natural crescents of her eyebrows. Even asleep, those lips seemed to smile at some private entertainment. He felt all of his repressed longings fold themselves around her shape. Brushing a lock of hair from her cheek, he inhaled her musk of perfume, perspiration and sex. He described all this to himself, a correspondent in love.

'Mae,' he whispered, 'it'll be dawn soon. They mustn't find you here.'

Without opening her eyes, Mae flattened the palm of her hand against the top of his head, urging him down towards her thighs, via her breasts.

Time passed memorably. He was well pleased with himself for having had the foresight to pack several 'riding coats'. Fashioned from the oiled and stretched intestines of lambs, they were not much protection from the pox. But they were fairly reliable at preventing what was known in polite society as an 'interesting condition'.

Outside the window, the sky began to shimmer with a premonition of dawn. Morrison slid under the warm quilt to bury his nose in Mae's bosom, occasioning all manner of delicious gasping and squirming. With great reluctance and greater willpower, he finally pulled away from her and sighed. 'We mustn't get caught. I don't want to cause a scandal for you.'

'Don't worry, Ernest, honey,' she said, snuggling close again. 'I am perfectly capable of causing my own scandals. I have been doing so since I was seventeen. Don't look so alarmed. You remind me of my father when you look alarmed and that won't do at all.'

He winced at the comparison. 'What scandal did you cause at seventeen?' The journalist in Morrison required information. The man in him wasn't sure he really wanted to know. Morrison had been relieved that she was not a virgin. Yet he would prefer not to discover that she was a tart. Even when it was a patently absurd presumption, he preferred to think that a woman had flowered uniquely under his tutelage.

'Oh, it was all rather silly. It happened about eight or nine years ago. The *Daily Examiner* reported that Fred Adams, who was in Oakland society, was to marry a divorcee who called herself Miss Potter. Can you imagine, a *divorcee*!' She threw her hands up to her face, her eyes and mouth perfect circles of mock horror. 'Well, the paper *would* report that he had met this unsavoury creature at a gathering I had hosted. My father was furious.'

Morrison, his hyperactive imagination having produced far worse scenarios, was relieved and amused. 'Scandal, as Oscar Wilde wrote in *Lady Windermere's Fan*, is but gossip made tedious by morality.'

'I must store that one away.' She tapped her temple with her forefinger. 'I am quite sure it will come in handy.'

'So what did your father do? Were you punished?'

'He was away in Washington at the time. You know he's a senator. He wrote a letter to my mother, urging her to tighten my reins.' Raising herself on one elbow, Mae switched into her father's voice: '"It seems that this Miss Potter was a friend of one of Mae's friends and had been passing herself off as a young girl, although she was at the time a divorced woman!!!" There were three exclamation marks, the final one of such vigorous a pen stroke that it tore the paper. He said, "As long as I let Mae do as she pleases, wear *bangs*" — he underlined the word — "and run around having a wild time with questionable boys and girls, I am a dear, good papa, but when I insist that she must go to school and socialise with respectable young people, why I am another kind of man!"'

Morrison shook his head. 'You frighten me. For a moment there, I could have sworn your father had slipped into bed between us. Have you ever thought of becoming an actress?'

'Of course. I've loved the theatre ever since Mama took me to my first play at the Alcazar in San Francisco. Do you know the Alcazar? It's the most elegant Moorish hall in all world, or at least that's what is printed on its playbills. Gas-jet chandeliers, classical busts on pedestals here, there and everywhere, and all society dressed in their finest, raising gold opera glasses to the stage. From the first encounter I wanted to be on that stage, to be the one they were all watching. And so I declared to Mama then and there that I would become an actress.'

'What was her reaction?'

Mimicking her mother's light Anglo-Irish lilt, Mae slipped into character: '"Young lady, are you so determined to disgrace the family? An actress is but another name for a fancy woman! It would kill your father!"'

'If your talent for mimicry is any indication, I would think you could have enjoyed a stellar career on the stage.'

'So you say. But I might as well have told her I was running away to join the circus. Which, like being a sailor, is something I also dreamed about when I was little. I wanted to be the girl with the feathered headdress who rode the pony and got the tigers to leap through hoops. But speaking of ponies, let's find some and ride out to the seabeach at the end of the Great Wall.'

'Now?' Morrison recoiled. 'But it's so pleasant in bed.'

'I will go alone then.'

'You mustn't do that. It wouldn't be proper. Or safe.'

'So come with me.'

'Can't you linger with me a while longer?'

'And if we are discovered?'

'Hmm. I feel a sudden desire for exercise.'

In Which Miss Perkins Demonstrates That She is Good in the Saddle and It Is Seen How the Meaning of a Parable Depends on Who Is Telling the Story

As the hotel *mafoo* saddled up two little Mongolian ponies, Mae pointed to the feisty chestnut. 'I'll have that one.'

The gelding's ears lay flat against his head and his lips were tight; he regarded Mae's approach with his head back and eyes rolling. When she tried to pat his neck, he jerked it away. Morrison signalled curtly to the *mafoo* to fetch a more tractable horse but Mae stopped him, insisting she liked that one. She calmed the pony with soft words and stroking until his ears rose to a happy angle and his lower lip loosened and trembled. Now, when she patted the white star on his forehead, he nuzzled her.

'See? That wasn't hard,' she remarked and vaulted into the tall, wooden-framed saddle before either man could offer a hand, then settled her skirts over her legs.

Morrison marvelled that not even beasts were immune to her charms. He hoisted himself up onto the pony's companion, a stocky bay, the *mafoo* slapped the horses' flanks, and they were off, Mae in the lead.

As they cantered alongside the Wall towards the sea, Mae's hair escaped its pins and streamed behind her. Snow flew from under the sure-footed ponies' tough hooves.

Morrison's spirits rose until he felt he had never been happier. With Mae's scent still in his nostrils and her taste on his tongue, all of his frustrations with editors, the war, idiotic colleagues, missionaries, his health, ageing — everything melted into insignificance. *What jowls?* He almost laughed aloud at the memory of the previous morning's perturbation.

Dismounting at Old Dragon Head, where the Great Wall jutted into the sea, they led their steaming ponies across the snow-crusted sand.

'You ride well,' Morrison said.

'Back in Oakland, I had the dearest pony. He was a chestnut like this one, but with a white blaze and socks on all four legs. I rode him everywhere when I was young.'

'You still are young.'

'Not at twenty-six, not according to Mama, anyway. She worries that I will remain a spinster. So what if I do? It is most unfair. Men like you may remain bachelors without fear of censure. Why can't women do the same?'

Morrison felt a rush of curiosity. For all the revelations of the night, he realised he knew next to nothing about her. 'Have you ever been engaged?'

'Three times.'

'Three lucky men.'

'One unlucky man three times.'

Morrison had so many questions it was hard to know where to begin. 'The fellow you mentioned last night, the one I remind you of, was he your fiancé?'

'No. That was a different one … Oh, Ernest, if you could see the expression on your face. It makes me want to kiss you again.'

A thick, tangy mist hung over the beach and the steely sea, laying a film on their hair and clothes and obscuring the ruined citadel at the Wall's end. The sun's first rays chiselled fine grooves in the fog and neat lines of waves licked at the beach's edge. Gradually, the crumbling, cannonball-pocked enceintes and fortifications came into focus and, in the shallows, dark amorphous shapes solidified into volcanic boulders.

'"To watch the crisping ripples on the beach, and tender curving lines of creamy spray,"' Mae quoted dreamily.

'Tennyson, *The Lotos-Eaters*. You recite beautifully.'

Mae smiled. 'I wish Papa could hear that. He was always accusing me of neglecting my studies. He once wrote to Mama: "If I were the daughter of a senator, I should think much more about my education and manners than I did about dress! It is character and education that is the true standard of womanhood." Oh, and that followed by three exclamation marks as usual.' She peered at the surface of the Wall, probing one of a series of symmetrical hollows with her finger. 'What happened to the Great Wall here? All these holes? I imagine some great battle between ancient warriors with shining helmets and bright silk banners of war.'

'Actually it was the foreign troops who had come to relieve the Siege of Peking four years ago who did this.'

'What a pity.' She traced the rim of a bullet hole with one finger in a manner Morrison found most distracting. 'Couldn't they have rescued you all without damaging this beautiful old wall?'

'As I said last night, sometimes there is adequate reason for military action. Had the Allied Forces not fought their way to the capital, I might well and truly have merited my obituary, at least in the sense I would have been dead. By then, we had been holding out for fifty-five days. The booming of their guns, when they finally reached Peking, was as welcome as music.'

'I am well pleased you are alive. On the other hand, I still don't see why there was the need for so much destruction. I have heard there was a great deal of burning and looting by foreign troops and residents. It seems wanton.'

Morrison did not answer immediately, abashed and uncertain as to how much she knew. His part in the looting that followed the defeat of the Boxers was minor compared to some. He knew foreign diplomats who'd had to hire entire railway carriages to transport their bounty out to the ports. But he was not entirely blameless. There was that jade citron, encrusted with gold, taken from the Imperial Palace. And other things. Yet he considered it barely adequate reparation for his near-fatal wounding and the loss of his first home in Peking.

Something he had not thought about for a long time came back to him now as a painful memory. A fortnight after the foreign troops had swept in, Morrison had encountered a Chinese friend, a teacher. The man's eyes were vacant. Russian soldiers had raped his moon-faced baby sister, sixteen years old, who wrote poetry and played the zither; they had battered and used her and left her for dead. Seven members of this friend's family had swallowed lumps of raw opium and lain down side by side to die — their joint suicide a reproach to the perpetrators. It went unnoted. Morrison, appalled, had roundly slandered the Russians as an army and a race to his inconsolable friend. If British troops committed comparable crimes, he did not know about them — had not wanted to know.

Mae's voice broke into his thoughts. 'What are you thinking?'

He shook his head. 'Just that they were … interesting times. But to return to your original point — if men destroy monuments from time to time, don't forget it's men who build them, as well.'

'And the tears of one woman can bring them all down,' Mae declared. 'Yesterday, Mrs Ragsdale and I visited the Temple of the Virtuous Woman on Phoenix Mountain. Our native guide told us how Lady Meng-Chiang's husband was abducted on their wedding night and dragged off to work on the Great Wall. When winter came and he still hadn't returned, she took a bundle of warm clothing and went searching for him. By the time she found him, he was dead and his bones interred in the Wall itself. She wept until the skies darkened and the earth grew black and an eight-hundred-mile stretch of the Great Wall collapsed into rubble. Hearing of this, the Emperor ordered her killed. But when he laid eyes on her and saw how beautiful she was, he wanted her for a wife. She demanded that he give her first husband a proper burial first. As soon as he did, she jumped into the sea and drowned herself. Two stones rose from the waters, which you can still see today — her tombstone and her grave. Why are you smiling?'

'They also say that Lady Meng-Chiang was born from a gourd, from which she sprung fully formed as a little girl. It's just a native legend. Besides, in the end, although the Emperor did not get to have Lady Meng-Chiang for a wife, he did unify the country, standardise its system of writing and currency, and in many ways made it what it is today. And he rebuilt that section of the Wall.'

'That may be so. But all I could think was that Lady Meng-Chiang was young and beautiful and scarcely knew her husband when he was taken away. I certainly wouldn't have thrown myself in the sea. Not for a man I hadn't even slept with yet.'

'And for one you had?'

'Oh, honey. What a question.'

He went to embrace her but she seemed distracted. 'I fear Mrs Ragsdale will soon be rising and calling me for breakfast. I probably should have left a note.'

'And Dumas and I hold tickets for the morning train to Peking.'

'I shall pine for you,' Mae sighed. 'Promise you will come to see me in Tientsin as soon as possible. Sooner, if you can. And promise that you will write. And that you will think of me often.'

'I will, I will and I will,' Morrison pledged.

In Which Morrison Contemplates the Nature of Promises and Romance and Receives Further Confirmation of Granger's Incompetence

'And what did she promise you in return?' Dumas asked as the train pulled away from Mountain-Sea Pass.

'Nothing,' Morrison replied. 'It was implicit. A woman always has more cause to worry and thus to extract promises than a man does, in the beginning at least. Our attention is easily and quickly turned. Women, on the other hand, normally require a certain amount of time and structure to grow faithless. That is why the institution of marriage plays such a useful role in encouraging infidelity in the female.'

'Ever the cynic.'

'A romantic, actually. But I would classify my view of human nature as realistic rather than cynical.' Morrison looked out the window for a moment. 'I must admit, I am immensely taken with her. She is a gem, full of life and happiness.'

'And with ten million gold dollars behind her.'

'Now who is the cynic?'

'Not me. Like you, I am merely a realist.'

Morrison rolled his eyes, more impressed with the notion of her wealth than he cared to let on. 'Ah, good. Here is Kuan with our tea.'

The train, steaming away from the mountains, cut through a flat mosaic of fields. Snow was thinner on the ground here. Garlic shoots poked their jade heads up through the dusty soil. Wisps of smoke curled from farmhouse chimneys, ears of corn lay stacked in flat woven baskets on the roofs, and pale bundles of native cabbage peeped out from under the eaves. Despite the cold, the peasants were deep in industry. A man flicked a straw switch at the straining flanks of a donkey that was pulling a cart stacked three times its own height with cornstalks. Swinging heavy mallets, other men pounded stones quarried from the distant mountains into gravel. At the back of one house, a young girl hobbled on bound feet, scattering seeds amongst a clutch of hens.

Morrison found it hard to imagine that many miles west, across the Gulf of Bohai, war was being waged on land and sea. Or that he had spent such a night — and morning — of intimacy with one so enchanting.

'Your Miss Perkins is certainly quite a specimen,' Dumas remarked. 'Her style and manner call to mind Alice Roosevelt, whose father once said that he could either be President of the United States or control Alice, but not both. It would not have surprised me in the least if, following Miss Roosevelt's example, Miss Perkins had jumped into a swimming pool fully clothed or shot a pistol into the air to enliven the party, had there been a pool or pistol at hand, or a party for that matter.'

'You seem obsessed with Miss Perkins,' Morrison commented. 'Perhaps it is you who ought to be having the affair.'

'You don't mean that.'

'Of course I don't.'

'*Buon giorno!*' Guido Pardo, correspondent for *La Tribuna*, materialised in front of them, and with an embarrassment of Mediterranean enthusiasm, kissed them both on the cheek. He had just travelled from St Petersburg, where the Russians claimed they had already amassed one hundred thousand soldiers in the Manchurian city of Harbin, five hundred and forty miles northeast of Port Arthur. They were sending five thousand reinforcements to the war zone each day. Inclement weather, however, was creating difficulties: an entire engine had fallen through the ice.

'Well, that at least is welcome news,' said Morrison.

Pardo then gratified Morrison with further proof of the incompetence of his colleague-cum-nemesis Granger. In Newchang, Pardo said, he'd taken on Granger at billiards. Russian officers were playing at the next table. Granger, boasting of his fluency in Russian, eavesdropped on the Russians with droll diligence before turning to Pardo and whispering smugly, 'Forty-five wounded.'

'Which battle?' Pardo asked, expressionless. Russian was his second language.

'Not sure,' Granger said, eyes darting about as though searching for the answer elsewhere in the room. 'Latest one.'

'I didn't bother telling him that the Russians had been discussing the game's score,' Pardo told Morrison and Dumas. '*Buffone!*'

The three shared a hearty laugh at Granger's expense.

Pardo's company helped make the time fly until, at just past three in the afternoon, the massive walls of Peking appeared in the distance.

As the train pulled up alongside the entrance to the inner city at the ruins of the Ch'ien-men Gate, which had been chewed to rubble in the Boxer conflagrations, Morrison felt the medieval capital enclose him once more in its mighty grey-brick arms — oppressive, comforting, familiar, safe. Lonely.

In Which a Sneeze Leads to a Discovery, Kuan Offers an Insight Into the Nature of Mischief, a Dangerous Secret is Revealed and Morrison Thrills as a Storm Penetrates His Inner Sanctum

Dumas would be staying the night at the British Legation before returning home to Tientsin. A carriage was waiting for him. Pardo was to rest with friends. The men parted warmly.

As Morrison and Kuan rattled through the familiar dusty streets on a hired cart, Morrison fell disconsolate. Mae had been to Peking and he hadn't known. How that rankled him! He would have loved to have shown her the city, the site of so much history, his own as well as China's. C.D. Jameson was an ass. Morrison was beyond certain that Jameson had never mentioned anything about an American heiress requesting his company at lunch; it was not the sort of invitation one overlooked or easily forgot.

Taking a deep breath, a prelude to a sigh, he inhaled dust and, feeling a sneeze coming on, dug his hands into his jacket pocket in search of his handkerchief. There he found something softer, fresher. He pulled out a lady's lace-edged handkerchief. It was embroidered with the monogram 'MRP'.

What a delightful thing for her to have done. Completely forgetting he had to sneeze, Morrison pressed the delicate square of fabric to his face. Her perfume lingered on it like a last kiss. *That flashing-eyed maiden! Such a picture of loveliness!*

The cart made its bone-jarring way north towards the Gate of Heavenly Peace, east past the walls of the palace, and north again up the Avenue of the Well of the Princely Mansions, a street so close to the Forbidden City that the palace walls cloaked it in shadow every sunset.

As they pulled up before the grey walls of his compound, formerly the residence of a Manchu prince, Morrison looked at it as if through Mae's eyes. He pictured her exclaiming at the sight of the stone lion sentinels with their fierce expressions and proud chests, a carved ball under the paw of the male and a cub under that of the female. He imagined telling her how the people of Peking were able to tell a man's status from the depth of his entryway as easily as they could read the position he held in court from the embroidered panel on his robe. A wealthy commoner might adorn his shallow entrance with murals and silk-fringed lanterns, but it would not fool anyone. His own entryway, Morrison would point out to the senator's daughter, was impressively deep.

He was smiling to himself as, trailed by Kuan, he approached the great carved wall blocking the view to the inner courtyard — a 'spirit screen' intended to deflect evil spirits, which the Chinese believed could only travel in straight lines. Something occurred to him. He gestured at the screen. 'Kuan, do you believe mischief only moves in straight lines? In my experience, mischief always surprises one by coming round the corner.'

Kuan considered this for a moment. 'It is people who do not travel in straight lines,' he replied with a little smile. 'They can't help themselves. Always turning corners. Mischief just waiting for them there.'

'Ha.'

In the immaculate courtyard behind the screen, the crab-apple tree was swollen with buds and, within the bamboo cage that hung from one of its branches, Cook's Mongolian lark trilled. The spring festival had begun on the sixteenth of that month and everything still looked New Year's-fresh, from the brightly painted latticework of the windows to the newly calligraphed couplets on either side of the doorways. Miniature mandarin trees in ceramic pots wafted a faint note of citrus into the air. From somewhere in the compound with its thirty-odd rooms drifted the uvular sounds of conversation in the Peking dialect. Morrison's grey mare whinnied in her stable.

Morrison usually savoured that moment at the end of a trip when the sounds and smells of travel — the whistle and jolt of steam engines, the push and pong of crowds, the cries of coolies and the clip-clop of hooves — began to fade and the rhythms and sensations of home reasserted themselves in a bittersweet return to the familiar. This time, however, he felt as though a solemn grey curtain had fallen across a stage, and the gay and colourful world in which he'd been absorbed just over twenty-four hours earlier had evanesced, an artful illusion.

A slight and delicately featured girl stepped into the courtyard, carrying a stick broom. Although not more than sixteen, she wore her hair in the style of a married woman. At the sight of the men, she shrank back and, clutching the broom, stared at the ground.

Turning to Kuan, Morrison was surprised to see that his normally unflappable Boy had paled.

Before he could ask for an explanation, Kuan and the girl entered into low, urgent conversation, speaking too quickly for Morrison to understand. He gathered that they somehow knew each other and were shaken by the unexpected reunion.

'Who is she, Kuan?' Morrison asked when they had finished speaking.

'She's ...' Kuan seemed to be choosing his words with care. He glanced back at the girl, who had resumed sweeping with a concentration Morrison found strangely affecting, her feathery eyebrows drawn into a barely perceptible frown. 'We were childhood friends. She's Cook's new wife.'

'Truly?' Morrison was surprised. He was fond of Cook, a taciturn old widower with a fanatical devotion to both the arts of the table and Morrison's wellbeing. But Cook was not the most attractive of men. His narrow eyes looked as though they'd been carved out of the tough leather of his face by the thin blades that were his cheekbones. His nose was unusually flat for a northerner, his mouth wide and graceless. Cook was certainly no Kuan, whose large, intelligent eyes, brushstroke eyebrows, proud nose and well-proportioned mouth inspired appreciative comments from even some of the Western ladies of Morrison's acquaintance. Morrison would not have expected Cook's new wife to be such a slender young beauty as the one standing before them now. 'Perhaps I'm wrong, but she doesn't seem like she was brought up to be a servant,' he observed.

Kuan straightened. 'No one is brought up to be a servant. No one's parents want this for their child. It is — how you say? — *circumstances.*'

Morrison realised his mistake. 'Of course. What I meant was, what circumstances brought her to this place, I wonder?'

By now the pair was walking in the direction of Morrison's library, a specially reconstructed wing on the southern side of the main courtyard.

Kuan gave Morrison a searching look. 'I will tell you, but you cannot tell anyone else. Not even Cook.'

Morrison's curiosity was piqued. 'Go on.'

Kuan's voice dropped to a whisper. 'Her father was a follower of T'an Ssu-tung. You know?'

T'an had been one of the 'Six Gentlemen' whose ideas for reforming the Chinese system of government in order to strengthen China and bring it into the modern world had found a sympathetic hearing with the young Kuang Hsu Emperor six years earlier. The reformers argued that China needed to modernise everything, from the way farmers planted their fields to the manner in which the government managed its railways and trained its army. They spoke of women's rights and of universal education. For one hundred heady days, the Emperor promulgated the reforms but his aunt, the Empress Dowager, and her conservative cronies in the court grew alarmed. The Empress Dowager arrested her nephew and had him locked up in a pavilion in the palace. Then she rounded up and executed the leading reformers, including T'an. A number of their supporters formed an underground anti-Ch'ing movement that blamed the Manchus for China's woes and believed it was time for China to move, like Japan, to a constitutional monarchy or even a republic.

Morrison had been enthusiastic about the reform movement. He had once even offered to help one of the reformers, an offer that had been turned down, most unfortunately as it turned out, as two years later the man was put to death.

Morrison looked back with renewed interest at the girl

sweeping his courtyard. He noticed then that her feet, whilst small, had only been loosely bound. 'I do indeed know who T'an was,' he told Kuan, drawing a forefinger across his throat.

Kuan nodded, glancing nervously at the girl.

'Her father — was he executed, too?'

'He ran away. Then my parents died and I was taken to the orphanage. I never saw her again. She was young then.' He looked pained. 'Just a girl.'

'She still looks young to me. What's her name?'

'Yu-ti.'

Morrison narrowed his eyes in thought. 'Jade something?'

'No. Not that *yu*. Means "waiting for little brother". She was the second child, both girls. You know Chinese families must have boy.'

'So they weren't that progressive after all.'

'This is China.'

'It certainly is.' They both watched as Yu-ti, having finished her sweeping, scampered back into the house. 'What do you think of the reformers, Kuan?'

'They are China's hope,' he replied fervently. 'Unless we make our country strong, we will always be victims of foreign powers.' As though catching himself saying something he should not, he bit his lip.

'Do go on,' Morrison urged. For all his complaints about Granger reporting the gossip of Chinese cart drivers, Morrison had always been professionally interested in the opinions of his Head Boy. But Kuan seemed reluctant to continue the conversation. That was fine, for Morrison had correspondence and other tasks waiting for him. He gave Kuan a few instructions, then stood alone in his courtyard, collecting his thoughts.

Two white kittens belonging to his servants came mewing and tumbling in together on the neat brick paving, the bells around their necks jingling. From his cage, Cook's songbird observed their antics warily, cocking his head first in this direction, then that. Morrison felt for the handkerchief in his pocket and stroked it with his fingers. He took a deep breath, almost a sigh. Where was she now? he wondered. Was she thinking of him, too? His chest filled with longing.

Morrison's library was narrow and high-ceilinged, a place of repose, order and scholarship. On the shelves, in addition to twenty thousand books in more than twenty languages, lay at least four hundred early manuscript dictionaries and grammars, four thousand pamphlets and two thousand maps and engravings, each one meticulously catalogued. Of all his collections, which included bibelots, silks and jade, Morrison cherished none as much as his books. He loved the written word for the way it secured thoughts and experiences, lending them structure, preventing them from passing out of sight and memory.

Morrison's greatest regret was that for all his accomplishments, he was not, he knew, a great writer. He had published a book and a good many reports and telegrams. But when he thought of poets and writers he admired, he felt humble — and not many things humbled Morrison — for great authors, like Kipling, his favourite, gave moral sense to the world. It was not just facility with language or even a rich imagination, he knew, that made an author great, but the way the writer reached for and honoured the truth. Morrison freely confessed to the limitations of his own craft; deep inside he knew that a worse problem was that in his public writing, at least, he was incapable of an unwavering allegiance to the truth. He could not deny to himself that how he understood the world did not always accord with the way he presented it to others. There was the odd doubt about an ally, which he thought unwise to voice, for example; information that for whatever reason he did not wish to share; strategic considerations; even, on occasion, necessary flattery.

Morrison confided only to his journal, *Lett's No. 41 Indian and Colonial ROUGH DIARY Giving an Entire Page to a Day*, a serious, manly notebook, bound in leather and bearing advertisements for Remington typewriters and Whitfield's Safes & Steel Doors on its inside covers, its pages faintly lined for convenience. Morrison had his eye on posterity, and to posterity he would be true. At the same time he would be loyal to the place that, for all his travels, he kept close to his heart: Australia. His journals would return there in the end, even if he did not. It was to his journal — and those who lived under the big, forgiving Australian sky — that he would confide his most awkward truths, the latest being that he was wildly infatuated with Miss Mae Ruth Perkins. His Maysie. *Maysie, Maysie.* But he would not dawdle now over sentimental matters. The unopened sack of mail on his worktable reproached him.

Morrison touched the precious handkerchief to his lips before folding it and replacing it in his pocket. Tipping the sack onto the table, he chose an envelope at random and sliced into it with his scrimshaw letter-opener. It was from J.O.P. Blunt, *The Times* correspondent in Shanghai. 'What news from the City of Dreadful Dust?' it began. Morrison could almost smell Blunt's lavender pomade. Next was a note from some busybody in the Church, harping that Morrison had still not reported on a modern college the missionaries had established somewhere or other. Morrison wrote himself a reminder to look into it. His old neighbour Prince Su, meanwhile, had sent a note addressed 'My dear younger brother'; Morrison knew enough of Chinese ways to perceive both the endearment and the condescension in the address. There was a letter from Bangkok: 'I hope you are happy,' wrote his friend Eliza R. Scidmore of the National Geographic Society. 'At last you have your war.'

As he sorted through the post, putting some letters on his desk to answer straight away and setting others aside, he stopped to dash off a line to Moberly Bell, pointedly noting to his editor how good it had been to be able to get out and see things for himself, and remarking, by the by, that his health had improved greatly since the outbreak of war.

Much to do. He pulled on his sleeve guards and, seated at his desk, set up blotter and inkpot.

Dear Mae. Dearest Mae. Maysie. Mae, dear. Dearest. After several false starts, his pen fairly flew down the sheet of paper, and the one after, and the one after that. He was just impressing his seal on the wax that fastened the envelope when a mighty sandstorm swooped upon the city. Howling winds rattled the windows and swirled yellow and orange dust through the air. Elsewhere in the compound he could hear doors slamming, flowerpots smashing and the cries of the servants as they rushed hither and thither securing the house. Morrison felt the excitement of the weather like a tremor throughout his body. *Maysie*.

From behind the padded quilt that in winter helped trap his study's meagre heat, the door banged in the wind. Snapping out of his trance, Morrison scrambled for the stitched bundle of rags he kept to stuff in the crack by the floor. He adored the thrill of a storm but not the disorder it brought with it.

When the winds abated, he emerged from his library to find Cook upset and cursing. Before Cook had been able to get to his lark, the cage had crashed to the ground and the bird had flown away. Yu-ti appeared shaken by his temper as she and the other servants busied themselves sweeping the courtyard and tidying up. Though brief, the tempest had left piles of grit on the roof tiles, piped sand along the latticework and deposited souvenirs of the Ordos Desert into the hearts of cabbages. Back inside, Morrison found it had insinuated sand into the pockets of clothes folded in wardrobes and chests, the pages of his books and the lens of his precious Brownie camera, which had been encased in leather and locked within a drawer in his study.

Morrison dismantled the lens and blew on it, then brushed it with a feather. As he watched the drift of sand on his desk, a tune popped into his head. *It won't be a stylish marriage, / I can't afford a carriage, / But you'll look sweet upon the seat, / Of a bicycle built for two!* How ridiculous he appeared, even to himself, humming out of tune. He could scarcely credit that just months earlier he had felt so debilitated by poor health that he'd considered leaving China altogether. *Maysie, Maysie, give me your answer do.* His blood flowed in his veins like that of a much younger man.

In Which Morrison Encounters the Bumptious Egan, Whose Excellent Teeth Remind Him of the Sorry State of His Own, and an Assignment from His Editor Proves Just the Ticket

The following morning, Morrison woke invigorated, organised his notes and had just begun drafting his telegram for *The Times* when Kuan entered with a letter from Granger.

'My dear Morrison,' it began, presumptuous in its familiarity. Cavilling over the course of nearly two pages that his telegrams were not being published as regularly as he had hoped, Granger then fretted over the reliability of both modern telegraphy and the post. He begged the indulgence of his esteemed colleague: would Morrison please ensure the enclosed report, obtained at the cost of much sweat and blood, reach the eyes of their editor in London? He would be eternally grateful.

Morrison extracted the report and read it carefully.

Damned badly drawn and inconsequential. Addle-headed idiot. He tore it up and tipped the scraps into the stove.

Yesterday's storm had scoured the sky to a cerulean magnificence. Morrison worked through lunch but, as the afternoon wore on, he found it impossible to keep himself at his desk. Buoyantly, he strode out into the breezy sunshine. The winds had strewn the candy-coloured petals of early-flowering apple and cherry blossoms about the streets like fragrant confetti. Through broad avenues and narrow *hutong*, Morrison wove his way through a dense traffic of merchants and peddlers, carters, ricksha pullers and palanquins. He passed Manchu ladies with lacquered wings of hair, beggars and Bannermen. The vendors' sing-song cries, the chatter from the wine shops, the clatter of cart wheels and the shouts of the children kicking shuttlecocks rang in his ears. His nose was simultaneously assaulted by the rotten-egg smell of thawing sewage and delighted by the scents of toffee and pancakes. The streets of Peking were exhilarating and claustrophobic all at once, and he quickened his steps until he reached the ramp that led to the top of the Tartar City Wall.

The wall was forty feet high and so wide in places that four carriages could be driven abreast. Hundreds of years old, the ramparts afforded an incomparable view of the city, including the golden-roofed halls, gardens and pavilions of the Imperial Palace itself. The Tartar City Wall was a place to contemplate history — China's, Peking's, one's own, and to order one's thoughts with the aid of the grand symmetry of the capital, with its north–south axis and clear, sacred geometry. It was a post from which one could observe the teeming, clamorous life in the streets below without having it present in every pore. Walking the Tartar Wall appealed for every reason to Morrison, himself a man of solid bulwarks, gated enceintes and complex fortifications.

Atop the wall, Morrison took a breath and gazed out over his adopted city. Box kites carved colourful grooves in a brilliant blue sky and from all directions came the music of bells: ringing on peddlers' carts, tinkling from the necks of camels and mules, and chiming from the flying eaves of the city's temples. It was not a day for guarded emotion. His heart sang. *Oh Maysie. What a type*, he thought. *She excites me passionately, pleases me infinitely.*

Infinitely. His thoughts jumped to Mary Joplin. Mary was the angelic Eurasian nurse who had aided his convalescence from fever in Calcutta at the end of his epic journey from Shanghai to the subcontinent ten years earlier. Sweet Mary, on whose fingers even hydrochlorate of quinine tasted like honey. He had written much of that ilk in his journal at the height of his infatuation: *the animation of her beautiful features ... the charming grace and noiseless celerity of her movements ...*

When he had recovered enough to leave India, Mary tearfully bade him marry a good girl of his own station in life. Yet he could not put her from his mind. In 1899, he persuaded *The Times* that he needed to visit Assam to report on advances in tea cultivation. He never came within a mile of a tea bush. Mary had fallen on hard times and pawned the jewellery he'd given her — for fourteen rupees, half its worth, he'd noted with displeasure. What was worse, this time quinine could truly compare to her. *She wired into me like blazes.* Shouted, cried, pummelled his chest with her small, caramel fists. Morrison had done his duty and helped her out as best he could, but his feelings had turned to stone. When he finally left, it was forever, and with relief. He had moved up in the world. Women like Mary, as achingly lovely and tender as she had been, would not perform well under society's glare.

A cheery baritone cut into his thoughts. 'And what are you frowning about to yourself on such a fine day as this, Dr Morrison? Is the war not going to your satisfaction?'

Morrison looked up with some chagrin. 'Ah, Mr Egan. What a surprise.'

The men shook hands. Egan's grip was strong, assured, his smile as big and white as a sail. He easily matched Morrison in height and athletic physique, though being ten years younger than the Australian was trimmer and tauter of build. Morrison had always found Martin Egan disconcertingly hale and hearty. He possessed the sort of bold good looks that his American self-assurance had a way of amplifying until they reached a state of near caricature. The United States may have been a place full of teeming slums and political corruption, barely recovered from civil war and only recently clean of the stain of slavery, and Americans could be presumptuous and their culture crude, but you couldn't beat the New World for its confidence, idealism and optimism. All the world loved America for its belief in progress, democracy and a better future for all, and admired its ruddy, irresistible youth. Egan's grip and his smile spoke of all this.

Morrison recovered his hand. 'What brings you to Peking?' He suddenly remembered Mae saying she'd met Egan in Tientsin and wondered how well he knew her. 'I heard you were in the country.'

'A bit of business, a bit of pleasure,' Egan replied. He had recently joined the Associated Press after a stint with the *San Francisco Chronicle*, and headed up the AP's bureau in Tokio. 'The bureau can run itself for a few weeks. There's no place like Peking, is there? Imagine, the capital of three dynasties and the current one alone older than the United States.'

'*Five* dynasties. Liao, Chin, Yuan, Ming, Ch'ing,' Morrison corrected. He then recalled that Egan had lent Mae his book. He owed the man for that. His tone softened. 'Of course, the first two were relatively minor as dynasties go.'

'I must read more Chinese history,' Egan conceded. 'I always thought the Mongol Yuan was the first. I do wonder what goes on in there.' He gestured towards the Forbidden City. 'It's like a dream of the Orient.'

'A dream of Oriental despotism more like it.'

Egan pursed his lips in thought. His lips were full, pouty, on the border of feminine, and Morrison experienced a flicker of revulsion.

'I always understood Oriental despotism, at least as Aristotle described it, to be despotism by consent, which implicates the people in their own slavery. I may be wrong.' Egan's relentless affability was getting on Morrison's nerves.

'But then again, your personal enmity towards the Old Buddha is well known.'

'There is nothing personal about it. You know what the Chinese call this gate here?' Morrison pointed at the wall's southeast corner. 'The Devil's Pass. That's because of the tax collectors there, imposing tariffs on rice and salt and cigarettes and the rest. Every Chinaman knows it only goes to keep the Old Buddha in fancy soaps and face powder, just as she diverted the funds for naval defence to construct her marble pleasure boats at the Summer Palace. The woman is a jezebel.' *That should shut him up.*

A camel train approached from the west and Egan pointed at it. 'I always wonder what marvels these caravans are bringing to market. I imagine beautiful tapestries or woven rugs, furs —'

'Coal. From collieries in the Western Hills.'

Egan shook his head in admiration. 'I only have to be in your company five minutes and I'm reminded why you're the doyen of the correspondents!'

Morrison mined for respect like other men prospected for gold. He decided he didn't really mind Egan. The man was not such bad company after all.

Egan then mentioned that the famous American novelist Jack London had arrived in Japan to cover the war for Hearst's newspapers.

'Ah yes. My colleague at *The Times*, Lionel James, said they were on the same ship over from San Francisco to Yokohama.'

'Yes, London remembers James well. Said it was the talk of the ship that he was travelling with a valet! The Americans were all greatly amused. Turns out —'

'Yes, I know. The so-called valet was in fact our colleague David Fraser. *The Times* said Fraser could cover the war if he paid his own way. Got a cheap ticket under the guise of being James's valet. Apparently the ribbing still hasn't ceased. As for London, James said he was good company. Drank everyone under the table. Young bloke too, apparently.'

'Yes, Jack is still short of thirty. Two years my junior. Have you read any of his books?'

'I enjoyed *The Call of the Wild*. I'm not convinced that he is the American Kipling, as some would claim, though I speak as an ardent fan of the English poet. I'm certainly not an admirer of London's socialist ideas. But he writes well. Manly sort of prose.'

'Jack and I are good friends — mates, as I think you say in Australia. It's true he still swaggers and drinks like the sailor he was. He's challenged me to arm-wrestling in bars once enough whiskies are down the hatch, but he's educated himself well, lived hard and is the best raconteur I've ever known. I must introduce you. I'm sure you'd like him. In spite of his socialism.'

'I look forward to it,' said Morrison, privately dismayed at the thought of another boisterous American. One who arm-wrestled in bars, at that.

'He's on his way to the front now.'

'Ha! Let him get past the Japanese. He'll be the first. One month into the war and they're still not giving anyone permission to get to the front.'

'Jack says the Japanese aren't going to stop him.'

Morrison raised an eyebrow. 'He underestimates their determination.'

'Oh, if anyone will get there, it'll be Jack. What's more, he says he'll report the real face of war — the mud on the soldiers' boots, the look in their eyes, the sizzle of their cookfires, the smell of gunpowder. Already he's got one of the Japanese soldiers to empty out his kit so he could take notes on it!'

'That's all very well for a novelist. A journalist requires harder facts.' Realising that Egan was about to launch into what would no doubt be a rather tedious defence of his friend, Morrison quickly switched the subject to that which was most on his mind. 'I hear you've been spending some time in Tientsin lately.'

'I certainly have been,' Egan replied with a broad smile, and Morrison was once again struck by how alarmingly white and orderly were the American's teeth. 'The attractions of that entrepôt have increased enormously in recent months. In saying that, I confess to feeling somewhat guilty. I promised someone there I would introduce you. A visiting American lass. She's very keen to meet you. I must say, however, that it's been hard not to try to keep her for myself.'

Morrison did not like the sound of that. 'You are speaking of the delightful Miss Perkins, I assume.'

'Ah, so you've met her already.'

'Only recently. At Mountain-Sea Pass. She was there with Mrs Ragsdale.'

'Her poor chaperone.'

'To all appearances, Mrs Ragsdale was rather enjoying Miss Perkins's company. It was probably far more agreeable than that of her husband.'

'Ha!' The American, laughing heartily, slapped Morrison on the back.

Brash pup.

Encountering one possessed of genuine youthful ardour left Morrison feeling considerably less suffused with that quality himself. Those teeth. Ridiculous. An infected molar suddenly pierced Morrison's jaw with arrow-like pain. As though the toothache opened a door through which other ailments could rush in, rheumatism flared through his joints and the damned spear wound threatened a nosebleed. He wondered how, just two days earlier, he could have felt so mindless of anything but the pleasures of the flesh when once again all he knew were the pains.

'Are you all right?'

'Grand. Never been better. But I must be off. Much to do.' Espousing an imprecise intention to see Egan again soon, and shaking hands with a grip that he thought compared well, Morrison took his leave and marched off with an air of purpose that he did not feel.

In the west, the sunset overlaid the violet hills with crimson and gold. The roofs of the Forbidden City fell into silhouette. His hand searched his pocket for Mae's handkerchief. She had still not written, though he realised it had only been two days since they'd met. Yet he had found the time to write and he was a busy man; he didn't understand why she hadn't even dropped him a postal.

He told himself to stop being obsessive. His mind wrapped itself around myriad anxieties.

He would try to get to Tientsin as soon as possible.

The following day, Morrison arrived home from a walk to discover Kuan in conversation with Cook's wife, Yu-ti. She scurried off at Morrison's arrival.

'Is she settling in all right?' Morrison asked.

'Yes. Oh, and I have asked one of the coolies to buy a pair of wedding quilts as a gift from you to her and Cook.'

'Very good. *Hen hao*.' Morrison shot his Boy a look of appreciation.

'Oh, and could we pay Yu-ti, too?'

Morrison's expression dimmed slightly. Cook, who earned twenty-five silver dollars a month, was the highest paid servant in his household after Kuan.

Kuan read his master's expression. '*Yisi, yisi*,' he said, using the Chinese term that meant 'just a token' but managed to imply both a negligible amount and a burden of thoughtfulness at the same time.

Morrison nodded, abashed at his own transparency and, thinking of how Maysie might view his natural parsimony, obscurely ashamed. 'You look after it.'

Later, en route from his library to the house to retrieve a book he'd left in the parlour, he spotted Yu-ti chopping vegetables in the courtyard. She was absorbed in her task and did not notice him at first. He tried to imagine how she might have felt when her red wedding veil was lifted and she first laid eyes on her middle-aged husband.

Morrison had heard Chinese defending the system of arranged marriage, saying that the love that grew out of it was stronger and more secure than that enjoyed by the romantic but fickle Westerner. The custom of arranged marriage did have a long history in the West as well of course. And he had certainly appalled himself several times in the past by his passionate attachment to women such as Mary Joplin who, in the end, proved less than deserving. His thoughts resting on Mae, he suffered a moment's doubt, then excoriated himself for it. *She is nowise like the others!*

Yu-ti bowed her head, colouring. 'Master,' she said in Chinese.

He realised he'd been staring. 'Carry on.' He strode back to his study, having entirely forgotten the errand that had brought him out. He would have liked to talk to Yu-ti about her father and her upbringing. According to Kuan, Cook did not know about his father-in-law. Then again, Cook had always refused to be drawn on the subject of politics, saying he was a simple man and that his concerns in life had to do with the freshness of garlic shoots and the quality of bacon.

The next afternoon a telegram arrived from Moberly Bell. His editor wanted him to write six hundred and fifty words for *The Times* on the progress of the war. *Well, here at least is good news!*

Morrison had every reason to travel to Tientsin now. As the hub of financial, academic and journalistic activity in north China, and a leading trade entrepôt, Tientsin was full of useful contacts — foreign and Chinese. It was said that whilst decisions were made in Peking, to hear of them one needed to travel to Tientsin. Morrison had no need to convince himself of the benefits of going to Tientsin. He would depart forthwith.

In Which We Are Introduced to Major Menzies and the Sound of a Lady's Footsteps Rattles Our Hero's Teacup

'You looking forward to Tientsin, Kuan?' Master and servant were at Ch'ien-men Station waiting for the train to Tientsin. It was Saturday, the fifth of March. 'Good chow there, right?'

'Number one. You want to eat Doggy Ignores Us buns?'

'Mmm. Maybe.' On their last trip, Kuan had taken him to a local eatery where Morrison had tried their famous meat buns, *kou bu li b'ao-tzu*. The buns were so popular that the chef, old 'Doggy' Kao, was too busy to chat to his customers, hence the name. Morrison was not entirely sure what distinguished them from other such buns he had tasted but he was reluctant to admit it. As Kuan suggested other local specialties they could try, including fried dough twists and mung-bean-and-sesame omelettes, Morrison's mind wandered.

How shall we greet each other in company? He wondered again why she had not written.

Around them in the train carriage the vapours of a dozen cigars mingled with the invisible exhalations of men with rotting teeth and inflamed gums, reminding Morrison that he needed to make an appointment with the British dentist in Shanghai. Bothered by a sudden vision of Egan's excellent teeth, Morrison levered open the window by his seat and was rewarded with a gust of cold air. He wrestled the sash back down. Noticing a Russian colonel he'd once met seated a few rows ahead, he got up to say hello but was unsurprised when his greeting wasn't returned with much bonhomie.

After some four restless hours, Tientsin appeared, rising from the alluvial plains. Though here too the Allied troops had laid waste to the centuries-old city walls, the odd gate and tower still stood sentinel. The train trumpeted its arrival into the station that serviced the foreign settlements with a long, piercing blast of its whistle.

Stepping onto the platform, Morrison breathed deeply of the Tientsin air, saltier and more invigorating than that of closed, dusty Peking. He scarcely had time to stretch his legs when a clamour of ricksha pullers descended upon him and Kuan. Following a short but intense negotiation during which Kuan strode away twice, only to be rapidly called back, a pair of runners efficiently packed them and their belongings onto the cushioned seats.

Morrison's runner stepped smartly over the shaft and lifted the ricksha with such vigour that Morrison was forced to grab the side rails for balance. They took off at a trot, tracked briefly by a brown hawk in the cloudless blue sky.

Morrison's heart beat in time with the quick rhythmic slap of the runner's feet on the macadamised road. As they crossed into the Italian Concession, the runner stopped to pay boundary tax to a pockmarked Chinese policeman and his curly-haired Roman counterpart. The transaction seemed to take forever. Then, crossing the iron bridge over the Pei-Ho River, they passed through the

French Concession, its grey-tiled chateaux a mirage of Paris. Another taxation stop at the stone boundary post for the British Concession, a salute from a black-turbaned Sikh with a waxed moustache, and at last they joined the busy traffic of Victoria Road, Tientsin's own Wall Street: hustling rickshas, broughams and drays; pale, important-looking men on horses; swarthy farmers with produce-laden wheelbarrows; and peddlers whose wares bounced off the ends of their carrying poles. North China's richest city had electric lights and a working telephone exchange; the ricksha in which he was riding even had rubber tyres. Westerners, Russians, Japanese and Chinese traders, entrepreneurs and investors bustled in and out of the grand public buildings, banks, trading firms and mining companies that lined the street.

If Peking was like a slow-moving, silk-gowned Mandarin who received his guests with rituals so arcane that one could learn more of his intentions from one's place at his table than from his words, Tientsin — the foreign sector, anyway — was a smartly dressed comprador with a trilby and fluency in two or three languages, one of which was always business. The solidity of Victoria Road's colonial architecture announced the British presence in the Far East as formidable and permanent. But on this day at least, the glories of empire were not foremost on Morrison's agitated mind.

Finally, they arrived at Victoria Park, a public garden built on land that was once a noisome swamp. A wrought-iron bandstand, paved walkways and an imposing fire bell adorned the park, which was intended for the pleasure of the foreign community — Chinese were admitted only if they were looking after the children of foreigners. Gothic Gordon Hall, with its crenulated battlements, guarded one side of the path and the colonnaded veranda of the Astor House Hotel, Morrison's destination, faced another.

In Tientsin the Boxers had fired more shells into the concessions than had fallen on South Africa's Ladysmith during the famous four-month siege of the Boer War earlier that same year. The luxurious Astor House had taken its share of hits but was now restored to its former magnificence. It was a sign of the economic vigour of the foreign concessions — and the reparations forced upon the humiliated Chinese government — that the Astor House bore fewer scars than did the Great Wall at Dragon's Head.

Whilst Kuan looked after the runners, Morrison swept past the potted palms and into the elegant lobby, boots squeaking on the lindenwood parquet. The manager, Mr Morling, looked up from his desk under the regal staircase, his look of surprise quickly giving way to deference. 'Dr Morrison. A pleasure to see you again.'

'A pleasure to be back.' Burning with impatience, Morrison followed the hotel boy down wood-panelled corridors to his room overlooking Victoria Park. It was fitted out with a pair of armchairs covered in an identical floral chintz to the curtains, a small table on which stood a porcelain vase of silk flowers, a dresser, a wardrobe and a double bed with an eiderdown quilt. The bedposts were turned in the Portuguese manner to resemble stacked wooden balls. It was not the grandest of the Astor House's rooms and suites, but it was the best Morrison could afford. Seating himself at the escritoire whilst Kuan unpacked his bags, Morrison fired off a series of chits for Kuan to convey to his contacts in the city, letting them know that he would be calling. Dumas, sadly, was out of town until the morrow. He then strode through the pale sunshine of early spring to the home of a fellow Australian, Major George Fielding Menzies.

Menzies was a man of standing in Tientsin and also enjoyed something of the aura of hero. During the Siege of Tientsin, when both British nationals and Chinese Christians gathered for safety in the basement of the Astor House, Menzies had taken charge of the defences. Under his command, the converts built barricades a mile long on the Bund Road out of whatever came to hand — cartons of condensed milk, bundles of camel hair, even furs. He currently served in the army of Viceroy Yuan Shih-k'ai, a man Morrison much admired. For all that, Morrison privately considered his compatriot *miraculously stupid*. In fact, he had also complained in his journal that Menzies was one of the most lethal, maddening bores in all of China. *My nose bleeds when Menzies is in the house.*

Menzies had no idea that Morrison held him in such contempt. Like most Australians, Menzies was in awe of Morrison's youthful feat of retracing the footsteps of the explorers Burke and Wills. With Menzies it was personal: Robert O'Hara Burke was his uncle. He was almost pathetically grateful to Morrison for paying him any heed at all. 'Bless you for all your kindness,' he once wrote. 'I always feel that I owe much of the interest you take in me to the memory of my uncle. My endeavour shall be to prove worthy of that interest.' Setting his jaw against his own hypocrisy, Morrison knocked on Menzies's door. It was time to let him show his usefulness.

'G.E.!' Menzies's expression was one of surprise and joy. He shook Morrison's hand warmly. 'To what do I owe this honour?' Menzies's voice was almost as resonant and deep as his own.

Morrison's features composed into a mask of geniality. 'I have a favour to ask of you.'

In less than an hour, the two men were standing at the gate of the Ragsdales' residence in the compact de facto American Concession, close to the British one. Morrison smoothed down the front of his jacket and ran his fingers through his hair. At his side, Menzies stood as though ready for military inspection, a foil for any suspicion that Mrs Ragsdale might have of Morrison's intentions.

The Ragsdales' Head Boy, Ah Long, opened the door. Collecting their calling cards, he ushered them into the parlour, returning with lidded cups of jasmine-flower tea before disappearing to inform the ladies of the house of their visit. Morrison, frantic with anticipation, attempted to calm himself by studying the décor. His eyes lit on a print of the famous late-nineteenth-century painting *The Doctor* by Luke Fildes, a depiction of a surgeon tending to a sick child. Morrison made a mental note to tell Dumas: it was their private theory that the more anxious people were to convince others of their respectability, the more likely they were to display a print of that very painting.

Menzies followed Morrison's gaze. 'Splendid painting,' he commented hopefully.

'Indeed,' answered Morrison, poker-faced.

A lady's footsteps could be heard coming down the stairs. Morrison replaced the lid on his cup with a clatter, and both men rose. The footsteps grew closer. They were not those of a lithe young woman.

'Mrs Ragsdale. Thank you for receiving us. I believe you are well acquainted with Major George Menzies.'

Mrs Ragsdale professed herself delighted to see them both. However, when Morrison enquired after Miss Perkins, their hostess's face dropped so steeply that for a scarifying moment Morrison thought Mae had either died or gone home to California, and his heart clenched.

'Miss Perkins is dreadfully indisposed,' Mrs Ragsdale informed them. 'I fear she is coming down with the grippe.'

Morrison, relieved, offered to see her. 'I am, after all, a medical doctor.'

Mrs Ragsdale clasped her hands. 'God bless you, Dr Morrison. But she's sleeping. I feel we ought not disturb her.'

'Of course,' he conceded, pierced by a vision of her in bed.

'I've applied a poultice of goose fat to her throat,' Mrs Ragsdale assured him. 'And she is well supplied with tea and lemon.'

Morrison forced a smile. 'She's in good hands. Please convey our sincere wishes for a speedy recovery.'

'I do hope you gentlemen will return to dine with us this evening in any case. Mr Ragsdale and I should be honoured if you would.'

Menzies politely declined, sensing he had done his duty. Morrison accepted. *Perhaps she will be well enough to come down to dinner. Please God.*

When he returned that evening, Mae was still too ill to join them. Yet just being under the same roof as that charming creature animated him to such a degree that, finding Edwin H. Clough of the *New York Journal* and several junior correspondents at the table as well, he was inspired to great wit and volubility, recording in his journal later that evening: *I entertained them very pleasantly, dare I say brilliantly.*

The following day, Morrison, this time on his own, called upon the Ragsdales once again. 'I'm sorry,' Mrs Ragsdale said, her voice laced with regret. 'Miss Perkins is recovering, but she is feeling too poorly to receive. She couldn't even accompany us to church this morning. Please, do have some tea.'

Morrison stayed for an obligatory ten minutes, invented a previous appointment and set about his proper business.

On the seventh of March, his third evening in Tientsin, Morrison joined Dumas, who had returned to the city, for a modest supper of fish soup, roast lamb, green peas, potatoes and plum pudding at the Tientsin Club. 'How does it go with our young heiress?' Dumas asked, pinching a splash of gravy from his moustache.

'It doesn't. She is ill with the grippe.'

'Have you seen her at all?'

'No.' It was not for lack of trying. He had dispatched as many loving notes as were feasibly consistent with a friendly concern for her health. None came back. He had stopped at the Ragsdales several more times, feeling as transparent as thinly blown glass. Each time, she was too ill to come downstairs. He saw no need to go into such detail. 'Of course, I've been awfully busy,' he said with a shrug. 'I haven't given it that much thought.'

'Well, you still owe me for keeping Mrs Ragsdale occupied that time at Mountain-Sea Pass. That woman could talk the ear off a brass jug. What have you occupied yourself with in the absence of your fair maiden?'

'Oh, I've been busy enough. I've seen the corruptible Chow of the China Merchants' Steam Navigation Company; dull, fat Admiral Yeh; the very stupid Fenton, full of mystery and brimming over with impossible facts; our Japanese friends, as gracious and unforthcoming as ever; railway men and bankers; Wingate; and Yuan Shih-k'ai, whom I have concluded is the only useful man in Tientsin. Present company excepted. I also called on Viceroy Yuan at his home on Wen-bo Road, accompanied by his interpreter, Ts'ai. I am consistently impressed by Yuan. I am convinced that he is the most forward-thinking and civilised Mandarin in all of China. His work promoting libraries, tree-planting, a unified currency, not to mention a Western-style police force, has been entirely meritorious.'

'And yet he betrayed the movement for reform that you support.'

'Tosh.'

'It's true,' said Dumas, fortified by the wine. 'You know it, G.E. At the crucial moment, the young Emperor, aware that his aunt was cooking up some plot against him, sent a note ordering Yuan to arrest her first. Yuan betrayed him. If Yuan hadn't told the Empress Dowager what was afoot, she wouldn't have arrested her nephew or had T'an Ssu-tung and the others executed. So —'

Morrison cut off his friend mid-sentence. 'I'm not disputing the facts or the outcome. But Yuan had reason to doubt that the Emperor's order to detain the Empress Dowager was genuine. Colour of the ink: it was written in black instead of the imperial vermilion. He had no choice but to reveal the plot to the court. The point is, if China has any hope today of becoming a strong and modern nation, it lies with the likes of Yuan. Even if not all of those on the side of the reformers can see this.'

'So you say,' Dumas replied mildly, 'and I have no reason to doubt you.'

'Anyway, I certainly have gathered far more material than I can possibly fit into a six-hundred-and-fifty-word telegram, and that's all that concerns me for the moment.'

'Very good. Oh, what do you make of the news that the Russians are rallying? They claim to have sunk four Japanese battleships.'

'I am sure the Japanese will retaliate,' Morrison responded tersely, attacking his peas.

In Which Morrison Ponders a Paradox of Female Literacy and We Are Introduced to the Audacious Scheme of Lionel James

Back in Peking, Morrison wrote to Mae twice on the first day, twice on the second. Not even a postal card came in reply. His pride could not countenance the notion that she did not care enough to respond. And so his mind focused on other explanations. Perhaps she'd been more ill than Mrs Ragsdale had realised. He castigated himself for not having insisted on seeing her. On the morning of the third day, his correspondence took on a tender tone, solicitous and concerned for her health. But then he worried about sounding too much like a doctor and not enough like a lover. And so that afternoon he expressed himself with greater ardour, straining awkwardly towards the poetic. Meanwhile, with each delivery of the mail sack, his hopes swooped and plunged like a kite riding the capricious breezes of the Peking spring.

But if Morrison fretted, he did not languish. Constitutionally incapable of idleness, he filled these days with rounds of contacts, catching up with correspondence and cataloguing his books. When an acquaintance mentioned the burgeoning coolie trade to South Africa, he investigated the possibility of investing. He hatched a plan to abet the Japanese cause by sparking a run on the Russo-Chinese Bank, the institution that funded the Russian administration in Manchuria.

One afternoon, as Cook set out for the markets, he thought to ask Kuan how Yu-ti was settling in.

Kuan's gaze flickered at the mention of Yu-ti's name. He took a moment to answer. 'Cook not like her to read. He take away her books.'

Morrison did not expect this answer and it interested him. 'So she reads. That's unusual for a girl. Ah — but of course. Her father was a follower of T'an Ssu-tung. But wouldn't Cook find it useful to have a wife who can read and write?'

Kuan shook his head. 'No. He has old thinking.' He seemed lost in thought. When he finally spoke, it was with the kind of passion that Morrison had never heard in his Boy's normally careful voice. 'Women are human beings, not slaves of men. Not property.'

'Very progressive thinking, Kuan. You got that from the missionaries, did you?'

'The ancient sage Mo-tsu talks about universal love, and Buddha about compassion. And Confucius spoke of *jen* — I think in English you say benevolence. We do not need Christianity to say woman equal to man.'

'So you say. But T'an Ssu-tung, K'ang Yu-wei and others who've spoken about women's rights — they themselves admit they were influenced by Christian ideas.'

'Confucius and Mo-tsu and Buddha all came before Jesus. Maybe Christians got their ideas from them.'

'Maybe so,' Morrison replied without conviction. 'Speaking of the reformers, I hear that the anti-Ch'ing movement is gathering steam. Have you heard anything about that?'

'People are upset about the war. They say foreign powers are slicing up China like a soft melon. They —'

Morrison interrupted. 'Surely they can see that's the fault of the Old Buddha, can't they?'

Kuan measured his words. 'She is not the whole problem.'

'If China enjoyed good, sound governance, its sovereignty would not be in jeopardy,' pronounced Morrison with an air of finality. Something occurred to him. He returned to the previous topic. 'So, Yu-ti was taught to read and write.'

Kuan nodded, seemingly wary of where this was going.

'And yet she's not allowed books or a brush by her husband.'

'Yes.'

'That's a tragedy, wouldn't you say?'

'Yes.'

'So why does a woman who is privileged enough to be able to read and write not do so?'

'I don't understand,' Kuan said, frowning. 'Maybe my English …'

'No,' Morrison replied. 'It's not your English. It's Miss Perkins. I don't understand it myself. Why doesn't she write to me?'

The men travelled in silence for a while. 'You know, Kuan,' Morrison ventured, 'it's too bad Yu-ti wasn't married to you.'

'Not good to speak of this. You know *yuan fen*? We say two people have *yuan fen* or no. If no *yuan fen*, they will never be together. It is will of Heaven. Yu-ti's *yuan fen* is with Cook.'

Something in Kuan's expression told Morrison it would not be a good idea to pursue the topic any further. Besides, having brought up the subject of Mae in what he intended to be a light manner, he found himself lost in the morass of his own confused feelings.

On the evening of the third day back in Peking, Dumas arrived for a visit. Morrison greeted him warmly and invited him to stay for dinner.

Over Ceylon tea and a plate of Kierluff's biscuits, the men exchanged news and gossip. Morrison was more than happy to reveal to his colleague Granger's latest crimes against correspondence. 'He claims in one breath that the Russians are holding out well at Port Arthur, and in the next implies they are about to crumble.'

'I admire the man,' Dumas said. ''Tis no simple task to contradict oneself in such a large and generous manner.'

'Naturally, I declined to pass on his report. He then had the gall to request a credit of five hundred pounds. I am quite sure it would be spent on the syphilitic American whore, an erstwhile resident of Maud's Brothel, with whom I understand he's taken up residence. Either the sex or the pox has addled his brain. I refused, of course.'

'Of course,' Dumas said, spooning pressed sugar into his cup. 'Have I mentioned that my wife has taken passage on a steamship. She'll soon arrive back in China.'

'Nervous?'

Dumas plucked a biscuit off the plate. 'I have no doubt that she will take advantage of my contrition in all sorts of unpleasant ways.'

'For example?'

'For example, she is prone to nagging about my weight. But I shall defy her, at least on that count, and ask what it matters. She's not going to leave me because I have a potbelly, so long as it is never again discovered resting against another woman.' He bit into the biscuit defiantly. 'Ah. I knew there was something I had to ask you. I hear that *The Times* has dispatched the famous war correspondent Lionel James to cover the war. How is he getting on?'

'All right, I believe, though the Japanese have yet to accede to his plan.'

'Which is?'

'To set up a wireless communications ship able to report freely from the theatre of war. It's never been done before. Imagine — James could witness a naval battle, fire off a report and see it published halfway around the world the following day.'

Dumas shook his head. 'It would be a miracle. But he'll need the cooperation of the Japanese. Will they guarantee him safe passage, do you think?'

'Hard to say. I'm not overly optimistic. The Japanese government and navy will certainly be worried by the thought of him getting out reports that haven't passed by their censors.'

'It sounds as though he will be thwarted then,' Dumas observed.

'Not necessarily.'

'Have you ever met him?'

'Yes. In London.'

'What's he like?'

'Serious and self-willed,' Morrison responded.

'I cannot tell if you are complimenting or undermining him.'

'I do like James. But I'll give you an example. When I met him in London, I asked him to take me to the theatre. I was hoping for a sprightly sort of spectacle, ideally with dancers. He took me to an earnest play about dying kings. Later he told me that it was out of respect for my position that he chose such an entertainment.'

'I suppose I should consider it fortunate that I haven't yet been taken for such a respectable man that I can't be afforded the occasional extravaganza,' Dumas remarked.

'Indeed. The point about James is that he is as serious in his purpose as he is in his tastes. I assume he will knock on every door — he'll knock down every door — if he has to, but he will get his way.' It occurred to Morrison that there was a lesson in this for him. 'What are your plans? Do you return to Tientsin soon?'

'No, I shall be delayed here. Mind if I stay?'

'Not at all,' Morrison replied. 'It's just that it's been four days. I am becoming concerned about the reliability of the post and was thinking you might deliver a note to Miss Perkins for me.'

'I've heard that C.D. Jameson leaves for Tientsin tonight. You could send it with him.'

'Jameson? That rum-soaked homunculus? Don't you recall that he diddled me out of a luncheon with Miss Perkins when she last visited Peking?'

'True, but he does go tonight. And I hear he has some business with Mr Ragsdale, so he shall be dropping in on them anyway.'

Morrison made a face. 'Oh, why not? He owes me.'

In Which Miss Perkins Comforts Our Suffering Hero with a Letter and C.D. Jameson Makes a Terrible Boast

Ernest, honey …

Can you forgive me for not coming downstairs that day? I was terribly indisposed. I fear you would have been much put off by my appearance, which was frightful. How I wish I had been well enough to go to dinner or to meet you at all in the days you were in town. I understand from Mrs R. that you were the very life of the party! Mr Jameson kindly passed on your latest letter, which I treasure along with the other letters you have sent by post … I know I have been a terrible correspondent in every way, and still am if you would count my penmanship. I was never very good at penmanship. Once, a letter I wrote to Papa in Washington (you know he is a senator) took months to deliver because the writing on the envelope was so very poor! Papa had much to say about that, as you might imagine.

Anyway, I am feeling much better now and would be so very glad to see you …

The dear, sweet girl. Morrison read the letter twice through, sniffed the perfume still clinging to its pages, and held it to his heart.

'Are you all right, old chap?' called out C.D. Jameson from just inside the library door.

Morrison started. 'Yes, yes, just … composing my next cable.' *How did that bandy-legged old dipsomaniac sneak in here unannounced?* Morrison hastily slipped Maysie's letter into a pile of papers on his desk and rose to greet his guest. 'Thank you for delivering my letter to Miss Perkins, by the way.'

Jameson, flashing a greasy smile, fell heavily into Morrison's favourite chair. ''Twas a pleasure,' he slurred. 'Handed it to the young lady myself just yesterday morning.'

Fighting his natural revulsion towards the man and in the hope of gleaning more news of Mae, Morrison invited Jameson to stay for dinner. 'Dumas is expected as well; he's been staying.'

'That'd be grand.'

Kuan brought in a tray with glasses and the good sherry. Jameson pounced on the drink.

'I've heard some interesting scuttlebutt,' Jameson said as he drained his first glass and poured a second.

'Go on,' said Morrison, a jealous eye on the decanter.

'I've heard …' Jameson hesitated and swept the room with his rheumy eyes, as though spies from the Empress Dowager's court might be hiding behind one of the towering bookcases or peering in through a high, latticed window. He lowered his voice. 'I have heard that her favourite eunuch, the one they call "John Brown" —'

'Li Lien-ying.'

'Yes, Li Lien … that Li is no eunuch at all!'

'Which is why he is her favourite,' Morrison said flatly. 'He has kept his "precious", and not in a jar like the rest of them. He's the only eunuch who doesn't fall into hysteria at the sight of a teapot with a missing handle or a dog without a tail.'

Jameson's laugh threatened an imminent expulsion of phlegm. He slapped at his chest. As he calmed down, he grew thoughtful. A smile played around his brutish lips. He leaned forward suddenly, causing the chair to creak in complaint. There was a conspiratorial glint in his eye. 'I have to thank you for something.' He smirked. 'You did me a great service the other day when you asked me to deliver that letter to Miss Perkins. I have seen something quite unforgettable as a result.'

An intuition told Morrison he was not about to receive glad tidings. Had Jameson discovered her with another suitor? It was settled. He would return to Tientsin as soon as possible. 'And what was that, pray tell?'

Jameson didn't answer immediately. Chortling to himself, he rose from his chair. Lifting the dustcover on one of the bookshelves, he rifled through a stack of rare pamphlets from the Diocese of West China. Dust motes flew into the milky light and hung there.

'Easy on,' Morrison snapped, for as little as he cared for missionaries as a species, he did treasure their publications. 'Those pages are brittle and liable to —'

'Keep your garters tied, old boy.' Jameson let the cloth drop into place. He grinned, exposing a mouthful of nicotine-stained false teeth. 'Miss Perkins is quite the nymphomaniac, isn't she?'

Morrison flushed with surprise and outrage. 'You dishonour Miss Perkins!'

Jameson laughed. 'Miss Perkins has as much hold on honour as the Empress Dowager.'

'Sir!'

'Tsk. The only thing keeping that girl from an asylum and a clitoral excision is the uncommon wealth and influence of her dear father.'

'How dare you!' Morrison leapt to his feet. Had there been a glove handy, he would have thrown it down before the man. *Crass-natured, whacking great liar! Cantankerous freak!*

'Hear me out, old chap.' Jameson waved him back down. 'You're hardly one to moralise. Besides, we have shared a woman before. Does the name Anna Bullard, of 52 Water Tower, Shanghai, mean anything to you?'

'Yes,' Morrison snapped. 'An ear-splitting laugh, the pox, and champagne at five dollars a bottle. It is hardly germane!'

'My dear Morrison, no need to dissemble. Miss Perkins told me herself what you two got up to.'

'She talked about me? I don't believe it for an instant.'

Jameson sniggered. 'Do the words "Mountain-Sea Pass" mean anything to you?'

'Yes.' Morrison fumed. ''Tis the place where the Great Wall meets the sea.'

'You are a true gentleman, G.E.,' said Jameson, bowing grandly and nearly tipping over in the process. 'I fear I am your inferior in this regard. I can barely keep from singing her name aloud as I walk the streets. It was only because the dear girl was still suffering the effects of the grippe that I could be persuaded to return to Peking at all.'

'Is that so?' Jameson was an extravagant liar and a lush. He'd heard gossip from someone who'd been at the hotel in Mountain-Sea Pass and seen Morrison stroll out with her that night. Morrison told himself it was nothing but a poor joke. There was no other possible explanation, no credible one anyway. Morrison regretted asking the lecherous old croak to dinner.

Kuan entered to say that Colonel Dumas had left word that he would be joining them soon and that, as he was off to Kierluff's for some supplies, Yu-ti would serve in the meantime. Did his master require anything?

The removal of this oaf from my presence. 'No, thank you, Kuan.'

When Jameson again extended a paw in the direction of his books, Morrison overcame his repugnance to place a hand on his guest's shoulder, the better to march him out of his library, across the courtyard and into the parlour. There, Jameson immediately spotted a fine ivory *netsuke*, a belt ornament, and began to fondle it. Morrison, gritting his teeth, bade him be seated.

Yu-ti appeared in the doorway, carrying a tray with more sherry. She hesitated.

'*Lai, lai.* Come in.' Jameson beckoned to her with his forefinger. She reddened as though slapped. Her eyes shone for an instant with something that, if Morrison was not mistaken, seemed like defiance. Giving Yu-ti an apologetic look, Morrison held out his hand palm down, and curled his fingers inwards.

'Jameson, in all your years in this country, have you not yet learned that in China only a dog is called with one finger?'

'Is that so? Well blow me down. That certainly explains a few things.' Jameson sniggered.

'Come,' Morrison urged the still reticent Yu-ti. '*Lai.*' Pointing to the table, he mimed setting down the tray.

The breath caught in her throat as she approached them. Morrison knew that to many Chinese, 'Hairy Ones', as Westerners were called, smelled nauseatingly of beef and cow's milk. Jameson was not fragrant even to Western nostrils. Holding her breath, eyes downcast, Yu-ti placed the tray where Morrison had indicated.

Jameson leered at her. 'Speakee English?'

'Not a word,' Morrison answered for her, wondering as he spoke if that was really true. He had never asked.

'Pretty little thing, isn't she?' Jameson observed. 'Bertie Lenox Simpson says that native women are exceptionally soothing in bed.'

Yu-ti blushed, though whether from general shyness or comprehension, Morrison was not sure. 'All right, *tsou, tsou*,' Morrison said, waving Yu-ti away. She bowed her way out and hastened back to the kitchen.

'Bertie says that once you've had a native, you'll never go back to Western women, who either view fornication as the ultimate sacrifice or are complete and natural harlots. Which of course leads us back to the subject of —'

'Bertie is a syphilitic dunderhead,' barked Morrison before Jameson had a chance to finish the sentence. 'He's also a liar, for he's certainly gone back to Lady Bredon countless times.'

'Interesting character, Bertie. Speaks five languages, can imitate the call of the Peking muleteers and wrote a rather amusing memoir of the siege. I believe it sold rather well.'

Stupidly well, Morrison thought. He'd heard some readers actually preferred Bertie's loose account of events to his own. His irritation momentarily drifted in the direction of Bertie Lenox Simpson before returning to its mooring. 'Anyway,' he said, with a pointed glance at Jameson's paunch, 'I don't really care what Bertie does. But I do have some affection for Lady Bredon and believe she could do better than Bertie, whose stomach enters the room long before his nose.'

'I heard that.' Dumas appeared in the doorway, one hand patting his own belly. 'I shall remind myself to enter rooms sideways from now. Hello, Jameson.' His voice contained some surprise at finding Jameson in Morrison's parlour but he shook the man's hand as if it were an everyday occurrence.

'What news, Dumas?' Morrison asked, relieved to see his friend.

'I met the Japanese military attaché Kamei today at lunch. It seems the Russian minister is trying hard to convince the Chinese to assist the Russians against the Japanese in Manchuria. Kamei, naturally, is insisting to the Chinese that they maintain their neutrality in the conflict.'

'A bit hard, don't you think, considering it's being fought on Chinese soil?' Jameson interjected.

The other two turned and stared at him.

'Think about it,' Jameson said. 'The last time the Japanese invaded Manchuria, what, ten years ago during the Sino-Japanese War, they massacred thousands of Chinese citizens at Port Arthur alone. Razed whole towns to the ground. Burnt crops. No wonder that although the Treaty of Shimonoseki gave the Liaotung Peninsula to Japan, the Chinese were only too happy to invite in the Russians.'

'Nothing to do with natural justice,' Morrison said with a dismissive flip of the hand. 'The Chinese let the Russians take Port Arthur only because the Russians helped pay off China's war debts to Japan.'

Jameson shrugged. 'Agreed. I'm just saying that the Chinese are bound to be wary of seeing Japanese troops in Manchuria again. That's all. But I'm not criticising the war. I've got mining interests in Manchuria and wish to see them protected just as much as the next fellow.'

Morrison was still working out his retort when Kuan, who'd returned, rang the bell for dinner.

Morrison's table was not the most fashionable or elaborate in Peking but, unlike its host, on this particular evening it was welcoming enough. Candles in tall silver candelabras flickered warm light over a damask tablecloth. Branches of cherry blossom protruded from a modest vase at one end, and an unpretentious epergne stacked with sweetmeats and dried fruits occupied the centre.

The men took more sherry with their soup, and hock with their fish. They worked their way through mutton with fried potatoes and beer, rice and curry with ham, a custard, some cheese and salad, bread and butter and port wine, all delivered to the table in good order by Kuan. But Morrison was in a choler. The food, as good as it was, incited his dyspepsia. He said little as Jameson nattered on about gold mines in Jehol and passed on more spurious news from the Forbidden City. He nodded with exaggerated enthusiasm as Dumas shared some minor revelations about the Russian army's difficulty with supply. They'd just started on their liqueurs when Morrison, unable to contain himself a minute longer, turned to Dumas and announced, 'Jameson here is in love.'

'Is that so?' Dumas asked, turning to Jameson. 'And who is the lucky girl?'

'Miss Mae Perkins,' Morrison answered for him.

'Oh, truly?' Dumas could barely contain his mirth. That he doubted Jameson's chances very much was clear from the twitch of his eyebrows.

'Truly,' Morrison confirmed, as gloomy as a eunuch contemplating his 'precious'.

Dumas cocked his head. His smile dimmed.

'Jameson here says the girl is a confirmed nymphomaniac. He says he has confirmed it himself.'

Dumas looked alarmed. 'Well, isn't that remarkable?'

'She's quite the coquette.' Nodding and smiling like the cat that had swallowed the canary, Jameson popped a cherry into his mouth. 'Completely man-crazy.' He followed the cherry with a finger, making a minute adjustment to his false teeth. 'Nice little mole above her left hipbone.' As if the others might not be aware of that anatomical part, he poked at his stomach where his own hipbone might possibly be found, if only by way of excavation.

Morrison was filled with such a hot fury that he half expected his brandy to ignite in its snifter. He took a deep breath and counted to himself before raising his glass. 'Here's to Miss Perkins.' *That little courtesan. That strumpet. That trollop.*

'Miss Perkins,' the others chorused.

In Which Our Hero Passes a Damned Stupid Day, After Which He Is Both Revived by Beauty and Thwarted by Duty

The following morning, Morrison awoke with an aversion to sunlight and a head pounding from the previous night's excesses of alcohol and revelation. He thought despairingly, then crossly, of Mae. *Jameson. How could she?* He told himself that that was it. He was finished with her. Lesson learned. He was a busy man. He had more important things to think about than some faithless little American tart with such poor taste as to succumb to one such as Jameson. She was uncommonly charming and as accomplished in bed as any prostitute. But none of that was worth a farthing in the face of such duplicity and betrayal — not to mention lapse of taste. *Jameson?* Morrison had only had her that one time. It wasn't as if they were betrothed. *Thank ye gods!*

No, he thought. *It is impossible, inconceivable that she has ever been with Jameson as she has been with me. And yet, that mole ...* Perhaps she had mentioned it to Jameson. She was, after all, a most uninhibited conversationalist and, for all her mother's strictures, something of an actress as well. She might have spoken of it just for effect, much as she'd declared her intention to marry a native that night after dinner in Mountain-Sea Pass. As much as it pained him to think that she would make such a personal revelation to the undeserving other, he concluded that he'd been a fool to have taken Jameson at his word. Jameson was an accursed liar. Morrison had done Mae a terrible disservice to think otherwise. He leapt out of bed and splashed his face with cold water. Hair wild, thoughts feral, he raced into his study.

Snapping open his rolltop desk, he snatched up the letter he had received from her the day before, reread it and smiled with relief. He smoothed down his blotting paper and dipped the nib of his pen in his inkwell. In a melting reply, he kissed her from the palms of her hands to the inside of her elbows, stroked her hair, held her close, called her 'my darling Maysie' and beseeched her to be true. He added a few barbed witticisms at the expense of C.D. Jameson, asked after her health and expressed his wish to be remembered to the Ragsdales. Sealing the envelope with wax, he impressed it with his seal and bid Kuan to post it forthwith. There would be no more entrusting of such missives to unreliable messengers, that was for certain.

The day passed in a flurry of work as Morrison gathered the material for another telegram to *The Times*. There were rumours that the Japanese were bombarding Vladivostok. Morrison did the rounds of Japanese diplomats and military attachés, each one of whom claimed to know less about it than the one before. When he tested some of Granger's information on the Japanese military attaché Colonel Aoki, Aoki's response was a single word, as dismissive in English as it was in French: '*Canard!*'

That afternoon, a new cable arrived from Granger with the instructions, 'Say it comes from a reliable source but not from me or Newchang.'

Granger's ineptitude nettled him. The whole point was reliability. If one was to make a reasonable judgment about a situation, one needed to know the facts. He could not rely on the bungling Granger for the truth about the war. It would be like relying on the malign Jameson for news about Mae. 'All my work comes from a reliable source, otherwise I would not send it,' he muttered as he consigned Granger's work to the fire.

He was just replacing the poker when Kuan entered with another telegram, this one from James. A vision of himself as Gulliver in Lilliput, assailed and tied down by small men, came to Morrison as he took James's cable to his desk to read. *Good god.* The report, intended for publication, was replete with news and speculation as to present and future movements of the Japanese army. Morrison considered this a shocking failure of judgment coming, as it did, from a correspondent who had seen action in the Boer Wars and the Sudan. How the Russians would have relished this information! Screwed up into a ball, James's telegram followed Granger's into the potbelly stove.

Younger men like Granger and James — and Egan for that matter — had vigour on their side; Morrison would happily acknowledge that. But discretion, reasonableness, calm-headedness and wisdom — such was the province of age.

As night fell, Morrison agonised over whether to write Mae another letter. He was not sure why he felt such a desperate need to persist. The pride that drove him also gave him pause. Jameson's calumnies had rattled him more than he cared to admit.

On the following morning, Morrison slapped on his trilby, slung his cape over his shoulders and loped through the dusty streets towards and then through Ch'ien-men Gate. Once south of the gate, he plunged into the familiar, roiling public excitement that the Chinese called 'the hot and the noisy', which characterised that part of Peking just south of the Tartar Wall known as the Chinese City. Here was enterprise, from the streetside barbers, scribes and fortune tellers to the bustling shops. Overhead dangled painted shop signs in the shapes of the goods on offer — wooden combs, decorative glass grapes, gourds for wine, the soles of men's boots. From a pharmacy, with its infinite small drawers of herbs, wafted the mysterious, close smells of Chinese medicine into the street. From a teahouse came the staccato of a storyteller's clappers, and already a crowd was forming outside the Heavenly Happy Tea Garden in Polishing Street, where one could watch moving pictures — 'electric shadows' — on equipment brought all the way from Germany. Further south were the wilder diversions of the Heavenly Bridge district, famous for its sing-song girls, flower houses and efficient gangs of tatterdemalions who could strip a man of his watch and purse before he sensed them coming.

Other foreigners of Morrison's acquaintance were wont to declaim at length about the quotidian delights of the ancient capital. His friend Lady Susan Townshend was even writing a book about them — *My Chinese Notebook,* she was going to call it. She had shown him the draft. It was full of vivid descriptions of such adventures as riding in rough Peking carts (once was enough for Lady Susan) and visiting opium dens. Morrison was not immune to the exotic, the strange, the constant sensory assault that was China. Yet he could not help but feel that such literary effusions were the proper domain of women, dilettantes and professional travellers — not the professional journalist. Since the publication of *An Australian in China* almost ten years earlier, he'd barely confessed them to his journal.

Coming now upon a crowd gathered around some entertainment, he happily joined the throng. At its centre stood a man holding a stick on which three songbirds perched. A flick of the showman's wrist sent the birds wheeling through the air. When he whistled, they landed back on the stick in turn, taking their bows by bobbing up and down. The onlookers laughed and applauded, rewarding him with a rain of copper coins.

Finally, Morrison arrived at his destination, Liu Li Chang, originally the site of the imperial kilns that produced the thousands of golden roof tiles for the palaces within the Forbidden City. Liu Li Chang was a thriving street of curio merchants and booksellers and one of Morrison's favourite haunts in the capital. Past the ornate shopfronts lay treasure troves of rare books, fine calligraphy, old paintings and stone rubbings, as well as bibelots such as jade archery rings, snuff bottles and belt ornaments. The clicking of abacuses, the chink of lidded teacups on saucers and the rolling hum of negotiations were sounds that gladdened Morrison's heart today more than usual.

Half an hour later, a small paper-wrapped parcel under his arm, Morrison passed whistling back through Ch'ien-men Gate. In a generous mood, he felt in his pocket for a few coins to throw the hollow-eyed beggars who were huddled against the wall like sacks of rags. These were the survivors; every morning a cart came to collect the bodies of those who had not made it through the night.

Back in the Tartar City, Morrison quickened his footsteps in the direction of Rue Marco Polo in the eastern part of the Legation Quarter, not far from the Ch'ien-man Gate, and the home of Sir Robert Hart, Inspector-General of the Chinese Customs Service. Hart was the most influential foreigner in the

Celestial Empire — 'Our Hart', the Empress Dowager him.

'Ah, Dr Morrison.' Hart emerged from his cluttered study with Morrison's calling card in his hand. He was immaculate in grey-striped trousers and black vest and coat, his white beard neatly combed. The only discordant note in the ensemble was a tie of blue ribbon. Once, on a holiday in Peking's Western Hills, Hart had famously reached for what he thought was his black tie, recoiling just in time, for the 'tie' was in fact a small, venomous snake. Since then, the Inspector-General had only worn ties of blue.

Though he was greeted cordially, Morrison never could escape the sensation that Hart viewed him with a similar wariness to that with which he beheld narrow black ties. He knew that Hart disapproved both of his harsh views on the Empress Dowager and his warmongering on behalf of Japan. For his part, Morrison suspected the Irishman, who had only returned to Europe twice in forty years and who had scandalously taken a native concubine, of viewing the world through Chinese lenses. Hart had outrageously described the Boxers as patriotic, their movement 'justifiable' in theory. It made Morrison's blood boil. Yet for all his acquaintances in the Mandarinate, he trusted only Hart to provide him with an accurate sense of the court's thinking on the war.

On this day, Morrison managed to extract only the most general sort of information from Hart: China would *most likely* remain neutral. With ongoing threats to Chinese and particularly Manchurian lives and property, however, Hart warned that neutrality might not be enforceable. The court should not be held responsible if there was some resistance to the Japanese incursion by the population. Beyond this, Hart could not or would not say.

As Morrison was taking his leave, Hart's niece, the charming and clever Juliet Bredon, came in from a walk, apples in her cheeks. Five years earlier, on a group excursion to the Western Hills, Morrison and Juliet, then eighteen, had ducked into a Chinese temple to hide from a tedious old missionary. The crusty old man of God had found them anyway and insisted they join him for biscuits and tea. 'Bad biscuits, worse tea,' Morrison had observed afterwards, and young Juliet had laughed musically.

'Hello, Dr Morrison,' she greeted him with a happy smile. 'We haven't seen you for such a long while.'

'Hello, Juliet.' He smiled back. 'You're looking lovely this fine morning.'

'Dr Morrison was just leaving,' her uncle said.

Useless old sleevedog, thought Morrison as he trudged towards his next appointment. It was with a Mandarin named Hwang and was ostensibly to congratulate him on winning one of the Ch'ing Court's highest honours. Hwang and his interpreter, Kwang, received the Australian with elaborate courtesy, a plate of sesame-flavoured sweets, and cups of fragrant leaf tea from Hunan. Yet when Morrison tried to steer the topic on to the war, Hwang brought up the invasion of Tibet by British forces several months earlier.

'The Tibet Expedition is wholly in China's favour,' Morrison argued. 'The Russian Empire, as you know, is trying to encircle British India. If they succeed, it will benefit neither of our countries. And yet, as you are aware, the Thirteenth Dalai Lama is so friendly with the Russians he has a Russian courtier. It was widely rumoured that the Ch'ing Court was thinking to allow him to invite in the Russians. England does not wish Tibet to remain a wild and barbarian country without rulers. But neither does it want to see Tibet fall under the shadow of the Tsar's empire. No, it must become another province of China, governed as Yunnan and Szechuan are.'

Kwang translated for Hwang and then conveyed Hwang's response: 'Does England itself really have no territorial designs on Tibet?'

'We would not take one foot. It is China that must make Tibet strong.'

'Correct me if I am mistaken,' Kwang said after a thoughtful pause, 'but I recall that in 1900, Mr Younghusband wrote a letter to your own honourable newspaper. I read it and memorised it, for a facility for memorisation is the benefit of my poor education in the Chinese classics. If you will permit me, I'd like to recite a line in the letter that I have never forgotten ...'

Morrison nodded, setting his jaw against the inevitable. He had a fair idea of what he was about to hear.

'He said, and I quote, "The earth is too small, the portion of it they occupy is too big and rich, and the intercourse of nations is now too intimate to permit the Chinese keeping China to themselves."' Kwang translated what he had said for Hwang before returning his attention to their guest. 'What do you think of that, Dr Morrison?'

'I do believe,' Morrison replied in a voice that didn't admit any doubt, 'that the intercourse of nations has benefited China as it benefits Britain.'

Hwang, upon receiving the translation, smiled and urged more tea on his guest. Morrison understood that to be a signal to take his leave.

Damned stupid day, Morrison thought as he trudged home. But then he noticed the glow of buds on the tendrils of the capital's willow trees and how the canals had begun to thaw, though a fringe of ice still clung to the edges of the man-made lakes. A swooping music filled the air. Lifting his gaze, he watched a flock of snow-flower pigeons soar past, lacquered bamboo whistles fastened to their tails with fine copper wire. The birds circled against a brilliant blue sky, looping over the sparkling golden roofs of the palace. His spirits rose. The remnants of his gloom evaporated in the spring sunshine. He picked up his pace.

Back home, Cook's new lark was singing in its bamboo cage and the Lion's Head goldfish, beloved of all his servants, chased the dragonflies that hovered over their blue-and-white ceramic tub. The potted orchids lovingly cultivated by Kuan had days earlier erupted in delicate white-and-pink blooms. Grass was sprouting anew between the paving stones of the courtyard and in tufts from the roof tiles. Nature's pulse was quickening. Morrison would not wait on the mail or fret for one minute longer.

'Kuan!'

His Boy hurried out of the house in response.

'We're going to Tientsin.' Then his face fell, for Kuan handed him a telegram. Lionel James was on his way to Peking. Tientsin would have to wait. Whilst a visit from Granger wouldn't have kept Morrison from his travels, James, unfortunately, was a different story.

More than two weeks had passed since he'd met Miss Mae Ruth Perkins, and one month since the outbreak of the Russo-Japanese War. Both seemed as distant as history.

In Which the Famous War Correspondent Describes a Skirmish with Tofu and Morrison Enlists Himself in the Battle for the Future of Correspondence

'So there we are in Yokohama, in this room with walls made out of, what, toothpicks and paper, and I've got my boots off. I don't feel happy about that at all. We're sitting cross-legged. It's putting my legs to sleep. Brinkley's pushing all these damned oddly shaped little dishes at me. I hardly recognise a thing. All very pretty but it doesn't look like food. *This* is food.' Lionel James pointed to his plate of boiled mutton with caper sauce. 'You know what all that sushi-shimi stuff looked like to me? It looked just like the titbits of information on the war that the Japanese government is doling out to correspondents in lieu of access to the front. Nicely packaged, wholly insubstantial. This doesn't bother our colleague Brinkley, though. Neither the quality of the information nor the food. Our man in Japan has gone completely native. Speaks the lingo, eats raw fish with sticks, has taken a little Japanese missus. He's telling me the Japanese have the most developed aesthetic in the world; couldn't be more proud of his adopted country's achievements if they were his own. He pushes a plate towards me. On it is something that looks like wet shoelaces left behind by leprechauns. "Seaweed," he says, as if that will really make me go for it. Then he urges on me something that looks like a block of milk. It falls apart on my camp fork and tastes like damp. He tells me it has as much protein as a plate of chops. That's when I know he has passed the point of no return. I had a damned hard time keeping him on the subject.'

'Did you meet his wife?' Morrison asked.

'No. I hear she is a pretty sort.'

'That she is. It's interesting to observe them together, for you can find the key to Brinkley in their interaction. She appears frail and ladylike, and makes a great show of deferring to her husband. In truth, she leads him by the nose no less surely than if she'd put a ring through it, as the farmers here do with their buffalo. Our uxorious colleague submits to her — and to her country — as wholeheartedly as a Mohammedan submits to Allah. I am guessing that your plan to report from the scene of the action makes him nervous, though he chooses an approach of Oriental indirectness by which to communicate his concerns.'

'I don't understand his reservations. The plan is a boon to our mutual employer and to journalism itself!' James thumped the table. The crockery danced. Kuan poked his head in to see if anything was the matter. 'Sorry, old chap,' James apologised as the vibrations settled.

When Morrison had described James earlier to Dumas, he'd mentioned his determination. He'd forgotten that his colleague's other leading quality was rampant excitability.

'G.E.,' James continued, 'I've reported from Africa and India. I've had to get my reports out by pigeons, camels, horses, skin-floats, heliographs, bottles, field telegraph, boats and flags, cut-throat Pathans and long-limbed Ethiopians. It is ludicrous in this modern age, with all the advances made in wireless telegraphy, that we must take such risks. We have steam-powered rotary presses that can print hundreds of thousands of newspapers in an hour. But what's the point if the news is stale?' He went to bang on the table again but stopped himself just in time. 'The public deserves better. *We* deserve better. The future of correspondence rests with the science of Hertzian waves.'

'Indeed. This is the twentieth century after all.' Morrison unexpectedly found himself infected with his colleague's enthusiasm.

A grateful smile lit James's face for a moment as he fumbled in his pockets for tobacco pouch and pipe.

'Here's the problem with Brinkley,' Morrison said, watching James prepare his smoke with practised, yellow-stained fingers. 'It's two problems really. One is pressure from the Japanese. They're worried about the difficulty of censoring your reports. As you know, they're fanatical about controlling news from the battlefield. Brinkley knows that if the Japanese have any complaints, they will go to him.'

'I will take full responsibility for my reports.'

'That's not how it works in the Orient.'

'I'm not an Oriental. What's the second problem?'

'It's obvious. The Japanese have been refusing all journalists, and most military attachés, access to the front. And so any news that they had given *The Times* permission to steam straight into the Siege of Port Arthur, on its own boat no less, would incite the rest of the correspondents violently. Your reports will make their dispatches look even more belated and second-hand than they are. Never mind the Japanese navy — the other correspondents will be watching you like a hawk. This naturally places Brinkley, as your colleague, in a deucedly awkward position.'

James sucked on his pipe, unmoved, filling the room with the scent of tobacco and a cloud of stubbornness. 'That's not my concern.'

Morrison liked James. He wanted him and *The Times* to succeed. He would try to make it happen — no, he *would* make it happen. It occurred to him that he was at an age and in a position in life where he ought to be able to forgo the sort of compromises forced upon youth. He did not need to sleep in short beds any longer. He had been recently unbalanced by romantic obsession and underemployment; a focus, a mission, would restore him. 'We will get Britain's minister in Japan, Sir Claude MacDonald, to help us.' Morrison heard himself say the words 'we' and 'us'. He was committed. It felt good.

'Do you know Sir Claude?' James asked hopefully. 'Brinkley said that Sir Claude has already told him that we're wasting our time and our employer's money. Noel, the admiral in charge of the China Station, is apparently applying considerable pressure on the minister to go against us. Brinkley says Noel is furious at the thought that through some blunder or indiscretion we might compromise British neutrality. Or create some sort of precedent by which journalists could demand access to any future theatre of war and the right to report from it unhindered. I suspect that is the real problem, *franchement*.' James pronounced the French word like a true Englishman, biting down on the 'ch' as though it were crackling.

'You'd be right about that,' Morrison said. 'The thing about MacDonald is that he may have been a good military officer but he doesn't have the marrow for diplomacy. He needs to be able to stand up to the likes of Noel. You know, they say Lord Salisbury only appointed MacDonald minister because Salisbury believed that MacDonald was in possession of evidence proving that he, Salisbury, was Jack the Ripper.'

James's eyes nearly popped out of his head. 'Is there any truth —'

'No of course not,' Morrison replied. 'It's just scuttlebutt. But it's true that MacDonald is a vacillating and selfish old dry-as-dust who, just as water always flows downhill, will always do what's easiest for himself. Especially if he is being pressured. You know the old joke about the difference between a diplomat and a virgin?'

'What's that?'

'If a diplomat says *yes*, he means *perhaps*. If a diplomat says *perhaps*, he means *no*. If a diplomat says *no*, he's no diplomat.'

'And the virgin?'

'If a virgin says *no*, she means *perhaps*. If a virgin says *perhaps*, she means *yes*. If a virgin says *yes* — well, she's no virgin.'

'Ha. I must remember that one.'

'Anyway, the point is — best to act discreetly for the time being. And work on the Japanese. The rest will fall into line if you can get past them.'

'I am the soul of discretion,' James asserted. 'And I am working on the Japanese.'

There was something in the way James said this that made Morrison think there was something else to the story. But if he had been hinting at something, he offered no further clues.

'All right then,' Morrison said after a pause. 'I shall write to Sir Claude forthwith. I shall not mention anything about the neutrality issue as that could be tricky. Instead, in my letter I shall impress upon him how, if you are allowed to report directly from the front, *The Times* will be the paper of record on this war. It will reflect well on all of us and be to the glory of Britannia. I shall compliment him on the foresight and spine that he will have displayed in standing with us and make it clear that his hand will be one of those that has written this new page in the history of journalism.'

Morrison drank in the admiration on James's face like a tonic.

In Which Jameson Shows That, Whilst Undeniably Vile, He Is at Least Consistent, and Our Hero Reads a Most Immoral Book

When Dumas arrived from Tientsin on the evening train, Morrison related the gist of his conversation with Lionel James.

'Let us hope permission is forthcoming,' Dumas said. 'Where is your man now?'

'On his way back to Japan.'

'And your plans?'

'I am stuck here for another day doing the rounds of the ministers and attachés on his behalf. As for my own best plan of action, I am still mulling that over.'

'With regard to Sir Claude? It sounds to me like you've worked it out rather well.'

'No. I'm speaking of the whole distasteful business with Jameson. It has been eating at me.'

'Ah. Why not call Jameson's bluff?' Dumas suggested. 'If he's telling the truth, then it's better that you know. If he was only trying to rile you, that should become apparent soon enough. Ask him over in company and see if he sticks to his line.'

'Good thinking.'

Morrison dashed off a note asking Jameson to luncheon the

next day. He also invited some others to whom he owed invitations, including the British military officer Colonel Bagshawe, a man so placid he appeared somnambulant, and his excitable wife; Mrs Williams, a platitudinous Englishwoman whose husband owned a Yangtze steamer; and, gritting his teeth, the Nisbets.

And so it was over lunch the next day that Jameson, unprompted, regaled Mrs Bagshawe and Mrs Nisbet, between whom he was seated, with the details of what he claimed to be his ongoing affair with Miss Mae Perkins. The shock on Mrs Nisbet's face and the delight on Mrs Bagshawe's roused Jameson to deliver an oration as slanderous as it was detailed.

Villainous man, Morrison seethed. *Clearly a sordid fantasy all of his own and nowise amusing! He's read* Venus in Furs *and let his wretched imagination run away with him! She is not that way inclined.* She had suggested nothing of the sort to him anyway, not that he would have submitted to it. Jameson's own perversions, he concluded, were clearly of the most wretched nature.

His mood grew acerbic. When Colonel Bagshawe playfully mentioned British Legation Secretary Reginald Tower's propensity to fall asleep at formal dinners, Morrison snapped, 'No one is ever sorry about that, much preferring Tower asleep to Tower orating.' Mrs Williams mentioned that on their last visit to London she and Mr Williams had seen 'that other famous Australian', Nellie Melba, in concert. 'Madame Melba!' Morrison exclaimed. 'That woman has the manners of a lime-juicer. She drinks, uses foul language and at her table permits a ribald conversation that would shock any decent lady.' *Though probably no worse than I have just tolerated at my own.*

His guests bent to their plates. Dumas worried his sideburns until they stood at angles from his cheeks. Jameson remained offensively cheerful.

Morrison was as relieved as everyone else when the luncheon drew to a close. Worn out by his own cantankerousness, he tidied his correspondence, went out to pace the Tartar Wall and retired early that evening to read. Two days before, Menzies had sent him a gift of a large box of books from the English bookseller in Tientsin. On top of the pile, a slim volume with an attractive dustcover caught his eye: *Anna Lombard,* the latest novel by Victoria Cross. *Anna Lombard* had sold millions of copies worldwide to become the bestselling book of its time. Morrison had heard that the author identified with the New Woman movement and that the novel had stirred considerable scandal. This had intrigued him but he had not been able to procure a copy before now.

Turning up the spirit lamp, he settled himself in his favourite reading chair, tie loosened and carpet slippers replacing his brogues. Despite the advent of spring, the northern Chinese evenings were still chilly. He pulled a woollen rug over his lap. Kuan had placed a brazier at his feet. The kettle on the potbellied stove wheezed softly. A cart mule clip-clopped along the lane with heavy footsteps, bell tinkling with every sway of its neck.

Morrison lost himself in the voluptuous Indian night of the novel, in which the purple sky was 'throbbing, beating, palpitating with the light of stars and planets', and in which the 'soft, hot air itself seems to breathe of the passions' and tropical flowers released their cloying perfume. He chuckled to himself at the male narrator Gerald's description of the cackle-headed females at a colonial ball. He grew as interested as Gerald himself in the appearance of the cultivated and passionate beauty Anna Lombard. He nodded with recognition as Gerald remarked that, having come to the East, he wished never to return, for the Orient 'holds one with too many hands'. And he suffered a shock almost equal to Gerald's when he discovered that the brilliant Anna had not only taken a native Pathan for a lover but, outrageously, a *husband*. The authoress lingered long on her staggeringly wanton descriptions of the Pathan's masculine yet sensual beauty — as if that excused the white woman's passion. His indignation mounting, Morrison turned the pages ever more swiftly, appalled by how Gerald passively accepted every insult to his British manliness. Loving Anna with a steadfast heart, Gerald waited for her to come back to him with almost — it had to be said — *female* devotion. Reaching the last page, Morrison snapped the book shut. He now understood why some of the critics called the book 'disgusting' and 'thoroughly impure', even as others — no doubt women hiding behind male pseudonyms — pronounced it 'remarkable' and 'difficult to praise too highly'.

The illusion of subcontinental heat disappeared from the cold Peking night. He would go to bed, but not before recording in his journal in a firm, certain hand that *Anna Lombard* was *the most immoral work* he had ever read. George Ernest Morrison could be very assured in his opinions about the immorality of other people and particularly women: Nellie Melba, the Empress Dowager, Anna Lombard and … No. Jameson was a liar, a masturbatory fabulist.

Morrison's dreams that night were dense and scented with jasmine.

The following morning, the eighteenth of March, snowflakes swirled through the air. Spring may have been retreating but Morrison was advancing. He bounded out of bed.

'Kuan! We're going to Tientsin. Get us tickets on the first train out.'

119

In Which Morrison Is Vastly Relieved by Miss Perkins's Attentions, and Bonnets Are Discussed and Immediately Forgotten

Stamping snow from his boots, Morrison stepped into the oasis of the Astor House Hotel. Soon he was following the Chinese bellhop through the familiar panelled corridors to the second floor. Sending Kuan out on some errands, Morrison sat down at the escritoire and penned a note. *My dear Mae, I must know … Jameson said … of course. I don't believe …* He tore it up and wrote another, far milder in tone and neutral in content, blotting it carefully. He told Kuan to deliver the chit with utmost expediency after which he could take the day off. *I will confront her in person.*

Morrison did no such thing. He knew from the first sight of Mae that C.D. Jameson was nothing but a mendacious old windbag. From the manner in which her eyes softened at the sight of him. The way she flung herself into his arms. The urgency with which furs and hat and gloves and shoes were discarded and top bodice, under bodice, gored skirt, petticoat, corset cover, busk, corset, chemise and drawers whispered to the floor. The tattoo of their hearts. Her inquisitive lips. Her delicious unfurling. Her nimble pleasure at his own excitement and the inventiveness with which she sought to increase it. Her own quivering hunger. Nothing existed outside the intoxicating dance, the mingling of flesh, the mutual conquering and vanquishing. Not China, not war, not care nor suspicion — and certainly not C.D. bloody Jameson.

Afterwards, he wrapped her tightly in his arms, inhaling the sour-plum smell of their spent passion. He excoriated himself for listening to Jameson's calumny. He could have wept for his lack of trust. But Morrison was not the sort to weep. And there was only so long a man could hold such a magnificently buxom and callipygian form in his arms before rising once more to the siren's song.

But for a commitment to a late luncheon with Mrs Ragsdale and Mrs Goodnow in the Astor's glass-domed dining room, they would never have left his room at all.

Mrs Goodnow was the wife of a prosperous British merchant who was a notorious seducer of other men's wives and who also kept a Chinese concubine on the side. Society was much tested by the question of whether Mrs Goodnow was aware of her husband's infidelity, for she was of an invariably cheery disposition — only increasing public sympathy and kindness in her direction as all awaited the thrilling moment when all would be revealed. The truth was that Mrs Goodnow, an attractive and vivacious woman in her forties, not only knew but was complicit in her husband's debaucheries. She took a range of interesting lovers herself, including, on one apparently spectacular occasion, a Khamba warrior from Tibet, and occasionally slept with her husband's concubine either in front of him or by herself. Morrison had long suspected she was not the innocent victim she seemed to be. Mae, who had become Mrs Goodnow's confidante, confirmed it. She told Morrison that Mrs Goodnow had confessed to greatly mourning the passing of Queen Victoria;

should sexual mores grow too relaxed under the reign of King Edward, already famous for his womanising, Mrs Goodnow had declared, she would have to find another vice with which to amuse herself. Mrs Goodnow was more than happy to provide Mae with alibis; that day, the pair of them had supposedly been at Bible study, a ruse that pleased Mrs Ragsdale no end.

Morrison, nerves sparking and limbs languid, was barely able to focus on a word any of the ladies said. And though the Astor's dining room was famed for the excellence of both its cuisine and wine cellar, Morrison did not know or care if he was eating fish or ham, and if blindfolded would have been unable to say if the wine he was drinking was white or red. Mae did not aid the project of concentration with her outrageous half-mast gaze and hinting lips, nor Mrs Goodnow with her barely suppressed hilarity. After the coffee and petits fours, Mae remarked that she wished to purchase a bonnet before the shops closed and asked Morrison if he and Mrs Goodnow would accompany her to the department store on the Ho Ping Trade Road. Bonnet shopping was not high on Morrison's list of favourite recreations. 'I would be delighted,' he said. Mrs Ragsdale, amiably stupefied by food and drink, allowed them to see her into her carriage.

After the three of them waved her off, Mrs Goodnow, eyes twinkling, bade them a pleasant afternoon and departed for an assignation of her own. Mae snuggled her hand into the crook of Morrison's arm — 'Shall we?' Fresh snowfall had left a hush over the garrulous streets. Drifts lay across the branches of trees like lazing cats. The air's cold breath tingled in Morrison's nose and mouth. She fixed him with an irresistible look.

'I take it that Miss Perkins is not too pressed on the matter of bonnet shopping?' he asked in a voice full of hope.

'I do wish to purchase a new bonnet. But perhaps this is not the best time for it.'

Blessed relief! 'And what would mademoiselle prefer to do?'

'Ernest, honey, need you ask?'

Mae knew better than any woman he had ever encountered how to make a man happy without for a moment neglecting her own pleasure. In fact, her capacity for pleasure was so voracious, Morrison worried a little for his heart.

Dinner that night with Mr and Mrs Ragsdale, Menzies and other anodyne company was *dull passing belief*, Morrison later recorded in his journal. It was nonetheless entertaining to hear Maysie explain, in answer to Mrs Ragsdale's enquiry, how she'd tried on 'dozens of bonnets, and yet none suited me; isn't that so, Ernest?' He'd replied that she had looked lovely in all of them and that it was the bonnets' loss that none had been chosen to accompany her home.

After the meal, the men gathered in Mr Ragsdale's library for cigars and brandy. Out of habit and curiosity, Morrison scanned his host's bookshelves, finding nothing to impress him and several titles that provoked his contempt. He was just beginning to enjoy himself when the men clustered around him, quizzing him about 'his' war. Was he surprised, after his predictions of a swift victory for the Japanese, that Japan had still not taken Port Arthur from the Russians? And what of his colleague Lionel James's wireless scheme — did he really think the Japanese would allow it? Were the difficulties experienced by the Japanese military behind its reluctance to open the war to the correspondents generally? Morrison expounded with more confidence than he felt on Japan's chances and intentions, though in truth, after such a day, he struggled to keep his mind on the war at all. After the weeks of agonising doubt as to whether Mae cared for him, his relief was visceral. He stifled an uncharacteristic urge to fling open the room's french doors, sail out onto the balcony and proclaim her name aloud to startled streets, to dance, to sing, to rush back into the room where the ladies were gathered, to scoop her into his arms and carry her off. He felt young with joy. He willed the evening to a close, for he wished to hasten with sleep the coming of the following day and his next assignation with the lover he named in his journal the *flashing-eyed maiden*.

In Which Morrison Impresses Miss Perkins with the Mark of his Spearhead, Miss Perkins Confesses to Having Engaged in a Certain Amount of Diplomatic Activity and a Question About Love Receives a Most Surprising Answer

The following morning Morrison awoke in good cheer and, he fancied, with the energy of a man twenty years younger. Whistling, he set out for his various appointments, interviews and meetings. To Westerners he spoke of gold and tin and quicksilver and the many ways Japanese control over Manchuria and Korea would benefit Britannia and her allies. To Chinese he spoke of the advantage to their country of allowing this to happen by remaining neutral. He filled his head with facts and his journal with information, ruminations and figures.

'Do you think Japan and England rule China better than Chinese?' asked Kuan as they were hurrying between appointments. His expression was itself a perfect model of neutrality.

'No, of course not. Not in the sense that China should abandon its sovereignty. But if the Chinese government was smart, it would let the English look after China's defence. It'd be as quiet as Sunday school then. You could bring in all sorts of changes — your reforms — and you wouldn't have any more problems from the likes of the Boxers. Or anyone else for that matter.'

'If China had a modern army we would not need British. It is better, I think, to defend ourselves.'

'It'll be a long while before that happens, Kuan. You know that.'

Kuan started to say something, then caught himself.

Morrison did not pursue the conversation. His mind was already on other things.

At the age of twenty, Morrison had packed a swag with a bedroll, a billy can and some beef jerky. He soaped the inside of his stockings, slapped a panama hat on his head, and stuck a sheath knife in his belt. Breaking a raw egg into each of his boots for lubrication, he set out to walk more than two thousand miles from Normanton, near the coast of the Gulf of Carpentaria, to Adelaide. His goal was to retrace in reverse the footsteps of the explorers Burke and Wills. They had died attempting to traverse Australia twenty-one years before that, just before Morrison was born. People told him he was mad, suicidal. They warned of poisonous spiders and snakes. They said that if the critters didn't get him, the blacks would. He smiled and waved goodbye. And when he found himself up to his armpits in swamp, or tramping across clay flats on which grew little but salt-bush and mallee, or when he was tortured by heat and thirst, or tested by cyclones, he exulted no less than when he found himself in sun-dappled thickets of yapunyah or watching mobs of kangaroos grazing at sunset or sitting around a friendly campfire with the people of the bush. Humbled by the great sky above his head and covered in red dust from the earth below his feet, he knew he wouldn't die. Not when there was so much to do in life. And certainly not in the midst of such life, such beauty.

Optimism and confidence, vital to the overlander, are helpful traits for a lover as well. Nestled with Maysie later that afternoon, Morrison felt happy to the point of giddiness. In a moment of egg-down-the-boots optimism, he whispered into her hair, 'Maysie, dearest, dare I think that you are as happy as I am right now?'

'Oh, honey,' she answered, 'it's in my nature to be happy.'

He had anticipated a number of answers to his question. This wasn't one. 'I meant —'

'I know, honey. Of course I'm happy here, now, with you. You should know that.'

The way she said it, and a look in her eyes that seemed a lot like pity, made him uneasy.

'Let me explain it another way,' she said. 'I went to the Chinese opera one night last week.'

'I see,' said Morrison, more confused.

'The costumes, the make-up and the gestures were magnificent. And the story was wonderful, all about a scholar who finds a painting of a beautiful woman and falls in love with her.'

'*Peony Pavilion*. I know it. It's a famous story.'

'I felt it had such universal truth in it. Perhaps a particular truth, too.'

'And what would that be?'

'That men fall in love with an ideal image of woman,' she replied.

'And women don't do the same? I believe that the heroine first died of a broken heart after meeting the scholar in a dream. He came upon that picture after her death, dreamed about her in turn, and brought her back to life.'

'True, but the story was written by a man, so of course he wrote it that way. I think that, contrary to general opinion, we women are the less romantic sex. Don't look so incredulous. We may be mistaken for the more romantic, due to the sentimentality of expression that's so common in women's books and magazines. But don't ever forget that we have an inherent — or perhaps well-taught — desire to please. That commonly entails letting a man feel that he is the centre of our world when that centre might just as easily be ... I don't know ... bonnets or novels or entertaining.'

''Tis a sad day when a man feels he must compete with a bonnet. You're teasing me. But what are you saying, my dear Maysie?'

'Maybe that what you see is not who I am.'

'What — that this charming, sensuous, joyous, intelligent and loving creature in my arms is, in fact, some dour and doughy old spinster? Or perhaps one of those mischievous sprites the Chinese call fox spirits? Or, I don't know, a Mandarin in the Imperial Court?' Morrison found it hard to respond with any seriousness.

'You see, you are proving my point. Your affection for me makes you blind, though I'd be a daisy if I didn't appreciate that. There's another thing about the opera that reminds me of us.'

'Do tell.'

'Let me get this right.' She closed her eyes for a moment, thinking. 'You see, laughter in the Chinese opera is so stylised that it is far more than just a laugh. It is all laughter, laughter everywhere, laughter of every type and for every joke on Earth.

Weeping is the same, it's like a Platonic ideal of crying. When an actor weeps on stage in the Peking Opera, he's weeping every tear ever shed by anyone. Also, every movement is subtly circular. To look up, the actor looks down and around first; to point, the fingers circle back before they move forward. And so we enact scenes of love that, when played so well, take on meanings greater than the actual gesture, and contain within them the notion of returning to the same point, again and again.'

Morrison was unsure how to respond. 'Interesting thesis. Quite a metaphor.'

'I ought to own that it's not original. Chester told me that.'

'Chester?'

'Holdsworth. It was he who took me to the opera. He understands much of Chinese ways.'

'Holdsworth,' Morrison repeated. An acetic taste in his mouth recalled him to the fact that the Chinese phrase for jealousy was to 'eat vinegar'.

'You are surely not denying it, honey. That book of his, *The Real Chinaman*, is full of insight.'

He was on the brink of ridiculing Holdsworth's book, which had refuted *An Australian in China* on several subjects. Certainly Morrison had been a trifle hasty in concluding in his own book that the Chinese were affected by pain less than other races. But such had been the evidence before his eyes when he saw the seeming equanimity with which men tolerated such punishments as being placed in stocks or how they harnessed their naked bodies to tow-ropes and pulled heavy boats against the currents of the Yangtze. Still, Holdsworth had not needed to get on his high horse about it. But not wishing to spoil the mood, Morrison kept his thoughts to himself. The hoary Holdsworth had as little chance as the liar

Jameson with Mae. Morrison, as her lover, could afford to be magnanimous. Besides, it was very difficult for one to maintain an ill temper when Miss Mae Ruth Perkins was caressing one's backside.

'That's quite a collection of scars for one pair of buttocks,' she observed.

Making it seem like such things were all in a day's work for an adventurer like himself, he launched into his stories of being shot whilst defending the Legations in the siege and speared whilst attempting to walk across New Guinea years earlier. *Top that, Holdsworth!*

'I should have known about the bullet — that's when your newspaper thought you had died.'

'Yes, and the bullet nearly did kill me. But what happened in New Guinea was worse. There were a few moments there when death seemed the better option, especially as I took another spear below my eye. Some years later I was operated on in Edinburgh by Professor Chiene, who removed a number of fragments from my sinuses, though he couldn't get them all. It remains a source of some misery. Chiene also extracted an entire three-inch wooden spearhead from my iliacus muscle.'

'Where's that?'

'Here.' He pointed to a scar on his stomach. 'There's a funny story about this.'

'Oh?' She stroked it curiously.

If I were twenty, he thought wryly, *I should not be able to continue speaking right now. Age has its advantages.* 'Professor Chiene later held a dinner in honour of my recovery. He said that he was going to send my mother and father a replica of the spearhead in gold. I wrote to my parents straight away to tell them about the gift that would soon reach them. But it was never sent. In 1895, I was again in Edinburgh and met the professor to whom I owed so much. He said, "I have long intended to send your father a model of that spearhead in silver."'

Mae chortled. 'I thought he'd promised gold.'

'Precisely. I again wrote to my parents, informing them of the imminent dispatch of this slightly less valuable souvenir. But it never arrived. Years later, I met the good professor a third time. I only regretted that he did not announce his intention to send my parents a model in bronze.'

Bathed in Mae's bright laughter and sweet gaze, Morrison felt a surge of euphoric energy. He remembered belatedly the gift he had bought for her that day he went to Liu Li Chang in Peking's Chinese City: a pair of tiny embroidered slippers, made for bound feet. Her exclamations and the shower of kisses that followed gratified him immensely. He had been absurd to allow her mention of Holdsworth to disturb him as it did. 'I wish I hadn't promised to meet Dumas for dinner,' he said ruefully, stretching to reach the switch for the electric light.

'And I the Ragsdales.'

Morrison watched like a lovestruck boy as, seated at the dressing table in her chemise, she brushed her hair. He helped her tie a black ribbon with a silver horseshoe charm around her neck, the open part facing upwards, she explained, in order to catch good fortune. She asked him to fasten a delicate platinum chain with a vertical triplet of gold hearts around her neck as well. 'Luck and love,' he observed.

'The essentials.'

He kissed the back of her neck.

Outside, the clatter of shod hooves and the rattle of cart wheels could be heard. Down the corridor of the hotel, a longcase clock struck the hour. Beyond the curtained window, twilight lay its veil over the city.

'It's a fine hotel, isn't it?' she remarked.

'Mmm,' he murmured into downy skin.

'I was here not long ago with Zeppelin, the Dutch consul.'

His lips froze on her nape. His heart skipped a beat. *She couldn't possibly mean … Surely not.* Optimistically, he envisioned the lobby, high tea, cucumber sandwiches. An avuncular diplomat, his stout wife, the garrulous Mrs Ragsdale. 'Not like this, I presume,' he said, expelling a short, harsh laugh.

'Oh yes, Ernest honey, just like this.'

He stared at her reflection in the mirror.

She smiled back, her expression free of malice. She stood up and walked over to the bed, extracting her stockings from the pile of clothing on the floor and rolling one and then the other up her legs. 'Now where has that garter gone?'

Morrison had endured lone treks across deserts and through jungles. He had raised his head above the parapets to fire at Boxer legions. He had cheated death a dozen ways in as many countries. He was not easily daunted. Yet he could be thrown. He lowered himself down on the bed next to her and chewed his lip for a moment before speaking. 'A few years back, a Chinese man ran at a foreign consul in Peking with a knife.'

'Goodness,' Mae gasped, looking up. 'Did he kill him?'

'No, the consul ran faster. The police apprehended the man and declared him insane. But a witness objected. "Insane? For trying to kill a consul? There could be no clearer evidence of his sanity!"'

Her gaze was steady, cool and nowise encouraging.

'You know the old ditty,' Morrison ploughed on, bursting into song: 'The English, the English, they don't amount to much; but anything is better than the goddamn Dutch.'

Mae pursed her lips. 'Don't be jealous, honey. I don't like it. If you are to be my beau, then there are things you ought to know about me.'

'And what is it, precisely, that I need to know?'

'Now, honey, have you ever attended the Fancy Dress Spring Ball here in Tientsin?'

'Once or twice, yes.' The ball, held at Gordon Hall in a grand room hung with tapestries and lit by magnificent chandeliers, celebrated the spring thaw that heralded the re-opening of the port and capped the winter social season in Tientsin.

'But you didn't attend the most recent one.'

'No.'

She shrugged. 'If you had, perhaps things would have turned out differently. I had finally recovered from the grippe and was very excited about the ball. Weeks earlier I had decided to go as Marie Antoinette. It took the seamstresses and woodturners of Tientsin that long to make my *robe à la française*. I wanted every detail perfect, down to the V-shaped stomacher and panniers. The night before the ball, I had Mrs Ragsdale's maid, Ah Lan, wash my hair in beaten egg-whites and rinse it with rum and rosewater. I think she was quite scandalised by that — I'm quite sure she saved the yolks for the servants' kitchen. Oh, Ernest, you would have laughed at me that morning. I had flung open every last one of my steamer trunks, hatboxes, shoeboxes and jewellery boxes. Things were everywhere.'

She piled detail upon detail, of pearls pooling on the bedspread and jewelled necklaces cascading from the bedposts, of eggshell-blue crepe de Chine, of accordion flounces and chiffon ruffles, parades of satin roses, of beauty spots, cream-coloured slippers and elbow-length gloves, Morrison was simultaneously appalled and enthralled by the extravagance and luxury her words conjured. For the son of a frugal Scottish schoolmaster from Geelong, it was a titillating vision.

'I'm sure you were the belle of the ball,' he said at last.

'That's what he called me.'

'Who?'

'Zeppelin, of course.'

'Of course,' Morrison repeated, recalling the point of the story with a sinking heart. 'Did you meet this … *consul* there for the first time?'

'I'd danced with him at one of Tientsin's weekly Kettledrums not long after arriving here. But I hadn't known him well.'

Mae told Morrison how over dinner at the ball she grew rather crazy for the Dutchman with the bright blue eyes and cheeky smile. She admired the stylish cut of his dress uniform and the flash of red silk socks at his ankles. He turned out to be an excellent dancer. Morrison, he of the pale blue eyes, mercurial smile, poetically casual dress sense and tolerable competence on the dance floor, found no cheer in these particulars. 'And so, after a generous little bottle of champagne,' she told him, 'we slipped away from the ball.'

By the end of the remarkable recitation, which spared no detail, Morrison's head spun with visions of Mae as Marie Antoinette, legs akimbo upon some anonymous clerk's desk deep inside Gordon Hall, the damnedly handsome blond head of the Dutch consul navigating complex channels of petticoats towards the split in her bloomers, murmuring just before docking, 'The gates of Heaven are always open.'

'What a sparkling wit he must be to have come up with that old chestnut.'

She smiled, oblivious to Morrison's sarcasm. 'He kissed me for the longest while.'

Kissed! Such is the euphemism. 'Lucky you.'

'I really did need to get out of that costume. That's when we came across the street and took a room here at the Astor. Are you sulking?'

'Of course not,' he lied, then, with the air of a convicted man enquiring after his sentence, he asked, 'Are you in love with Zeppelin, then?'

'Oh no. He is not all that amusing, for all his obvious talents. I prefer a man of wit and intelligence.' She drew a finger down Morrison's chest. He had begun to pull his shirt on, but had not buttoned it. She circled his nipples. 'And one who is tall and handsome, and strong and manly as well.'

Morrison's chest inflated, along with his pride.

'I am in love with —'

How sweet she is!

'Martin Egan.'

'Egan?' *Egan!*

'Yes. Oh darling, why the long face? It doesn't make me happy to see that. I told you I don't like jealousy. Anyway, Martin hasn't had me for many days.'

'Days?'

'A week, probably. Oh dear, look at how the time has flown. You will call for me again at three o'clock tomorrow, won't you, honey? I shall pine for you until then.' She turned her attention back to her stockings.

Anna Lombard, who at least married her Pathan, seemed almost chaste by comparison. Zeppelin was one thing. Too much champagne, a heady evening at the ball. As much as it pained him,

135

Morrison could almost understand that. But Egan, that cheerful bastard — in love? When did that happen? *Damn him!* His mind flew back to the day they had met on Peking's Tartar Wall. Egan had said something about the attractions of Tientsin having increased in recent months. Something else, too, which had niggled at the back of his mind. Something about wanting to keep her for himself. In hindsight it was obvious that the American had been hinting at something. He had failed to pick up on it. He was a deuced fool.

Morrison tried to think rationally about where all this left him, and what it said about the woman beside him, happily absorbed in tying a pink ribbon around her stockinged thigh. A violent rush of emotion, shame and desire overcame him. *I will not come second to a Dutch consul or an American whippersnapper!*

He reached over, pushed her hand away and firmly tugged at the bow until it fell open.

'Now look at what you've done!' Mae watched her stocking slither down to crumple around her ankle. She pouted but did not bend to pull it up again. Nor did she push his hand away when it travelled up the inside of her thigh, trailing the ribbon. 'This is very naughty of you,' she said, opening her legs wider. 'We will both be awfully late.'

'We are already awfully late. And you do not seem to be resisting.'

'I could resist,' she murmured. 'Would you prefer that?'

When they finally parted, each doomed to arrive at their respective dinners too late even for the fruit macédoine and cream mousse, he was confident that her goodbye kiss did not say, 'I love Martin Egan.'

In Which We Learn One Difference Between Morrison and the Japanese Army He Supports, and Our Hero Goes Down in a Sea Captain's Wake

Zeppelin! Egan! As he stared at the ceiling of his hotel room, kicked from his dreams by misery, Morrison entertained the notion that perhaps Mae was simply goading him. She would no sooner fornicate with the Dutch consul on a desk in Gordon Hall than look for a Chinese husband in order to secure a cultural education — or have sexual relations with C.D. Jameson. The passion he and Mae shared was palpable, enveloping, consuming. She saw how it enlarged with provocation, so she provoked. *Egan. Really!* He laughed aloud, rolled over and ground his teeth, knowing he deceived only himself — and even that not well.

Early that morning, a brisk stroll took him to Tientsin's native city. There he caught sight of a Chinese policeman leading three miscreants by their queues, the ends of which he'd tied into a knot that he held in his fist. The unfortunate trio made for a comic sight, tripping over their own feet and each other's, cursing and yelping. Morrison had a sudden and unpleasant vision of himself, Zeppelin and Egan being led by a no less self-satisfied

Maysie. He walked with a burdened gait back towards the concessions and a luncheon with Menzies and Viceroy Yuan's interpreter, Ts'ai Yen-kan.

Ts'ai was a veteran of the Sino-Japanese War of 1894–95. That war had also been sparked by conflict over Korea, then under China's suzerainty, as well as Japanese designs on Manchuria. It ended badly for China. The Treaty of Shimonoseki granted Korea nominal independence whilst ceding the island of Formosa and the whole of the Liaotung Peninsula, including Port Arthur, to Japan in perpetuity. That had led to Germany, France, Britain and Russia demanding more 'spheres of influence' for themselves: ports, mines and the railways to access them. When the Russians offered to pay off Chinese debts to Japan in return for access to Port Arthur, the seeds of the present conflict were sown. Morrison was eager to hear Ts'ai's views on the situation, for he was certain they'd reflect Yuan's own.

The luncheon got off to an agreeable start. Ts'ai informed Morrison that for months prior to the outbreak of the Russo-Japanese War he had translated every article Morrison had written on the subject of the inevitability of war for Viceroy Yuan. 'You were most prescient,' he said. 'The Viceroy considers you a true prophet.'

'I'm not worthy,' Morrison replied, laughing to himself. *No one ever praised Zeppelin or Egan as prophets!*

'You were also right about the strength of the Japanese army. We have heard that advance forces have already crossed the Yalu River.'

'Yes,' Morrison confirmed, hoping that for once Granger was right. 'Our correspondent says the Japanese have arrived within seventy miles of Newchang.'

'It is said,' Menzies added enthusiastically, 'that the Japanese army carries no white flags.'

Ts'ai exhorted both Menzies and Morrison to eat more. Had they tried the Four Treasures dish? A Tientsin specialty.

Morrison understood that Ts'ai was not as pleased with the news of the Japanese advance as he was. 'I have written that the Chinese will remain neutral in this conflict. Am I correct in believing this to be the firm stance of the Chinese government?'

Ts'ai nodded. 'We would not act rashly. But as I believe you are aware, Prince Kung wishes to mediate between the belligerents. Perhaps we could bring about a reconciliation.'

'This would only benefit the Russians.' Morrison had just begun to argue the case when Ts'ai pushed the brocaded sleeve of his robe up his arm, reversed his chopsticks and, with the blunt ends, levered a choice portion of braised fish onto Morrison's rice. 'Please, Dr Morrison. You must eat as well as talk,' he urged. 'And the fish is a local specialty.'

Morrison, recognising that this subject was closed for the moment, brought up that of the Russo-Chinese Bank. 'It's the beating heart of the Russian administration in Manchuria,' he stressed. 'Bring down the bank and you cut off their financial supply. If you persuade enough investors to withdraw their funds, it will collapse like a house of cards. This is in China's own interests; surely the Viceroy can see that he must decline all dealings with the bank forthwith.'

A brief silence ensued, broken only by the sound of a peanut accidentally dropping from Menzies's chopsticks onto the table.

When Ts'ai spoke, his tone was measured but no less forceful than Morrison's. 'I do fear that the neutrality your honourable self so keenly enjoins upon my country does rather circumscribe our actions in aid of the Japanese cause. That would naturally include any actions against the Russo-Chinese Bank. Please, do try the duck.'

Once the luncheon was over, Morrison glanced at his fob. One-thirty. 'Well, that was less satisfying than hoped,' he conceded to Menzies. 'Ts'ai can be deucedly obtuse sometimes.'

'He will assuredly report everything you have said to the Viceroy.' Menzies then suggested the name of a British investor in mines and railroads who might be persuaded to shift his money out of the Russo-Chinese Bank if Morrison spoke to him about it personally.

It was one and a half hours before Morrison's next assignation with Mae. 'Let's go then,' he said, setting off at a brisk pace, which it satisfied him to see Menzies struggle to match.

By five minutes to three, Morrison was pacing in front of the bandstand in Victoria Park, ordering his thoughts and bridling his emotions. He was resolute. Strong. He would make it clear to the young lady that he was not the sort to play second or third fiddle and certainly not to a damned consul or junior reporter. She could have them, and they her, and he would wish all three of them supreme happiness and bliss but he would not himself be part of any harem or compete for her attention. He was George Ernest Morrison, doyen of the China correspondents, Hero of the Siege, 'a true prophet' to Viceroy Yuan, overlander, author. Alpha and eminent in every way. Not some young gull to be toyed with. And what with the war, the project to bring down the Russo-Chinese Bank and the normal burden of correspondence for his paper, he was perfectly capable of filling his days without her assistance.

'Hello, honey, I'm sorry I'm late.'

He turned. He would not mince words. But the moment she trained those heavy-lidded eyes on his and folded her arm into his own, his stomach unclenched, his fury melted. He was conquered territory. Everything he had planned to say seemed petty, small and senseless. Around Miss Mae Ruth Perkins, Morrison carried nothing but white flags.

Back in his room, Morrison did his jaw-aching, marathon best to assert himself over the memory of Zeppelin. He was rewarded with rosy moans and undulations. After a long while, he raised his head and wiped his chin on the back of his hand. Her arms were flung behind her on the pillow and her eyes were closed. Her peachy nipples were alert; he was briefly disconcerted by the sensation that her breasts were looking at him and not the other way around. He coasted upwards until they were face to face. Her eyes fluttered open.

'Australian versus Dutch. Who is the superior man?' he demanded.

She licked her lips and thought for a moment. 'Technique or endurance?' she asked.

'Both I suppose.'

'Mmm, victory belongs Down Under. Naturally. Of course,' she drawled, wriggling underneath him, 'with regard to endurance, Captain Tremaine Smith did kiss me on the *Siberia* all the way from Honolulu.'

Morrison, en route to what from his perspective were greater pleasures, froze. The image in his mind was too vivid for comfort. He remembered her mentioning Smith before — in that first conversation they'd had over coffees at the hotel in Mountain-Sea Pass. He wondered if he'd been a fool not to have suspected. But was he thus to understand that any male name, however casually mentioned, indicated a history of carnal relations? 'Surely,' Morrison rasped, 'he looked up from time to time to check his bearings.'

'He steered a straight course through the waves. We used to joke about that. About that and his rigging. But don't stop, honey.'

Determined to drive the enemies from the contested land, Morrison headed south again, where he performed valiantly and strategically. Mae spent herself spectacularly. Her face was beaded with perspiration. Sweet, sweet victory.

'So,' he said, before it occurred to him that he was well and truly opening Pandora's Box, 'I take it that you've had one or two lovers before me. Three. Three that I know of. Zeppelin, Egan and Smith.'

'It's true. I have had lovers before you. And before them as well.'

There comes a point in every love affair when the lover's desire to know everything about the beloved crashes up against what there is to know. Morrison had a choice: to retreat and shore up the defences or advance on the heartland; to remain in relative comfort or set out into the wilderness. By virtue of stubborn nature, Morrison could do only one thing: advance.

'Who, dare I ask, was the first?'

In Which the Practices of Modern Dentistry Are Explicated, with Particular Reference to the Filling of Cavities

'I had a toothache. Our parents were in Washington and my older sister Susie was in charge of Fred, Milton, myself and Pansy. Fannie and George had both married by then and were no longer living at home. The four of us younger children could be quite a handful. Susie made an appointment for me with the dentist Jack Fee in San Francisco.

'On the day of my appointment, things were a bit hectic. Milton had been expelled from school again, Pansy had an appointment with the seamstress and our cook had taken ill. Susie had recently given birth herself. Well, I say that to you, though to society her Alice has always been referred to as my father's "niece" and our "cousin". So Susie couldn't escort me into the city. She wanted to ask our frightful old chatterbox of a neighbour, Mrs Merton, but I convinced her that I was perfectly capable of getting there and back on my own.

'Truthfully, on the day I was to see Dr Jack Fee, the toothache began to settle. But I didn't care to give up an opportunity to escape Oakland, even for a few hours. Everyone calls it the Bay

City's Brooklyn, and Oakland does have lovely broad avenues and meadows full of oak trees, but compared to San Francisco it can be awfully staid. Even at that young age, I preferred the salty excitement of San Francisco.'

Morrison lifted the champagne from the ice bucket, filled their glasses and settled back against the pillows. He had learned that there was no such thing as a short story with Mae Ruth Perkins; besides, it was a good idea to gird himself for whatever revelations were in store.

'My, my, how you've grown, Miss Perkins,' remarked Dr Fee. 'You're quite the young lady now, aren't you? How sails the Good Ship George C. Perkins?' He hummed the tune 'Good Ship George C. Perkins', which had served as her father's theme song in 1880 when he ran, successfully, for Governor of California. A brass band had played it everywhere that he made his stump speeches. People often hummed the tune when they asked after him, thinking they were the only ones ever to have thought of it.

'He's very well, thank you, and in Washington with my mother. Senate is sitting.'

'Leaving you and your sweet baby sister, Pansy, all alone?'

'Susie looks after us when we're not at school and we do have housekeepers and nannies. Anyway, Mama will be catching the train home from the East Coast in a day or two.'

A look passed over Dr Fee's eyes, as though he was measuring the precise distance between the present moment and that of her mother's arrival. He smoothed down the cotton bib over her bosom. Something about the flutter in his fingers and the look in his eyes made her nerves tingle. She was experiencing *that feeling*. A glow, a congestion, a warm slide of moisture on her inner thighs, disruption to the breath, urges felt everywhere from the scalp to the stomach to her feet, which arched, tense, in their narrow boots. As he fussed about her, tilting back her head, opening her mouth and spreading her lips with his fingers, her blood quickened.

Mae had accidentally discovered the art of self-pleasure in another doctor's office a year or two before. She'd had a kidney infection. The doctor had wiped between her legs with wet cotton, recommending that she do the same at home twice or three times a day and after urinating. What revelations that had led to!

One rainy afternoon soon after, aimlessly knocking about the house, she had come upon a cache of books in her brothers' closet of the sort known as the 'Curious & Uncommon'. Amongst these were a rare copy of *1601* by Mark Twain, Sir Richard Burton's translation of *The Perfumed Garden,* and Émile Zola's *Thérèse Raquin*. Her schoolgirl French had to struggle with the last but it rewarded her with a portrait of a woman who never hesitated in the pursuit of pleasure. 'I had already seen how self-sacrifice had dulled my own dear mama and her friends, women who lived in service to everyone's gratification but their own,' she told Morrison. And so, in the perfumed gardens of erotic writing, her unfocused yearnings found expression.

'Did it occur to you that this could lead to trouble? I understand the libertine impulse, having lived with it for much of my own life. But it's different for a woman, surely. Especially given the expectations that would have been on you with your father's place in society and all.'

'It's true that it would have been easier had I not been born into society. It's not expected of women of lower station that they will guard the "citadel of love" quite as zealously as do those of the upper classes. Less is presumed to be at stake.'

Morrison thought obscurely of the famous Chinese military 'empty town' strategy, by which a general makes a show of not guarding the citadel at all, then captures and annihilates the enemy the moment they pass triumphantly through the gates.

'I have never understood what is so virtuous about keeping one's knees pressed tightly together until marriage,' she continued. 'I know many a girl who does that whilst engaging in the most vicious gossip and slander. Their *soi-disant* virtue has nothing to do with kindness or generosity or care. Others will publicly censure a fast girl whilst privately outrunning the field. I abhor hypocrisy. I think it is a far worse sin than free love.'

Morrison was capable of dining amiably with a man one moment and describing him as a dullard, a sleevedog or a bore in his journal the next. He revelled in gossiping about women who were loose, bold and bad as much as he revelled in such women themselves. He noted aloud who was said to have the pox whilst confiding only to his journal his own bouts with orchitis and worse. In this, he was like most people. Also, like most people, he professed to detest hypocrisy. 'You must know, my dear Maysie, I have never been an advocate of women keeping their knees too tightly pressed together. So please, do continue.'

Mae obliged. She told of how she had inched her chest up towards Dr Fee's fingers, pretending that they were those of Tommy, the shy, freckle-faced teen from down the street. Two weeks earlier, on a whim, she'd taken Tommy behind the woodshed of Palm Knoll, the beautiful home her father had built for the family in Oakland's Vernon Heights. She lay down on the grass and told him to kneel beside her. He obeyed as if hypnotised. She lifted the skirt of her loose tea-dress and then, as matter-of-factly as if she were positioning one of her doll's limbs for a play tea-party, placed his hand where she wanted it. Her intuition that it would be more exciting to have someone else's fingers there proved correct. They met every day after that. One day, she guided his other hand to her breast. Three days before her dental appointment, after she had pulled her skirts down, he had thrown himself on top of her, rubbing himself against her until he spent himself in his trousers. He had rushed off quickly after that and did not return. In all those days together, he had uttered not a single word.

Mae's stories, however disturbing from the perspective of a lover, were, Morrison was finding, at least as exciting as any tale from the pen of John Cleland or Frank Harris. 'What did this Fee look like?' he asked.

'He had a waxed moustache, which he twirled into parentheses at the ends. His clothes were dapper and his neck rose strong and sinewy above his collar.'

Morrison raised his head a little, the better to display his own neck. Lost in her story, she didn't seem to notice.

'Okey dokey, young lady. Let's look in that mouth of yours. Where does it hurt?' Dr Fee had said.

As he tapped and probed her teeth, she felt the pressure of his body against her side. Her bloomers were growing damp. She thought she could smell the funny, close smell of her cunt, a word she knew from her reading. She knew it was a bad word. She liked it very much. She held her breath.

'Are you all right there?' He placed a manicured hand on her thigh. His wedding band glittered under the electric light.

Mrs Fee attended her mother's sewing circle; she was a nice lady with good teeth. This had nothing to do with Mrs Fee. Holding stock-still, Mae raised her eyes to those of her dentist.

It did not take long for Dr Fee to ascertain that there was nothing much wrong with the tooth that an icepack and some drops of laudanum wouldn't solve. After administering the analgesic, he washed his hands, his back to her. 'Why don't you be my guest for lunch?'

Her mother had often stated that no respectable, or self-respecting, girl would dine alone at a restaurant with a man, intimating that something of that sort had been behind the 'trouble' that her older sister Susie had been in and was the reason that Susie now lived at home with little Alice. But her mother could be terribly old-fashioned. It was almost the twentieth century. 'I'd like that,' she replied, the opium and alcohol in her blood helping her shed any last inhibitions she may have held.

Tripping light-footed alongside Dr Fee as they strolled the two blocks to the restaurant, Mae was only just sensible of the eyes that fell on her from passing coupés. When a baker's wagon drawn by heavy dray horses came up behind them, the warm, yeasty smell of freshly baked twistbread made her even more giddy. She was giggling for no reason by the time they arrived at the corner of Grant and Bush. The restaurant was called Le Poulet and beside the door was a sign reading, 'Best dinner for a dollar on earth', and in smaller letters below that: 'fine food — and discretion'. Dr Fee put a hand on her back and guided her through the ground-floor dining room with its linen-covered tables, elegant settings and crystal chandeliers, straight to the elevator at the back. At the third floor, the operator clanked back the iron grille and a waistcoated attendant led them to a beautifully appointed private dining room with a curtain covering its rear wall. They hadn't said a word between them since entering the restaurant. Whilst Dr Fee ordered two bottles of Golden State Extra Dry, shrimp cocktails and a few other luncheon items from the waiter, Mae peeped behind the curtain. Her heart skipped a beat. She was staring at a bedroom with a big brass bed and satin coverlet. She released the drapery and sat down on the chaise longue, fussing with her skirts.

An air of uncertainty descended upon the dentist like a sudden fog on Fisherman's Wharf. When the waiter returned with their champagne and food, they clinked glasses. She felt like an actress in a play. That, the champagne and the laudanum gave her the courage to do what she did next.

Spearing a pink shrimp on the delicate tines of the cocktail fork, she performed a spontaneous debut version of the dance of the boiled pheasant that Morrison had witnessed that first night at Mountain-Sea Pass. The effect on Dr Fee was palpable. Without so much as a by-your-leave, he lay her down on the pink velvet chaise, spread her legs and slid his hand up into her bloomers. When his fingers touched the wetness there, he grinned. She let him undress her, though she was so nervous she was trembling. By the time he had rubbed and probed her with his fingers — so much more expertly than Tommy ever had — she was nearly fainting with pleasure. The sight of him unbuttoning his trousers to reveal his red and swollen cock gave her a fright. But he showed her how well it fit her mouth and her sex. It hurt down there at first but she would not have stopped him for the world. She had never felt so grown up or powerful.

Something occurred to Morrison. 'How old were you, Mae?'

'I'd just turned fourteen.'

'He took advantage of you. You were a child.' Morrison was choked with indignation and confusion.

'He made me a woman.' She shrugged. 'I was ready. I wanted it. There were things I could not learn on my own and that Tommy could not have shown me.' She reached out and rested her hand on Morrison's stomach for a moment before floating it southwards. 'It seems that you enjoyed the experience almost as much as I did. And I enjoyed the telling.' Although mortified, he allowed her to place his hand between her thighs. 'Can you see?'

By the time he escorted Mae out through the lobby, Morrison was in a daze. When the concierge approached with a telegram, he stuffed it into his pocket to read later.

He felt like King Shahryar in *The Book of the Thousand Nights and One Night*. Except his Scheherazade's stories were no fiction. Curious & Uncommon indeed. Morrison was a man accustomed to lucid thought and firm opinions. Mae Perkins defied both. She provoked him hugely, titillated him absolutely. The story of the dentist had disturbed him deeply. During his limited medical practice, he too had had young female patients who tempted him with their loveliness and corruptibility but he had not taken advantage of their trust. He felt a hot anger rise up against this Fee with his waxed moustache and dapper clothing. At the same time, he wondered at the apparent sang-froid with which she recounted the tale — and, for that matter, the stories about her affairs with Zeppelin, Egan and Smith. It was a strange combination, cold-bloodedness and hot passion, though he had to concede it was a combination not that foreign to him.

He was in such a state that, setting off for the Tientsin Club, he nearly walked straight into the path of a night-soil cart. The cart driver veered away sharply, only to smack into a coolie carrying the carcasses of a dozen chickens on his carrying-pole. Shit and meat rained onto the street. Death and excrement, the ways of the flesh. Morrison hurried away, curses raining down on his back and the grim slush that had been yesterday's charming drifts lapping at his boots.

Dumas and Menzies, who'd been waiting for him in the billiards room, looked up with an air of mutual consternation. Morrison hadn't realised how late he was. When he explained, in the broadest terms, the reason for his delay, the two exchanged glances.

As they entered the dining room, acquaintances streamed over to congratulate Morrison on *The Times*'s great scoop: the first wireless dispatch sent directly from a war zone. James had succeeded after all. The men were naturally interested in his assessment of the situation. Would the Japanese really be able to walk through the Russian troops as he'd predicted? And what of the other correspondents' chances of getting to the front? As Morrison ventilated the topic, Dumas and Menzies stood by with the dutiful interest and thin smiles of the retinue.

As the three were finally seated, Morrison remarked as if inconvenienced and not uplifted by the attention, 'It is a professional hazard of the journalist, who envisions himself as a hunter and gatherer of news, to be perceived by others as a mere pantry or storeroom of information to be raided at will.'

'You are much sought after,' Menzies replied, adding awkwardly, 'as ever. But more than ever. Now with the war and all.'

Morrison nodded. By force of will and discipline, he stayed on the topic of the war all the way through to the blancmange.

'Will we be seeing you tomorrow night?' Dumas asked as the men advanced on the line of rickshas outside the club. The Tientsin Amateur Theatrical Corps would be performing *The Yeomen of the Guard,* in which Mrs Dumas, who had arrived back in the country, had a minor role. As part of his general campaign of appeasement, Dumas had promised his wife he would bring along friends who could be counted upon to applaud cheerfully at curtain call. She had specifically asked him to invite Dr Morrison.

Morrison had forgotten all about it. 'Of course. I will see you there.'

His next rendezvous with Mae was the following morning. He slept poorly and awoke befogged from dreams in which he was back in the siege, though this time the tasselled spears of the Boxers resembled nothing more than giant dental probes.

In Which Morrison, upon Discovering What He Has in Common with an Almeda Pharmacist, the Son of the Richest Man in the World and a Congressman from Tennessee, Spoils the Linen

Mae turned up at the Astor House with a basket on her arm. In it lay neat stacks of letters, tied up with loving care in wide pink satin ribbon.

Taking up one packet, she loosened the bow and dealt the envelopes onto the table before choosing one, extracting the letter and reading it aloud. And then another. And another, the ribbons lining up on the desk like military decorations.

And so it was that Morrison, torn between reluctance and curiosity, heard yet more seductive and disturbing tales. She told him about her faithful three-time fiancé, George Bew, a pharmacist from Almeda with a plan to get rich by breeding Belgian hares, who called her 'my own darling little sweetheart' and wrote every day, even after she had broken off the engagements and despite the mockery dished out by rival suitors: 'poor George, his dough has been baked into cake' one had cruelly remarked. He heard about dalliances at cotillions and lawn parties with young naval officers with names like Edgar and Walton, and how she had made love in the fragrant, moonlit orange groves behind a quaint old Florida fort with a dean of law from Providence, Rhode Island. She told him about playing golf in summer with Judge Fred Clift, with whom she slept for seven months, and about sleighing in winter with Bobby Mein, who had her for five. 'I dropped Bobby because he drank too heavily. I do not like a man's breath to be eight parts whisky,' she explained.

'Indeed. It should be four parts champagne at least,' Morrison quipped, his head reeling. 'That is quite some catalogue,' he added. 'It's little wonder that women make better novelists than they do journalists.'

'Oh, it's not fiction. It's all true, honey.'

'I just meant,' he continued lamely, 'no editor could keep you to six hundred words.'

She was not close to finished. The Fifth Avenue heir Willie Vanderbilt Jnr had pressed her up against the cool Algerian-marble walls of the ballroom at his family's Newport mansion, given her gifts and proclaimed himself her 'most devoted' admirer. There were letters from Captain Kay-Stewart Thompson of the P.M. Agency in Hong Kong, whom Morrison knew, Harry Handford, and others too numerous to name or remember. His head swam with other men's endearments: *How lovely you were … The day is awfully dull for me when I cannot see you at least once … My darling little sweetheart … I think often of our drives — Sweet, oh! … A thousand and one kisses … How I longed for you last night, and how I wish you were here by my side now … Do not write such endearments on postals for I am often out when the mail arrives, and other boys at the Academy may read them … I wonder if you ever do think of your little boy out east … you little witch, you win, you got me too much interested in you … I never yearned for anyone as badly in all my days ... You cannot know one half the desire I possess in the longing for your letters ... Remember those 5 o'clock rides we had out on Castro and Market Streets ... My own darling little sweetheart — remember your promises to me ... you were so very good to come again this afternoon to see your lover ... I want you now ... I want you ever ... I beg you if you love me, please tear up these letters once you have read them ... I will try to get you to the phone — to hear once again the sweet voice that has been music to me so often ... My darling Mae ... I have learned to love you more than I thought any man could possibly love a woman ... My Dear Sweet Mae ... you charm and bewitch ... I am crazy to see you ... that wonderful ride in which you saw a marvellous thing of his ... I love you enough to promise always to yield to your pleasure ... I am crazy for a glimpse of you ... I knew you were a spoon but you beat my expectations ... kiss yourself for me a thousand times till I see you again ...*

Morrison heard about dancing the cakewalk in Chicago with this lover and bob-sledding in Maine with that one, tales of trysts and buggy rides, of long drives in four-in-hands with the storm-sides up, of assignations with Billie and Harry and William and Lloyd and Fred and others named and unnamed, until he was tormented by a vision of his darling Mae laid out under men from Oakland to Tientsin.

'Who was the most formidable?' Vain hope thickened his inflection.

'Hmm.' She inclined her head. Her gaze flickered as though she was reviewing the pages in a photograph album. 'Linton Tedford was the most formidable fornicator I have ever encountered,' she finally pronounced. 'But others wrote better love letters. They're good, don't you think?'

'Remarkable,' Morrison responded, dazed. 'Truly remarkable.' *Any one sufficient to convict her of unchastity. As if chastity were ever a possibility.* The fictional Anna Lombard was looking more and more like a shining exemplar of feminine virtue. 'Is that the whole collection?'

'It's all that's left. There were more. Mama discovered the rest and burnt the lot. Her health is frail and argument sends her to bed. I didn't raise it with her. There was no point. The letters were gone.'

Her fingers dawdled on his thighs. He tried to summon the will to push them off, but the will would not be summoned. His legs, long and hard-muscled from a lifetime of tramping, walking and riding, offered a sinewy landscape for tracing, even in repose. *Willie bloody Vanderbilt Jnr would not have such legs!* When she fluttered her hand upwards, he trimmed his stomach in anticipation for the more intimate caresses that would follow as surely as lover followed lover in her stories.

'Dare I ask which of the many beaux I have heard of is the one you say reminds you of me?'

Her hand stopped roaming. 'I have not yet told you about him. He's maybe one year older than you.' She wore a faraway look. 'John Wesley Gaines. They say he is the most handsome congressman in the whole United States.'

'Congressman?'

'Democrat from Tennessee. Women have been known to trip over their own skirts for staring at him as he passes. You should see how parasols twirl and handkerchiefs drop when he's about.'

'And what is it exactly about him then that makes you think of me? I have never noticed much parasol-twirling or handkerchief-dropping in my vicinity.'

'Ha! You are so much alike. He does not notice either. Or pretends not to.'

Even worse. 'What else do I have in common with this acme of manhood?'

She narrowed her eyes. 'Jealousy, darling. Not attractive.'

'Ah, he was jealous too.'

'That's not what I meant. Though it is true. And it was a problem. Also like you, he was intelligent, witty, accomplished, strong in his opinions and highly regarded. And agreeably talented in bed.'

Such a style of compliment! 'How did you make the acquaintance of the lucky Mr Gaines?'

'At a social function in Washington when I was visiting Papa about six years ago. I was nineteen or twenty at the time. Papa and he are not even on the same side of politics — isn't that funny?'

'Very droll.'

Mae reproached him with a look. 'Oh, and like you he is a medical doctor, though he has studied law besides. He also has great acumen in business. And his career in Congress has been a brilliant one.'

Morrison hated him more and more.

'There was this one time — it still makes me laugh to think of it — the House was debating pensions for soldiers who had served in the Civil War. The President had put forth some bill that would override the decisions of the Commissioner of Pensions, arguing that the commissioner was doing injustice to the soldiers. At this, John Wesley stood up and asked, most ironically, "Why does not the distinguished President turn that commissioner out and put in one who *will* do justice?" Isn't that just so very clever?'

'Very.' Morrison's voice was steeped in vinegar.

Morrison could have stopped her from then describing how John Wesley Gaines stroked her with his hands and with his voice, a mellifluous deep Southern drawl she imitated to perfection. How she'd been his bad little girl and how he had spanked her for it. How he'd tied her hands with ribbon and had her against the walls of his office, hard and powerful. She confessed that she still ached for him. She missed his keen wit, and keener desire, to which his careful letters rarely gave expression. Letters written in a proud, precise attorney's hand. His deep-set eyes of green, their intense, sardonic gaze. His aura of wealth, intelligence and power, enhanced by his shock of thick brown hair, high brow, arrogant nose and proud, sensual mouth. His chiselled features thrilled her eyes; the soft bristle of his prominent chin excited her thighs. His tongue was so clever, and not just at speech. She had loved him so much her heart bled to think about it.

As if on cue, the site of the old spear wound in Morrison's sinuses haemorrhaged. Seeing the blood streaming from his nose, Mae gave a little cry and rushed to get a flannel. She then ministered to him with such unaffected kindness and devotion — and a considerable quantity of hotel linen — that he was brought to mind of his Calcutta angel, Mary Joplin.

As he had told Moberly Bell, Morrison had not long before considered giving up reporting from China on account of his chronic poor health. Meeting Mae had revived him and given him an illusion of youth. Now proof of the opposite was written all over the ruined sheets. 'You must be thinking what a poor specimen I am,' he mumbled, humiliated, feeling all the worse for having just heard tales of so many athletic predecessors.

She shook her head and stroked his cheek with a sweetness that made his heart ache. 'Not at all. I was thinking about the intrepidly adventurous life you have led and how marvellous it is that at your age you are suffering not from rheumatoid aches and pains but only from the effects of an old spear wound.'

Dear, dear girl. He was relieved that he had never mentioned his arthritis.

'Besides,' she said, her eyes alight with good humour, 'with all this blood on the sheets, the staff of the hotel, if no one else, will be quite convinced that I was a virgin before I met you.'

They hadn't left the room all day. The sun slowly sank over Victoria Park, sprinkling the room with golden light. Plates of half-eaten food and empty champagne bottles littered the carpet. There was the sound of a light knock and then an envelope slipped under the door.

Mae looked over Morrison's shoulder as he opened it.

Come WHW James Urgent.

'That sounds most mysterious. Who's James?'

'Lionel James. He must be in Wei Hai Wei.' He started to tell her about James when he remembered the unopened telegram in his jacket pocket. 'This one says, "Come WHW James." That was yesterday. Today it is urgent. *Deuced* nuisance.' He was more concerned than he let on. He was well aware that he had been neglecting his work rather badly.

'Perhaps you should go.'

'I don't want to go anywhere,' he said. They both saw the next envelope slide under the door. The content was identical to the previous two except it said "Very Urgent".

'You must go to Wei Hai Wei before that poor Mr James explodes with frustration,' she said. 'Have I mentioned that I will be accompanying Mrs Ragsdale to Shanghai in a few days? Come to Shanghai after Wei Hai Wei. We'll have a high old time there together. But first, Ernest, honey, promise me something.'

'Anything.' He was still ashen-faced from his nosebleed.

'You won't go with any fast women whilst we're apart, will you?'

Morrison blinked. She was perfectly serious. Astounding himself, he gave her his word.

In Which Our Hero is Taken Captive by 'Yeomen of the Guard' and the Perfidious C.D. Jameson Makes an Unwelcome Appearance

That evening found Morrison slumped in his seat in the auditorium at Gordon Hall, staring at the stage from under his lowered brow. In poor, untrained voices, the singers tortured the melodies whilst stout matrons old enough to be grandmothers coquetted about pretending to be fair maidens. Stolid bankers playing young gallants flung their pork-knuckle hands here and there in lieu of acting. The painted set fell over in the first act and, when one of the younger actresses made a hash of her lines, she burst into tears. *The most astonishingly rotten amateur performance I have ever seen*, Morrison thought morosely. *Dull ye gods! Not that much in the way of theatre could hope to compete with the performances to which I've been witness these last few days!*

On Morrison's right sat Menzies, rigid and dutiful even in his approach to entertainment. On his left, Dumas squirmed, apologetic. The only uplifting aspect of the evening was the sight in the crowd of a handsome and amorous young couple whom Dumas identified to Morrison as Zeppelin and his fiancée. She had arrived the day before from Holland.

After congratulating Mrs Dumas and company, Morrison pleaded exhaustion and an early start the next morning. He returned to a hotel room redolent of sex, perfume, blood and champagne and thickly haunted by the ghosts of other men.

That night, he dreamed feverishly of cakewalks and sleighing and buggy rides, of men, men and more men, around, on and in his Maysie, in her sweet cunt, her squeezable arse, her smiling lips, her soft, moist lips, her red, red lips. He woke with a start in the middle of the night, covered in sweat, though he had thrown the eiderdown clear off the bed. His tooth hurt. His joints ached. His nose threatened another eruption. Bloody Willie *Vanderbilt*. Son of the richest man in the whole world. How could one compete with that? Should one have to? Morrison rolled over in a huff, as though to leave Mae's vast collection of beaux out of sight on the other side of the bed. Her sweet cunt. Her squeezable arse. Her soft red lips.

With a great effort, he turned his thoughts to more appropriate concerns, the subjects of his other conversations in Tientsin. The war. The politics of the railways. The war. Shipments of coal and arms. The ongoing Siege of Port Arthur. The coolie trade to South Africa. The war. The port of Tientsin doomed by its sandbar worsening every year. The war. The arms trade. The war. And what the devil was up with James — URGENT, URGENT, URGENT? Morrison yawned, felt the ache in his jaw, and thought that if he met Mae in Shanghai he could see the dentist there as well. That, in turn, caused him to recollect the tale of Jack Fee. He groaned. Her smiling lips, her sweet cunt. Blood. He finally fell asleep, a paltry three hours before he was due to rise for his train to the port, where he would catch the steamer sailing southeast through the Gulf of Bohai to Wei Hai Wei.

Morrison was nervy with a dearth of sleep when Kuan, who had been distinctly underemployed for several days, woke him for the train. At the station they ran into C.D. Jameson, just off the train from Peking and plainly as thrilled to see Morrison as Morrison was to see him.

'Well, hello.'

'Morning, Jameson. What brings you to Tientsin?'

Jameson mumbled something about mines and concessions. He smelled of rum, even at that hour.

Jack Fee, Bobby Mein, George Bew and Willie bloody Vanderbilt were of the past, Zeppelin out of action with the arrival of his fiancée, and Martin Egan, he had ascertained, safely back in Japan for the moment. But Jameson? Even Mae had her limits, surely. Morrison refused to place Jameson within the frame of this increasingly crowded picture. The grubby old duffer had merely heard the rumours and thought to start one about himself.

'And you, old chap?' Jameson's rheumy eyes flickered. He adjusted his false teeth with his pinky. 'What's been your business here? Seeing Miss Perkins, I presume?'

Morrison, the nerves behind his eyes hammering, felt his hackles rise. *He is down after the fair Mae, that is certain sure.* He shoved his gloved hands deep in his pockets. 'I may have seen her in passing. This city of one million is a small town, after all. Ah, there goes the whistle. I shall bid you adieu. Good day, sir.'

In Which Morrison Is Reminded to Guard His Yang and His Old Friend Molyneux Offers Some Startling Advice

The *Hsin Yu*, piloted by the burly, red-faced Captain Richards, got away in good time. Kuan by his side, Morrison leaned on the rail of the little steamer and watched T'ang-ku recede into the distance. The noise of the engine and the ship's vibrations under his palms and feet compounded his headache and the sickness behind his eyes; he hid behind his sunglasses from the thin, milky sunlight.

As the wave of nausea passed, Morrison relished the sensation of being on open water. Breathing in, he let the viscid spray numb his face and hands. Tientsin had begun to feel claustrophobic. His world had shrunk to the size of his hotel room or, more precisely, his hotel bed, and that had suddenly seemed absurdly overpopulated.

Mae's attentions made him feel simultaneously cherished and diminished; despite all the virile evidence to the contrary, he had to admit he felt unmanned by her, a eunuch in her court. As much as he detested this image, he rolled it over and over in his mind like a child with a stick and hoop. He had confronted her, rather pathetically it had to be admitted, in the aftermath of his nosebleed, declaring that if he was but one face in a crowd to her, then he would not linger. She had fervently denied that this was the case. Challenged to say what she liked about him in particular, she did not need to stop and think. 'Your opinionated, cantankerous intelligence. The ginger in your beard. The spray of freckles across your knuckles,' she proclaimed.

He looked at his hands, wrapped around the ship's rail. They were broad and pale, with long, square-tipped fingers. He had not noticed the freckles before she had pointed them out, laying a trail of kisses over them. He smiled to himself.

At the same time, he couldn't help wondering what she had told the others. The thought that she might be promiscuous with her compliments grieved him more than the knowledge that she was free with her body.

Suddenly a woman screamed. Morrison whirled around. A Western lady was pointing at something in the water, her face pale as ash. Silhouetted by the sun, a sphere bobbed on the current in a collision course with their ship. A chorus of panic arose from the deck; the air was filled with shrieks and shouts.

For the first time in the history of warfare, the combatants were using mines as offensive weapons, rather than solely as a means to defend land and maritime borders. The Japanese had started it, setting explosive devices adrift in the direction of the Russian flotillas. The Russians quickly followed suit. Currents and winds wreaked their havoc. As Morrison and Dumas had learned in Newchang, hundreds of mines were on the move in the Yellow Sea and Gulf of Bohai. They had already taken down half a dozen Chinese junks; all the prayers in the world to Ma-tsu, Goddess of Compassion and Protectress of Fishermen, could not have saved their crews. It was only a matter of time before one found a passenger ship such as the one on which Morrison was now travelling.

The steamer tacked away, pitching vertiginously. Kuan, one hand gripping the rail, caught Morrison before he fell. Morrison's thoughts, had they been final, were of the war, his mother and Mae.

As the boat steadied, it became apparent that the 'mine' was nothing more than a shiny clump of dark seaweed. Beside him, Kuan expelled fear and nerves in a burst of laughter.

For the first time since the conflict broke out, Morrison experienced the visceral, gut, erotic thrill of war. He wiped his salt-encrusted sunglasses on his sleeve with enough vigour to disguise the fact that his hands were still shaking.

'Well, Dr Morrison, that was quite a scare. I thought for a moment that your war was going to catch up with all of us.'

Morrison turned at the sound of the familiar voice. 'Professor Ho! What a pleasant surprise.'

Professor Ho was a moon-faced Cantonese gentleman with an impeccable Oxbridge accent whom Morrison had met in Hong Kong some months earlier. Polished leather shoes protruded from the hem of Ho's traditional blue gown and he sported a bowler hat, from which the mandatory queue fell at the back. Ho, Morrison had been impressed to learn, counted amongst his acquaintances British admirals, members of Parliament and even Prince Alfred. The men shook hands warmly and Professor Ho introduced Morrison to his two travelling companions: Sir T'ing, a former governor of Kweichow Province, and Mr Chia, a curios dealer.

T'ing and Chia greeted Morrison in the Chinese manner, clasping their hands together and raising them to their chests.

Morrison reciprocated, though a blend of native Australian egalitarianism and British superiority ensured that he never bowed quite low enough to be genuinely polite. He produced his Chinese calling cards. Printed in red as was the custom, they bore a line of Chinese characters that read, also following tradition: 'In fear and trembling, this humble late-born bows respectfully.' When the others handed him their cards in return, Morrison pretended to read them, eliciting undeserved compliments on his language skills.

Chia, loquacious and cheerful and speaking in English that was almost as fluent, if not as polished, as that of Professor Ho, said that he had heard much about the famous Morrison.

Kuan, whom Morrison always encouraged to act as an extra pair of eyes and ears, remained by Morrison's side. The conversation progressed at first in the predictable way, with the men asking Morrison how many boy children he had. He had learned that telling the truth, that he was not even married, appalled the Chinese to the extent that they didn't quite know what else to say to him. It was a Confucian axiom that of all ways in which one might commit the sin of being unfilial, the worst was to produce no sons. So Morrison obliged his interlocutors with a fabricated family of wife, three sons and two daughters, all healthy, and the expectation that he would have grandchildren before too long. In turn, he heard all about their little 'bugs' — the Chinese always speaking dismissively of the children they loved lest the gods grew jealous and stole them away.

The conversation, one Morrison had had a thousand times with small variations since he'd first stepped foot in China ten years earlier, left him feeling more than usually discomposed, for he would not have minded had his answer been true. He adored children, and though he spoiled those of his servants as though they were his very own little nieces and nephews, he craved a family of his own.

As the gulf slipped past, slate blue under a cloud-streaked sky, a muddy current came into view, a vast stream of silt flowing out from the eastern shore where the Yellow River disgorged into the sea.

'They don't call it the Yellow River for nothing, do they, Dr Morrison?' Professor Ho remarked. A coffee-coloured tendril broke off from the stream and curled around a patch of blue. T'ing, gesturing with his fan, made a comment in Mandarin.

Chia explained. 'Sir T'ing says it is like the *t'ai-chi* symbol, *yin* and *yang*. The learned Dr Morrison has been long in China and knows *yin* and *yang*.'

'Yes, of course,' Morrison responded with the air of an actor who'd just been asked if he knew who Shakespeare was. 'Feminine and masculine, dark and light.'

'That and much more,' Professor Ho said. 'The concept is as old as the ancient book of divination, the *I Ching*, as I am sure Dr Morrison is also aware. In the hexagrams of the *I Ching*, *yin* is represented by a broken line and *yang* a continuous one. They are passive and active. Downward flowing and upward climbing. Water and fire, earth and wind, moon and sun, cold and heat. A closed door and an open window.'

'All the opposites,' Morrison stated.

'Ah,' demurred Professor Ho, 'yes and no. In fact, *yin* and *yang* do and do not exist in opposition. One flows into the other as night becomes day and day becomes night. Neither is inferior or superior — *yin* is to *yang* as bamboo is to an oak, the plains to the hills, a sheep to a horse. And they are prone to shifting. If metal is hammered into the shape of a wok, it is *yin*; if it is forged into a weapon, it will be *yang*. Fire is *yin* when held within a lamp, *yang* when released by the sun. *Yin* and *yang* complement and contain one another; *yin* cannot exist without *yang*, and *yang* without *yin*. *Yang* limns *yin*, and *yin* limns *yang*. Thus, the *t'ai-chi* symbol, with its teardrops of *yin* and *yang* chasing one another round and round in perpetuity, each containing a dot of the other. I fear that Western notions of masculine and feminine do not contain such subtlety or nuance.'

Listening to Ho, Morrison had a sudden insight into why the character of the faithful Gerald in *Anna Lombard* continued to rile him — whilst assuredly masculine, he was as compliant and yielding before the assertive Anna as any woman. *Altogether too big a dollop of* yin *in his* yang! *Only a female novelist could invent such a personality.*

'Of course,' Chia added, his smile making crescents of his eyes, 'woman's place of *yin* can absorb man's *yang*. So if man not release — you understand? He doesn't lose *yang*. The danger,' and here he grinned slyly, 'is that one may encounter the sort of woman whose *yin* is so powerful that it can steal all of the man's *yang*. There are creatures called *hu li ching*, fox spirits, who dwell in the — how do you say? — *borderlands*, where the edges of *yin* and *yang* blur, for example.'

'I have heard of Chinese ghost stories in which the good-hearted scholar, bent over his books, fails to notice a beautiful woman, in reality a fox spirit, passing through the window of his study. Personally, I cannot imagine not noticing such a thing,' Morrison said.

'Perhaps Dr Morrison would not be so easily seduced. But fox spirits are powerful creatures, and clever too. They say a fox spirit is as sophisticated, intelligent and tough as the man she haunts, as lovable, canny and dangerous as his own reflection. And thus it is that a ruffian will pull to him a rogue; a sharp-talker, a wit; and a lustful man a succubus, who steals so much *yang* from her lover that the man is left a shell and may die.'

'Fox spirits belong to the realm of superstition,' Morrison insisted with a vehemence that suggested the topic had provoked him more than he might admit. 'You received a Western education, Professor Ho. Surely you don't believe in such whimsy.'

Before Ho could answer, T'ing asked in Chinese what they were talking about.

Ho translated Morrison's words for the Mandarin.

T'ing spoke, his words measured. Ho translated: 'We are aware that our humble country is backwards-looking and lacking in scientific knowledge and outlook. We hope that Dr Morrison will share with us the benefits of his scientific thinking. Perhaps then, China might reach the exalted standards of modern Western nations such as Great Britain in government administration as well as agriculture and defence.'

There were moments when even the most assured of old China hands could not be sure if he was being given a polite dressing down, a genuine compliment or an invitation to explore the topic further.

A brief silence descended on the group, broken only by the steady thump of the ship's engine. The sun, which had been quivering fat and red above a corrugated horizon, dropped out of sight. Night fell heavily upon the gulf. In the light of the lanterns that had been lit on deck, the men's faces flickered in and out of focus as though they were spirits themselves. A shiver ran down Morrison's spine.

'It's getting cold,' Professor Ho observed. 'Dr Morrison must watch his health. *Shui-t'u b'u fu.* It is hard for a foreigner to adapt to conditions in China. I suggest that we retire to the smoking saloon and wait for the dinner bell.'

As the little group made its way inside, T'ing in the lead, Morrison looked around for Kuan and caught sight of him in converse with Chia. *These men are exceptionally polite to my Boy*, he thought.

In the saloon, Morrison moved the talk to politics. He pressed the three gentlemen for their views on the reform movement, the Empress Dowager and, of course, the war. They in turn professed themselves most interested in his views. They asked him many questions. It was only later that he realised that they had answered very few of his own. He suspected that he had been the loser in a subtle contest of 'push hands', in which the master allows his opponent to unbalance himself with the force of his own blows.

Morrison woke the next morning to the squawk of gulls. That and the engine's slackening beat told him they were approaching the shore. *In whose arms does she lie today?* His chest was ballasted with woe. *What an infatuation it is.* Dressing against the damp chill in the air and that in his thoughts, Morrison hurried up on to the deck.

The steamer had cut southwest through the gulf to arrive at Chefoo, a British treaty port where it would stop before continuing on to Shanghai. He and Kuan would disembark here and catch the mail packet to Wei Hai Wei, fifty miles east, an easy trip. He thought how improvements in steam technology, particularly the invention of the screw propeller, had revolutionised travel in his lifetime. Ocean voyages that had taken months in his parents' day were now but a matter of weeks. Steam made the world a smaller place. It had not even been twenty-four hours since they'd left Tientsin's port of T'ang-ku. And yet there was already enough sea and air between the two places that, for all his fretting, Morrison felt relaxed, bigger, expanded into his normal self, a man amongst men once more.

Kuan joined him on deck in an animated mood. The rising sun was burning off the morning fog. Kuan pointed to an outcrop silhouetted in the mist. 'It is called Horse Island — see the horse?'

Morrison squinted. 'I'm not sure.'

'That one easier.' Kuan indicated another. 'Shoulder-pole Island.'

Morrison smiled. 'Yes, that's clear enough.' Something occurred to him. 'Say, Kuan, what do you think of Ho and his companions?' The men, who were travelling on to Shanghai, had bid them a warm farewell the night before and were still resting in their cabins.

'They are good men,' Kuan replied enthusiastically. 'They love their country.' A look of caution flickered across his face. He turned back to the view. 'Firewood Island. See?'

Morrison didn't, nor did he exert himself trying. He studied his Boy. 'Is there something about the men I might be interested in knowing, Kuan?'

'My master is very smart,' Kuan said carefully. 'I think maybe they are — how you say? — sympathetic to the reform movement.'

'Interesting,' Morrison replied. 'Would they be active, in your opinion?'

'How can I know? I am only a servant. Why would they tell me?'

Chefoo's golden pebbly beaches, crumbling stone forts and smart rows of two-storey brick godowns hove into view. Overlooking the port was Beacon Hill with its Ming Dynasty signal tower, nearly three centuries old, the cliff-edge Temple of the Dragon King and the grandest of the homes, offices and consulates of Chefoo's foreign community. Further inland stood the old walled city. Behind sprawled the undulating hills, mountains and farmland of Shantung. A province larger by seven thousand square miles than England and Wales put together, it had been the home of Confucius. With the exception of modest Chefoo and tiny Wei Hai Wei, it was also almost entirely, and to Morrison's mind infuriatingly, within the German sphere of influence.

In Chefoo's harbour, wooden-hulled junks with patched concertinaed sails and gaily painted high sterns wove in and out between British and Japanese warships and passenger steamers. Skiffs swarmed around the junks like pilot fish, the boatmen loading cargoes of vermicelli, beancake, peanuts, fruit, silk, hairnets and lace bound for Shanghai.

As they cast anchor, Morrison's eye was caught by the outlandish sight of a Chinese fishing junk crowded with Europeans. The passengers sat slump-shouldered on the deck as though weighted with sadness, hunched over suitcases and bedrolls. Morrison had heard that with land battles looming and the siege dragging on, European, Russian, Chinese and Japanese residents of Port Arthur alike were giving up their jewels and cash to the captains of junks willing to run the Japanese naval blockade. Chefoo, being a mere eighty-nine nautical miles south of Port

Arthur, was, along with Wei Hai Wei, a first port of call. He would try to speak with the refugees before going on to Wei Hai Wei and his appointment with Lionel James. But he wouldn't do so straight away. Seated on the customs launch headed for the steamer and waving his hat was Morrison's dear friend J.L. Molyneux, the customs service's resident surgeon. Molyneaux's mischievous wit and knowledge of the indiscretions, follies and infelicities of the foreign community were second to none. *Now this is a balm!*

'Ernest! Good to see you, man!' the irrepressible Molyneux called out. 'There is much gossip here for you. Scuttlebutt from all corners of the Empire: Tientsin, Shanghai, Chefoo, Wei Hai Wei, Port Arthur and Japan. I was only afraid it was going to go to waste. It's been lying about in great piles awaiting collection.'

'Oh, that is good news,' Morrison replied, clambering down the boarding ladder and into the launch, followed by Kuan with the luggage. 'What's on the menu?'

'The usual: journalistic slapstick, diplomatic indiscretion, sexual peccadilloes.'

'Let me see. I'll start with the first. Journalistic slapstick.'

'I thought you might.'

There was nothing better calculated to cheer up a frustrated journalist than news of the imbroglios of his peers. Morrison only hoped that his beloved's beloved Martin Egan would be amongst those whom his friend was about to lampoon.

'With breakfast?' Molyneux offered. 'There's still plenty of time before the mail packet departs for Wei Hai Wei.'

'Even better.' The customs launch reached the docks. Morrison instructed Kuan to arrange passage for them both on the mail boat. Leaving his Boy with the luggage, he and Molyneux turned their footsteps towards Beacon Hill.

Molyneux began. 'So, McCullagh of the *New York Herald* recently got into such a funk trying to compose his telegram that, in order to hold the wires whilst he pushed it out, he telegraphed home two whole pages of a novel — at fourteen shillings a word. He blew his editor's budget and nearly got the sack.'

Morrison chortled. 'I should think so.'

'Meanwhile, Norris-Newman of the *Daily Mail* did so poorly, despite managing to pass himself off to the Japanese as a British Lieutenant-Colonel, that he actually did get the sack. And Ernest Brindle sank certain Japanese warships that to all other observations were afloat and in action, whilst evacuating Port Arthur all on his own.'

'My colleague Granger did the same for Newchang the other day.' By the time the men reached the colonnaded officers' mess, Morrison was much revived.

'Oh, and Paul Bowles has demanded his employers at the Associated Press produce the sum of eighty thousand dollars for a yacht to give him steady access to Chefoo. He says this is the only place where he can send off telegrams uncensored by the Japanese.'

'Audacious. And I suppose he told them no steamers were arriving in port, either. I suppose if Lionel James has got himself a boat, the others don't see why they shouldn't have one as well.'

'Your James has caused no end of excitement. Dispatching poor David Fraser, whom I fear will ever be known as "the valet", to set up the wireless land station for the *Haimun* at Wei Hai Wei, he ordered him to raise a one-hundred-and-eighty-foot mast. It needed to be that tall to receive signals from the boat if it got as far as Port Arthur. James didn't realise that the peasants had already chopped down every tree on every hill for miles around

Wei Hai Wei for fuel. Fraser had to cobble together something out of the half-rotting masts of abandoned junks. When he set about raising it, it broke in two and nearly dragged half a regiment of bluejackets with it into the sea.'

'Half a regiment?' Morrison sounded dubious.

'I exaggerate.' Molyneux shrugged. 'As one normally does in pursuit of a good story.' He prodded his friend.

'I never!' Morrison pulled away from the offending finger. 'All my mistakes, and I admit they're manifold, are honest ones.'

'Anyway, whilst all this is unfolding, the indefatigable James is sending one telegram after the other to Fraser — "Expedite Forestry", "Expedite Forestry".'

'Ah. The De Forest wireless system. Forestry. Of course.'

'After the same message arrived day after day after day, several times a day, the pun ceased to amuse them.'

'I can imagine. James summoned me to Wei Hai Wei with a similarly persistent, if pun-less, deluge.'

'On a more serious note,' Molyneux said, 'you should probably know that he has put some rather prominent noses out of joint.'

'That's quite an image,' Morrison replied. 'How big are these noses, exactly?'

'Big. You see, strictly speaking, only the government, the British administration of Wei Hai Wei, may sanction the building of a new wireless station. He failed to square with the commissioner first.'

'Lockhart?' Morrison knew the commissioner well. 'Maybe I can have a word.'

'That would be useful. But I'm not sure what you can do about the Admiralty. Fraser talked Colonel Bruce into volunteering the help of the Royal Engineers, entangling the military in *The Times*'s project as well. Hence the involvement of bluejackets. Wholly illegal, as you might imagine. All things considered, it's a miracle that he managed to get the mast up and working at all, and without anyone getting arrested or court-martialled, at that.'

'It appears that I'll have my work cut out simply trying to keep people from trying to sink the *Haimun* with James on board — and I mean those ostensibly on our side. It must be said that, just over a week ago in the midst of all this ballyhoo, James did manage to send his first wireless news message from the *Haimun*, the first ever transmitted from a war zone.'

Molyneux opened his mouth and shut it again. His lips twitched.

Morrison fixed his friend with a wry look. 'I know what you want to say: the only fact James reported in said dispatch was that he was at sea aboard the *Haimun* en route to Korea. Oh, and that the "military developments" that he had previously foreshadowed ought to be taking place "very soon".' After that night at the Tientsin Club, when Morrison had been surprised by the news of James's breakthrough, he'd found and read the dispatch in question. 'The second telegram, which he sent the day after, was more satisfying.'

'About the landing of Japan's main expeditionary force on the Korean coast.'

'Yes, with good detail. The building of pontoon jetties and so on. He was properly discreet, too, declining to give numbers or designations of the troops, saying it would be "unfair" to the Japanese to do so.'

'I understand there's been a third telegram. It was sent two days ago. He provides much information on Admiral Kamimura's bombardment of Vladivostok earlier this month. He does seem to have won the trust of his Japanese sources.'

'Yes. Even if the Japanese navy is still prevaricating about how close they will let him get to any real action. I look forward to hearing more when I join him in Wei Hai Wei. Speaking of which, I spotted a junk carrying European refugees earlier. I'd like to speak with them before leaving Chefoo.'

'Let's go then,' answered Molyneux. 'When you're done, I shall have the customs launch deliver you to the steamer.'

The men set off. An hour or so later they boarded the customs launch at the jetty.

'So,' Molyneux said, 'I believe that you are keeping the best story of all to yourself.'

'What do you mean?'

'One hears that you're seeing the famous Miss Perkins.'

'Famous?'

'Most certainly. She is widely discussed. The wife of a customs official — no, don't worry, not *that* one — arrived back from Tientsin a week or so ago full of information, though I admit it was so excessively sartorial in nature that I ceased to pay attention at the third mention of taffeta. My Boy told me about her in more interesting detail. His cousin Ah Long works for the Ragsdales. That's how I learned you knew the lass.'

'How small China is. Nearly four hundred million people and every single one of them knows my business.'

'And, to be fair, you know theirs.'

'It's my job. But touché. So, what exactly have you heard?'

'She seems to have charmed everyone except the missionaries, whose disapproval commends her more highly to everyone else. Even the women appear to be entranced, with the exception of those whose husbands have embraced the cult of Miss Perkins too heartily.'

Morrison affected insouciance. 'In which case they may be embracing more than the cult, one would think.'

'Indeed. She is quite the courtesan, from all reports.'

'Quite,' Morrison replied, as tightly wound as his watch.

'Do I detect a note of sourness?'

'Not at all. I'm enjoying myself and haven't felt so young or vigorous in a long while. She does me good, even when she does me bad.'

Molyneux grinned. 'That's apparent. You're looking in ruddy good health.'

'On the other hand, one does struggle. Like most explorers, I have an instinctive dislike of the beaten track.'

'And her track is well beaten.'

Morrison shot Molyneux a malefic look.

'That was crude, I admit. But I am curious, G.E. Is it possible to make an honest woman of her?'

Morrison was about to answer with a wisecrack when a realisation struck him. 'That's the thing about her and why separation from her causes me to feel downspirited. She is the most honest woman I have ever met. She has no pretence, no hypocrisy. And that is rare and lovable in a woman.'

'It is rare and lovable in a man as well,' Molyneux noted.

Morrison paused. 'I feel that if I can only hold on to that appreciation, I might find happiness with her. But I confess it is damned hard at times.'

'What does she want from you? Did she say?'

'For me not to go with any fast women whilst we're apart.'

Molyneux guffawed.

'I'm serious.'

Molyneux wagged his finger at Morrison. 'There is only one way to deal with a woman like that, G.E.'

'And that is?'

'You must marry her. Whoa!' The wake from a passing warship caused the launch to roll. Molyneux caught Morrison before he tumbled straight over the gunwales.

In Which Morrison Finds Lionel James in the Queen's House and Resists Duty in the Name of Temptation

Marry her?

The packet made the coastal run in good time and it wasn't long before Wei Hai Wei, much smaller than Chefoo, slid into view. Morrison looked towards the low brown denuded hills with their sparse covering of scrub oak and rough grass, imagining Fraser's dismay at being ordered to erect a sturdy mast. Without the right raw materials, any enterprise descended into folly.

The man has a sense of humour.

The boat juddered to anchor at Port Edward, the compact settlement that was home to Wei Hai Wei's small European community. Atop a flagpole, one of the British Empire's more eccentric flags snapped in the breeze. A Union Jack in the upper left corner. Centre right a circular badge with a delicate Chinese watercolour of Mandarin ducks, the classic symbol of love and fidelity. They represented the marriage of sound colonial administration and local custom, which was intended to transform the sleepy fishing village into a veritable Hong Kong of northern China. It would be more than just a British naval base and rest station: it would be a model of colonial administration. And so the British established school and clinics. They planted trees. They vaccinated children against bubonic plague and puerperal fever, mandated the covering of night-soil buckets and organised villagers into rat-catching associations. Yet for all the energy of the administration and hopefulness of the symbolism, Morrison knew neither the British nor the Chinese expected the union to last. The 1898 convention under which the Ch'ing Court leased Wei Hai Wei to Britain granted the tiny territory to the British only for so long as the Russians held Port Arthur. Thus both sides viewed the arrangement as a makeweight by which a more stable balance of imperialist powers might be achieved. If Japan won this war, the union would dissolve. It was hard to put much stock in love and fidelity when the groom knew the bride was liable to wander off with someone else at any moment.

Morrison told himself to stop reading meaning into every deuced thing.

He and Kuan caught the first launch for hilly Liu Kung Island, the natural breakwater at the mouth of Wei Hai Wei's harbour, which the British navy had made its base and recreational ground. It was not a big place, only two miles long and one and a quarter square miles in area. The north of the island rose steeply from the sea in forbidding cliffs. Chinese fishermen lived on the island's pointy east and blunter west ends in stone houses thatched with seagrass; the British erected their barracks, churches and public buildings in the sheltered south and centre. Kuan pointed out a Japanese man o' war steaming past, en route to Port Arthur.

They disembarked at the crowded quay on the island's south side. Directly across the way was a grand old building that had formerly housed a Chinese temple. At the top of a low flight of stone steps stood massive vermilion doors. Painted with the fierce figure of the Chinese God of War, they had been swung open in welcome. A sign at the side of the door announced the premises as 'Queen's House'; it served as the Royal Naval Canteen. Making plans to meet Kuan later, Morrison strode up the stone steps, stepped smartly over the wooden threshold and looked around. In a courtyard where Buddhist idols once 'ate joss' and spirit food offered up by worshippers, British officers and civilians consumed light meals and 'temperance drinks' such as beer served up by the management. Seated at a table on which the latest edition of the daily *Wei Hai Wei Lyre* lay open and unread, Lionel James puffed furiously on his pipe, looking no less red-faced or wild-eyed than the God of War himself.

Morrison had barely sat down when James let loose a barrage: 'the hide of …', 'gross insult …', 'outrage …', 'provocation …' Morrison had to wind him back like a clock.

Admiral Alexieff, the Tsar's viceroy for the Far East, James said, had decreed that should the Russian navy discover that any correspondents travelling on neutral vessels were utilising wireless technology to communicate war news to the Japanese, the Russians would arrest them as spies and seize their vessels and equipment. 'I am, of course, the only correspondent who fits the description!' James fumed. 'And all this just as I've finally begun to make a mark with my telegrams. The *New York Times* is now publishing them after *The Times*. Somebody has to stare down Alexieff!'

'Agreed,' Morrison said. 'But if you are not actually communicating war news to the Japanese, the Russians would have no grounds to complain. I say write a telegram for *The Times* in which you make clear that you use a cipher that neither Japanese nor Russian instruments are capable of recording. Put it on the record. You are doing nothing that compromises the neutrality of your position or the ship's. If the Russians dare to act then, it will be seen as a hostile act.'

James grunted assent. His brow remained furrowed under his slouch cap. He relit his pipe and drew on it for a while in silence, his features growing hazy behind the cloud of smoke. 'That is certainly the position of the editors of both *The Times* and the *New York Times*,' he confirmed in a gruff voice. 'The *New York Times* is making much of the fact that our wireless operators are young Americans. There is talk that if the Russians are going to threaten American lives, the State Department will have to get involved. The *New York Times* has gone so far as to say that Russian seizure of the *Haimun* would be tantamount to a declaration of war against both the United States and Great Britain.'

'And the American government?'

'The American State Department is considerably more cautious in its own pronouncements.'

'What about the Foreign Office?'

'More cautious still. The legal adviser of Foreign Secretary Lord Lansdowne is appalled that we may have compromised Britain's neutrality in Russian eyes. He has not been shy about letting our editors know it. And thanks to Admiral Noel's opposition to the project, the Admiralty Lords have weighed in as well.' James paused to gauge Morrison's reaction.

'You're right,' Morrison said. 'It's a perfect night for a stroll.'

Having delivered that non sequitur, Morrison rose and strode towards the exit. James, snatching his tobacco and matches from the table, scurried after with a perplexed expression.

It was a mild and moon-silvered night. 'Our conversation was attracting attention,' Morrison explained once they were on the waterfront. 'In their eagerness to eavesdrop, several correspondents were listing dangerously from their chairs. Now that we are no longer placing them in harm's way, we are free to talk. What exactly is the opinion of the Admiralty Lords?'

'It is that issues of neutrality aside, allowing journalists with wireless apparatus to steam willy-nilly about the theatre of war in press boats could set a dangerous precedent. They don't want anyone trying that when it's Britain at war.'

'They have a point,' Morrison conceded.

'To make things worse, the commander of Britain's China Fleet, Sir Cyprian Bridge, was furious to learn that Fraser had enlisted the help of the Royal Navy to raise the wireless mast. Fulminated that it was "a piece of great impertinence". He learned about it from a guest at his table on board the HMS *Alacrity*.'

'Insult to injury,' observed Morrison, imagining the scene. 'At least you've got a fine ship there with the *Haimun*. I'm rather fond of it for its role in transporting the British troops who came to put down the Boxers four years ago.'

'The *Haimun* is a good vessel,' James agreed. 'She can do sixteen knots if pushed. Jolly good crew, too. Captain Passmore is a mulatto who claims a wealthy uncle in Melbourne and a place in the bed of the actress Lillie Langtry. You'd enjoy Passmore. Biggest gossip on the China coast. Our quartermaster's a hardy Malayan, the wireless operator, Brown, is a good bloke, and Tonami, my Japanese translator, a capital sort. He's spent time in Europe. Knows Paris as well as he does Tokio. G.E. ...' James turned and gripped Morrison's arm. 'We sail for Nagasaki at dawn. Come with us. You'll get a taste of the *Haimun* in action. You'll see for yourself just what's at stake. We're going to change the future of correspondence, G.E.! We just need to be left alone to do it! Well? Will you come?'

Morrison's mouth tightened. *I should go. Of course I should.* 'Can't do. Business in Shanghai. Urgent business. Very urgent.' He wondered if he was as transparent as he felt. *What an ass I am.*

'You can't delay?' James asked.

'No.' Morrison shook his head. 'Sadly not.'

In Which Morrison Travels to the Charing Cross of the Pacific, Lectures Kuan on the Benefits of Western Imperialism and Receives a Surprise at Journey's End

Two days it took to steam the nearly five hundred nautical miles down the China coast from Wei Hai Wei to the mouth of the Yangtze Delta, two days in which Morrison had plenty of time to wonder, fret, imagine, burn and hope, though he couldn't have said what exactly he was hoping for. Early on the morning of the twenty-sixth of March, lying in his bunk between sleep and wakefulness, Morrison felt the shift of the engines. The steamer had left the East China Sea and entered the delta. The world outside his porthole was thick and grey, opaque air, turbid water.

He ought to have gone with James to Japan. There was no question but that the Russians were looking for trouble. James would not willingly give it to them. Yet Morrison was not convinced that James, irascible, stubborn and obsessive as he was, could avoid provoking it.

Dressing warmly against the dank air, he took himself above deck. Though the fog was still impenetrable, the earthy, estuarial breath of paddy fields and vegetable gardens told him land was close.

A lightship arrived to guide the steamer through the treacherous shallows into the channel. The ships chugged in concert past low marshy banks to the mouth of the Whampoa River. Farms pitched into view, then mills and factories and graving docks, and waking industry proclaimed itself with a cacophony of clanging, scraping and whistling.

As the steamer arrived in sight of Shanghai itself, the channel grew crowded with a circus of sampans and steam liners, skiffs, paddle arks, junks, gunboats, launches and the tramps of a dozen nations and two dozen companies, all, it seemed, sounding their sirens, whistles and bells at once.

Yet for all the purposeful energy of the 'Charing Cross of the Pacific', there was a fecund, promiscuous, feminine sensuality here with which arid north China, for all its intellectual and political vitality, could not compete. Morrison felt both unnerved and stirred by Shanghai's sultry breath, its sly dialect, its savage *t'ai-chi* of cosmopolitan and parochial. Peking and Tientsin were male, purposeful, important, *yang*. Shanghai, with its steamy, moist exhalations, was *yin*. A woman, and a loose one at that. Anyone could have her. It didn't matter if you were an honest man or a pirate, a foreigner or a native-born, if you came from Canton or Paris, London or Szechuan, she offered herself up as easily as the vendors and hawkers on the Bund proffered tea eggs, steamed bread or their own — they swore — virginal sisters. If you were smart, you'd take her with one hand on your purse and your eyes wide open. It was an unsettling place in which to be meeting Miss Mae Ruth Perkins.

As they passed a hulk full of bonded Indian opium, Morrison

noticed Kuan's frown. Most Chinese whom Morrison knew were unhappy with the British importation of opium to China. They saw the Opium Wars, in which Britain forced China to accept the importation of opium as part of the terms of trade and which began the process by which imperialist powers carved out concessions from Chinese territory, as the supreme humiliation.

'I know what you're thinking, Kuan,' Morrison said. He ploughed on: 'But you have to admit, Shanghai would not be Shanghai or Tientsin Tientsin for that matter, the Chinese Customs Service would not be so efficiently run, and places like Wei Hai Wei would be festering stink holes of disease and backwardness if it wasn't for Western intervention. Japan had the Meiji Emperor. He put Japan on the right track, what, fifty years ago? China needs to do the same. And if it won't, if it can't, then it is up to the civilised nations of Europe to drag it into the modern age.'

'*Shi*,' Kuan said after a pause. His answer was not less polite for being monosyllabic, but, whilst implying agreement, it also had the connotation of obeying an order.

Morrison's thoughts turned to his arrangements. He would stay at the home of his colleague J.O.P. Blunt, he of the lavender-scented pomade. Blunt lived with his wife and children in a grand Western-style residence on Bubbling Well Road in the joint British and American International Settlement, of which Blunt was also Secretary. The Japanese consulate was conveniently close to the Blunts' home. As for Mae, he had wired her hotel from Wei Hai Wei to inform her of his arrival, promising to send a note as soon as he had settled.

In his head, Morrison had composed numerous possible scenarios for their reunion. In some he gazed upon her with a curious indifference, for which he was thankful. In others — the work of his heart rather than his head — they flew into one another's arms. Certain versions allowed for the possibility of additional revelations from her, occasioning further moral outrage and passionate consequence. One variation that caused his chest to swell with hope had them agreeing that what was past was past; she was his and his alone now. That preferred by both pride and sensibility involved him enjoying her intimately one final glorious time and then splitting from her, occasioning tears on her part but demonstrating an unshakeable firmness on his own. That which caused him to gnash his teeth involved her having been so rushed by some bounder or another in the interim that she had entirely forgotten having bid him come. None of his fantasies took into account the possibility that she would be perched on a bench in the public gardens at the Bund under an enormous hat trimmed with pink flowers, waving at his launch. Paradoxically relieved by the sight of the source of his torment, he asked himself how he could ever have doubted her.

In Which Talk of Railways Is Derailed, Our Knight in Burnished Armour Fails to Protect His Most Vital Organ and the Science of Hypnotism Is Elucidated

'I am quite mad for Shanghai,' Mae proclaimed as their carriage, piloted by two smartly uniformed Chinese drivers, made its way down the Bund toward Nanking Road. One driver, regal and straight, held the reins and whip. The other flourished a bell, scattering pedestrian and other traffic before them. Their carriage passed in front of the foreign shipping offices, hotels and *hongs*; the hustle of Shanghai's river was reflected in the bustle of its streets. Western women paraded in the latest fashions and both foreign businessmen and Chinese compradors dressed with élan. Morrison, casual by inclination and bedraggled by travel, felt blurry and rustic in comparison.

If Mae minded, she gave no sign. 'I am so happy you've come. We shall have such a glorious time here.' She pressed her foot in its narrow boot against his.

The knots in his stomach loosened. All his tension, misgivings and foreboding — in short, every consequence of the use of his rational faculties with regard to the young lady beside him — evaporated like morning mist.

'Did you find out what that Mr James was being so terribly urgent about?' she asked.

Morrison delivered a witty rendition of his meeting with the excitable James in Wei Hai Wei. 'And it's not just the Russians, the British and the Americans who are stirred up by the *Haimun*. A Japanese naval commander wasn't too thrilled the other day when, instead of his Admiral's orders, he received on his wireless set James's dispatch to *The Times*!'

Mae laughed. 'And how is your war going, anyway?'

'The Japanese have yet to capture Port Arthur but I expect that good news is not far off.'

'And once Port Arthur falls, that will be the end of it?'

'For all intents and purposes. Port Arthur is both strategic and symbolic. The Japanese have already overrun Korea. They still need to confront the Russians in engagements on land but they are doing what they can to disrupt the railways and block the ports so the Russians' supplies must come over the mountains by cart and packhorse. They will easily be exhausted.'

'I would think so. I'm exhausted just hearing about it.'

Now it was Morrison's turn to laugh. Relaxed, invigorated and absurdly happy again, he reminded himself that if he was to justify this trip to Shanghai, to himself as well as James and their employer, he could not afford to be so distracted that he neglected his work. Folding her hand into his own, he mentally reviewed the tasks at hand. Molyneux had mentioned rumours of a naval engagement off Port Arthur in which the Japanese, dazzled by the flashlights from Russian-operated lighthouses, had failed to sink any enemy ships. Apparently, the officers responsible had shaved their heads in shame. No one in Chefoo or Wei Hai Wei could confirm this story but he had better hopes here in Shanghai, where sources were looser lipped.

There was also the matter of the Chefoo–Port Arthur cable, which the Japanese had cut to punish Russian communications, acting on information he himself had provided them. The cable company had sent a ship to repair it but the Japanese navy turned it back, claiming the repair would breach neutrality. The company had protested but retired the ship south so as not to provoke an incident. Again, he expected to be able to get more detail in Shanghai. Finally there was the vexed issue of the railway concessions …

'A penny for your thoughts.'

'Ah … That's a complicated one.'

'Why? Are you thinking of another woman?' She nudged him.

In his experience, such a question, however playful in phrasing, was rarely lighthearted in intent. 'Such would be impossible in your presence. It's just that I fear boring you.'

'I cannot imagine how you could possibly bore me.'

Tentatively at first, Morrison began to expound on the politics of China's cable communications and railway concessions. 'Baron Rosen … General Dessins … the Lu-Han prospectus …'

A commotion erupted ahead. A motorcar had only narrowly avoided smashing into a dray. The Chinese cart-driver's curses flew like shrapnel, aimed at everything from eighteen generations of the other driver's ancestors to the likely possibility that his children would be born without arseholes. The driver of the automobile, a European, gave back as good as he got in a stream of language as evidently defamatory as it was incomprehensible.

'Jànos!' Mae exclaimed.

'Jànos?' Morrison echoed warily.

'Yes. He's a Hungarian and the first person to own a motorcar in Shanghai. It is quite a big deal. Everyone is much impressed with him.'

As she nattered on about Jànos, describing a dinner the previous night where he'd been the life of the party, Morrison sank into a sulk. The possibility that this Jànos might already have been added to her list of lovers was bad enough. Morrison was even more put out by the fact that, having encouraged him to talk about his interests, she'd obviously not taken in a word he'd said. Recalling his intention to love and thence leave her, he felt both fortified and brightened — like burnished armour. The metaphor pleased and comforted him.

'I'm sorry. What were you saying about the Lu ... Lu-something prospectus?'

She exceeds all expectations. The guards of Morrison's inner fortress threw open the gates, let down the drawbridges and breached their own defences. He was hers for the asking, and she had not even needed to ask.

They were in the relatively open country and fresh air of Bubbling Well Road in no time. The Blunts' Head Boy, Ah Chang, hurried out to greet them. He told them that the Blunts were upcountry. They'd be back that evening and were expecting Morrison. Relieved of any need to dawdle, Morrison instructed Ah Chang to have Kuan, when he arrived from the port with the luggage, send the washing to the steam laundry on Hanbury Street. Having reserved the carriage, he instructed the driver to deliver them in good speed to Mae's hotel.

Once in her room, she drew him down onto her bed with a familiar urgency. 'I have missed you so much.'

Clothing piled up on the carpet. No one else existed. No one ever had. No one … Morrison abruptly recalled her telling him that Martin Egan had once had her for days in succession in Shanghai. *Don't ask*, he warned himself. *You won't like the answer.* He seethed. *Don't.* He struggled. *Ask.* 'Was it here?'

'Was what here, honey? What are you talking about?'

'Egan.'

A pause. 'Martin? What about him?' She rolled onto her side, draping the sheet carelessly over her curves. With one arm stretched under her head and the other hooked over it, she regarded Morrison with lazy eyes. She toyed with a curl whilst awaiting his answer.

Morrison squeezed out his words through a rigid jaw. 'Was it here, this hotel I mean, that he … he *had* you?'

'Yes, I believe it was. Why?'

Why? It was as though he could see, clear as day, the younger man, the damned American with his damned handsome features and excellent teeth, lying in the bed betwixt them with a hand on her breast. Once this vision had taken purchase, he was unable to evict it.

'Does it ever occur to you …' His lungs filled with anguish. He could not finish the sentence. *Racked with jealousy!*

'What, honey?'

That this. 'That this.' *Hurts.* 'That people.' *Me.* 'Might talk.' *Damned pompous. Why did I say that and not what I meant? Distraught with passion!* 'They see you flirting with every Tom, Dick and Harry.'

Mae studied him for a moment and then erupted into merriment so hearty her breasts quivered. Her stomach rippled with waves of laughter.

'Why is that funny?' Petulance fluted his words. *Humiliating. Damned humiliating. As though I cannot satisfy you alone.*

'Ernest, honey, don't you understand me by now? I don't care what people say. You will never please people. Well, maybe *you* will please people. Not me. Not that way. I promise you that if I were to take up a nun's habit tomorrow, by the day after they'd all be whispering about the scandalous manner in which I wore my wimple. I do not doubt that my own parents, whilst professing in their letters to miss me ardently, are relieved to have a holiday from the obloquy that my presence always threatens.'

'I just don't like to hear that people are speaking ill of you. That's all.'

'If to note that I have desires and urges and the wherewithal to act them out is to speak ill of me,' she responded hotly, 'then I shall save everyone the trouble and speak ill of myself. I make no pretence of propriety. Propriety interests me not in the least.'

That is self-evident.

She studied him for a moment. She kissed him on the nose. 'Oh, honey, if that's what's troubling you, please don't worry. You've been awfully moody. Is that what's been on your mind?'

He nodded stiffly. *Of course not. It is that you can need another when all I need is you.*

'Oh, Ernest, let's not quarrel — not today, not ever. Certainly not over something as silly as whether people are pretending to disapprove of behaviour they envy.'

'Hypocrisy is rife,' Morrison conceded between clamped teeth. 'Don't think that I don't also detest it.'

'Well then, come, let us be honest with each other and to heck with the rest of the world. If you're really upset with me,' she said with widened eyes, 'you can spank me and I'll tell you I've been a naughty girl.' She propped herself up on her hands and knees so as to better display the realm of punishment and peered around at him with an irresistible expression. 'Come on, honey, my Cinnabar Gate, my Open Peony Blossom, my Jewel Terrace awaits your Jade Stalk, your Heavenly Dragon Pillar.' She giggled. 'Your Swelling Mushroom. I'm sure I've forgotten one.'

'My Coral Stem.' Morrison fought back a smile.

'That's it! I will even allow you to bring the Flowering Branch to the Full Moon as long as you're gentle.' She wiggled her bottom at him. 'But I do think I need a little slap first, don't you? Considering how bad I've been?'

Morrison raised his hand.

'You know, in my experience,' she observed, 'men of the cloth are inordinately fond of this particular practice.'

Morrison stayed his hand.

Did he recall Reverend Nisbet, whom they'd met at Mountain-Sea Pass that night?

He did. Not happily. And less so by the second.

Within the Reverend Nisbet's breast, it seemed, his ordained love for mankind wrestled with an innate revulsion of same. She had discovered not long after that evening that a similar struggle occurred between an abhorrence of sin and a natural predilection for it.

It took a moment for her words to sink in.

'God no.'

'God yes.' She put particular emphasis on the word 'God'.

Desolation! 'Did you ...'

'All he desired was for me to sit naked but for my stockings and shoes in an overstuffed reading chair in the mission in Tientsin when Mrs Nisbet was absent and play with myself in front of him. He took care of his own pleasure. There was a terrible moment when his face went crimson and I feared he was about to be struck with apoplexy. It would have been most awkward. As it turned out, the congestion was the normal precedent to his eruption. Also, it would have been more pleasant if the chair I was sitting in had not been stuffed with horsehair. I could feel it on my buttocks and thighs and back for a week, I swear. After, he spanked me for some time. My skin went very red. I could only just tolerate it. But by far the worst part was that he forced me to endure a sermon on the nature of lust and sin for at least half an hour afterwards.'

If there is a hell, here is a vision of it. 'But why?'

'Because he felt guilty, I presume.'

'I didn't mean why the sermon. Why did you do it?'

'Because he asked. Begged, really. I felt sorry for him. Anyway, no harm done and it made him happy, for a moment, anyway. I like making people happy. It is my gift.'

Morrison was unable to argue with that. In as nonchalant a tone as he could summon, he asked, 'And did you derive pleasure yourself or was it an act of charity — *Christian* charity in this case?'

A sweet laugh rewarded the bitter pun. 'My pleasure was in being observed. Anyway, you should know that when I touched myself I was thinking about you.'

'Is that so?' Morrison asked, his voice arid.

'It was certainly so.'

'Enough, Mae. No more stories.'

She looked surprised. 'I thought you liked my stories.'

'Not that sort. Not that way. Not any more.'

She studied his face. 'All right. As you wish.'

Morrison reached for his shirt. His mood had soared and plunged so many times in the last several hours that he was exhausted. He wished to return to the Blunts' to speak with his host about ships and mines and war. For the first time since meeting Mae Ruth Perkins, he looked upon her voluptuous languor with only the desire to flee from it.

'Honey. What are you doing?'

'Getting dressed.'

'But we haven't made love.'

Morrison, too wretched to respond, was fumbling a cufflink into place when she embraced him from behind, throwing her arms around his chest and burying her face in his back.

'I have a gift for making people miserable sometimes, too,' she whispered. 'I know that. I'm not happy about it. But if I let go of my honesty, I let go of myself. You understand that, don't you?'

'I have to leave, Mae.' The air in the room was close, suffocating. He pushed her hands off his torso and stood up, feeling her eyes on him as he finished dressing.

'I have reserved a carriage for us tomorrow,' she said as he made for the door. 'I thought you could show me the native city. Meet me here around eleven, won't you?'

When Morrison was a boy, a carnival had come to Geelong. Amongst the sideshow acts was that of a hypnotist. He had watched, arms crossed in defiance at the spectacle, as before the man's spinning wheels and gentling voice the volunteers grew glassy-eyed and pliable. He found it horrible. As long as he lived, he had vowed to himself that day, he would never surrender control of his actions to another in the way those sad, suggestible sods had done.

'Eleven?' he replied. 'I shall see you then.'

'Kiss?'

I should not do this. I must not do this.

The mesmerist had assured his audience that he could not make anyone do what they did not, deep in their hearts, wish to do themselves. This knowledge did not lessen the hilarity of the entertainment; in fact, it heightened it.

It was several hours before Morrison left the hotel for the Blunts' house.

In Which It Is Seen That, in Times of
National Crisis, Even the Wives of Tycoons
May Turn Radical, J.O.P. Blunt Cautions
Our Hero About the Dangers Posed by Feminism
and Mrs Blunt Demonstrates the Superiority
of Women's Intuition

Having missed dinner with his hosts the night before, Morrison
joined John Otway Percy Blunt and his wife, Constance, for
breakfast the next morning.

'It's grand to see you again, G.E.,' Blunt pronounced in his
soft Irish brogue. 'And what will occupy your time in Shanghai?'

'I'll do what I can to advance the case of the *Haimun*. I also
have several stories to pursue.' Morrison elaborated on all but the
story that was occupying him most completely and was, in any
case, of no consequence to *The Times*. 'And I would like to do
some shopping,' he added, turning to Mrs Blunt. 'I should seek
your advice. I wish to get a number of things that are difficult, if
not impossible, to find in Peking, including a bicycle and a good
tea service.'

'That's easy in Shanghai,' she replied. 'You'll want to visit Lane
Crawford. It's a most marvellous emporium.'

'My dear,' Blunt interrupted, 'before you enumerate your reasons, which I know to be manifold, I must enquire of our guest if he has heard of Tso Jung.'

'Is that a bazaar to which you would send me instead?' Morrison asked, po-faced. He saw how Mrs Blunt contemplated her husband with the sort of resigned sullenness that, from his observation, appeared to be the glue of long marriages.

'Uh, no, Tso Jung is —'

'The eighteen-year-old author of *The Revolutionary Army*,' Morrison interjected with a half-wink at his hostess. She seemed cheered by the gentle poke at her husband's expense and Morrison silently thanked Kuan, who, ear to the ground as usual, had alerted him to the growing movement around the young Shanghainese radical. 'Preaches from within the safety of the International Concession that China has become a race of slaves that needs to free itself from both tyranny and foreign domination. Wants to annihilate the "hairy and horned" race of Manchus, institute American-style constitutional government, bring about equality of the sexes — that sort of thing. Typical of the more radical of the heirs to the failed reform movement of 1898. What about him?'

'I should never think to stump you on any point of Chinese politics,' Blunt said. 'So you are undoubtedly aware that the Russo-Japanese War is giving new impetus to Tso and his adherents. They talk of China being "carved up like a melon" by the foreign powers.'

'That's interesting, though such talk is nothing new. I have heard this before from Kuan, and others as well, of course.' Morrison chased a scrap of bacon across his plate with his knife and fork. 'It was widely current at the time of the Boxers, as you know.'

'True, but support is growing for the anti-foreign cause amongst the intellectuals. The Boxers were but pig-ignorant peasants.'

'I have not yet met a peasant in China who is ignorant when it comes to pigs,' Morrison replied. 'That is one subject they tend to know much about. But I take your point. There is much disaffection abroad.'

'Indeed,' Mrs Blunt said. 'And not all of it aimed at the Ch'ing Court. There is anger at this war.'

'My wife is suddenly a follower of politics.'

'I have always been a follower of politics.' Constance Blunt turned to Morrison. 'My husband thinks that a woman's attention to the details of shopping and other entertainments prevents her from having a brain for more serious matters.'

'My wife has discovered the writings of Mary Wollstonecraft,' Blunt observed mildly. 'They have caused no end of trouble and upset.'

Mrs Blunt smiled in her husband's direction as though he were a young and stupid boy whose idiocies were not worth refuting.

'Mrs Wollstonecraft makes the odd valid point, of course,' Blunt continued, 'but she does stir up the ladies terribly. When you do find yourself a good woman to wed, my dear Morrison, check first that she is not one of Wollstonecraft's disciples.'

'He teases,' Mrs Blunt said, 'but he would have it no other way. Everyone knows that the measure of a civilisation is the position and progress of its women.'

Blunt widened his eyes at Morrison.

'I saw that, dear. To return to the topic of Chinese radicalism,' Mrs Blunt continued, 'last year there was a significant public protest against Russian designs on Manchuria. You would know of it, of course, Dr Morrison.'

'I heard something, yes.'

'Well, a diamond ring turned up amongst the donations. People said it was from Liza Roos. You know Liza Roos?'

'Wife of the Baghdadi Jew Silas Hardoon, wealthiest man in Shanghai, or near to it. Eurasian lady but considers herself Chinese before anything else.'

'Precisely. And is most sympathetic to the patriotic cause.'

Morrison shrugged. 'Interesting position for the wife of an opium importer. But that the patriots of all classes are aligned against the Russians means that I have no quarrel with their patriotism.'

'I believe they're equally opposed to the Japanese,' said Mrs Blunt.

The image of the man of God spanking sweet Maysie, suppressed by Morrison with the utmost effort since the night before, welled up unbidden, bringing bile with it. Blades of fury, humiliation and jealousy stabbed at his heart. *How could she? Why do I put up with it?*

'I know,' Mrs Blunt conceded, 'that's not what you want to hear.'

Morrison fell silent, in no mood to argue.

Blunt studied their guest over the rim of his cup. 'You appear unusually distracted,' he said.

'Distracted? I hadn't myself noticed. Then again, if I was truly distracted, I wouldn't have, would I?'

'I wonder,' Blunt ventured, 'if you are not as sanguine about the war as your dispatches would suggest.'

'Nonsense.' Morrison stirred a lump of pressed sugar into his coffee. His spoon clicked so forcefully against his cup that he saw he gave cause to Mrs Blunt to fear for her porcelain. 'If I am distracted, it is not by lack of optimism about Japan's victory.'

Then, for a woman's instincts were strong and Morrison no stranger, Mrs Blunt mused, 'Personally *I* wonder if your distraction is not something to do with a fascinating young maiden we have been hearing much about.'

'Which fascinating young maiden would that be? I should like to meet someone of that description.' Morrison was normally happier extracting gossip from others than revealing it about himself. Yet he was fond of Mrs Blunt. Replacing his cup and rising, he added with a glimmer of a smile, 'And if you will excuse me, I am going to do just that. I'm to meet her in just over an hour's time.'

In Which, to Morrison's Relief, Mrs Ragsdale Refuses to Go Native and Morrison Falls in Love with an Honest Woman

'I don't know that it is such a good idea, Mae, dear. Besides, the ladies of the American Women's Club in Shanghai were looking forward to meeting you.'

'Oh, Mrs R. There'll be other occasions. It's not every day one has the chance to visit the Chinese quarter in the company of such an eminent expert in Chinese ways as Dr Morrison.'

'Of course,' Mrs Ragsdale agreed, her voice seesawing between anxiety and deference. 'I didn't mean to imply … But I worry.'

'There's nothing to worry about,' Mae responded breezily.

'My dear,' said Mrs Ragsdale, searching without luck for back-up in Morrison's neutral expression, 'I should hardly call smallpox and other such maladies "nothing to worry about".' Mrs Ragsdale pressed her lips together so tightly she appeared to have swallowed them. 'Even if, praise God, you are not infected with something fatal, there is always the likelihood of being rudely … *jostled*. The Chinese mob is not well-disposed to those of the fairer races, not to mention the weaker sex. Anything could happen.' Sweat beaded her forehead. '*And* the smells are reputed to be quite overwhelming. Mrs Clarkson said that her son went there one afternoon and came back smelling like a stable; it took days to wash the stench of garlic and joss and who knows what else out of his clothing.'

It would be a most unusual stable that stank of garlic and joss, Morrison thought. Growing impatient, he said, 'I'll look after Miss Perkins.'

'Oh, bless you, Dr Morrison,' Mrs Ragsdale replied. 'I know you will. I never meant to imply otherwise. It's just that —'

'The great traveller and author Isabella Bird did it some years ago,' Mae interjected. 'She wrote that she was similarly warned but, in fact, was allowed to explore the streets unmolested. She wrote that the smells were no worse than anywhere else in China.'

'Isabella Bird is an *adventuress.*' Mrs Ragsdale's enunciation of the word suggested that it signified an entirely alien life-form.

'Really?' Morrison affected a scandalised tone of voice. 'I had no idea. On the occasions I've met Miss Bird, I've always found her to behave most modestly.'

Mae giggled and Mrs Ragsdale blanched. 'Oh, I didn't mean to insinuate ...'

'Ah,' Morrison said with an amiable air, 'of course not. That's all very well then.'

Mae stood up. 'We should probably be off.'

Mrs Ragsdale bit her lip. 'What will I tell your father ...?'

'My dear papa is busy in Washington making laws for the United States of America. I'd imagine that he would be most astonished, if not displeased, to be told anything at all about some innocent excursion. Mrs Ragsdale, please don't worry. I'm a big girl.'

The previous day, Morrison had departed with decidedly mixed feelings. He had, in truth, misgivings about the wisdom of continuing the relationship with Mae at all. But her spirit of fun and adventure was too adorable, not to mention contagious. He recalled how it had drawn him to her in the first place. By the time they said goodbye to the fretful Mrs Ragsdale, he was quite looking forward to the outing.

'I would hate to go through life so fearful of everything,' Mae said as they set out in a hired two-in-hand. 'I am certain that you could not be so fearful of anything if you tried.'

'You may find this odd,' Morrison replied, 'and I don't always confess this, but I understand timidity more than you might think. My saintly mother has expended much ink over the years beseeching me not to seek out unnecessary danger. Every instinct tells me that her worry is neither misplaced nor foolish. Indeed, I have very nearly come to grief a dozen times in as many countries. It is an effort of will not to become a cautious man as a result. You could say that my whole life has been a combat against a natural shrinking from danger. I might not have attempted half the feats I did had it not occurred to me that running from them was the more sensible option. If I may be so bold as to say so, one of the greatest of your myriad charms, dear Maysie, is what I perceive as your native, unabashed and unaffected courage.'

'Thank you for saying so. But we are not so dissimilar. It has also often struck me that when we think of soldiers valiantly charging the frontline, we don't always remember that something else may be in pursuit from behind. We all have our demons.'

'And what demons could possibly be in pursuit of you?'

'I have told you about George Bew, my three-time fiancé. I don't believe I mentioned his mother, Mattie. For years, Mattie Bew wrote the dearest, most heartbreaking letters to me.

She traced them in faint blue pencil on nearly transparent paper, as though trepidatious of leaving any bold mark on the world. She was almost pathetically keen to hear of my adventures, even when they might have been prejudicial to the interests of her own son. Once, I asked her what she wanted for herself. She baulked, as though it had never occurred to her to think about it. This vision of life lived meekly and through the agency of others — for she was in thrall to both husband and son — has never left me. It chills my blood. It is this demon that makes me run, and run fast.'

Ever a mystery, the alchemy of love. With Mae, Morrison had quickly progressed from lustful curiosity and delight to obsession. Then his passion had begun to gutter, the flame burning less hotly as more and more contenders appeared to steal its oxygen. The day before, he'd nearly walked away from her entirely. But for whatever reason, and despite his most rational intentions, Morrison now felt his heart clench around a stronger emotion. He saw in that instant that he and Mae were kindred spirits, fellow adventurers who shared a secret about courage and a fierce commitment to it. The tide of affection swept away all consciousness of rivals past and present as effectively as if they had gone down together with all the warships, Russian and Japanese, sunk to date in the Yellow Sea.

By now they had reached the Chinese City's distinctive curved walls. Instructing the driver to wait for them, they dismounted and walked through the city gate.

Inside the walls, the brackish tang of the Whampoa River was complicated by wafts of pork, joss and tobacco, as well as less salubrious vapours rising off the foul drift of sewage, horse droppings and raw humanity. It was a far worse concoction than even Mrs Ragsdale had imagined but, to Morrison's delight, Mae did not appear at all fazed by it. A coolie pushed past, on his bent back the jiggling corpse of a fat sow bound for a restaurant. Everywhere was activity, industry, hubbub. Mae wanted to sample it all. The joss houses where the air hummed with the monks' sonorous chanting and where the fragrance of sandalwood incense clung to one's hair. An opium den where men lay on hard beds in soft dreams, the sickly sweet smoke curling around their heads. Above the laneways, a tassel of freshly laundered footbinding bandages, quilt covers, silk trousers — 'the flags of a hundred nations' — fluttering from a horizontal forest of bamboo. Ahead, a wedding procession led by blustering brass horns and spanking cymbals, red on red; behind, a funeral with its wailing trumpets and sackcloth mourners, white on white. Shanghai's seductive world of sensation. Everything interested her. Everything delighted her.

When travelling with other Westerners, Morrison had frequently noticed the odd phenomenon of China — so alive to him when he was on his own or with Chinese people — appearing to flatten out like wallpaper. Mae, in her sparking excitement, caused everything to quicken and appear more vivid. It had been some time since Morrison had experienced the heart-stopping wonderment that China in all of its teeming life, art and invention could induce. Around Mae, he experienced everything as freshly as when he had first landed. It occurred to him now that this was due to her astonishing, albeit confronting, honesty. Most people held between themselves and the world a shield of deception, little lies, social poses, self-delusions, pretend responses and rank hypocrisies, himself included. She, miraculously, had retained the openness and directness of a child. As he'd said to Molyneux, if there was a more lovable quality than such honesty, he did not know what it could possibly be.

In Which Dr Kellogg's Injunctions Are Roundly Ignored, Morrison Is Shanghaied, Old Friends Come and Go, and a Word Beginning with the Letter 'F' Is Spoken Aloud

They left the Chinese City before the gates closed for the night and took the carriage to the Chang Gardens in the International Settlement to round off what Mae called 'our Chinese day'.

It was dusk and the lanterns set out along the artfully landscaped paths and swinging from the upturned eaves of the park's pavilions glowed against a pastel sky. A courtesan in a robe the colour of plum blossoms peered at Mae from behind the swaying beaded curtains of her palanquin and Mae waved, eliciting a smile. On the lake, men and women idled in painted pleasure boats, their laughter and the sounds of flute and zither floating on the moist breeze. 'I could stay in China forever,' Mae murmured dreamily and Morrison was filled with dumb hope.

They took a table on the second floor of a teahouse overlooking the lake. The waiter placed a miniature terracotta teapot and small cups on the table along with a selection of dainties. There were crisp biscuits coated in sesame; steamed, see-through 'crystal dumplings'; parcels of meat wrapped in withered beancake skins; boiled peanuts. Morrison watched, besotted, as Mae set to the feast with abandon.

Selecting a steamed bun filled with a paste of peanuts, sugar and salt, she cried, 'Peanut butter! How funny. It's all the rage in New York. They served it with watercress in sandwiches at the Vanity Fair Tearoom last time I was there. Have you been?'

'New York or the Vanity Fair Tearoom?' Morrison asked, mustering shards of pink ginger around a 'little basket dumpling' of minced pork.

'Either.'

'I've been to New York but my travels were not so well funded that I could aspire to tea on the Upper West Side. I was renting a room on 19th Street for two dollars a week. I was far better acquainted with the ten-cent pork-and-potatoes special at Beef Steak John's, and *that* I could only afford to eat once every two days.'

'Goodness! It's hard to imagine. You know, I don't think I shall ever tire of your stories. Even if you have tired of mine. But what on earth were you doing there under such circumstances?' She levered up a slice of mock goose with her chopsticks.

'Looking for work. I was fresh out of medical school and still hopeful of inflicting my poor talents on the sick. But when I applied for the post of warder at the New York Hospital on 15th Street, the secretary took one look at my testimonials and demanded, "How do I know these haven't been written by yourself?"'

'What did you say?'

'Had they been written by myself, they'd have been much more flattering.'

Her laughter sparkled. She truly was a gem, every facet gleaming with happiness. He watched with contentment as she tested the braised eel, exclaiming over its subtle texture and taste. 'You know, Mrs Ragsdale is terrified to dine in any Chinese eatery, certain that if she manages to cheat the plague she will be shanghaied into service in a Chinaman's brothel.'

'Mrs Ragsdale has a most fertile imagination.'

'Yes, and for someone so averse to contact with the male germ, one that frequently occupies itself with sexual matters.'

'I would not have guessed.' Morrison's expression in no way forbade further confidences.

'When I lace my corset tightly, for instance, she frets that it will prevent my venous blood from returning to the heart, collecting instead in organs where it might cause "unnatural excitement". Men are lucky not to be the subject of so much vigilance.'

'As a boy, we were warned about sliding down banisters, but I didn't understand why at the time. And at medical school there was much talk about the lecherous daydreams induced by the smoking of tobacco.' Morrison bit into a dry pastry covered with toasted sesame seeds and felt doughy flakes stick to the roof of his mouth and the back of his teeth. He worried them with his tongue. He was so focused on the woman before him and performing this operation without undue uncouthness that he did not notice, amongst the Chinese coming and going, their felt-soled footsteps soft on the stairs, Professor Ho, Sir T'ing and Mr Chia.

'Mrs Ragsdale,' Mae said, 'is a great devotee of Dr Kellogg and his theory that late-night meals and tasty foods like flesh and chocolate are the work of the devil, prone to exciting "morbid sensibilities" and "harmful instincts". She doesn't go so far as to follow him into vegetarianism, primarily because Mr Ragsdale will not countenance it. But every morning she urges upon me a bowl of Dr Kellogg's cornflakes, which have been scientifically formulated to dampen unbidden sexual urges. I have assured Mrs Ragsdale that I do not suffer from unbidden urges, an answer that seems to satisfy her.'

'You must have much to hide from her.'

'You never need to conceal anything from people who don't want to see the truth.' Mae shrugged. 'Once, she walked in on me when I was playing with myself. Ha, Ernest, don't look so shocked. What did you think, honey? I play with myself every morning, even if I've had sexual intercourse the previous night. Even if I'm ill. Don't you?'

Morrison sipped his tea to cover his temporary loss of words as his complexion reddened. 'I wonder what the good Dr Kellogg would say about that,' he said finally, in as jocular a tone as he could manage.

'He would say that masturbation leads to sin and crime, not to mention indigestion, imbecility, dimness of vision, weakness of the knees and backaches. They say he is a virgin who never consummated his marriage, in which case he should know all about masturbation.' She bit into a glutinous rice ball filled with black sesame paste. 'Mmm. I fear all this tasty food is rather exciting my harmful instincts. I do hope you're planning to shanghai me.' She treated him to a look of pure burlesque. 'It would seem only right, this being Shanghai and all.'

Morrison patted his brow with his handkerchief. It was already the twenty-seventh of March. He had not written much of import in some weeks — not that his editor seemed to have noticed, for Bell had demanded little else of his star correspondent lately than that he keep track of his colleagues in the field. Although feeling diminished, Morrison was determined to keep up appearances. Besides, such was the nature of journalism that, if one kept looking, a story was bound to turn up somewhere. 'I'm afraid I have some calls to make. I've been neglecting my duties …' His voice did not carry a great burden of conviction.

Mae's foot travelled up the inside of his leg. 'You are surely not going to start tonight.'

If anyone is being shanghaied, it is I. Morrison did not struggle.

As the trap rattled towards the hotel, Mae remarked, 'You know, I could have sworn I saw your Boy entering the teahouse just then as we were leaving.'

'Really? I suppose it is a popular place. I wonder why he didn't come over to say hello.'

'Perhaps he didn't wish to disturb us. Maybe it wasn't even him. They do rather look alike to me, as I am told we look alike to them, hard as that is to credit. I didn't take too much notice. I had other more amusing thoughts with which to occupy myself.'

'Like what?'

'Like how I was going to try doing this once we were in the carriage.' She drew the blanket over their laps. Her fingers made their nimble way towards his trouser buttons.

The next morning, Morrison took Mae sightseeing. He suggested they start with the Woosung Forts, where he inspected the field guns on the parade grounds and made rather a big deal about taking notes. After that, they visited a church she'd heard about where the missionaries had painted frescoes of Jesus and his Apostles all in Chinese dress, complete with pigtails.

Shanghai offered many divertissements. Whilst mentally making a list of contacts he really ought to call on before dinner, Morrison was content to squire his own, two-legged divertissement about town in pursuit of this or that amusement.

He had been gratified to see that she was determined to keep her promise not to speak to him of other lovers. And if the odd tale about going on an outing in a four-in-hand or a Valentine's Day card party for which she smothered the chandeliers at Palm Knoll in cascades of fango grass and huckleberry ended a little too abruptly, he silently thanked her. Other men floated like spectral presences at the margins of her stories. But Morrison was a practical sort: not the type to see ghosts and certainly none he did not wish to see.

His plan to return more seriously to his work ended up, like his trousers, shed carelessly in the vicinity of her bed. Yet he told himself he felt happier and younger than he had in years. 'If only it could be like this forever,' he said aloud without thinking.

Her eyes narrowed for a second. 'Ernest, honey,' she purred, 'it's like this now.' She leaned over to kiss one of his nipples. A loose strand of her hair, soft and fragrant, tickled his stomach. 'Why wouldn't it be like this forever?'

That night, back at the Blunts', Morrison confided to his journal: *Days foolishly spent. Her company stimulates me greatly. My head in a whirl of excitement. I feel that the foundation of our affection has been driven even more deeply and strongly. Our natures are curiously dissimilar and yet … she so strongly attracts me and interests me. We are in closer intimacy than ever, in more affectionate converse. This has been a time of unsullied happiness.*

He reread the words and blotted the ink before closing the journal. He shook his head. *Unsullied indeed.* He had scarcely done a jot of work. With a twinge of guilt, he wondered how Lionel James was faring.

In Which Our Hero Loses the Heat but Wins the Race, Has a Revelation About Crockery and Decides to Take a Friend's Advice

'They are saying that Japan is too small a country. She will not be able to withstand the strain on her finances of prolonged war,' Dumas remarked. He had just arrived in Shanghai for a visit and was taking tea in the Blunts' parlour with Morrison.

'Similar doubts were voiced ten years ago at the start of the Sino-Japanese War. It's good to see you here, old boy.'

Dumas answered with a flash of teeth. The leather upholstery of the sofa creaked as he swivelled around, cup in hand, to examine the décor. Amongst the fine Chinese screens, French grandfather clocks and other acquisitions reflecting the taste of Mrs Blunt were scattered Mr Blunt's hunting trophies — an elephant's-foot umbrella stand, a bearskin rug and on the wall the mounted heads of a tiger and an oryx.

'The Blunts' drawing room is every bit as fine as I've been led to believe. Though I don't like how that tiger's head observes me. I feel rather like prey. It is something I have grown used to at home, of course.'

'How *is* Mrs Dumas?'

'Fighting fit. Or so she was when I left Tientsin and so, in all trepidation, I expect to find her upon my return. She has recently discovered the clitoris.' Dumas lapsed into ruminative silence.

'Do go on.'

Dumas sighed. 'She has become impossibly sensualised. Oh, stop looking at me like that. Where are your hosts?'

'At Mrs Mudhurst's for a dress rehearsal of some private theatrical,' Morrison replied after satisfying himself that no further revelations were forthcoming. 'One prays that it is at least as fine an amusement as *Yeoman of the Guard*.'

'It could not be worse. I do owe you, G.E.' Dumas launched into an account of his recent trip to Newchang. He'd learned that an unscrupulous arms merchant had sold the Russians 4200 rounds of German powder that did not contain any cordite. 'I doubt it will be able to fire the Armstrong guns,' he said, and Morrison noted the fact in his journal with satisfaction. The men speculated next on the purpose of the arsenal that the Chinese were establishing in Wuhu, and Dumas passed on the heartening intelligence that sales of gunpowder and ammunition to the Japanese side were already netting British firms thousands of pounds. 'Oh,' Dumas noted, 'I almost forgot. Outside Newchang, I ran into a Jewish surgeon gone absent without leave from the Russian army. Claims at least forty thousand of the Tsar's conscripts are Jews. They're dragging them out of the *shtetls* to fight the war. The Jews, he says, mutilate themselves, taking out their own eyes or severing tendons, anything to keep from having to do service, for Jews are badly used by the Russian officers. Eyvin says tormenting Jews is both habit and prime entertainment for the Russians. The Poles and other conscripts, meanwhile, would just as soon bite the finger off a Jew on their own side than shoot a Jap on the other. He says the Jews all go off to war carrying canvas boxes that their mothers have stuffed with bread, herring, chicken fat — which they call "schmaltz" — and sausages. "God forbid we should eat Gentile meat whilst fighting the Japanese on behalf of the Tsar," he said, and spat for emphasis. He then issued what he told me was an old Yiddish curse: "May an onion grow from all their navels.'"

Morrison chuckled. 'How did he get away?'

'Another Yiddish saying gave him the will: "A man should stay alive, if only out of curiosity."'

'Confirms everything I've ever thought about the Russian army, not to mention the Jews,' said Morrison. 'Add cases of vodka, an absence of discipline, wild Cossacks and the picture is complete. And yet … have you read James's account of the Japanese bombardment of the Russian fleet at Vladivostok?'

'Most vivid. All that business about the Russian bluejackets mutilated by shell; the rush from the conning tower; and the two Russian stokers who leapt overboard and were rescued by the Japs to become the sole survivors, along with two other wounded, out of a crew of fifty-five.'

'And yet the blasted Russian navy will still not be port-bound. Enough Russian ships have escaped the attentions of the Japanese to patrol the entrance to the gulf rather effectively, as James also reports on the basis of Japanese intelligence. He has got close to his sources, despite the action remaining at some distance.'

'I shall be making another northern excursion soon, if you wish to join me. The War Office wishes me to go, and my wife, for all her newfound enthusiasm for the marital bed, has no great wish to prevent me.'

I should go. 'I still have some things to do here in Shanghai. I fear I shan't be able to get away that quickly.'

'May I ask how goes that other theatre of war?'

'I don't know what you're talking about.'

'Don't forget that I was present at the first battle.'

'Ah. So you were. The truth is, I spend most of my time here in Shanghai driving backwards and forwards between my supposed and actual places of residence. I cannot claim absolute pacification. *Hors de vue, hors d'esprit* seems to be her rule and I would be foolish to forget it. Still, I am hopeful. The flashing-eyed maiden has been most, shall we say, *consistent* in her affections of late.'

Dumas had the appearance of a man who, if he thought or knew otherwise, did not deem it apposite to say so.

'Indeed, she has requested our company this afternoon at the races. You can see for yourself what passes between us.'

Arriving at the grandstands, they saw exactly what passed between Morrison and Mae: to wit, nearly every eligible man on the China coast, and quite a few ineligible ones as well. For Morrison and Dumas found the maiden at the centre of what could only be described as a male vortex. The swarm gyred about her, jousting for attention. In steady orbit were the bald and bespectacled Paul Bowles of the Associated Press; wily old Chester Holdsworth, whom Morrison had since learned was, like Ragsdale, connected to Mae's father through the Republican Party; the blasted handsome Martin Egan and by his side none other than the famous Jack London; Zeppelin *sans* fiancée; and a dozen or more other bounders, cads and vile opportunists. Even Captain Tremaine Smith, he of the tireless tongue, was there. Only the

Reverend Nisbet was missing. *But not missed*, thought Morrison as he completed the gloomy inventory, refusing to consider the question of Jameson. Mrs Ragsdale hovered nearby with some of the women of the ladies' auxiliary, her expression flickering with worry.

'Goodness,' said Dumas. 'The enemy is out in force.'

Bowles, Egan and London appeared to be having the most luck in capturing the lady's attention. They worked in concert: London acting the raconteur, Egan spurring him on, whilst Bowles played a hearty audience. Bursts of Mae's merry laughter lit the air like fireworks, soaring, fading away and exploding afresh at each new witticism offered up by her collection of swains. *Sheer provocation*. She was so busy shining up to her other suitors that she didn't seem to have noticed Morrison; if she was looking for or expecting him, it wasn't obvious.

In his book *The Real Chinaman*, Holdsworth had made much of the concept of face, *mien-tse*, as though it was alien to those of Occidental disposition. Thinking of his own *mien-tse*, Morrison regretted that he had not presented the situation between himself and Miss Perkins to Dumas in somewhat more casual terms than he had. His toothache, which had been dormant for the last few days, flared.

'At least she stays faithful to the press,' Dumas said finally.

'I am only relieved to see that she will not expire from loneliness when I am gone. Which shall be soon enough. May onions ... how does that go?'

'May onions grow from their navels.'

'Precisely. Now, before she espies us and attempts to impel us into the uncharming circle, let us go seek out those of Shanghai's menfolk who have not yet turned themselves into metal filings before her magnet. We shall probe them for information whilst attempting to overcome the usual Shanghai passion for inaccuracy. I have wasted too much time in this useless city.' Morrison affected insouciance badly. He knew he did not fool Dumas in any case.

The report of the starting gun followed by a din of cheers made this mission impossible, as the attention of all was drawn to the track. The field was a hodge-podge of barrel-solid Chinese griffen ponies, sway-nosed Arabs, Indian-bred mounts, English saddle ponies and sturdy Australian steeds. The griffens galloped with their heads down, oblivious to direction. As they tended to skitter wildly across the track, spooking the others, they provided considerable diversion. In the end, a South Australian rode to victory on a horse belonging to the Welsh Fusiliers, devastating an English taipan who had entered a horse at his own expense. Having noted that the taipan had recently numbered amongst Mae's captives, Morrison was pleased to see the taipan's wife glare at her husband as if drawing a causal relationship between his inattention to the field and losses on same.

'Let's go,' Morrison muttered to Dumas. 'I am growing bored with the entertainments.'

They were making their way towards the gate when a hand on his arm and a dulcet voice in his ear stopped him in his tracks. 'Darling. I have been desperate to see you. The others were making me crazy. Ah, Colonel Dumas,' she added with a sweet smile, 'lovely meeting you again.'

Morrison recalled the showman he'd seen juggling songbirds that day in Peking near Liu Li Chang. Mae was the magician, the trainer, the whistler holding the stick as the birds performed their tricks, landing and taking off on cue. *Bowles! Holdsworth! Egan!*

Zeppelin! Jack bloody London! And let's not forget the fiancé! The dentist! Willie Vanderbilt Jnr! Et cetera et cetera et cetera. And me of course. Her artistry easily surpassed that of the bird man of Liu Li Chang. He had three birds in the air. She played the entire aviary.

The dentist. He had made an appointment with the British dentist and would see him soon. It was comforting to know that for some kinds of pain there were known remedies.

Morrison returned in a funk to the Blunts' house for supper. Their guests that evening included Lord Robert Bredon: brother-in-law of Inspector-General Hart, father of the vivacious Juliet and husband of the philandering Lady Bredon. Lord Bredon, who was also Chairman of the Shanghai Race Club, the Shanghai Club and the St Patrick's Society, was high on Morrison's list of the most enervating men in all of China, worse than Menzies and with fewer redeeming features. Bredon dominated the conversation, boasting about his many honours and accomplishments. According to him, these included the drafting of several major diplomatic treaties. *Damned empty windbag. I do hope Lady Bredon is taking precautions against the syphilis.*

A diversion was afforded by Bredon's startled discovery that he was eating mille-feuille off his own monogrammed dessert plates. 'I've warned Cook a thousand times,' Mrs Blunt apologised. One of the peculiarities of life in the foreign settlements, as they all knew, was that the servants were forever borrowing dishes from other households; guests often found themselves dining off plates from their own homes. It was, Morrison thought, a perfect metaphor for the incestuous existence they all led: he, Zeppelin, Martin Egan, and God knows how many others were each supping from the same precious bowl, after all.

That night Morrison went to bed with an icepack pressed against his jaw and Rudyard Kipling's new novel *Kim* propped up on his chest. He lost himself in the world of the young Irishman gone native in India, with its wandering monks, scheming Pathans and overlay of British intrigue. Then a random sentence gave him a jolt: 'The voice told him truthfully what sort of wife he had wedded and what she was doing in his absence.' Slipping in a leather bookmark, he closed the book and lay it on the bedside table. *Ridiculous. I am not wedded to anyone.* He and Mae were lovers in the sense they shared a bed from time to time; that was all. He had been deluded to believe it was anything more than that.

He turned down the lamp, threw himself down on one side and then rolled onto the other. The urge for sleep had gone. He lay on his back and stared at the ceiling. The bamboo rattle of the nightwatchman sounded in the street.

It came to Morrison like a bolt. He had been an ass, a fool, an idiot. Molyneux was right. She would behave as she did until he took a decisive course of action. No woman was *terra nullius* and Mae had been extensively mapped, it was true. What was required — and the obviousness of it stung him — was a man resolute enough not just to explore but to conquer. She may have been the gay centre of attention at the races but she had not left with anyone but himself.

He vaulted out of bed and composed a letter. There were things he needed to say and things she needed to hear. Things to do with future happiness, stability and security that they both needed to consider. Ought to consider. *Ought or needed or should?* He scrunched the sheet into a ball and started again. It took several drafts but he felt that he had it right in the end. He went back to bed and dreamed, uneasily, of Lord Bredon and borrowed crockery.

In Which Morrison Mines for Gold and Makes a Bid for Peace, Prosperity, Longevity, Happiness and Health

Thanks to some clever investments, Morrison had a bit of capital behind him. When he had been with his Parisian grisette, Noelle, with Pepita and with his Calcutta angel, Mary, his finances, though poor, had matched and even exceeded the expectations of his paramours. Mae's wealth and her profligacy in the ways of the purse placed him in a different position altogether. 'That's the good thing about heiresses,' Dumas had said. 'They keep themselves.' Perhaps that was true in the long run. In the short term they required a certain standard of maintenance.

He sent the letter with Kuan and went to the bank.

'One thousand?'

'Yes.' Morrison took a deep breath and addressed the stout young broker sitting across the desk from him. 'One thousand pounds.' He was seated on a leather settee in the man's dark-panelled office on Shanghai's financial street. Even vocalising such a sum of money made him breathless. He felt as though the words had been scraped from his throat. A stack of documents lay before him.

The broker, Flatyre, leaned in towards Morrison, lowering his voice conspiratorially. 'Korean goldmines, Dr Morrison — very sound investment.' His eyes glinted as Morrison drew a thousand pounds sterling in notes from his case and placed them on the table between them.

'You won't regret it.' Flatyre had a smile like a baleen whale. The word 'cetacean' came into Morrison's head.

'I hope not,' Morrison replied, picturing Flatyre inhaling his money like plankton and then swimming off, never to be seen again. *I cannot afford to come down to first principles.* He thought of his tall, thin schoolmaster father, loping along the campus of Geelong College, his frock coat streaked with white from his chalk box, the elbows patched where they'd become threadworn. To his father, a thousand pounds would seem a prodigious sum. *Think big,* he urged himself. He rocked his seal on the pad of red ink and pressed it to the paper by his signature. *Think like a man with an heiress for a wife.*

'Rest assured, Dr Morrison.' The broker gathered in the notes like a croupier. 'Once the Japanese have consolidated their hold over the peninsula, the value of those shares could easily increase to two and a half thousand. The war will result in some tidy dividends for those banking on the right side. You've made a wise decision.'

Shaking hands and pocketing his contract, Morrison strode out to the Bund, full of fresh resolution. 'Come, Kuan,' he said. 'We're going shopping. I am not Willie Vanderbilt Jnr. But I am not such a bad prospect.'

Kuan gave him a quizzical look.

'Never mind.'

At a Chinese jewellers, he found a gold bracelet with charms in the shape of the characters for Peace, Prosperity, Longevity, Happiness and Health, all of which he dared to think he might share with Mae. A vision of himself shaking the hand of her wealthy and powerful father flashed before him; he had been relieved to learn that, at sixty-five, Senator Perkins was twenty-three years his senior. It could have been deucedly awkward otherwise. The starting price for the bracelet was seventy-five Mexican dollars but with Kuan's help he beat it down to fifty-eight, still such a princely sum that he nearly choked on it before reminding himself it was worth every last Mexican cent.

It felt good to be so resolved. He walked briskly to the Shanghai Club, where the former military attaché 'Monkey' O'Keefe, who had fallen on hard times and was living, it appeared, half upon the bar itself, fell upon him in a soused and lugubrious embrace. Morrison irrigated O'Keefe further and reaped an excellent harvest of gossip: O'Keefe was able to name all the arms traders, Chinese and foreign, who turned a profit supplying both sides of the conflict. Leaving the Irishman in the care of the Chinese bartender, he paid a call on his Japanese contacts, who offered him green tea and no news. Only when it came time to return to the Blunts' house did he feel the claw of anxiety upon his vitals. *Has she answered?*

Waiting for him were a letter and a telegram. The letter, from Mae, summoned him to the French Hotel des Colonies on the Bund in an hour's time. The telegram, from James, was even more peremptory. Morrison swore under his breath and addressed his Boy in a resigned voice. 'Kuan I need a clean suit of clothes, a ricksha and tickets for the first boat to Wei Hai Wei that leaves tomorrow afternoon. Straight after my dental appointment.'

Whilst Kuan hastened to his tasks, Morrison scratched out a quick reply to James. By the time he was seated in the ricksha, he was already running late. Her telegram had revealed nothing of her intentions. Though her urgency was clear enough, he was tormented by the thought of what it might portend. Further down Bubbling Well Road, a horse had shied and a carriage overturned. Even the agile ricksha runner had trouble extricating them from the snarl of traffic and onlookers. Morrison's handkerchief grew damp from the sweat streaming off his brow and neck. Fearful that she might not wait for him, Morrison realised he was not as confident as his actions that morning suggested. He fingered the parcel containing the bracelet as though it were an amulet. By the time he arrived at his destination, he was a full hour past the time she had set to meet. Tossing more cash at the runner than the man had asked for, he flew into the hotel, only to find her in the parlour absorbed in a book.

In Which the Road to Hymen's Altar Is Seen to Be Paved with Obstacles, a Terrible Truth Is Revealed and Our Hero Is Left with His Mouth Open

'Maysie. Darling. I'm so sorry I'm late.'

She held up her book so that he could read the title on the dustcover: *The Ambassadors*. 'It's fortunate that Henry James is such a good writer. A girl could get restless if made to wait too long without entertainment. Oh, honey, I'm only joking. Come here.' She stretched a gloved arm in his direction. He pressed his lips to her hand, tasting satin. Her perfume, French and redolent of fig, tickled his nose. Reaching into his pocket, he extracted the new bracelet and fastened it onto her wrist, over the glove. She turned it this way and that. 'Ernest, it's stunning.'

'Like its owner,' he replied awkwardly. Compliments did not so much trip as stumble off Morrison's tongue. He envied men who knew how to flatter a woman, but not so much that he'd ever tried to emulate them. Yet on this particular day he yearned for such skills, for Mae, never careless with her toilette, was attired in an especially fine lilac-and-cream gown, one, he did not fail to note, that showed off her voluptuousness to perfection. 'Beautiful,' he added, his vocabulary, vast on the subjects of war and politics and human frailty, exiguous on the topic of ladies' fashion. 'Exceptionally … beautiful.'

Two days earlier, she'd casually mentioned that the only man she knew who appreciated the effort made by a woman in her costume was her hairdresser, Strozynsky. An Eastern European who wore corsets and rouged his lips and cheeks, Strozynsky danced as lithe as a maid as he plucked and teased, curled and trimmed. Her mother feared Strozynsky was homosexual, pronouncing the newly minted word in an uneasy whisper. Mae didn't care. She adored Strozynsky. Not only was he the most fashionable hairdresser in the entire Bay area but he noticed one's fashions — and *understood*.

Morrison read the expectation in her eyes but he could not compete with a dandy and invert and would not try. He called over the waiter and ordered oysters and champagne for them both. Mae made small talk, about the weather, the food, and some of the hotel's other guests, until Morrison couldn't stand it a minute longer. 'Maysie. You got my letter.'

'Yes, I did, thank you.' She played with the charms on the bracelet.

'And? Have you considered my proposal?' The words flew from his mouth like a shot from a cannon. Realising to his chagrin that he probably ought to have dropped to one knee, for that was how things were done, he sat as though nailed to his seat.

'Oh, honey,' she said with an unfathomable expression, 'we have all the time in the world to speak of such things.'

'Maybe not,' Morrison replied, unnerved.

'Why not?'

The conversation had taken a decidedly unromantic twist. 'My colleague Lionel James. He's landed himself in a spot of trouble.'

'Really?' Her eyes lit up. 'Who is she?'

'Not that sort of trouble.' He did not wish to discuss Lionel James's predicament. His own was pressing enough.

'How disappointing,' she pouted. 'There are so many types of trouble in the world and so few of them truly amusing. I suppose I shall be losing you to Wei Hai Wei again. If that's the case, I may return straight away to Tientsin. I'm getting bored with Shanghai.'

'Maysie.' He took her hand and gathered his courage. 'Will you consider my suit?' The waiter arrived just then with their oysters and, oblivious to the drama, fussed about, setting the table with plates and special forks.

The moment passed.

Retrieving her hand, she undid the buttons at the wrists of her gloves. With precise, practised moves, she tucked the fingers back under the sleeves, leaving her hands bare. Plucking an oyster from the platter, she tipped it into her mouth. Morrison wondered if he'd actually proposed or only imagined he had done so.

'Delicious.' She patted her mouth with her napkin. 'You're going to have to breathe, honey.' She sighed. 'I love you too. But for us to join at Hymen's altar is not a good idea. So, no, I cannot marry you.'

Morrison blinked. 'May I ask why not?'

'Because I love you.'

'Maysie, you're being perverse. That's normally the reason one gives for saying yes.'

'I've given it thought. You would not be happy with me. I attract gossip like the hem of a skirt attracts mud. When the first blush of romance wears off, you would want to change me, tame me, make me the sort of wife you could take out to the races or home to Mother without fear of incident.'

Her words rang true even as they stung him. 'But I love you.' He steeled himself. 'I sense there's something else behind your refusal. Please tell me.'

She shut her eyes for a moment. When she opened them again, Morrison read desolation there. 'You know how I told you about John Wesley Gaines? The congressman?'

'I remember.' He tensed.

Her voice dropped to just above a whisper. 'You won't like this. I was "that way" with John Wesley.'

Morrison's stomach churned. He put down his fork. 'What did you do?'

'What could I do? French cures.'

Morrison knew 'French cures' — potions whose labels promised to restore a woman's 'regularity' and whose contents boded searing pain and wretchedness. It took a while before he was able to speak. 'And how did he feel about that?'

'He was grateful — the first three times, anyway.'

Pain sliced through the site of the old spear wound. He gripped his handkerchief, praying he would not suffer a nosebleed. *The first three times?*

'He told me he would never forget my loyalty. He called it "loyalty to the marrow". I will always remember those words. He said I touched him very deeply with my discretion. I can be discreet, you see, when I want to be. I did not fear scandal for myself so much as for him — and my father, of course. John Wesley did joke that if the scandal had broken, at least it would have been bipartisan.' She smiled faintly.

Morrison's head reeled. 'You said "first three". And after that?'

'The fourth time I told him I was going to keep it. We argued.'
She lowered her eyes. 'He accused me of trying to force his hand.
He said that every young woman is a free thinker until she is tested,
or until she finds the man she wants to marry. That hurt me
profoundly. The truth was that the doctors had warned me that
another French cure could kill me. I didn't tell him though, lest he
think I really was trying to entrap him. So I went into seclusion.
But Baby Wesley was stillborn, two months premature. In the end,
that's what decided me on this trip. There were rumours, as always,
but for once I could not bear them, or the sorrow, or John Wesley's
anger, or anyone's sympathy.'

Morrison's wit failed him. 'And your parents?'

'Mama knew. I'm sure Papa did too, though we never spoke of
it. He is the kindest man in the world. He's famous for the number
of criminals he pardoned when he was governor, for his
philanthropy and for the good works he does keeping impoverished
young people from crime and degradation. I told you he pretends
that my sister's girl, Alice, is his niece. I'm sure he would have done
the same with my son. It was he who had the idea of sending me to
stay with the Ragsdales.'

'So it wasn't just a fascination with the Orient or wanderlust
after all.'

'No. Although it's true that I adored the *Mikado* and travel.
What I told you that first night was not a lie. But I admit that as
our ship passed out from the Golden Gate and I caught my last
glimpse of the Seal Rocks, I was inconsolable.' She reached out
and touched Morrison's wrist. He started as though electrically
shocked. 'I could not have predicted how much my spirits
would pick up on arriving in the Orient, and particularly on
meeting you.'

'I *am* special to you then.' He heard the thinness in his own voice.

'Of course you are.'

'Does Mrs Ragsdale know? About the child, I mean.'

'Yes. She is sworn to secrecy of course. Mrs R. has convinced herself that I was seduced, taken advantage of, and probably believes it was only that unlucky one time. I believe the cornflakes are by way of prophylactic against any relapse. I'm rather fond of her, for she is a good soul and well meaning. She's been through much with her husband. I don't wish to cause her more grief. She believes what she wants to believe and that's fine with me. In fact, it's been most convenient.' She allowed herself a rueful smile. 'As I'm sure you've realised.'

'I confess I'm at a loss as to what to say. But ... that's all in the past. It is not impossible that you and I could make a fresh start.'

She shook her head. 'The doctors have assured me that I have been left barren. That is why, on the few occasions we have neglected to use a riding coat, I have not panicked. But I've always been mindful of how much you love children. It would break your heart to marry a woman who could not give you any of your own.'

He was shocked by this revelation. He wanted to say he didn't care, that he loved her and that was all that mattered. In his heart, though, he wasn't sure — about any of it. All he knew was that she attracted him like danger. And as he'd told her, it was his habit to run at danger. It had never been his experience to have danger flee in the opposite direction. It occurred to him that this wasn't necessarily a bad thing. Through his confusion he heard himself telling her that it would be best for both of them if they stopped seeing each other. He sounded more resolved than he felt.

She went quiet for a moment. 'All right then,' she murmured and stood to leave, gathering up her book, her beaded purse and her fan with an air of finality. 'I'm sure you're right.'

I'm not, he wanted to say, but it was too late. He was left with a barely touched platter of oysters and bottle of champagne, feeling absurdly like the scorned heroine in a Victorian melodrama. Like Gerald in *Anna Lombard*. Except there wasn't even a Pathan lover involved — Mae Ruth Perkins was leaving him for herself.

The toothache bombarded Morrison's nerves all night long. In the morning, his testicles ached, his sinuses were afflicted with an abundance of phlegm and his joints felt as though they'd been rusted. It was as if the sudden departure of pleasure had presented a vacuum that all the maladies of his ageing body rushed to fill. By the time he dragged himself across the threshold of the dentist's surgery, he was a bundle of self-pitying misery. He sat glumly in the chair as the chatty Dr Tooth treated him to an exposition on the origins of his surname — either a modern version of the medieval 'Tot', the actor who played Death in travelling morality plays, or the name assigned hundreds of years earlier to someone who'd managed to keep most of his teeth past the age of twenty. Dr Tooth preferred to think it was the latter and assumed his patients did likewise. He was young, baby-faced and intermittently flatulent — nothing like the mental picture Morrison had formed of Maysie's Dr Jack Fee. And yet Morrison felt, with a sense of despair greater than any dentist could induce by dentistry alone, that he would be cursed for the rest of his life to think of Dr Fee whenever he had a toothache. And that was the least of his woes.

Dr Tooth advised Morrison to relax, gave him a swig of rum and got out the medical pliers.

An hour and a half with the dentist left Morrison's jaw swollen and bruised as though he'd been punched. He felt it most apt.

In Which We Are Introduced to the Indiscretions of Major F.S. Bedlow and Our Hero Turns for Succour to the Poet Kipling

The SS *Hsin Fung* steamed up the Whampoa River towards the Yellow Sea and Wei Hai Wei. From the bridge, Morrison watched Shanghai disappear into the distance. To one side stood Kuan; to the other a stocky Englishman with mackerel eyes and unpleasantly fleshy lips. Major F.S. Bedlow of the Royal Dublin Fusiliers was the latest correspondent dispatched by *The Times* to bedevil him, a human blunderbuss capable, Morrison was quite certain, of flattening any enemy with garrulousness alone. Before the SS *Hsin Fung* had left the Whampoa, Bedlow had confided all manner of inside intelligence about the war to a subaltern with whom he had formed a casual acquaintance. The subaltern told the chief mate who, in turn, told Morrison. *A nice discreet man is our correspondent!* Morrison rued inviting him to stay in Peking. Battered by Tooth and bruised by Mae, he was already downspirited enough.

Over dinner at the captain's table, an American woman *d'un certain age* named Lara Ball flirted with both Morrison and the handsome chief mate. Not in the mood, Morrison excused himself to search out a comfortable nook in the smoking saloon where he might nurse a whisky and his disappointment in relative peace. He was obscurely rattled by the behaviour of Miss Bell. She was too old, he thought, for such shenanigans. *Forty if she were a day!*

Almost his age in fact.

Anxiety flared in him along with his sinuses.

In came Bedlow in search of fellowship. Vainly attempting to deflect conversation, Morrison huddled over his journal. Bedlow, oblivious, pulled up a chair. Morrison scrabbled in his mind for the glorious solitude of the Australian wilderness and a clarity of thought he feared he might never recover.

Gossip welled up from Bedlow like a spring. Morrison, giving up any hope of writing in his journal, found himself almost admiring the man for the tirelessness of his news gathering. And Bedlow did convey the titbit that Paul Bowles — last seen amongst the crowd sniffing after Mae at the Shanghai racetrack — had so exasperated his employers at the Associated Press that only yesterday they had recalled him to San Francisco. *One down*, he thought and then remembered he was no longer in the competition himself. An acute sense of loss walloped him in the guts. Muttering some excuse, he stumbled off to the cabin he was sharing with a Japanese bean merchant called Yendo.

As Yendo snuffled and snored, Morrison pitched from cold, dank thought into tempestuous dreams and back again, waking more tired than when he had gone to bed. His jaw still ached from the dentist's mallet. Stooping in the cramped cabin, he shaved, drawing blood. In the looking glass, a sallow man with downturned mouth stared back at him. Soaking his flannel in a basin of cold water, he pressed it to his face and eyes. A marginally pinker and more vital man looked back. The corner of Morrison's mouth twitched as he recited lines from Kipling that had given him comfort in the past:

A million surplus Maggies are willing to bear the yoke;

And a woman is only a woman, but a good Cigar is a Smoke.

God, he missed her.

In Which Lionel James's Tales of Derring-Do on the High Seas Recall Our Hero to His Proper Position in Life

Tailed by the scombroid Bedlow and having left Kuan to his own devices for the evening, Morrison entered the canteen on Liu Kung Island, where he found James drinking what looked like flavoured milk.

'Local specialty. Not sure why I didn't discover it earlier. Ichiban. Jap for "number one". Egg, milk, brandy, gin, crème de Macao, Angostura bitters, all the usual devices of the devil. Midshipmen write home to their mothers about it but only mention the first two ingredients. Does wonders to keep out the cold. G.E. — there's been an incident.'

James had been on deck on the *Haimun*. It was a cold night. He looked up the coast towards Port Arthur, then across to Dalny. Twenty-five miles of darkness. Not even a passing convoy. He was about to go below deck when a steamer flying the flag of a Russian admiral suddenly appeared at stern, all four funnels belching smoke. 'Damned fast boat, that one,' he told Morrison.

He raced into the saloon. Brown, the *Haimun*'s wireless operator, was deep in a novel by Jack London; he might as well have been in Alaska. 'Brown!' James yelled and Brown jumped. 'Spark up the wireless! We're about to be boarded by the Russians! Tell Fraser that if they don't hear from us within three hours he should inform the British commissioner, the senior naval officer and *The Times*.' James then raced up to the bridge.

Captain Passmore was glued to a pair of binoculars. By now the Russians were running parallel. 'Bloody hell, James.' Passmore spoke without removing his eyes from the glass. 'That's the *Bayan*.'

At this revelation, Morrison sat bolt upright. 'Makarov's flagship?'

'Yes, the flagship of the Commander of the Russian Pacific Fleet himself,' James confirmed.

Morrison could have sworn Bedlow's ears actually angled forward at this.

'Brown sent the message. At that moment, the *Bayan*, which had passed the *Haimun*, suddenly changed course. Just then a great booming flash of yellow fire screamed across the *Haimun*'s bow.'

Bedlow's eyes popped.

'Ye gods,' exclaimed Morrison.

James continued. 'Brown, white as a sheet, raced back into the cabin as Passmore shouted the orders to weigh anchor. I whipped around, looking for Tonami.'

'Your Japanese translator.'

James grimaced and took a swig of ichiban before continuing. 'The quartermaster said Tonami had made a dash for his cabin. I pushed open the door. His shirt was off and he was pointing a dagger at his own stomach.'

A shiver went through Morrison. 'Let me get this right. Your interpreter was going to commit *hara-kiri*.'

'*Seppuko*. I mean, that's what they call it.'

There was more to this story, that was for certain. Morrison was beginning to get an inkling of what it was. 'Go on, man.'

'I shouted at him to stop. He told me he knew what he had to do and thrust a sheaf of papers at me.'

'Papers? What papers?' Bedlow could scarcely contain himself. His eyes gleamed with interest, his moustache with milk. Morrison felt his hackles rise. There was enough to be concerned about here without worrying about the human wireless sparking up next to him. He glanced around the room. His eyes lit on the eccentric Reginald Johnston, a genial thirty-year-old Scot who served as Wei Hai Wei's chief magistrate. Johnston, Morrison knew, travelled with an entourage of imaginary friends who had been with him since boyhood. Johnston could keep a man entertained — or trapped — for hours with his stories of The Quork, with her bonnet box and scandalous behaviour; the libidinous Mrs Walkinshaw, who could 'shock a geisha'; and the strange malefic beast Hopedarg.

'Bedlow.' Morrison's fingers closed around Bedlow's wrist like a manacle. 'There's someone I want you to meet.'

Returning alone to James, Morrison scowled. 'Indiscreet little jackanapes. He's been a barnacle to my hull ever since I met him. Nearly impossible to scrape off. Now tell me all about Tonami and tell me fast. He's no civilian translator, that's for sure. Officer in the Japanese navy, I take it. Rank?'

James attempted a smile. 'Commander.'

'The papers?'

'His ciphers. He said if he died I should destroy them.'

'When were you going to tell me?'

'I am sorry, G.E. It was part of the deal.'

'The deal?'

'To keep quiet. The Japs swore me to secrecy.'

Morrison raised one pale eyebrow. 'I take it our employer is as in the dark about this deal as I am.'

James nodded. He confessed that the Japanese navy had finally agreed to give him limited access to the theatre of war on one condition: that he carried on board a Japanese naval officer pretending to be a civilian translator. Tonami would act as an official censor. His job was to ensure that James's reports contained nothing detrimental to the Japanese cause. It was true he also translated but that was rather a bonus.

Morrison digested what James was telling him. 'An arrangement that compromises the neutrality of the ship, and, by extension, Great Britain as well. Not to mention the operation and good name of *The Times*. And yet the Japanese have done next to nothing to fulfil their part of the bargain, which is to grant you protected access to the front.'

Digging in his tobacco pouch, James focused on refilling his pipe. 'If you put it that way, yes.'

Morrison put one hand on his forehead as though to shield himself from further revelations. 'So go on. Tonami, the Japanese naval commander posing as a civilian translator, was about to commit *hari-kiri* aboard a putatively neutral vessel leased by *The Times*.'

'*Seppuko*. I said we could disguise him. They'd never guess who he was. Alive, anyway. I'd have had a bloody hard time explaining the presence of a freshly disembowelled Japanese translator to the Russian search party. But Tonami shook his head. "They'll know. The Admiral, Stephan Makarov, and I were in Paris together. *Il est génial. Intelligent, aussi. Tout le monde lui trouve ça.*" There was more. Something about a French girl. Makarov had never forgiven him. Marvellous, I thought. Bloody marvellous. I forbade him to do anything foolish and dashed off, returning moments later with the uniform of the Malay quartermaster. By the time Russian boots were clomping across the gangway, Tonami was at the ship's wheel, the brim of the quartermaster's cap low over his eyes.'

James had extended a hand to the leader of the boarding party and introduced himself in English and French, doing his best to look calm.

The Russians exchanged glances. Also speaking in French, they asked if there were any Japanese on board.

James shook his head. '*Mais non, bien sûr.*'

The Russians demanded to be taken to the wireless and shown what had been transmitted. James handed over a ream of fake, innocuous telegrams they'd prepared for just such an emergency. Checking these against the equipment, the Russians noted that the latest transmission was missing. James found it and showed them: it was the notice to Wei Hai Wei that they were about to be boarded. The Russians took in the fact that since the *Haimun* seemed to be a neutral ship engaged in nothing that would compromise its neutrality, holding it beyond three hours might precipitate an international incident. Seeing his chance, James chose that moment to tell them he had earlier seen four Japanese cruisers steaming towards Port Arthur. He intimated that it would be a shame, a tragedy even, if ships of the Russian navy — including the Admiral's own flagship — were cut off from the home port due to their dealings with such an irrelevant person as himself. The Russians raced up onto the deck, thundered down the gangplank and were gone.

James exhaled. 'We returned here straight away and I cabled you to come. I wanted to inform you in case there were any repercussions. I knew I could count on your support. I am not so sure our editor will be as sympathetic.'

Morrison swirled his drink in his glass. 'Just out of curiosity, what was in the real record of transmissions that the Russians could have objected to? Were they not just submissions to *The Times* and so on?'

'They don't call you the great correspondent for nothing, G.E.' James took a few quick puffs on his pipe. He lowered his voice until it was barely audible. 'Tonami uses our wireless equipment to transmit intelligence and orders to the Japanese navy.'

'Ye gods, man! Are you reporting a war or trying to start one?' Morrison was about to ask James when he'd planned on telling him the truth when he realised that James had been hinting at it from that time they'd met in Peking. What's more, James had asked him to travel to Nagasaki with him and Tonami on the *Haimun*. He'd clearly wanted to tell him then. Morrison was certain that if only he'd gone, he'd have been able to work out some strategy to prevent the disaster that was now threatened by the Russians. But no, he'd gone to Shanghai in pursuit of the cackle-headed Miss Perkins instead. *From the evidence, it is I who is the cackle-headed one!* Well, that strange episode in his life was over. And thank goodness for that. His work needed him and he needed it.

In Which Ambushes Are Laid, an Abandoned Post Is Bombarded and a Bullet Both Finds and Misses Its Mark

In Tientsin again, and having barely set down at the Astor House, Morrison heard from the faithful Dumas the disconcerting news that Miss Perkins, whose return to Tientsin had preceded his by less than one day, had been spotted earlier that same morning seeing off Martin Egan at the train station.

Morrison shrugged as though the news was of no concern. 'At least Egan has the decency to make himself scarce upon my arrival. But they can do as they like. She and I are through. I told her I will not be seeing her again.'

'Ah, now that is a new development,' said Dumas with a dubious air. He turned to Kuan. 'Your master has come to his senses, don't you think?'

'*Shi.*' Kuan nodded. 'I think Miss Perkins … she was like fox spirit.'

Even the most unsuperstitious minds have a tiny crack in them into which, at the right moment, a suggestion of the supernatural might seep. *A fox spirit is as sophisticated, intelligent and raw as the man she haunts, as lovable, canny and dangerous as his own reflection*. Professor Ho's words flooded back to him. *Ridiculous*. He pshawed. 'Come, come, Kuan. Next thing you know, you'll be telling me again how, according to the laws of geomancy, the placement of my bed is impeding my chances for marriage. And my dear Dumas. My senses have been a part of the deal from the beginning. It is my rationality that went missing from time to time. I see from your expression that you crave further detail but, I assure you, there's nothing worth telling. We're through and that's that. It was but an inconsequential dalliance and, as is the way with such trifles, it has come to an end. It's already the first week of April and I'm feeling somewhat derelict in my duties. I've much to do. I should like to request a meeting with the Viceroy. Would you care to join me there, Dumas?'

As they discussed that and other arrangements for the next several days, a powerful wave of relief swept through Morrison. It was his firm opinion now that Mae's rejection of his proposal had prevented a moment of foolishness leading to a lifetime of regret. *A fox spirit, indeed! Whatever she is, she's incapable of fidelity, nothing more than a born prostitute — albeit one without desire for money or present.* Miss Mae Ruth Perkins, Morrison concluded, was beyond doubt the most immoral woman he had ever met.

Dumas looked through the papers as Kuan unpacked and Morrison changed into a fresh suit. As the three men descended the stairs into the lobby, a sultry 'helloo' caused Morrison's breath to stick in his throat. Mae rose from the settee, a vision in rose velvet.

'Major Dumas. Dr Morrison. Kuan.' She curtsied genially. 'Oh, Dr Morrison, I was so pleased to receive your note about going to the hockey. It is a very fine day for a ride. As you suggested, I've engaged a horse and carriage for us.'

A chill travelled down Morrison's spine. It would be useless, not to mention risible, to protest that he had sent no such note, made no such suggestion. *Besides, has she not just been with Egan? I, George Ernest Morrison, do not eat the crumbs off another's table! Look how her eyes flash with mischief. Her waist, cinched to nearly a handspan. My bracelet upon her wrist. She is shameless. Outrageous. That smile. Brazen beyond belief.* He expelled the breath he realised he had been holding. 'Very good,' he said at last. 'I suppose we should be off then. Dumas, I shall see you later at the Club. Kuan, you have those chits I have written to the Viceroy's interpreter and others. Please wait on the answers.'

'How was your ride?' Dumas asked that evening.

Morrison raised an eyebrow. 'Ride? Ah. Suffice it to say that the horse was less fatigued after four hours than his passengers.'

Morrison, Dumas and Menzies were at the bar in the Tientsin Club. At this revelation, Menzies appeared to duck for cover behind his own face.

'So, let me get this straight.' Dumas swirled the ice in his whisky. 'You proposed to her in Shanghai. She turned you down — or at least declined to accept — because, employing impeccable feminine logic, she loved you.'

Morrison winced. He had not gone into unnecessary detail. 'Yes. That's what she said.'

'So you forswore both your suit and her company. You duly arrive in Tientsin, mentally fortified against further offence to reason and good sense but, upon the first sight of the fair maiden, surrender all your forces.'

'It was an ambush.'

'It is a poor army that does not make some allowance for the possibility of entrapment in its strategy,' chided the military man. 'Wouldn't you agree, Captain Menzies?'

Menzies looked as though he'd rather be lying in a muddy trench somewhere.

Morrison grimaced. 'I have, I swear, no emotion on seeing the body clad. But hair down and body discovered — I confess this thrills every fibre in me.'

'Ah, youth,' said Dumas.

'She *is* young,' Morrison replied, knowing full well it had been a jibe.

Staring into his glass of gin, Menzies mumbled, 'Perhaps you could take a break, go into the country, find some restful brick-kiln.'

'A restful *what?*' He stifled a laugh. If Menzies had his odd moments, Morrison thought, they were also one of the man's more endearing traits.

'I think what Menzies is saying,' Dumas interjected, 'is that a holiday might not be a bad idea.'

Morrison cleared his throat. 'I appreciate your concern. I have far too much work, however, to consider a holiday at the moment.' For all his dallying with Miss Perkins, he informed them, he had also managed that afternoon to see the Manchurian Prince Na. After that, he'd persuaded the head of a missionary body to withdraw all of his organisation's funds from the Russo-Chinese Bank. He had requested a meeting with the Japanese consul, had got word that the Viceroy would see them, and he intended to look up many other contacts over the next several days before returning to Peking. 'Including Professor Ho, whom

I encountered recently aboard the steamer to Chefoo. Interesting man. Although he has not said it in as many words, it is obvious that my Boy, Kuan, holds him in almost reverential awe. Says he is one of the country's most progressive intellectuals and a leading light of reform and progress. Very critical of the Empress Dowager and the Ch'ing government. He speaks blessedly excellent English, too. In fact, Granger and others I know could take some lessons from Ho. He speaks with great irritation of the Old Buddha and her profligacy.' As he spoke, Morrison could see Dumas and Menzies relax, as if he had once again become the man they knew and expected him to be. *I have worried my friends. I shall say no more to them of my relations with the cackle-headed maiden. Indeed, there is nothing really to say. My senses may still be captive to her but she no longer has any purchase on my heart.*

And so it transpired that over the next two days, up and down the high streets and low of foreign Tientsin, Morrison collected and dispersed information, facts, figures and rumours, dined well, drank moderately, slept poorly, and, as was his wont when disturbed by other matters, fretted about the state of his health. When temptation threw herself into his path, which she did on a regular basis, he failed to resist and he stopped pretending that he was interested in doing so. But he was very clear in both head and heart — it was not love. Like him, she was a hunter, an explorer, a collector. A conqueror. He had been a fool not to have understood this earlier, to have become so emotionally involved. He took her more roughly than he'd ever done before on that first day back in Tientsin, more like a whore and less like a lover, and was both scandalised and titillated to see how readily she responded to it. The second day, *she* took *him* the same way — and he was equally astonished by how much it electrified him. He realised that, as a great actress, she not only played any role on offer but made it her own. And she had a few scripts she'd written herself. He stayed in Tientsin longer than anticipated. There was, of course, much there to be done.

'The dentist,' she suggested one day, 'the boy, Tommy,' the next. 'Willie Vanderbilt Jnr and his maid.' He had drawn the line at Zeppelin. She asked him to propose some scenarios as well, and, overcoming his initial reticence, he told her about Noelle and a time in the Bois de Bologne. Whether acting out fantasies or just revelling in sensuality, the sex he had with her made all that had come before it seem like curry without spice, bland and meaningless. But it was not the stuff of eternal union and on that point he was as clear as the spring skies over Tientsin. She was the quintessential courtesan. He didn't raise the issue of marriage again and she acted as though it had never come up in the first place. He could see no reason not to partake of the pleasures that were so freely offered to him. He was just a man, after all, even if she had never been just another woman.

On the train back to Peking, Morrison met a Miss McReady who was travelling in the company of a British diplomat's wife. She was in her early twenties, small-chinned and thin; Morrison guessed that the attractively generous appearance of her hips was aided by bustle pads. She was pretty enough, however, with cornflower-blue eyes, clear pale skin and glossy black hair. She had a practical, demure air about her, and the habit of pausing before speaking, as though tasting her words first to ensure they were not too salty. There was nothing extravagant about her clothes, constructed from more workaday fabrics than those with which Maysie adorned herself, and she wore them with an appealing modesty. Miss McReady, he caught himself thinking, was the sort of girl he could introduce to his mother.

As she related her experiences in China to Morrison, which included a recent boat trip up the Yangtze, he stifled his boredom. Her observations were hackneyed, those of every other traveller. On the other hand, he was flattered by her keen interest in his own experiences as well as his work. The conversation flowed all the way back to Peking. If Miss McReady had none of Mae's demonic spark, he told himself that this commended her to him all the more. She'd be staying as a houseguest at the home of the diplomat. When he bade her and her hostess goodbye at the station, he promised to call on them soon and was immediately overcome with enervation at the prospect.

He saw a plausible version of his life stretch out before him, full of predictable small joys and sorrows; children, yes — and that would be wonderful; his mother happy — and that would be more than grand; and himself respectable at last in the eyes of all — Chinese and foreign.

Dull, dull, dull.

He had just met Miss McReady. He didn't have to marry her.

But if that was not the whole point with a woman like that, what was?

Morrison expelled a long breath.

He and Kuan bounced along in the back of a covered Peking cart on their way home. 'What do you think, Kuan? Would Miss McReady be a suitable match for your master?'

'I think,' said Kuan, 'my master is very smart. I think he knows the answer. He does not need his poor servant to tell him.'

'That's a "no" then, is it?' Morrison chortled. 'You're probably right there, old boy.'

They arrived home. In the main courtyard, they ran into Cook, off to the markets with empty baskets dangling from the ends of his carrying-pole. 'I think my master is very lucky,' Kuan said as they waved Cook off with some requests for the evening meal. 'He can choose who to marry.'

'That's the theory,' Morrison replied abstractedly.

Inside his library, Morrison greedily inhaled the comforting animal smell of leather bindings, the woody scent of paper and the mineral wafts of ink that hung in the air like motes of dust. His dominion, his kingdom. He reflected, cringing, on the amount of time he had spent over the previous six weeks in feverish thrall to that *incantadora*, that *fox spirit*. He'd neglected the war for her — *his* war. Morrison was supposed to be keeping a watch over those colleagues dispatched to cover the war. If a scandal blew up now over the *Haimun*, he would have to answer to his editors.

The drone Bedlow arrived from Wei Hai Wei two days later and installed himself in the main guest room whilst awaiting his papers. He brought word that a Japanese mine had blown up the Russian warship *Petropaulovsk*. Admiral Makarov perished with all his crew. Tonami and James, at least, should be content with that glad news.

Morrison called on Miss McReady and offered to ride with her to the Western Hills, though already he knew that he would not pursue her.

On his fourth day back, a letter came from the malevolent Jameson. 'She is like a bitch on heat,' wrote the indefatigable knave. Hands shaking, Morrison ripped the note to shreds. He ceased to think about Mae every waking minute.

As for the war, rumours flew as fast as the telegraphists' hands could punch out the dots and dashes. Facts — reliable, verifiable — remained scarcer than hen's teeth. 'They're certainly scarcer than the journalists who come to hunt them down,' Dumas remarked. He was visiting Morrison and the pair had gone walking on the Tartar Wall to avoid what Morrison called the 'damned nuisance' of Bedlow.

'I have been up and down the China coast a fair bit in recent weeks,' Dumas told him, 'and everywhere I go they're there — correspondents, illustrators and photographers come to cover the war, stagnating in watering holes, sinking men o' war and evacuating towns before the advancing armies with every whisky. And still the Japanese control access as if the frontlines were their own virgin daughters. They say this will be the most reported war in history, but the devil knows what the reports are going to contain if this situation continues.'

'Indeed. Thanks to all the work done on Japanese customs by war correspondents unable to reach the front, readers in the West now know more about the balloon man of Uyeno Park, the intricacies of the tea ceremony and the routines of the geisha than they do of the diversions of Paris or New York. I have heard from my colleague Brinkley in Tokio that a Japanese nobleman, Baron Mitsui, is personally funding the veteran war correspondents to compile an anthology of their writings on previous wars. It will be called *In Many Wars*.'

'Just not this one,' quipped Dumas. 'And how goes Lionel James with his quest?'

'He goes. Mainly back and forth between Wei Hai Wei and the Korean coast. The Japs still won't let him get close to Port Arthur. He told me he once picked up a fellow in Korea, a journalist from a rival newspaper who'd managed to witness a land battle before getting arrested by the Japanese and dumped on the Korean coast. He was half-starved, filthy and desperate to get to a telegraph station. James had just wired a report on the same battle but based on Japanese sources. He hadn't received confirmation from the station at Wei Hai Wei that his report had been received and relayed to *The Times*. He didn't want to be scooped, especially by an eyewitness. So the *Haimun*'s crew prepared a hot bath and fresh clothes for their exhausted guest and plied him with food and drink until he put his head down on the table and snored. Captain Passmore then ran the *Haimun* into Wei Hai Wei as fast as he could. James checked that his report had gone off to *The Times* and they steamed off again. When the correspondent finally woke up, they deposited him somewhere safe and sound and none the wiser.'

Dumas squeaked with laughter.

'And what are you gentlemen smiling about on this fine spring day?' The speaker was Koizumi, a Japanese diplomat of Morrison's acquaintance.

'The rumour that the Japanese have recently taken Vladivostok,' Morrison bluffed. 'Is that battle won, then?'

Koizumi sucked air in through his teeth. 'You are a good friend of Japan,' he said. 'I can tell you that the truth is that the assault on Vladivostok was less than successful. Our navy expended considerable time and materiel bombarding an abandoned post.'

I did the same thing recently. Morrison had attained, he thought, a certain philosophical distance from his affair with Mae. He was almost beginning to see the humour in it. 'And so you have given up on Vladivostok?'

'Of course not,' Koizumi replied. 'The Russian stores will not withstand even one more month of blockade. It is the same at

Port Arthur. I am sure that we will have good news for you soon. Ah, and by the way, my government is not very happy with the dispatches of your colleague Granger. He seems to be rather too well embedded on the Russian side.'

'More well embedded than you know,' Morrison acknowledged, for his sources told him that Granger had thrown aside his American whore for a Russian one of even less appealing aspect. 'But if the Japanese government wishes to see the Japanese side better represented, then it needs to open up access to the front to the foreign correspondents.' Arguing eloquently on behalf of the foreign press, Morrison realised that he had found a worthy new outlet for his energies.

He continued to champion the journalists' cause to a sympathetic Dumas for some time after they'd taken leave of Koizumi.

'You're back with us,' remarked Dumas as the pair ambled back towards the Avenue of the Well of the Princely Mansions.

'I never left,' Morrison lied.

He smelled the perfume before he saw the envelope with the familiar, disgracefully poor penmanship. He tore it open with a sense of dread. *Ernest, honey, come back to Tientsin. I am dying to see you. I send you many kisses and many more after that.*

Scratching so hard with his pen that he nearly ripped through to the blotter, Morrison composed a telegram: DEEPLY REGRET NO IMMEDIATE PROSPECT COMING TIENTSIN. ADVISE YOU ENJOY YOURSELF. GOD BLESS YOU. THINK OF ME SOMETIMES.

It tears my heart strings!

He poked his head outside the library door. Kuan was in the courtyard, talking quietly with Yu-ti. Something about the tenor of their conversation made him hesitate a moment before calling Kuan's name. At the sound of his voice, both servants jumped. 'Kuan. Take this to the telegraph office, chop-chop.'

That night, Morrison went to bed with a copy of Rudyard Kipling's new volume of poetry about the Boer War, *The Five Nations*. He always found Kipling's full-blooded pride in the Empire as heartening as his virile wit was inspiring. But the unrhythmical nature of some of the verses in this collection left Morrison feeling discomposed. He closed the book just as the nightwatchman called the Hour of the Tiger. Three a.m. He was still tossing and turning when the watchman called the Hour of the Hare at five. He was beset with an overwhelming sense of foreboding. His knees were sore. His sinuses ached. A dull throb in one testicle prompted worried thoughts of gonococcus; dragging himself out of bed, he measured out ten grams of sodium salicyl and swallowed it down as a preventative.

He was plagued by the thought that something, somewhere, had gone horribly wrong. He took a sleeping draught and awoke late and alarmed to find an over-excited Bedlow bursting into his room.

'Bedlow. What on earth —'

'Last night, Secretary Kolossoff — you know him?'

Morrison's head ached. 'Yes. Kolossoff. Of the Russian Legation. I know him. And to ascertain this you've come to disturb my sleep?'

'I'm sorry for that, G.E. But I thought you'd want to know. Early this morning he shot himself in the head.'

Morrison jerked himself upright. 'Dead?'

'No. The bullet lodged in his brain but he did not die. He'd apparently been drinking for days. Blames himself for failing to give his government adequate warning of Japan's intentions.'

'Leave me. I'll be down in a few minutes.'

As Bedlow closed the door behind him, Morrison slid back under the covers. He felt sorry for Kolossoff, whom he'd always considered an agreeable enough sort — for a Russian. He wondered what it would be like to care about something — war, love, anything — so strongly that one could raise a gun to one's own head and fire. He feared knowing the answer.

In Which Bedlow Stays, Granger Goes and Our Hero Endures a Veritable Fusillade

The following morning a crashing downpour transformed the capital from dustbowl to mudpit, slicked the paving stones of Morrison's courtyard and made dank the lime-and-plaster walls of his study. In the streets outside, the open sewage ditches overflowed, a festering, perilous slurry. The weather was unpleasant enough to keep even the most intrepid indoors. And so indoors on this mid-April day Morrison stayed, working, pacing, cataloguing a year's worth of missionary journals, tending to his correspondence and pacing again, full of roiling emotion. A second missive had come from Mae, insisting he come to see her. *The lady's tone is most imperious.*

Morrison marvelled at her newfound enthusiasm for correspondence. It was eminently clear that she was displeased with how he had cooled towards her. She once told him that as a little girl she had always got her way; her renewed overtures seemed the petulant act of a spoiled child. She wanted everything — and everyone — on her terms. That might work on the likes of Egan but not him. He retained fond remembrances of their times together. He did not discount the possibility of future liaisons of the sort they enjoyed this last time in Tientsin but he was not her plaything; the scales had well and truly dropped from his eyes.

Morrison was in the midst of these ruminations when Bedlow stomped into the library in a funk, his hair plastered to his head by the rain, giving him a more fishfaced appearance than normal. He was waving a sodden telegram. 'The War Office has ordered me back to London "as soon as possible". It is most unfair. I have only just got here. I am keen to see action and keener to be published, as action I have seen before. What am I to do? You must help me.'

Must I? Not only am I expected to act as hotel, concierge, encyclopaedia and exchange clerk for these colleagues but now I 'must' solve all their problems as well. 'Calm yourself, Bedlow. I shall wire *The Times* and get them to cancel the order to rescind you.'

'Thank you, thank you, thank you.'

Damned nuisance.

'Oh, by the way, gossip is Lionel James has secured a Japanese commander on board the *Haimun* — but you probably know that already.' Bedlow, beady eyed, studied his host for confirmation.

'I'm not sure you'll need to be repeating that last fact — if it is indeed a fact — too widely.' *His indiscretion knows no bounds.*

Bedlow shrugged. 'You don't mind if I stay for a few more days, do you?'

'You're most welcome,' Morrison replied, grinding his teeth.

Kuan entered and handed him a telegram. His heart gave a jolt when he saw who'd sent it. From a poor correspondent, this was quite a fusillade.

IF YOU HONESTLY CARE YOU WILL COME. GO TIENTSIN DO.

Go Tientsin do? He shook his head. *Fairly lucid for a feminine dispatch.* Telegrams worked well for professional purposes but they lacked nuance. *What in heaven's name is all this urgency?*

'Is it about me?' Bedlow asked.

He'd forgotten Bedlow's presence. 'No.'

Bedlow looked disappointed. 'I'll leave you to it then, shall I?' He rose from his seat with a tentative air.

Morrison did not stop him.

It stormed all that night. *Raining like heaven's wrath.* The following day snow fell. *Where has spring gone?* The new leaves on the trees shivered under the onslaught. The city walls seemed to hunch under a squat sky, grey on grey. Morrison, his mood in tune with the weather, lunched with Miss McReady. Stripped of travel's shine, her conversation struck him as more banal and predictable than previously, her humour weak, her mode of speech schoolmarmish. Even her eyes were less blue than he remembered. He returned home dispirited, only to receive yet another telegram from Mae.

AM STAYING TIENTSIN TO SEE YOU. WIRE IF PLEASED.

If pleased? Of course I would be pleased. I will not respond. I am not her toy!

Kuan informed Morrison that Bedlow would join him for dinner. Life was one test after another.

After dinner, a telegram arrived from Bell giving him the power to act with regard to Granger. He wasted no time in drafting his letter: *Sir, your retention in our service has been left to my judgment. In my judgment your retention is undesirable. Please send resignation by telegraph.*

Kuan entered with a telegram. For a spine-tingling moment, Morrison imagined that through some extraordinary act of

262

telepathy, Granger had realised what he was doing and was attempting to pre-empt him.

It was not from Granger.

WHY DON'T YOU ANSWER IF ABLE MEET ME TIENTSIN?

Why don't I answer? As if it is not obvious! She only wishes to complete my humiliation. I am only fooling myself — I am quite sure I am fooling none of my friends — if I think that I will remain unaffected by her. It must not continue. I must stay strong and guarded.

The next morning, Molyneux, up from Chefoo, dropped in for a visit.

'*Comment va la mademoiselle?*' Molyneux asked.

'*Elle va, par habitude.* She wants me to follow. It is absurd under these circumstances. I am entirely disinclined to do so.'

'And yet,' Molyneux rejoined, 'you are tempted. I can see that from the ferocity with which you deny your interest.'

'It is true,' Morrison conceded. 'Have you ever done such a thing?'

'Invariably I do. Then again, I'm married. It makes things simpler.'

'So you say. I have yet to see any evidence that marriage makes anything simpler.'

'And your life, my dear G.E.?'

'A paradigm of simplicity. And so it shall stay.'

About an hour after Molyneux left, Kuan returned with another telegram. Morrison braced himself: Maysie or Granger? It was from Moberly Bell. Morrison's jaw dropped in disbelief.

RESCIND BEDLOW YOURSELF TAKE PLACE.

So now, after all, I am to go to war. They might have asked me. It rankled him that he had been ordered to go in such a summary manner. For all his complaints about being left behind and all his grousing about the quality of the roustabouts, amateurs and dunderheads employed by *The Times*, he was not eager to take Bedlow's place amongst the war correspondents. The *Haimun*'s problems were still unresolved and there was no guarantee, even with his connections, that the Japanese would let him get to the front when they were blocking all the others. He loathed the thought of how it would look if he, George Ernest Morrison, turned out to have no better access to the front than the rest of the rabble; it was insupportable.

He replied to Bell, stating that he would not shrink from going whilst also implying that he was too big a man to be ordered to take the place of a much smaller one. He girded himself for the drama of informing Bedlow that he himself was to replace him. He made a list of instructions for Kuan, whom he'd leave in charge of the household. He asked Blunt to take over as *The Times*'s chief correspondent in China while he was gone. He considered what he would need and what he could carry if on the march with the Japanese army. There was much to think about, much to do. STOPPING TIENTSIN EN ROUTE JAPAN. STAYING ASTOR HOUSE. *And thus I am guided by an inscrutable Providence back into her orbit. Back into her arms. And thence to war.*

In Which Tolstoi Chooses Between War and Peace and Miss Perkins Reveals That She Is Expecting Quite a Lot of Our Hero

The brass band of the Sherwood Foresters was playing an afternoon concert in the octagonal alcove of the Astor House and all Tientsin was there for the diversion. He had not realised such would be the case when he had suggested in his note to her that they meet there for tea. By the time he arrived, she was already seated and it was too late to suggest a change of plans. Morrison sensed that the entertainment was considerably enhanced by the sight of the famous correspondent and the scandalous American together again. He caught eyes darting in their direction from behind raised teacups and fans. It was all so intriguing that it was a miracle the Sherwood Foresters even got a look-in.

'And so I'm off to the front. Or at least that's the intention. The Japanese are still being most obstreperous on the topic of permissions.'

'If the war is as righteous as you claim,' she said, 'then why are the Japanese so reluctant to be observed in the practice of it?'

Flibbertigibbet. 'Strategic reasons,' he said with more conviction than he felt. Her question irritated him. 'But as I remarked in our first conversation, women are natural pacifists. That is why they are unsuited to govern nations. They do not have the marrow to enact the necessary.'

'You didn't answer my question. Besides, does that make Tolstoi a woman?' Mae retorted, responding to his tone. 'He has written a most moving pamphlet arguing the case against war in general and this one in particular, calling it contrary to the teachings of both Jesus Christ and Lord Buddha. He says war brings needless suffering and stupefies and brutalises men. I found his reasoning quite persuasive. *Bethink Yourselves!* is the title in English by the way.'

'I know it. And yet,' Morrison countered with a dismissive air, 'one of Tolstoi's own sons is so much in favour of the war that he has enlisted to serve. And the old man himself rides out from Isnaia Poliana every few days all the way to Tula to catch the latest news from the front.'

'Well of course he is eager for the news if his own flesh and blood is fighting. Do you deny that Tolstoi has any point?'

'He makes a very good point. He states that Manchuria is to Russia an alien land over which it has no rights.' *Why are we arguing about this?*

'Who has rights to Manchuria except the Manchus? I, at least, am persuaded by Tolstoi's words.'

Morrison had never appreciated Russian literature less. He took a deep breath. 'You're very feisty today, Maysie. But surely you didn't send me all those telegrams urging me to come to see you only because you wished to argue the case against war.'

'No,' she replied, her fire suddenly extinguished. 'Honey, you will be careful, won't you?'

'Of course. I'm not foolish. And I'm not going to do battle — only report on it.'

Her lips trembled. 'I'm afraid.'

'Please don't worry, Mae. I'll be fine.' He patted her hand. This was becoming tedious.

Her eyes filled with tears.

Now what?

A teardrop fell onto her gloves, leaving a damp spot. She blinked down at her hands for a long while.

Truly she has missed her calling. The stage is the poorer. Her carryings-on, her stories and her flagrant infidelities had finally registered with the saner part of him. Though he could not have known for certain until he had seen her again, observing her now he was satisfied that he had banished her from his heart.

Another tear fell. He grew irritated and restless, thinking of the many appointments he still had to attend to in Tientsin before sailing to Wei Hai Wei and thence Japan.

She took a sip of tea and replaced the china cup in its saucer. 'There is something I have to tell you.'

Morrison waited, his patience thinning.

She folded her hands in her lap again and looked him in the eye. 'It seems that I am not infertile after all.'

In Which Our Hero Hesitates and Is Lost, Following Which He Receives a Most Concerning Summons

Morrison reeled. He searched for the right words with which to frame a question as inescapable as it was indelicate. 'Are you certain it's mine?' he rasped.

Her upper body straightened incrementally. She placed the flat of her hand on her stomach. 'I feel that it is.' Her voice was steel wrapped in velvet.

That's it? She 'feels' that it is!

'A woman knows such things.' She poked at a sliver of cake with her fork, her eyes suddenly clear and dry.

Another moment passed. Then, an affection stronger than Morrison had ever felt for any woman welled up from God knew where and flooded his veins. All was forgiven, all could be forgotten. He'd be a father. He smiled stupidly.

She smiled back.

Morrison was forty-two years old. He had experienced alarums before, most recently with the sturdy Australian lass Bessie, whose menses obeyed no calendar known to Western science but did — *thank ye gods!* — eventually make their appearance. Bold bad Sally Bond had embarrassed and infuriated him some years earlier by insisting, to her husband no less, that he, Morrison, was the father of their child; Morrison had denied it absolutely, despite the boy's suspiciously ginger complexion and preternaturally serious brow. From the time he was a young man, Morrison had wanted children — though assuredly not with Sally Bond or even Bessie. But he'd been in no hurry. He always figured these things would sort themselves out. Perhaps it was time. He was getting on. He owned a comfortable home in Peking, enjoyed an international reputation and high social standing and possessed solid, if minor, investments. She was the daughter of a senator and millionaire. She was undeniably charming, stylish and more accomplished in the arts of love than any woman he'd ever encountered. She loved him. She'd said so. And he loved her too. He might as well admit it to himself. He'd already asked her to marry him once before. She had said no because — well, mainly because — she feared she'd be unable to bear him children. That, clearly, was no longer the case. As for her rather elastic sense of fidelity, things would be different now. *That's it then. This it it.* 'Will you …?'

She looked at him, blinking, expectant.

She doesn't make this easy.

'Will you … would you … do you think you would …?' Doubt niggled.

She sat preternaturally still.

'Maysie, is it really mine?'

Her gaze frosted over. When she spoke, each word was an icicle, gelid, dagger-shaped. 'I told you it was.'

'I just need to know — is there any chance it's not mine? Have you been with anyone else lately?'

'I thought you banned me from speaking of others.'

'It is not the speaking that is at issue.' At the next table, the English teachers Mr and Mrs Lattimore had been sitting with their four-year-old son, who slipped out of his chair and wandered over. Mae bent to stroke the child's hair. In that instant, Morrison saw her as he'd never seen her before. As a mother. The vision melted him. He was lost again.

'Owen.' His father stood up with an apologetic air. 'Don't bother Dr Morrison and Miss Perkins.' He led his son back to their table.

'If you wish to know,' she said with a resigned air, 'I will tell you.'

'I don't need —'

'Martin Egan, of course.'

'You don't have to —'

'I can see you want to know. There was Chester as well.'

'Holdsworth.' Morrison felt ill. *She is entirely faithful to my memory.* 'That old goat?' His tone was bitter.

'Yes. The last time we were together, that "old goat", as you call him, had me four times in two hours. More like an old bull, really, when you think about it.'

'At his age,' Morrison spluttered, trying to keep his voice down, 'you're lucky it didn't kill him.'

'I told him it was a most impressive performance. He was tickled pink.'

'No doubt the result of cardial infarction.'

Mae burst out laughing. 'Oh, Ernest, honey, that's why I love you. You always make me laugh.'

Against all reason her treacherous lips looked sweet again, full and kissable. He could not believe he was thinking about her lips. *She's doing it again.* 'You take other lovers to provoke me.'

The sparkle faded from her eyes. 'Oh, honey, will you never understand me? I don't do it to provoke you. I do it to amuse myself.'

'Maysie, whose girl are you?' His voice crackled with unhappiness. Just minutes earlier he had intended to renew his proposal of marriage. He did not understand how things had gone so terribly awry.

'Whose girl am I?' She smiled thinly. 'My own. And lest you ask again, so is the child. That's that then. You are just like John Wesley after all. I should prevent myself in future from giving my heart to men who keep their own hearts for themselves, for whom career and ambition will ever be their only true wife and mistress.' She stood. 'It's been delightful. But I must run. I told the Ragsdales I'd be back at four o'clock. They will be expecting me to be prompt.'

'Not if they have paid any attention to your timekeeping in the past, I should think.' It was a poor joke. But he had been stung by the accusation that he had not been willing to give her his heart, even if — or perhaps because — there was an element of truth in it.

'I do not appreciate your sarcasm, Dr Morrison. Good afternoon. And I wish you well with your travels and your war.' A flurry of skirts and shawls and she was gone.

That evening, at a banquet with Chinese officials, the conversation swirled about Morrison like mist. For once, his tenuous grasp of the language seemed a kind of blessing. Back at the Astor, he dreamt a thick unpeopled dream of fern gullies with whispering leaves, of hard, clean sunlight, and of rocks crowned with the square dung of wombats. He woke with a head like an anchor stuck in sand.

Before breakfast, he sent a telegram to Bell saying he was delayed in Tientsin, implying interviews. It was the nineteenth of April.

From a local curio dealer he bought a beautiful silver belt engraved with the character 'double happiness', the Chinese symbol for wedded bliss. He sent it with a letter addressed to 'My darling Maysie'. He begged her to see him.

No response came.

In Dumas's parlour that afternoon, Morrison confided that he was in trouble, in every state of every union but calm — and, for better or worse, marital.

'Ah, then there are some consolations.'

'I heard that, dear.' Mrs Dumas entered with a tray of tea and sandwiches. Her expression intimated that were she married to someone such as Dr Morrison, she would not have to endure such tedium as her own husband's humour afforded.

'You see my point?' whispered Dumas.

'I heard that too,' Mrs Dumas chirped. 'Anyway, I shall leave you two to your discussions. I am going to my room to read. I've discovered the most marvellous book.'

'And which one is that?' Morrison asked.

'*Anna Lombard* by Victoria Cross.'

'Ah.'

'You've read it? Don't you agree it's a wonderful novel?'

'Yes, fine book, hmm.'

After they were reassured by footsteps on the creaking floorboards above that Mrs Dumas had moved out of earshot, Dumas sighed. 'Thank goodness Tientsin is short of handsome, sword-bearing Pathans or I should fear anew for our marriage.'

'Awful book,' Morrison said.

'Terrible. So what news?'

Morrison described his conversation with Mae.

The tale sent Dumas into a frenzy of whisker-pulling. 'When do you see her next?'

'Her Grace declines to answer my notes. Mrs Ragsdale, however, has summoned me to her residence tomorrow morning for a chat.'

Dumas's eyebrows shot high and wide.

'My feelings exactly.'

In Which Morrison Endures a Most Curious Conversation

'Dr Morrison, thank you for calling.'

'Always a pleasure, Mrs Ragsdale.'

Overnight, the weather, as capricious as love, had turned springlike, almost sultry. A film of sweat sheened Mrs Ragsdale's upper lip as they stumbled through an exchange of pleasantries. Under his jacket, Morrison felt damp circles spread from under his arms. He held his hat in his hand.

'Dr Morrison,' she ventured at last, her eyes apologetic. 'As you know, Senator and Mrs Perkins have entrusted the guardianship of their daughter to me whilst she is in China.'

He nodded. His throat and stomach were a sheepshank, knotted top and bottom.

'I feel I must speak to you about a rather sensitive matter. I believe you know what I'm referring to.' Mrs Ragsdale attempted a smile. It died on her lips. She tried to resuscitate it without great success.

'Yes.' He felt his cheeks colour. 'I believe I do.' *Anguish gripping my vitals.*

'Dr Morrison, you know how much I respect you.'

Morrison held his breath.

'Back home, as you might imagine, Senator and Mrs Perkins are pillars of society.'

'Of course,' was Morrison's careful reply.

Mrs Ragsdale, eyes moistening, frowned. 'This is so terribly awkward.'

Morrison sat as still as a corpse.

'Miss Perkins is the apple of her father's eye. But she has always been a bit … man-crazy. She is, and I shall be frank with you, Dr Morrison, only kept from male company with the greatest of difficulty.'

Morrison nodded. 'I understand,' he said, though in truth he was struggling.

'I shall come to the point. Mae — Miss Perkins — has told me that you've been pressing your suit. That you have asked her to marry you. That you have been steadfast and persistent.'

Morrison blinked.

'I know your intentions are honourable, Dr Morrison.'

'They are.' *They were. They are.* 'And what,' he added, maintaining as neutral a tone as possible, 'does Miss Perkins say of her own intentions?'

In Which We Learn That Miss Perkins Had More Than One Ace Up Her Sleeve and Morrison Confides in the Sea

'You can imagine my astonishment as her circumlocutions finally spiralled towards the central point, which was that my fervently desired engagement — such was the dated quality of her newsgathering — was not to be. I digested this information, as well as the news that Miss Perkins had departed for Shanghai in the company of Mrs Goodnow, with some degree of heartburn, as you might imagine. But the moment I was truly threatened with reflux was when Mrs Ragsdale informed me, in a dramatically lowered whisper, that the cad, the scoundrel, the reprobate Martin Egan, whom she had always thought such an honourable gentleman and a pleasant man too, had gone and got the lass "into trouble".'

Dumas jerked forward in his chair as though mechanically sprung. 'No!' he cried.

'Yes.'

'No.'

'Yes.'

'Egan?'

'Egan. So she told Mrs Ragsdale, anyway. I cannot work out whether her motivation was to protect me or punish me. She's accomplished both. Mrs Ragsdale told me that Mrs Goodnow and Miss Perkins would soon be leaving Shanghai for Japan. There, the maiden will promptly marry Martin Egan, thus averting further scandal. Egan, conveniently, is from San Francisco as well and to San Francisco they will return, accidental man and wife, him to inherit a most eminent father-in-law and, in the long run, an obscene and undeserved fortune.'

Dumas's jaw bristled with questions. 'So was it Egan then, do you think?'

'In truth I am left no wiser as to whether the lucky father was Egan or myself, or perhaps even Holdsworth or someone else entirely. It could be the contagious wart Jameson for all I know. I rather doubt the lady knows herself, for all her protestations to the contrary. All I am sure of is that I am spared a future in which I would contend with Lord Bredon for the title of biggest cuckold in the Extreme Orient. That honour I shall happily concede to Egan. He can grin it away with those stupidly straight white teeth of his. And I shall go to the front. I have a ticket on a steamer departing T'ang-ku for Wei Hai Wei this very evening.'

In his cabin, Morrison smoothed the pages of his journal and secured his ink bottle. He wrote the date: the twentieth of April 1904. Then, out of long habit, he recorded the names of the crew: *Captain Bennett, Engineer Malcolm.* He noted various titbits of information and gossip culled from fellow passengers before turning to the topic that was closest to his heart. *For almost two months, all my movements had been guided by this infatuation ...*

The steamer ploughed through the gulf. The view from his porthole was unedifying. Darkness above and below. *Certainly the circumstantial evidence would suggest ... even now, every fibre of my body thrills with passion as her image passes before me ... capricious and wilful ... distraught ... blinding jealousy ...* He wrote solidly for an hour until his inkwell was nearly dry and his hand cramped with the effort of writing against the ship's vibrations.

As a much younger man, Morrison had thought the world would end when Noelle had run off with the sinewy Italian major-domo of Montmartre's notorious Chat Noir. There had been other devastations. And now Maysie was quitting him for Egan. *Is this to be the final parting?* he wondered, his chest contracting at the thought.

He reread what he had written and ripped the pages from his journal. Loping up the stairs two at a time to reach the deck, he sowed the sea with his hopes, dreams and disappointments. The white pages glowed briefly before being sucked down into the midnight waters.

In Which Bell Tolls for the 'Haimun', and Morrison, Quarantined from Miss Perkins, Goes Up and Down Like a Bandalore

A chill rain was falling. Liu Kung Island was shrouded in fog. Morrison had awoken with his throat as sore as if it had been scraped by razors. The muscles behind his eyes were throbbing hot, his neck felt as though it had been iced into position, his ears ached and his sinuses were in a worse than usual state of rebellion. Swathed in woollens, wrapped in misery and bound by duty, he dragged himself across the quay, past a medical boat unloading wounded Japanese soldiers and their civilian Chinese labourers and, with the moans of the injured in his ears, proceeded up the hill to the wireless base station. There, he found James in a right state.

James hurled a sheaf of cables onto the desk for Morrison's consideration. 'I am getting no support whatsoever from any quarter. The world is ruled by small and careful men.'

Morrison thumbed listlessly through the cables. 'And what from our editor?'

'The worst blow of all. Bell is not disposed to re-engage the *Haimun*. Says that unless we can get within sight of a naval battle, it's a waste of the paper's money and resources.'

'Your response?'

'We — you and I — sail to Nagasaki at daybreak. Passmore estimates that with the winds and currents it will take forty-eight hours and the *Haimun*'s remaining reserves of coal to get there. But we must convince the Japanese to allow us to proceed. It's our last chance. In the meantime, you have to stall Bell.'

'And if the Japanese still say no?'

'Then I shall give up the *Haimun* and seek attachment to a Japanese column. In any case, Tonami tells me you will travel with the Japanese Second Army Corps leaving Nagasaki on the first or second of May for the Yalu River. You should be able to witness the first major land battle of the war.'

Morrison had never felt less capable in body or less prepared in heart and mind for such adventure. 'Grand.'

At dawn the following morning, the *Haimun* steamed across the Yellow Sea towards the Land of the Rising Sun. Ichibans, for all the restorative properties of egg and milk, had not proven the best medicine for nasal catarrh. But Morrison's mood had brightened. A telegram had come overnight to him care of the *Haimun* from that impossible creature. *Dear, dear girl.* She was taking passage to Nagasaki on the *Doric* with Mrs Goodnow. She would be able to meet him there before joining Egan in Yokohama. Perhaps she had reconsidered. He found himself full of hope, though exactly what it was he hoped for now he would have been hard pressed to say. He dosed up on Tinct Cinchona. *By the time we meet, I ought to be well again. Please God. For all that she tests me, she brings me great happiness as well.*

Early on the morning of the twenty-fourth of April, the *Haimun* steamed into the mountain-cradled port of Nagasaki. Coal barges drew alongside the vessel as it tied up, and, on the jetty, women in plain blue kimonos queued, baskets of coal harnessed to their backs. Bare-legged boatmen, the hems of their calico robes tucked into their waist sashes and ropy muscles glistening, steered their skiffs across the calm water, gliding in and out of the moorings. A pungency of shellfish and seaweed infiltrated Morrison's consciousness; that he could smell again meant he was on the road to recovery. His senses were sparking back into life; the mix of travel and uncertainty — about Mae, about being sent to the front — gave everything an electric charge.

The *Doric* was expected that very evening. *And she is on board! It is almost too good news.* His mind raced with possibilities. She would not have told him to meet her if she hadn't reconsidered her plan to marry Egan. She had been rash and foolish. He would forgive her. They would be married and return to Peking, or return to Peking and be married, though it was possible she would prefer the wedding to take place in Tientsin or Shanghai. They would have that child and many more after. There was so much to talk about. Perhaps — *hope against hope!* — Egan did not yet know of her condition.

He was an idiot. She just wanted to have him again, on her terms, before leaving him on her terms. He should know that by now.

He should not be such a cynic.

It was in his nature to be a cynic.

It would be strange getting married at his age. But comforting, too. And children. He recalled the sight of her with young Owen Lattimore.

Ridiculous.

Lovely.

James was occupied with the refuelling of the ship, and Tonami with appointments that they all hoped would help break the official impasse with regard to the *Haimun*. Relieved of any immediate tasks, Morrison took a room at a hotel. He idly perused the guest book, only for Martin Egan's signature to leap out like a flare. He was relieved to see that Egan had checked out almost a week earlier.

He set out for a walk. A pair of middle-aged women in layered kimonos passed him on the street, bobbing along under oil-paper parasols and smiling from behind their hands. Paper charms fluttered from tree branches and chimes tinkled. There was a gentility here that Morrison found almost disconcerting after the robust hustle and bustle of China. He stopped at a tiny, immaculately clean eatery for an early lunch. Even the way the Japanese prepared food struck Morrison as discreet — the steaming, grilling, rolling; the delicate odours; the concealment in lacquered boxes as opposed to the hiss and crackle of the wok, the scrape of the spatula, the wallop of chilli and garlic and heaped platters.

Despite the impeccable courtesy of the Japanese, Morrison sensed that Japan had a way of coolly excluding the foreigner that China, for all its violent spasms of xenophobia, had never mastered. If China's government did not command Morrison's respect as Japan's did, China as a nation had won his love. For a man who craved order, who spent much of his time collecting, cataloguing and recording, Morrison had a weakness for the garrulous, the passionate, the chaotic, the unpredictable. China. Mae.

Walking out from the eatery, he found himself on a narrow street of open-fronted shops leading up to the Temple of the Bronze Horse. A doe-eyed little boy in a blue kimono played with spinning tops by the side of the road until, spying the tall foreigner with the pale hair and skin, he ran to his shopkeeper father and buried himself in the man's long skirts. The father bowed to Morrison, who bowed back, strangled with emotion. He burned so fiercely with anticipation he felt he might set the houses of wood and paper aflame. He had no patience for sightseeing. He turned and all but sprinted back to the docks.

The *Doric* had arrived but had been put into quarantine. A customs official told Morrison that a passenger had displayed symptoms of the plague. No, he didn't know the name of the passenger. No, he didn't know if it was a man or a woman. *Please ye gods, let it not be her.* Thinking of the danger to Mae and the baby she was carrying, and for once in no doubt that it was his, Morrison nearly doubled over with anguish.

Over at the *Haimun*, he found James in the engine room in heated conversation with the ship's engineer and gesturing sharply with his pipe.

'It's going to take days to fix,' insisted the engineer, a little Scot with wild red hair. 'You can rant and rave as much as you like, Mr James. But we have to get a new valve or we're not going anywhere, and they don't grow on Nagasaki's trees.'

Morrison, secretly relieved, led James back up to the deck. 'Think of it this way. Tonami will have more time to plead the *Haimun*'s case with his superiors in the navy here.' *And I will wait for the* Doric *to be cleared.*

'The engine is not the end of our trouble.' James thrust a letter into Morrison's hand. 'From our minister in Tokio.'

'Sir Claude? What does he say?'

'Nothing of any use whatsoever. He implies that he does not wish to use his position to argue our case with the Japanese government. He even intimates that he admires the efficiency with which the Japanese have managed to crush the curse of correspondents. The traitorous Brinkley, meanwhile, has published a leaderette supporting the Japanese position on keeping correspondents well away from the war. Says that information disadvantageous to the Japanese army, and hence the outcome of the war, could be disseminated by too much freedom of access to the front by the men of the press. He forgets he's one himself.'

'Bilge. The Japs thought this war would be swift. So, in truth, did I. Now that it's not going as well as they thought it would, they wish to hide this obvious fact from the world. Well, they can't. Bell should pull Brinkley into line.'

'Fat chance. His latest telegram read, "Obey the Japanese." And so the English, the Japanese, our own colleagues and even the bloody machinery are conspiring to keep me from doing my job,' James exclaimed. 'I can't speak for the engine but the others are doing this, from what I can see, not because I am not doing my job well enough but because I am doing it too well. The Russians, of course, would still welcome any excuse to hang me from the nearest yard-arm.' James lit his pipe and puffed furiously at it.

Tonami arrived back from an appointment with the commander of a Japanese man o' war berthed nearby, worry etched into his brow. He was clutching a telegram.

'What is it, Tonami?' James demanded before the man had even the chance to say hello.

'Not good.' He waved the telegram. 'Military Headquarters has overruled the navy and ordered the *Haimun* to remain south of the line of battle. Well south.'

'They know I am willing to play by their rules,' James spluttered. 'I just want to see the action with my own eyes. I am more than happy to accept censorship. Tonami, your welcome presence on the *Haimun* is testament to that.'

'*So*,' Tonami concurred. 'And James-*san* has been more careful in his dispatches than our own admiralty.'

'And as a reward I am threatened with capital punishment by one belligerent and warned off the high seas and neutral waters by the other. My own editor wishes to whisk my boat from under my feet. All because I have a vision for revolutionising correspondence itself!'

Morrison thought for a moment. 'MacDonald — Sir Claude — is weak and vacillating. But he's out best hope. James, draft a letter of reply to our minister. I shall have a look at it when you're finished.'

Morrison's air of authority clearly calmed James and brought a look of relief to Tonami's face as well.

'That's settled then,' Morrison added. 'We'll have dinner first at the hotel.'

The three men went ashore for dinner. Afterwards, Morrison returned to the docks only to find the *Doric* still in quarantine.

Gripped by foreboding and still suffering from the lingering effects of the flu, Morrison slept poorly. At dawn, he forced himself from his bed and discovered the *Doric* still had not been cleared. Composing a note, he sent it up to the ship. Whilst awaiting a reply, he obtained a copy of the manifest and ran his finger down the list three times. His heart sank. There was no

Miss Perkins aboard. No Mrs Goodnow, either. *The lady is constant only in her inconstancy*, he thought and was instantly struck with remorse. *What if something has happened to her?* Perhaps she just missed the boat. That was a plausible explanation. Enquiring as to the next boat out from Shanghai, he learned it was the twin-screw *Empress*, a fast boat due in the following day. He knew he could not wait indefinitely. Bell had ordered him to the front; he would have to go to Tokio soon to get his orders. He felt ill with worry — and glad for the *Haimun*'s troubles, for they gave him an excuse to linger in Nagasaki a bit longer.

Sighting him, James bounded down the *Haimun*'s gangplank with his draft letter to Sir Claude in hand. The pair returned to Morrison's hotel for breakfast. There, Morrison read the letter. He shook his head. 'You have rather let drift the faculties of diplomacy. Instead of moving the diplomat to come to the aid of the *Haimun*, you may be inciting him to sink it.'

James made a sound like a tyre deflating. 'It is a trifle uncompromising,' he conceded.

Morrison nodded. 'It's violent.'

'Violent,' admitted James.

'Worst of all, it's unconvincing.'

James grimaced.

'Moderation and a respectful tone might better aid the cause of a sympathetic result.'

'You see,' James said, 'this is why I need you, G.E. Please, help me redraft it.'

'My pleasure. I will get to it shortly. I've an urgent telegram of my own to send first.' He could see the question forming on James's lips. 'Our colleague in Shanghai, Blunt.'

'I'll accompany you to the telegraph office,' James offered as they walked out.

'You worked all night,' Morrison replied. 'Rest for a while.'

'I'm fine.'

'Rest,' Morrison ordered. 'I'll come to you shortly.'

Morrison had not been dissembling. The telegram was indeed addressed to Blunt: IS MISS PERKINS IN SHANGHAI. FIND OUT IF SAILING *EMPRESS.*

He feared his disappointment could be bitter. *Perhaps she has decided it would be folly for us to see each other again. She has made her decision. Egan is to be the happy one and I forever precluded.*

Plagued by pessimistic thoughts and craving occupation, Morrison was thankful for the task of revising James's draft. Several hours later, he handed James the new version. 'You will see that I have removed various random accusations and fulminations in order to stress the loss *The Times* would be forced to sustain if the *Haimun* was kept from sailing into the zone of war, the punctiliousness with which you adhere to the rules of neutrality, for so it must appear, and your sensitivity to Japanese military concerns. It most humbly requests Sir Claude, whose prestige and influence with the Japanese, not to mention our own government, is unparalleled, to render his most invaluable assistance in the matter.'

'I shall keep my original draft as a relic of barbarism,' James said humbly.

'Of course,' Morrison conceded, 'it is the reply that is the point.'

Morrison returned to the hotel to tend to his notes and correspondence, arriving just as the sky cracked open. Rain fell in sheets. James arrived for lunch, sodden despite his umbrella and bearing a telegram from Moberly Bell addressed to Morrison.

Made nervous by Morrison's poorly veiled dissatisfaction at having to stand in for Bedlow and fearful that his star correspondent might again threaten to quit *The Times*, Bell had rescinded the order for him to proceed to the front. He ordered him instead to concentrate on solving the problem of the *Haimun*'s access to the Siege of Port Arthur and other battles taking place in the Yellow Sea. And whilst he was at it, he was to convince the Japanese to allow all *The Times*'s correspondents access to the land battles unfolding as well.

Morrison hid his relief beneath a fit of coughing. 'So now I am not to go to the Yalu. I feel like a bloody bandalore. Up and down. Up and down.'

'I could use a bandalore myself. I like the newfangled ones with weighted rims. Yoyos, they call them. Picked one up in America when I was organising for the wireless plant. Good for relieving tension, or so they say.'

'So good,' Morrison responded drily, 'that it's said France's aristocrats played with them — the old-fashioned ones, anyway — all the way to the guillotine. Any reply from Sir Claude yet?'

'None.'

The rain fell all night long. Outside Morrison's window, bamboo creaked and groaned.

It is the hope deferred that maketh sick the heart.

In the club the following morning, Morrison perused the papers. Nearly every first-hand report or illustration was of troop movements or marches or such details as the weight of the Japanese soldier's kit. Those rare correspondents who'd defied Japanese controls to try to make it to the site of battle themselves told electrifying tales, which usually concluded with the correspondent himself being summarily apprehended somewhere in Korea and packed off back to Tokio with a reprimand.

The *Japan Mail* carried an article on the effect of stray mines on commercial shipping. He thought of Mae, pregnant, aboard a ship. Reading the notices as to who was staying at Yokohama's Grand Hotel, he saw Martin Egan's name. He looked up at the rain-streaked window; the world was grey and composed of tears. *Does she wish to be with me or Egan? Are we to be the two strings to her bow? And which of us really is the father?* He grimaced. *If it is indeed one of us at all.* He craved certainty.

The *Empress* arrived. There was no Miss Perkins aboard.

Morrison walked from the docks to the brothels of Mogi. He returned unconsoled.

Back on the *Haimun*, he found James chewing on his pipe stem in a state of fresh agitation. 'I thought he was on our side!' James exploded.

'Who?'

'Admiral Saito.'

'What on earth are you talking about?'

'Saito is the one who said that as long as Tonami was able to vet our transmissions and use our wireless, we would have access to the theatre of war. Now he's told Tonami that it would be a "tactical error" to allow us to leave Nagasaki at all! We have done nothing to deserve such treatment,' James fulminated, knocking the ashes from his pipe with undue force. 'Oh, by the way, a telegram has come to you from Shanghai.' He passed an envelope to Morrison.

Morrison read it and then reread it.

'Good news?' James asked hopefully.

'She says, "Do come Shanghai".'

'Who says?'

'Miss Perkins.'

'Miss Perkins?' James's voice ballooned with dread. 'I have heard … of Miss Perkins. What do you intend to do?'

'Go I will.' *Why fret my heart out here?*

'But the *Haimun* …'

'It is detained indefinitely. You have just told me so in great detail yourself. And now that I am not going to the front, I should check in with Blunt.'

'Tonami is going to Tokio to speak with Saito in person.'

'Nothing will happen and I can't do anything until he returns. He doesn't even leave here until tomorrow.'

'I cannot stop you,' James said unhappily.

'Good man.' Morrison clapped James on the shoulder and took himself to the booking office to procure a ticket to Shanghai on the *Empress* when it returned there in two days' time. Egan's name on the Tokio hotel list was looking propitious all of a sudden. They were not yet reunited. There was still hope. *Two days! How shall they pass?*

The following day, James solved that problem when he showed Morrison another letter he had drafted to Sir Claude, though the diplomat had yet to answer the first.

'I shall sober it down, shall I?' Morrison asked. It wasn't really a question.

At last the *Empress* was due to set sail. Arriving dockside with his bags, he presented his ticket only to be told that the steamer was delayed due to some problem with its engine.

At Mogi, the madam offered him a pretty little sixteen-year-old for five yen who, she claimed, had been only six months in whoredom.

He returned to find James pacing the deck of the *Haimun*, smoke signals of distress rising from the bowl of his pipe. Bell had sent another ominous telegram: FOR ONE MONTH AT A COST OF £2000 WE HAVE SUCCEEDED IN MAKING OURSELVES LOOK SUPREMELY RIDICULOUS.

'It is the Japanese who are making all of us look supremely ridiculous!' James ranted, and Morrison, for all his sympathy for the Japanese cause, could not argue otherwise. 'The latest news, from our colleague Brinkley in Tokio, by the way,' James added, 'is that they have now decided to allow sixteen correspondents to wire two hundred and fifty words a day from the front.'

'If the correspondents pooled resources,' Morrison calculated, 'they could come up with a comprehensive dispatch of four thousand words.'

'No, no — a total of two hundred and fifty *between* them.'

Morrison knew it was not the most felicitous time for him to be going to Shanghai.

In Which a Connection Is Missed, a Terrible Truth Is Revealed, and What Providence Taketh Away It Giveth Again

With steam pouring out of its two funnels and all three masts rigged, the sleek *Empress* managed seventeen knots but even that wasn't fast enough for Morrison. Why hadn't she come or telegraphed since that one urgent summons? He felt sick with apprehension. He thought again, inevitably, of the lantern-jawed Egan and was consumed with a furious jealousy. In the next instant, he told himself that he should be thankful to the clueless bastard for taking her and whoever's child it was off his hands and affording him some peace of mind. *This is peace of mind?*

Peace. Peace and war. War and peace. *To think that I should have been cajoled by a woman into proceeding to Shanghai when I ought to have pursued my duty for* The Times *— it is inconceivable.*

The *Empress* ploughed through the waves and Morrison's thoughts pitched and rolled from Nagasaki to Shanghai to London, Port Arthur, Tientsin, Isnaia Poliana and back to Shanghai again.

☯

'Checked out? Are you sure?'

'Yes, she left yesterday.'

'Any forwarding address?'

'Let's see. Ah, here it is. Care of Martin Egan, Grand Hotel, Yokohama. Oh, and she's left a letter addressed to you.'

❀

Dearest darling Ernest,

I know how often I have disappointed you. I hope that you know I've never set out to hurt you. I am sorry I was not on the Doric, *and sorrier to tell you why not. The day before I was to board, I began to bleed and then to cramp. Mrs Ragsdale called the doctor, but by the time he came it was all over. I cried an ocean. I am sure she was yours. I want you to know that, and also that I love you very much. I will think of you always, even when I am in the arms of others. I leave China today in the care of Mrs Goodnow to join Martin in Japan. I had hoped to see you before going but my boat was due to depart before yours could arrive. Anyway, Martin wants to marry me and I feel that perhaps it may be a good thing after all. At Mills College, we were given Ralph Waldo Emerson's essays to read. One line has stayed with me: 'A foolish consistency is the hobgoblin of little minds, adored by little statesmen and philosophers and divines.' Be good and sometimes think of your Maysie.*

❀

A foolish consistency? She has never ventured a consistency of any sort! Morrison realised that the hotel clerk was observing him with too much curiosity for his liking. He folded the letter and put it in his pocket. 'Good day, sir,' he said and strode out into the sunshine, liberated from his dreams. The promiscuous scents of Shanghai filled his nostrils, making him queasy. *The final parting.* He returned in a daze to the docks, where he had left his luggage at the office of the shipping firm. Hiring a rickshaw, he set out for Bubbling Well Road, stopping only long enough to send a telegram to Mae: ARRIVED SHANGHAI DAY LATE. DEVASTATED BY NEWS. WISH YOU PLEASANT VOYAGE UNBOUNDED HAPPINESS PROTECTED FROM ALL HARM. NEVER FORGET YOU. ERNEST.

☯

'I am stunned,' he confided to Mrs Blunt. He'd been relieved to find her on her own at the house.

'Did you love her?' she asked, a fount of sympathy.

'Love?' Morrison repeated, as though unsure what the word meant.

'Compared her to a summer's day, that sort of thing,' Mrs Blunt suggested. She poured out another cup of tea, and pushed a plate of sandwiches in his direction.

'You tease,' Morrison replied, oblivious to refreshment. 'I am too old to be reciting sonnets.' He could see that she saw straight through him. 'Perhaps. A little.' *I loved her so dearly I can scarcely express it. Unhappy me!* He emitted a low, self-mocking laugh. 'And now, she whom I loved so dearly and who loved me is leaving me for another. Without pretence or hypocrisy. As if it is the most natural thing in the world. It is an experience that chastens one in every way, for every reason.'

'Love always does,' Mrs Blunt said.

That night, hunched over the escritoire in the Blunts' guest room, Morrison wrote for nearly two hours. He expended more than half a bottle of ink and nearly wore out a nib. The result, he confided to his journal, was *one of the most beautiful and melting love letters that I have ever written in my life. And I will send it to the care of Martin Egan, my rival who has played the game so chivalrously, and into whose arms, younger and possibly stronger than my own, she will fall in several days' time. The thought fills me with pain as does that of my lost child. Alas, my happiness is for a long time ended.*

The prospect of returning to Japan did not cheer Morrison either, for he would not arrive in time to pre-empt Mae's reunion with Egan. He was therefore somewhat solaced to receive a telegram the next morning from Wei Hai Wei in which James reported that the Japanese had released the *Haimun* to return there. That was good news, but not the fact that en route the boat had run into a typhoon. The topmast had snapped off in the fierce winds, hurtling into the sea together with all the wireless attachments. It was one crisis after another.

Morrison left Shanghai for Wei Hai Wei on the first available steamer. It shocked him to see how, in dry-dock, the *Haimun* appeared far too small, vulnerable and broken a thing to have provoked as much passion and fury as it did.

Once he was with James, a cable came from their editor. James did not have the heart to open and so handed it to Morrison, who winced at the contents. It was a veritable philippic. Bell wanted to know how, for all the supposed advantages afforded to their paper by newfangled wireless technology, they had been scooped by the halfpenny *Chronicle*, whose reporter had got quite a long way towards the front before his inevitable arrest and expulsion by the Japanese.

'Let's hope that Fraser holds up the side,' Morrison said. In a concession to *The Times*, the Japanese army had granted Fraser permission to embed himself with General Kuroki's forces, who were crossing the Yalu River from Korea into Manchuria. With luck, he would be able to witness the first major land battle of the war. It would be a fierce fight, no one had any doubt about that. But according to Tonami, Japanese scouts, camouflaged amongst the local population, had managed to map every one of the Russians' trenches and trou-de-loups as well as the location of all sixty pieces of their heavy artillery. 'It will be a great victory,' Morrison predicted with confidence, wondering if it should have been him going and not the novice Fraser.

As it transpired, Fraser acquitted himself brilliantly. His reports from the scene of the battle, which took place on the first of May, were alive with detail. He wrote of brave Cossack battalions charging with their long spears, and the intrepid Japanese warriors who met them on the battlefield, swords raised and cries of '*Banzai!*' ringing through the air. He described how the Japanese army, forty thousand strong, annihilated the enemy force, which was half its size, sowing the Manchurian fields with Russian corpses. Blood irrigated furrows littered with snapped stalks of sorghum, broken carrots and crushed turnips. There weren't enough ambulance carts to collect all the wounded so the Japanese took only those with a chance of survival. Fraser could barely contain his admiration for the Japanese army: modern, skilful and displaying an 'utter disregard of life'.

His reports, conveyed out of the field by the usual uncertain methods, took between six and twenty days each to reach the paper. The Japanese army, having crossed the Yalu, swiftly advanced through Manchuria towards the commercial hub of Liaoyang. As May wore on, the trickle of refugees from the war zone became a flood. There were reports of famine in places. Morrison's Chinese contacts were increasingly vocal in their dismay, for there was no end in sight to the conflict. The Anti-Manchu movement gained strength; its adherents questioned what sort of government would allow foreign powers to fight over part of its territory, so hogtied by its promise of neutrality that it could not defend or rescue its own citizens.

The *Haimun* needed weeks in dry-dock. Morrison returned to Peking. One day, whilst he was in his library, a terrible keening rent the air. He jumped to his feet, every hair on his neck erect, and raced into the courtyard, almost colliding with Kuan, who stammered, 'The war ... *mafoo* ...' Morrison's eyes darted in the direction of the stables. His groom, surrounded by the other servants, was slapping his own face; the *mafoo*'s wife, Morrison saw, was the source of the awful wailing, though by now several of the other women had joined in as well. Morrison could see Yu-ti standing by Cook's side, pale, frightened.

The *mafoo*, Yang, like all of Morrison's servants with the exception of Kuan, Cook and Yu-ti, was Manchu. He had just received news of a battle near the town where most of his family, including his father and mother, still lived. After the Japanese routed the Russians, the Russians had returned and burned the entire town down to the ground. Nearly everyone perished. 'A cowardly proceeding and deliberate provocation,' Morrison told Kuan. 'It is proof, if ever needed, that the Russians never had

Chinese interests at heart.' He clasped Yang's hand in his own and felt the limitations of his spoken Chinese when he offered his condolences. It was a damned shame. *Russian perfidy.* He instructed Kuan to make appropriate arrangements, including giving Yang and his family time off to mourn.

☯

Morrison mourned too — for his lost child, lost love, for Maysie, for himself. At times, thinking of her with Egan, he was consumed with jealousy. Thankfully, as the weeks passed, he thought of her less and less.

At the end of the month of May, Morrison received one of James's urgent summons to meet him in Wei Hai Wei. Anticipating only a brief trip, he packed light and left Kuan at home in charge of the household.

He found James in his usual state at the mess on Liu Kung Island, a half-drunk ichiban on the table before him. 'It is not that I am unused to censorship,' James thundered before Morrison had even sat down. 'During the Boer War, we had to say "successful reconnaissance" when we meant "military failure". The censors there were cunning. But the Japanese are diabolical. Particularly with regard to the *Haimun.* It's been five weeks since they imposed their "temporary prohibition" on the *Haimun*'s movements, and a month since the Battle of the Yalu. It's time,' he said, reaching over and gripping Morrison's arm, 'we went to Tokio.'

'We?'

'You and me. As you know, the Japanese are allowing more reporters to ride with the army. Others are sneaking out through

Korea and across Manchuria to reach the lines of battle with greater success than before — if only because there are too many of them for the Japanese to catch. Some have attached themselves to the Russians. It is said that the Russo-Japanese War will be the most reported war in all history. Just not by us, and in the most path-breaking way conceivable.' He took a breath. 'G.E., you have known Sir Claude from the time of the siege. I know the bonds such an experience can forge. If anyone can get him on side, it is you. And the Japanese too. You have been most useful to them with your telegrams in support of the war and their cause, even before the conflict broke out; they know your loyalty and your value. You have a sound and almost uncanny judgment in dealing with people, a quality I do not claim for myself. You are imperturbable in debate. Most of all, you are untainted with the personal irritation that at this moment is liable to vitiate my own considered opinions. You are the *Haimun*'s final hope.'

'And you propose … ?'

'We sail in two days to Nagasaki and then Kobe, from where we will proceed overland to Tokio.'

Morrison nodded. 'Jolly good.' *What Providence is this that, following each separation, apparently final, sends me back to her again? This time to find her, no doubt, in the arms of Martin Egan, where she has been ensconced for this last month.* 'If you'll excuse me,' he said, 'I need to send a telegram.'

In Which Morrison Meets a Young Lady in Men's Clothing and Learns That They Have Interests in Common

Under James's stewardship, the *Haimun* had transported the odd refugee, lady translator and rival correspondent. Morrison was thus not unduly surprised when James told him that a fellow journalist would be travelling with them back to Japan. He was, however, taken aback by the fellow's extreme youth — his suit hung loosely on his boyish frame and he had nary the shadow of a hair above his lip. As James was below deck attending to some business, Morrison introduced himself. All became clear when the curious passenger offered a firm handshake in return and by way of introduction said, 'Eleanor Franklin, war correspondent.'

Morrison could not hide his amusement. 'And for whom do you correspond, Miss Franklin?'

'*Leslie's Weekly.*'

Morrison cocked his head, unexpectedly impressed. *Leslie's Weekly* was one of America's most popular illustrated magazines.

'And you didn't need to tell me who you are. Everyone knows the great Dr Morrison. Like the rest of the world, I devoured your report of the Siege of Peking. It's an honour to meet you. And a particular pleasure to meet someone, coming as you do,

Dr Morrison, from the second country in the world to give women the vote.'

'Did we do that?' Morrison teased. 'Whatever were we thinking?'

'Clearly you had nothing to do with it. But it happened two years ago. The first place to grant suffrage, in case you were wondering, was New Zealand. In America, we only have the vote in a few states. It's a source of vexation.' She sighed. 'Anyway, it's an honour to meet both of you.' She turned to James, who had just joined them on deck. 'I ought to have mentioned earlier that your dispatches from the Boer War inspired me to take up war correspondence in the first place. I read Winston Churchill's report in *The Morning Post* as well, of course, but I felt yours to be its superior.'

James beamed. 'I don't wish to boast, but my telegram appeared two days before Mr Churchill's. A minor miracle considering the only way to get reports out of Ladysmith at that point was by carrier pigeon, and I'd run out of pigeons. I was expecting a new batch when I noticed some flashes of light in the distance. The enemy was sending me a message by heliograph: "They were delicious."'

Miss Franklin, Morrison noticed, had an endearing giggle. 'It is unusual to find a woman in the job of war correspondent,' he commented.

Miss Franklin gave a little snort of derision. 'The age we live in celebrates feats of daring and acts of genius, as long as they are performed by men. Society's highest expectations of women are that they are obedient, orderly and modest. I see you two smiling, but you cannot deny that when men praise our virtue they are normally lauding our passivity and tractability. When they say we are looking beautiful, it is usually because we have tormented our feet into narrow, heeled boots and our bodies into tightly laced corsets.' She gestured down at her masculine attire. 'I would not be able to do the job I do were I dressed in women's clothing.'

She is another sort of handful. The young women of this new era, it seems, have myriad new ways of confounding us. Morrison could not help but admire Miss Franklin's spirit and intelligence; she was going to be a boon companion. 'Why then,' he asked with a twinkle in his eye, 'do not more women abandon their corsets and other fripperies and adopt the male style of dress outright, I wonder?'

Miss Franklin was quick to respond. 'Because most women are complicit in their own oppression.' She went on to deride the tendency of women her age to devote themselves to pleasure and trifles over education and duty. 'I have a friend — perhaps you know him? — Martin Egan.'

Until that moment the conversation had been so genuinely diverting that Morrison had ceased to ruminate upon his nerve-racking situation. Upon hearing Egan's name, his heart skipped a beat. 'I am acquainted with Mr Egan. What of him?'

'I shouldn't speak of it,' Miss Franklin replied, although the rush of her words made it evident that she was pleased to be able to do so. 'Mr Egan is such an intelligent and forthright sort of man, and not old-fashioned in his thinking either, so I would have thought that he would be attracted to, well, a more modern sort of woman. A woman who takes a responsible, active place in the world. But no, he is well enamoured of a creature of leisure, a woman devoted to little more than her own pleasure, and it is ...' Her words seemed to dam up all of a sudden. 'It is all too distasteful,' she said finally.

'You would be referring to Miss Perkins.' Morrison's voice gave nothing away.

Miss Franklin appeared nonplussed. She spoke her next words carefully. 'Are you acquainted with the lady?'

'We are acquainted, yes,' said Morrison.

'What is your opinion of her?' Miss Franklin asked after a pause.

'I agree that she is just the sort of woman you describe,' Morrison acknowledged. 'And more.'

'How ... fascinating.' She started to say something, but stopped herself.

'Her father is a Republican senator in the US Congress,' Morrison added.

'Yes, I know. He is an interesting case. Member of the Freemasons and Knights Templar, shares in mining, shipping, milling, ranching, whaling — you name it. Whilst governor, he pardoned many of California's young prisoners after interviewing them personally. Has a reputation for being so well-disposed towards business monopolies in his law-making that people joke that should he ever get into deep water, Standard Oil would send a tanker to rescue him.'

'You know much about Miss Perkins's father,' Morrison remarked. Even he had not done so much research.

'I am interested in politics, that is all,' shrugged the precocious Miss Franklin.

The topic turned to the *Haimun* and its wireless. Miss Franklin's interest and sympathy for their project gratified and somewhat mollified the fretful James. As they conversed, Morrison's mind stayed on the vexatious problem of Egan. He would see him and speak to him, man to man, about Mae and everything else. *That's it — I will see Egan first.*

He couldn't. It wouldn't be right. He'd see her first.

He'd see them together.

He'd see neither of them.

He'd see only Mae.

She would have got the telegram he'd sent from Wei Hai Wei. Unsure how long they would be staying in Nagasaki, he'd told her she could contact him in Kobe.

Night fell on the Yellow Sea. Morrison looked to the stars for guidance. It was not forthcoming.

In Which Our Hero Considers the Possibility That an Oyster Pirate Has Been Diving in Home Waters and Receives an Urgent Summons

The time spent aboard the *Haimun* and then in Nagasaki, where another small repair delayed them for some days, passed agreeably enough, though Morrison's anxieties increased as they got closer to their destination. Finally, Kobe came into view with its red-brick godowns and sprawling foreign settlement, the lush Rokko Mountains rising in the distance. Japanese boatmen, naked but for their indigo loincloths, unloaded passengers, luggage and other cargo. It was hot and humid. The throb of the ship's engines still in his ears, Morrison loped through Bund Park and along the orderly streets, past neat cricket pitches, tidy homes and bustling shops. Kobe, almost odourless even in June, thanks to its underground sewers, well deserved its reputation as the 'model settlement of the Far East', as far as he was concerned.

At the Telegraph Office, he found a long line of people waiting to be served. Just ahead of him was a Japanese man in a Western suit, a young European lady with an air of Gibson Girl about her, and a Chinese merchant in vest, silk shirt and loose pants, his hat lifted clear off his head by the coiled queue underneath it. The line inched forward. *I nerve myself and bow to the will of Heaven. What is to be the decree? Am I to meet Maysie, and under what circumstances? Is she still to love me or am I displaced forever by the* beatus providents? *Am I to have happiness or pain?*

'May I help you, sir?' The Englishman in charge of the Telegraph Office looked as though he'd rather be in Clacton-on-Sea. Morrison introduced himself and asked if any telegram had come for him.

The pace at which the man looked through the poste restante suggested he was reading the addressees' names one letter of the alphabet at a time. Morrison stood on one leg, then the other. Under his straw boater, sweat coursed down his temples; he could also feel it trickling from his underarms. At long last, the man turned and gave him an anaemic smile. 'I'm afraid not, Dr Morrison. Is there anything else I can do for you?'

The clouds burst as he emerged from the Telegraph Office. Rain splashed off the brick footpaths, and pastel-coloured parasols bloomed in a field of black bumbershoots. Morrison, raising his own umbrella, hastened towards the haven of the Kobe Club. He had time to spare before meeting James and Tonami for the overnight train to Tokio. Catching up with the newspapers in the club's reading room, he scanned the published list of guests at Yokohama's Grand Hotel. The names Miss M. Perkins and Mr Martin Egan appeared side by side. *It pains me, though who can blame either? Am I to be forever excluded by the lucky Egan?*

Morrison composed a wire to the Grand Hotel informing Mae he'd be checking into the Imperial Hotel in Tokio by two the following afternoon. HOPE YOU ARE WELL HAPPY ENJOYING YOURSELF. ERNEST.

It stopped raining. The mountains' steamy exhalations hung over the landscape. Morrison, more restless than usual, strode up the hill to Kitano in search of diversion. He wandered past the dollhouse-like homes of the foreigners, which, with their lush green lawns and neat flower beds, presented a vaguely sinister vision of domesticity. Then he stalked the streets of Native Town until it was time for the train.

Aboard the sleeping car for Tokio, Morrison, Tonami and James talked of ships and politics — concerns solid and masculine. Comforting. *Yang*. The following afternoon, the train pulled into Tokio, the blast of its whistle cutting into Morrison's nerves like a knife.

The neo-Renaissance façade of the magnificent Imperial Hotel abutted the Imperial Palace and rose out of the surrounding neighbourhood like a hallucination of Paris. Fourteen years old and modelled after the grand hotels of Europe and America, its décor was an artful mélange of East and West, its service the best of both. The Emperor himself had held his birthday ball there the previous year.

The impeccably attired Japanese manager greeted Morrison in French, ran his finger down a ledger, and sucked in an apologetic breath. '*Je suis desolée, Docteur Morrison.*' The world's correspondents, still only intermittently and selectively able to cover the war, had spread themselves rather more efficiently over the hotel. They had taken all the rooms. The manager regretted that the hotel could only accommodate Morrison in two days' time.

Disappointed, Morrison took a hired trap to the British Legation. Having settled into a guest room there, he telephoned the Grand Hotel in Yokohama, heart banging like a steam hammer.

'Darling.'

He was astounded by how quickly the music of her voice erased a month's accumulation of jealousy, anxiety, heart-worry and sorrow.

'Mae. Maysie. I've been so worried about you. Ever since I heard about ...'

'I'm all right, honey. Please don't worry about me.'

'The baby ...'

Her voice quavered. 'Really, I'm all right. It was such a shock. I mean, the whole thing. I never expected ... anyway, this is for the best.'

Morrison sensed some hesitation in her voice. 'Are you alone?'

'Yes. Martin's gone to Tokio to see off Jack London.' Her voice recovered its normal bounce. 'Jack has had his fill of the war.'

'Has he?' Morrison felt the familiar sour taste of jealousy on his tongue.

'Well, I suppose it would be more accurate to say he's had his fill of no war. He said,' and Maysie lowered her voice to what Morrison assumed was pitch-perfect imitation, '"There's nothing to see, nothing to write about save the woes of correspondents, swimming pools and peaceful temple scenes."' She laughed. 'It's funny. He grew up in Oakland, too, though our paths never crossed. He lived in the poorhouses and worked in a skittle alley and then a cannery, all before he was fifteen when he became an oyster pirate. Exactly the sort of boy we were warned never so much as to look at for fear he would take advantage or sully us in some way.' She sighed. 'I shall miss dear Jack.'

Morrison, grim-lipped, derived consolation from the fact that if the oyster pirate had indeed boarded the good ship Maysie, or 'sullied' her in some way, it would have caused even more acute distress to London's good mate Egan.

'I can't talk long, Maysie. James is waiting for me. What are your plans?'

'Martin doesn't return till tomorrow. Come down to Yokohama for dinner tonight. I'm crazy to see you.'

He felt the silken web close around him once more.

In Which Our Hero Battles with the American Military for Access to the Front

An appointment in Tokio with James and their colleague Brinkley detained Morrison beyond the hour at which he had hoped to get away. By the time he stepped off the train at Yokohama, it was eight-thirty.

The deep-water port of Yokohama was the Wild West of Japan, seething with *gaijin* of every description, from beachcombers, deserters and adventurers to scholars and correspondents. The whores in 'Dirty Town', as numerous as in the London Haymarket, spoke English — at least the madam at Number Nine promised they did — and Yokohama's Bloodtown brawled like New York's Bowery and San Francisco's Barbary Coast rolled into one. Morrison had explored the darker places of Yokohama in the past, but on this balmy June night he travelled towards the Grand Hotel along streets that were lit by arc lamps and that wouldn't frighten a Mrs Ragsdale. The only untamed darkness was that which he carried within himself.

Mae was waiting for him on the hotel's wide veranda, seated on a wicker throne and sipping a lemon squash. From the hem of a skirt trimmed with shimmering silk bows, one white court shoe with a small Louis heel and glass beading waggled. The extravagance of her outfits had already begun to strike Morrison as excessive. He recalled her prodigal habits and was pleased, for he wished to cling to at least a modicum of rationality.

On a plate before her was a half-eaten array of tiny Japanese cakes sculpted to resemble the flowers and fruits of summer: hydrangea, azalea, iris and plum. There was an empty chair by her side. As Morrison approached, she affected surprise.

'Goodness gracious, it's Dr Morrison. What a pleasant surprise to run into you here.'

'Miss Perkins.' He bent over her gloved hand. *What is this new game?*

'I'm so glad to see you, Ernest, honey,' she whispered quickly, 'but we must be awfully careful.' Before she could elaborate, a little American military man with an air of complacency and a face like a desiccated apple strode towards the empty chair, his air proprietorial. Mae introduced him as Captain Haymes of the US Artillery.

Captain Haymes shook Morrison's hand with the firm formality of the congenital bore. 'Yes, of course, pleasure, pleasure, how do you do?' His smile revealed teeth like a row of old tombstones. 'Miss Perkins speaks most highly of you, Dr Morrison, yes. Of course, there can hardly be a soul in the Extreme East, not one, who has not heard of Dr Morrison of Peking.'

Anxiety rose in Morrison's breast like a miasma.

'You are acquainted with Mr Egan as well, one hears. Fine chap, Egan, fine chap.'

Morrison's heart could not have sunk lower if it had been dropped into Yokohama Bay. 'Indeed.'

'Captain Haymes kindly escorted me to Moto-machi today,' Mae cut in a tad too brightly. Morrison regarded her uneasily. 'We had a bully time, didn't we, Captain Haymes?'

Captain Haymes nodded. 'A bully time,' he repeated, the youthful argot echoing in the necropolis of his mouth.

'I bought so many splendid little things. An *obi* with circled dragons and phoenix, and a kimono with the most delightful pattern of thatched pavilions, gingko trees and bamboo; did you know it takes nine thousand silk cocoons to make one kimono? I also found a black lacquered jewel box with mother-of-pearl inlay, which I will give to Mama, and another box for pens in a fine burnt-orange lacquer for Papa. I bought a bowl for tea, too. The shop owner told us it was once owned by an imperial concubine —'

'So he claimed, yes,' Captain Haymes interjected.

'Oh, Captain Haymes did not believe the story about the concubine. I wish to believe it and so I shall believe it, Captain Haymes.' She patted his arm with a show of fondness.

He shall have to get used to that logic if he wishes to keep her company.

'Anyway, it's either for thick tea or thin tea — I forget now. Tea drinking is a very complicated business here, it would seem. As is buying and selling, isn't it, Captain Haymes?'

Haymes nodded gruffly. Maysie turned again to Morrison, who was amused despite himself.

'But the best part was when we called in on a seller of native artworks. I bought some lovely old woodblock prints.'

Captain Haymes harrumphed. 'It's not much like our notion of painting, no, though one or two make a stab at perspective. One knows something of art, of course, being an amateur watercolourist oneself, yes.'

'Isn't he clever?' Mae batted her eyelids at Morrison.

'Quite,' Morrison agreed. He had no doubt that Egan had put Haymes up to the task of occupying her time and watching over their assignation. Surely even Maysie could not consider taking such a man to her bed. *Those teeth!* Then again, he reminded himself, that's what he had thought about C.D. Jameson.

Haymes pivoted in Morrison's direction. 'So, Dr Morrison, what brings you to Yokohama? The war, of course, yes?'

Morrison rapidly established that Captain Haymes had nothing useful or new to offer in the way of information. Feeling that he could tear out his own hair from nervous tension, Morrison was glad when Mae suggested they go in to dinner.

A row of ionic columns bordered the hotel lounge. Mae suddenly extended her arm and swung herself around a column. As she flung herself back into the men's company, she took Morrison's arm and gave it a squeeze. *What a creature she is!* He could not tell if the gesture had been intended as consolatory, comforting or conspiratorial. Her expression, fiercely gay, gave nothing away. Haymes, Morrison was pleased to see, looked most disconcerted.

The Japanese waiter poured the champagne into crystal glasses and took their orders in French.

The conversation over dinner was excruciating. Haymes had much to say to Morrison, none of it interesting. Morrison had nothing to say to Haymes. He and Maysie had much to say to one another but nothing that could be said in front of Haymes. Morrison, poking listlessly at his duck with his fork, had the unpleasant sensation that, thanks to the knot in his stomach, each beautifully presented course was piling on top of the last one inside him, until the dessert — cream pudding — threatened to turn the whole lot into gorge.

Captain Haymes thought they should take a stroll after dinner. He suggested they follow Kaigan Dori — Seashore Street — to the famous Tamakusu Tree, where Admiral Perry had signed the Treaty of Kanagawa that had opened Japan to the outside world fifty years before. Or, if they were feeling equal to more vigorous exercise, perhaps they could climb up to the scenic General Cemetery on the Bluff. *Where his teeth would feel right at home.* Mae protested that she'd done so much walking that day that her poor feet couldn't take another step. She urged Haymes to go ahead, saying she'd sit in the lobby for a while with Dr Morrison before retiring. Haymes then suggested a game in the hotel's billiards room. Morrison pleaded work commitments; he would only be able to stay the shortest while. Mae insisted that Haymes at least take a walk. When they finally managed to wave him off, she looked at Morrison, opened her eyes wide and exhaled. 'Room 105,' she said, spun on her heels and, with pert footsteps that nowise indicated pedal difficulties, exited in a cloud of ribbons and French perfume, her heels clicking over the marble floor and a wave of bobbing hotel attendants marking the trail to her room.

Churning with nerves, Morrison rose to follow.

In Which Our Hero Suffers a Most Staggering Interview and Is Afforded More Than Just a Glimpse of Heaven

Morrison glanced around the suite, lushly decorated in Louis XIV style, a European fantasy in powder pink. Martin Egan had left subtle but unmistakable signs of his presence: a necktie here, a bottle of shaving lotion there, a pair of socks and garters, and even a signed copy of *Call of the Wild*. Morrison wondered if this was happenstance or a tomcat's spray, or perhaps mines left floating in the sea.

He made a tentative move in Mae's direction but she stepped back, an apologetic half-smile on her face. Indicating that he should sit on the chaise longue, she settled her skirts over a chair. 'Ernest, darling, I am so glad we have this chance to talk.' She twirled a ribbon around a finger. 'We've had some high old times, haven't we?' Her eyes searched his for confirmation.

He yearned to touch her. The chasm that yawned between chaise and chair seemed unbridgeable.

'It's been most agreeable,' Morrison concurred between clamped teeth.

'So perhaps we should leave it at that. Oh, look at me, honey.'

'I thought we could … especially after … you know. I don't understand why you told Mrs Ragsdale that it was Egan's,' he said under his breath.

She leaned forward and put a finger on his lips. He sucked it into his mouth and she laughed — her true, free, natural laugh — for the first time since they'd seen each other this time. 'Ernest, honey, you know I'm crazy for you. But I know that in your heart you were never comfortable with the idea of marrying me. You're an ambitious and important man.'

'You mock me.' His voice was choked.

'Not at all. But I know my own concerns often strike you as frivolous, even dull.'

'Frivolous, perhaps, at times. Dull is the last word I'd ever use to describe you.'

'Thank you for saying that. You say it — the word "dull" — of so many people, I did occasionally fear for myself. It's true. Ever since I've known you, you've complained that so-and-so is an insufferable dullard and so-and-so is a terrible bore, that this dinner party was damnedly dull and that luncheon disagreeably stupid. Every day you dine with men you consider irksome or insipid — you cannot deny it. The only exceptions are Molyneux and Dumas, and you still cavil at the former's lack of discretion and the latter's dearth of ambition. As for your associates, I have heard an entire litany of complaint. James is fractious, Menzies fawning, Granger inept, Bedlow vexatious.'

'You have a point about the others, but Maysie, you are not dull, and no dinner at which you have been present has ever been dull on your account. Good God, woman, if there have been dinners and luncheons this past few months that have not been dull, it's only thanks to you.'

Maysie toyed with the buttons on her sleeve. 'I don't wish to get stuck on this matter of dullness.' A smile played over her lips. 'It is true that I have never been accused of it before.'

'You do have a talent for enjoyment — and for sharing it.' *That did not come out quite as I intended.*

Her lips pursed. 'I know you've never approved of my seeing other men.'

'It's not about approving or disapproving, Maysie.'

'Although I must accept a certain decorum for my family's sake, modesty is not in my nature. And, as you know, I cannot countenance hypocrisy, even if that means that some of my deeds, and not a few of my words, must give those around me pain.'

'Any pain you may have given me has been more than compensated for by pleasure. I do think we have more in common than you think. I detest hypocrisy too, Mae. With all my soul.'

'So you have said to me many a time, but do you really, Ernest, honey? For all of your scathing comments about people, do you ever tell them what you really think? I have heard you express different opinions in private than you do in your telegrams, on the way the war is going, for example. You don't always write what you think; you write what you think needs to be said. I think you love your place in society more than you detest the hypocrisy it requires to maintain it.'

Though his mouth opened, Morrison had no words with which to answer her. She had hit her target squarely.

'Oh Ernest, honey,' she murmured, 'I'm so sorry. I didn't meant to be so harsh and I don't wish to quarrel.'

Morrison, miserable, stood and held out his arms. 'If you don't despise me, hold me.

She pressed the back of one hand to her forehead in a gesture worthy of the stage. 'I can't. I've given my solemn promise to Martin to be faithful.'

I will perish on the spot. 'Why did you ask me to come to see you? Simply to torture me?'

'Of course not, darling. It's because I love you.'

'Why Egan then?'

Mae's voice fell to a whisper. 'He does not put my heart in danger the way you do.'

'Then I was wrong about you.'

She stiffened. 'What do you mean?'

'Remember our conversation that day when we visited Shanghai's native city? You told me that you embraced risk, that you abhorred the idea of a life lived timidly and in thrall to others. I believed you, but now I wonder if that was just an act.'

She went limp, like a marionette whose strings had been severed. 'Touché,' she said in a barely audible voice. 'But it wasn't an act. I meant every word. And yet,' she wavered, 'I don't know what to do. I *promised* Martin, you see.'

'Yes, but you also promised —' He was about to say that she'd previously promised him such things as well when it struck him that she never had.

'No, I never did,' she said, reading his mind. 'I try not to make promises I can't honour. And I try to honour the promises I do make. Perhaps some might scoff but that's my way of being a moral person.'

Morrison took a moment to absorb this. 'Are you marrying him?'

'No. Yes. Maybe. I am not all that eager. But he is.'

Tied up in the ribbons and bows of her preposterous logic,

Morrison could offer no argument. He was contemplating his exit, the better to retain his dignity, when she jumped up, threw herself around his neck and whispered, 'Oh honey, you and me, we're a bit hopeless, aren't we? Anyway, Martin isn't back from Tokio until tomorrow.'

A boat's horn sounded in the port. The electric fan creaked as it traced slow circles overhead.

What a type it is! One moment she is the tragedienne, the next the temptress and provocatrix! She incites me and plays me for her own pleasure and with only the present in her mind, the past erased, the future unconsidered. She is Diana, goddess of the hunt, though no virgin. Her wit is her bow; her charm, her arrow. There would scarcely be a white man in all of China or Japan by now, I should imagine, who has not been wounded by that exquisite barb. She is as honest as whisky, as direct as a shot across the decks. I kiss her and am intoxicated. Her candour is breathtaking, admirable, enviable. She promises me nothing more than fleeting joy and surely that is enough. She will not be owned, and Egan will learn that to his detriment, poor sod. I kiss her and she folds herself around me until I can scarcely breathe. She moans, she sighs, she creates drama wherever she goes; I still don't know if the baby was real, a hallucination or just a clever twist in her script. What is certain is that the world is her stage, hers is the limelight and we poor men but her supporting cast. She was right that I would not be long content with such a role. I understood her John Wesley's reluctance, his vacillations, more than I cared to let on. For whilst Mae Ruth Perkins is absolutely, eternally, true to herself, she will never be true to anyone else. And though she does not actively seek

319

scandal, it falls like the rains of June in Japan on those around her. As much as I detest the thought that C.D. Jameson ever laid his vile hoary paws upon her, I must admit that he was right. She is a nymphomaniac of the highest order and proves it with every action and indeed every breath. And yet … Her capacity to communicate happiness is unparalleled. Her buoyancy, her mischievous humour, her theatrical extravagance, her sensuality. Her wetness. Her plump breasts. Her heavy-lidded gaze. Her welcoming thighs. Her cunt. Her natural, indefatigable joie de vivre is a great wellspring from which we all drink. Or perhaps, like her fathomless eyes, it is a pool where we kneel, only to fall in love with our own reflections. Whatever it is, it is deep and seductive and liquid. And it is what keeps me chained to her, on my knees, my face towards Heaven.

Mae's voice, kittenish, small and breathless, broke into his thoughts as her hand grabbed his hair, pulling him upwards. 'Honey, you're making me crazy. I need you inside me now.'

In Which the Truth of the Old Saw About the Diplomat Meaning No When He Says Yes Is Illustrated In the Person of Sir Claude, and Our Hero, Inspired by Talk of Sieges Past and Present, Decides to Persevere with His Own

Before leaving the following morning, and whilst Mae's back was turned, Morrison tipped Martin Egan's cravat over the back of the bed. He was reluctant to go, but Sir Claude MacDonald had agreed to see him. He and Mae parted with tenderness. The thought of Egan's imminent return to her side tormented him. He had not been so foolish as to try to extract a pledge of faithfulness.

Morrison stepped off the train at Dzushi, where the minister had his residence, into a field of sultry heat. Insects strummed the air and pine needles baked in the sun. Dragonflies skimmed over a puddle and, in the distance, mountains faded to a grey-blue wash like a painting in ink. Although nervy from lack of sleep, his mood was elevated and he felt open to sensation in every pore.

Sir Claude's wife, Ethel, greeted him warmly. Morrison considered her the most attractive of the diplomats' wives and had been ever mystified by Sir Claude's luck. As she kissed him hello, he noticed that her hair was still thick and dark — not one grey hair. For a woman who had lost one husband and two children to cholera in India and then survived the siege with Sir Claude, this was no small miracle. The minister's welcome was not so much cold as damp, his basset-hound eyes lugubrious, his handshake weak.

In the MacDonalds' parlour, amongst the usual Far Eastern mélange of Western and Oriental furnishings, Ethel asked after old friends in Peking. Had Lady Susan finished her book on China? Was the I.G. well? How was the eccentric Edmund Backhouse — still translating the imperial gazettes for him? Was Bertie Lenox Simpson still up to his usual mischief?

Sir Claude, twirling the waxed ends of his moustache, noted that it was the thirteenth of June, four years to the day that hordes of Boxers launched their attack on Peking's Legation Quarter.

'So it was,' said Morrison, surprised at himself for not remembering.

'It was a terrible time.' Ethel looked down at her hands, veined with age yet still graceful and fine. 'And yet sometimes I find myself reminiscing as though they were almost halcyon days, even glamorous. Is that strange, do you think?'

'No,' Morrison replied, 'not at all. Sometimes the worst of times make the best of memories.'

Over cups of Indian tea, they slipped into shared remembrances. Of the French minister, Pichon, in his nightshirt patterned with red songbirds, wailing '*Nous allons tous mourir ce soir*' — every bloody *soir* — until they almost wished they *would* die, just to be free of him. '*Nous sommes perdus!*' he would weep, and how they all wished he would get *perdus* himself, the sooner the better. They recalled how old Von Below of the German

Legation banged out Wagner's *Ride of the Valkyries* on the piano as though to usher in the apocalypse — and sometimes, Sir Claude reminded them, just to drown out the screams from outside the Legation walls. Morrison and the MacDonalds fell silent for a minute.

'I remember drinking from a bottle of vermouth that had been sliced through its neck by a bullet.' Morrison chuckled and the mood lightened again.

'And those dinners of curried racing pony or pigeon ragout washed down with champagne,' Ethel said. 'Dinners for which the Italian minister always dressed in formal attire.'

Morrison recalled how less than a month before the siege, on the twenty-fourth of May 1900, the MacDonalds had hosted a magnificent celebration for Queen Victoria's eighty-first birthday. The afternoon of the party, in a *hutong* not far from the Legations, Morrison had observed a young Boxer acolyte chanting himself into a trance and slashing at the air with his sword. It had made a good anecdote that evening. He had led Lady Ethel into dinner on his arm. They had waltzed on the tennis courts under red paper lanterns to the Inspector General's own dance band.

Morrison could see the scene as if it were yesterday. He had danced with his hostess, as well as the outrageous Lady Bredon, the lovely Juliet, the eminently squeezable Miss Brazier and the fat and gushing Polly Condit Smith, whom, not long after, he would rescue from the Western Hills together with Mrs Squiers. They had toasted the Queen again and again and the revels had lasted until the wee hours. The following morning, Morrison awoke to the news that whilst they'd been feasting, the Boxers had committed a horrific massacre of missionaries, only eighty miles outside of Peking. Throats slit. Limbs hacked off. Women defiled. On the eighth of June, the Boxers entered the outskirts of the city and burned down the grandstands at the Peking racecourse. Three days later, they dragged the chancellor of the Japanese Legation, Mr Sugiyama, from his cart and stabbed him to death, ripping the heart from his chest. Two days after that, the Boxers, encountering no resistance from the imperial Ch'ing forces, tore into the city and began torching the foreign buildings and slaughtering the converts. The siege began in earnest.

'We have lived through remarkable times,' Sir Claude said. 'But,' he addressed his guest, 'you have not come here to reminisce.'

It occurred to Morrison, as he followed his host to the study, that whilst he had never lived life by halves, some time towards the end of the previous year, 1903, the adrenalin had run out and he had slumped into middle age. He had begun to surrender to his body's complaints. He'd grown cautious and cynical in spirit. And from the start of this new conflict, he'd been obsessed with minutiae (the number of rounds of ammunition smuggled in mail bags, the names of warships, even counting how many Russian troops guarded the platform of Newchang's railway station), the whole time dogged by the feeling that he was missing the real story. Not just of the war but of life. He hadn't dwelt on it, for his quotidian existence never lacked for stimulation. When he'd met Mae, he could hear his heart beating fast again. He still could not say if that quickening was the source of love, proof that it was possible, or something else entirely.

He was pleased with himself for having prepared for this meeting the day before, as, face to face with Sir Claude, he suddenly felt very tired. 'We have decided to surrender the charter of the *Haimun*,' he opened, testing the diplomat's reaction.

'Don't do that.'

'No?' Morrison kept a poker face.

'Not until I see Baron Komura.'

Komura was Japan's foreign minister. 'When will that happen?'

'Thursday. But before that, you, James and I will meet with General Fukushima.'

Morrison wondered if he had underestimated MacDonald.

On the train back to Tokio, the surfeit of tension and dearth of sleep caused him to nod off, his chin tipped forward onto his chest. He could barely keep his eyes open at dinner that night with James, to whom he delivered the following assessment of MacDonald's promise to help: 'Weak, flippant, garrulous and possibly insincere. But our main hope.'

The following morning, Morrison awoke to the sound of rain. *Pouring like blue blazes.* After moving to the Imperial, he wrote a loving note to Mae, telling her he was tied up with work but would call her after his meeting with Sir Claude and Fukushima at the British Legation. He felt light as air.

General Fukushima didn't mince words. The *Haimun* was nothing less than an impediment to Japanese military operations; it interfered with their communications and, given the Russians' overt hostility towards it, was a danger to itself. Japan did not wish to concern itself with the protection of such a vessel when it was fighting a war. Morrison suggested that if they did give up the *Haimun*, at least James should be guaranteed special accreditation and assistance in reaching the front.

'We'd be pleased with such a concession,' Sir Claude said, backing the request.

'It won't be necessary,' Fukushima responded, the picture of geniality.

'Why not?' James's question was a controlled explosion.

'Because we shall be taking Port Arthur in such a short time that no correspondent could make it there in time by land to see the victory.'

'Of course.' Sir Claude nodded, evidently satisfied with the answer.

The minute James was alone with Morrison, all restraint evaporated. 'The vacillating bastard agrees with our case one minute and is persuaded by Fukushima the next! Can't he see that the problem lies in a lack of understanding between the Japanese navy, which sees the advantage to itself of the *Haimun*, and the rest of the Japanese military — represented by the infuriating Fukushima — which does not! You must do something.'

Morrison did not see what he could do. Advising James to calm down, he excused himself to make a phone call.

'Hello?' A sleepy purr.

'Maysie.'

'You always sound so urgent. It makes me feel like the heroine in a melodrama.'

'And so you are.'

'How's the war?'

'We haven't won it yet. Two excruciating hours with Sir Claude and General Fukushima and all we managed to extract was the promise of greater frustration.'

'Ohh. Poor baby,' she cooed.

'I am dying to see you.'

'Don't,' Maysie said. 'It's not attractive.'

Morrison's heart skipped a beat. 'Don't what?'

'Oh, not you, honey. I'm talking to Martin.'

Martin? Morrison's voice cramped, tight and narrow as a woman's boot.

'Hello? Are you there, honey?' she asked.

'I had wanted to ask if you would like to come to Tokio tomorrow.'

'Of course I will. I look forward to it. Meet me at Shinbashi Station. Kisses for now.'

Picturing Egan having to listen to that, Morrison actually felt sorry for his rival.

In Which Morrison Learns About the Cultivation of Bonsai, No News Is Not Necessarily Good News, and Martin Egan Neglects to Show Off His Excellent Teeth

The following day as they drove in a hired carriage from Shinbashi Station into the milky sunshine, Morrison sensed a dark undercurrent to Mae's mood.

At a French restaurant in Uyeno Park, she pushed her food around her plate with a fork, her lips a moue of discontent.

'What's wrong, Maysie?'

She put down her fork and sighed. 'Martin quarrelled with me. He was most disagreeable. He fiercely opposed my coming here to meet you.'

'Ah.'

'He demanded to know where Mrs Goodnow was hiding herself, saying she was a shockingly poor chaperone. I retorted that she was no doubt enjoying herself with a certain Yokohama sea captain and that her failures of duty had never bothered him before. He claimed then that I was humiliating him. He said that his friends had warned him that I would never be faithful but that he had assured them that I listen to him.'

Morrison suppressed a smile. 'And do you?'

'Would I be here if I did? I was incensed at his boast. "Actions speak louder than words," said I, and grabbed my hat and gloves. He then told me to go to blazes. I said, "Fine with me; wasn't it your friend Jack London who said, 'I'd rather be ashes than dust'?"'

'What did he say to that?'

'That he would see me tomorrow evening as planned for an official reception hosted by the American minister in Tokio in honour of the visiting Under Secretary of State.'

His hide will stand any rebuff. 'He is constant, I will give him that.'

Mae tsked. 'I don't wish us to speak of this unpleasant topic any longer. I shall remain quite unable to eat if we do. Tell me something amusing, honey. Tell me how things are going with your little boat.'

After lunch, they strolled along the edge of Uyeno's Shinobazu Pond under a swollen, celadon sky. Waterfowl honked, *oh-up, oh-up,* and wagtails twittered. The park was filled with the pastel fireworks of hydrangeas. A quick, sulphurous smell told of an impending shower. Almost instantaneously, fat drops of rain began pearling on the lotus pads in the pond. Morrison raised his umbrella. A pink-breasted wigeon whistled noisily for its mate, the eerie note wending through the patter of the raindrops.

The circumstances were close to idyllic. But although they had not spoken of it again, Mae's quarrel with Egan had laid a pall over their mood. And Morrison did have the *Haimun* — his 'little boat' — on his mind; were he to see her off at the station now, he could make good use of the rest of the afternoon. 'Should we ...?' he began.

'Go to the hot springs? Why not.'

'Because —'

'I've reserved two rooms there. One for myself and one for my protector and medical attendant.'

She didn't even consult with me. 'And that would be …'

'Honey, do you really need to ask?'

'Sometimes, yes, I think I do.'

'Oh, Ernest, don't sound so cross.'

Morrison thought of the work he could — *should* — be doing.

'Besides, I don't want to go back to Martin tonight.'

Somewhat mollified by the realisation that he would be besting Egan once more, Morrison put on a happier face. 'Now that you mention it, a bath at the hot springs would be delightful.'

It was a cosy and beautiful inn that Mae had booked. Seated opposite her in a tub crafted from lemon-scented hinoki wood, their naked bodies reddening in the near-scalding water, her feet flat against his shins, Morrison listened to the gentle music of the rain on the roof tiles and felt himself fill with a light-headed contentment. Afterwards, they towelled each other dry. Mae grew playful and it was not long before they were wrestling on the plump futons.

Resting in identical cotton *yukata*, they took dinner in the room — slices of raw fish rolled with rice and pickles into little packages tied with seaweed and displayed on a bamboo raft, grilled vegetables and bowls of a cloudy, piquant soup washed down with tiny cups of heated rice wine. Sated, they fell asleep under a quilt filled with goose down, the silver rain outside a welcome barrier between them and the rest of the fretful world. They awoke at four-thirty, Maysie absurdly fresh and Morrison, hearing it was still pouring and knowing he faced a day of meetings, somewhat less so.

After breakfast, Morrison called for the bill and suffered a palpitation when it was presented: sixteen and a half Mexican dollars. The tide of contentment receded. He extracted the notes from his wallet, painful as pulling teeth, and watched her as she hummed and preened, no doubt thinking of her imminent return to the other.

James leapt from his seat with an expression of relief the moment Morrison entered the hotel. Sir Claude would be meeting the Japanese foreign minister at two. He and James were to take afternoon tea with the influential elder statesman Count Matsukata. Best of all, that evening they would be the guests of Admiral Saito. James had sent a note to Brinkley asking him to lunch with them. Their colleague, though lacking in enthusiasm for the project, might at least be able to offer some useful advice for the day's meetings.

Brinkley brought his wife to lunch at the Imperial. She was very pretty, with a sweet manner and intelligent eyes. When Morrison told them that they were to be entertained by both Matsukata and Saito, Brinkley's eyes widened. He looked at his wife. The faintest shadow of a frown clouded her brow. 'I thought so,' Brinkley said, turning back to the men. 'It would appear,' he said, 'that they are determined not to grant your request.'

Morrison noticed Martin Egan enter the dining room. Egan crossed to the other side of the room as though he had not seen Morrison, though their table was in clear view of the door. *He is being unusually petty.*

As it turned out, Egan was the only correspondent who didn't approach their table that day. Word had got out about Morrison and James's appointments. The first to steam up was burly Bennett Burleigh, reporter for London's *Daily Telegraph*, carrying along the mild-mannered war artist Melton Prior in his wake.

'Tell them we need more access,' Burleigh demanded, pounding fist into palm. 'Less courtesy and more frankness.' He had tramped all over Manchuria when he'd first arrived and hadn't asked for anyone's say-so. He'd be filing first-class reports if it wasn't for the damned Japanese. 'I mean no offence, madam,' he added, with a nod in the direction of Brinkley's wife, who inclined her head as if to say none taken, though Morrison expected, even hoped, otherwise. *Boastful braggart.* Morrison had no sooner sent Burleigh and Prior on their way with vague assurances than other correspondents swarmed up. *My editor's demanding ... bored senseless ... must get to the front ... they listen to you ...*

When they were left alone again, Brinkley nodded as though to himself. 'Never mind the *Haimun*,' he said. 'If anyone can argue the case for more general access to the war, it's you, G.E. Good luck.'

James and Morrison took advantage of a break in the rain to take a stroll after lunch. Up and down the streets came the newspaper boys with their bells, extra editions of war news stacked high in lacquered boxes on the ends of their carrying-poles. Men and women crowded around them, eager for news. Finding a vendor with copies of the *Japanese Graphic*, Morrison and James pored over the Western-style illustrations with their English captions.

The news was less then encouraging. The Russians had recently sunk Japanese transports carrying heavy siege guns, railway building materials and some 1400 men. And whilst the

Japanese were making some advances on land, occupying several Russian positions, it had been at the cost of thousands of additional lives.

James shook his head. 'No one foresaw the Russians putting up such resistance.'

Just then, they sighted a woman crossing the street with her little daughter. Her kimono was patterned with portraits of generals and drawings of battleships. Her daughter's costume was decorated with even more vivid illustrations of torpedoes and submarine mines.

'This is a nation that will not lose,' Morrison said. 'And there's a lesson for us in their determination. Let us see what the day's meetings have in store.'

Count Matsukata's residence was grand, but without ostentation, its splendour in the fine craftsmanship of every carved lintel and sliding-door handle. The reception room opened onto a garden that had been manicured into a simulacrum of natural beauty, studded here and there with stone lanterns and arched bridges painted ochre. On the walls of the reception room itself hung an ink painting of Mount Fuji that consisted of a single expressive brushstroke.

Morrison could not help but think of Mae and how she would delight in the artfulness of the residence. At times her irrationality and frivolousness confounded him to the point of irritation. Whereas he had occupation, she had recreation. And yet for all he had applied himself to the study of important matters such as politics, economics and empire, he knew that when it came to appreciating beauty, whether that of a vase, a scroll or a touch, she would always be his teacher.

Their host entered. His powerful build seemed at odds with his graceful bearing. All bowed. The Count invited Morrison and James to seat themselves on silk cushions on the tatami floor, then took his place in a rich susurrus of settling brocades.

Aided by his interpreter, the Count welcomed them warmly, saying he had long wanted to meet the legendary Morrison. He had relatives who'd been in Peking during the siege; they had spoken with awe of his valour. Despite Brinkley's warning, Morrison felt his hopes rise. Over bowls of whisked green tea, Matsukata spoke about the gold reserve, asked after mutual acquaintances and showed them the finest collection of old and rare photos of Japan that Morrison had ever seen. In response to a comment on a miniature pine in one of the photographs, he discoursed eloquently on the art of bonsai and its origins in Han Dynasty China. Not a word about ships or correspondents passed his lips and he deflected any attempt to bring the conversation round to that topic. Morrison's hopes fell once more. His leg muscles burned and cramped and rheumatism agonised his knees. When the audience was over and they all rose, he had to concentrate to avoid stumbling. Mae came into his head again, but this time it felt like a blessed relief that she was not there to see him looking so much like a pathetic old man.

'Blast this damned Oriental obfuscation!' They had barely finished their leave-taking when James expressed his opinion of the meeting with typical bluntness.

'Perhaps we shall have better luck tonight,' Morrison said. Although he considered that Brinkley and his wife were probably right after all, he didn't deem it propitious to share the thought with James. 'In any case, I suggest you do something to get some Oriental calm and patience about you before we proceed to dinner.'

When they met to share a carriage to the dinner, Morrison was intrigued to see James looking not only calm but smug.

'Saito is to tell us that the *Haimun* is free to sail at last,' James announced.

'Your source?'

'Sir Claude.'

'His source?'

'He promises it is a good one.'

Morrison again kept his doubts to himself. In front of a gracious, two-storey wooden building down a quiet lane, an aide-de-camp of Admiral Saito, a man with a deep voice and a deeper bow, welcomed them and led them into an exquisite room with walls of gold lacquer blackened by candle smoke.

Admiral Saito, the son of a samurai, had a broad forehead, melancholy lips and a heavy-lidded stare that conveyed both understanding and weariness. His hospitality, like his pedigree, was flawless: thirty-eight delicately flavoured courses, each displayed with the utmost artistry and served on a unique piece of porcelain; ethereally beautiful geishas whose long, shimmering sleeves brushed the floor as they made their fluttering entrance; and musical entertainment. The Admiral gave Morrison and James everything but the response they craved. He gave them no answer at all — and no chance to ask the question, either.

Like a rumbling volcano, James seethed all the way back to the hotel. Morrison remained silent, worn out by the anticipation, the unflagging courtesy of their host and the quantity of sake he had drunk at his urging.

James finally erupted. 'Sir Claude gave me his word!'

Morrison imagined lava trickling from the crown of James's head. 'You know what they say. An ambassador is an honest man sent abroad to lie for his country. As for giving you his word, Sir Claude has used me often and given me nothing in return but bad dinners.'

Entering the Imperial, James glanced up at the ancient bonsai pine that commanded the centre of the hotel parlour. 'Well, I may never be able to witness the battle for Port Arthur but I could write a picturesque on the art of the bonsai.'

Morrison's lips twisted into a wry smile. 'That's what they do to us,' he said, tracing the little tree's twisted, cramped branches with his finger. 'The Japanese, our editors, our diplomats, colleagues, censors, all those who would limit and control us. They tie us up with copper wires of querulousness and nitpicking when we should be out in the field doing our job. They twist and torture every impulse for greatness out of us.'

James shook his head. 'Perhaps it's time, G.E., that I gave up this dream of mine and accept that I am simply a man ahead of my time. Perhaps I should take what the Japanese offer me in the way of accreditation and hope it's more than just a sop. I shall mount my horse and take it to the line of battle along with my usual anxieties about messengers and pigeons and all the rest, and leave the revolutionary advances of which I've dreamed to future generations of correspondents.'

'It's not fair.' Morrison frowned, more distressed than he had expected he would be by James's proposed surrender.

'As in love, so in war — and especially in war correspondence — all is fair,' James replied. 'Or so they say. Not sure I believe it myself.'

'Let's give it one more shot.'

The next four days passed in futile discussion with both British and Japanese contacts; the nights for Morrison passed either in bliss or, if it was Egan's turn to enjoy Mae's company, agony. On the afternoon of the fifth day, Morrison was strolling out the door of the Imperial when Martin Egan accosted him. 'Good afternoon,' he said, greeting Morrison with his firm, American handshake and an expression of studied affability. 'I understand from Miss Perkins that we're dining together tomorrow night at the Grand.'

Morrison was grateful that Egan's smile showed no teeth. 'I look forward to it.' *What the deuce is she playing at now?* Whatever it was, he did not have a very good feeling about it. Sleeping in a comfortless bed that night, his dreams were thick with anxiety.

In Which the Correspondents' Quest for Access Is Afforded a Definitive Answer

The following day dawned cloudless and warm, a perfect summer day. Morrison had rushed to Yokohama straight after breakfast only to learn that Mae had gone yachting with her putative chaperone Mrs Goodnow and that lady's sea captain in the cliff-lined bay just south of Yokohama, which the Japanese called Negishi and the foreigners Mississippi.

He took a walk to a street where postcards were sold and distracted himself for an hour or two by shopping for war-themed postals and illustrated journals. He was particularly cheered by the find of an excellent woodblock print illustrating the battle between Japanese and Cossack cavalry on the banks of the Yalu the previous month and a magnificent triptych showing the destroyers *Hayatori* and *Asagiri* sinking Russian men o' war during a snowstorm in one of the earliest battles for Port Arthur. He returned to Kaigan Dori but since there was still no sign of the yacht, he settled himself on the veranda of the Grand with a lemonade and some English-language papers to await Mae's arrival.

Cackle-headed, that's what she is. Cackle-headed, controlling, presumptuous — and breathtakingly lovely when she finally appeared back at the hotel in a splendid white dress, windswept and sun-kissed and, best of all, wreathed in smiles at the sight of him waiting there for her.

'Honey, thank you for agreeing to come tonight. Martin's been dreadful. Threatened to break off our relationship and everything. He said he knew that we had been together because whenever you and he run into one another, you look sheepish.'

'Sheepish! He's the one who just yesterday, upon seeing me in the dining room, walked the long way round just to avoid having to say hello.'

'I know, I know,' she soothed, weaving her arm into his as they strolled into the hotel. 'He's just being childish.'

'You're not making me look forward to this evening's dinner, I must say.'

'We'll have a bully time, honey. He has promised to behave. I reminded him that he'd always liked and admired you and that the two of you were friends.'

'It is not such a great sign of friendship when friends must be reminded that they like one another,' Morrison countered glumly as they waited for the hotel boy to open her suite. 'Where's Egan now?'

'He had some meetings or interviews or something.' They entered the room. 'Let me show you some of the things I've bought since I've been here. So much silk and brocade that I had to buy a beautiful carved tea chest to hold it all. That makes thirteen pieces of luggage, by the way. Yesterday I found the most beautiful hairpins, including one made from the shinbone of a crane that I shall give to my darling sister, Pansy, and matching ones of tortoiseshell for my dear mama.' She burbled on, giving him scant opportunity to return to the topic of the evening's entertainment. When she ran out of things to show him, she related how she'd spent the previous evening lounging about her suite in a satin dressing gown whilst eating Japanese bonbons and reading about the life of an ancient courtesan. Then, scarcely pausing to draw breath, she launched into details of Mrs Goodnow's affair with her sea captain. 'He lashes her to the mast, imagine that!'

Mae pressed herself against the bedpost and held out the silk tie of her dressing gown. 'Imagine that!' she repeated. 'Can you?'

Morrison could.

Her skin was seawater-salty and rosy from the sun. He took her like a sailor, urgently and hard against the bedpost. He wanted, on this day more than ever, to fill her up completely and in every way possible. She responded with a hunger equal to his passion. She would go to dinner, he was determined, with his impress upon her every cell.

By the time they untwined their bodies, slick and limp with bliss, it was getting late. Singing to herself, she went to run a bath. Morrison stretched, looking around for reading matter. Something on her dressing table caught his eye. He picked it up and his heart jolted. It was a ticket for passage on the *Mongolia*, which was sailing for San Francisco on the twenty-sixth of June, only five days away. The passenger's name was listed as Miss Mae Ruth Perkins.

He rushed into the bathroom. 'What's this, Maysie?'

'Oh, honey, I had to go home eventually. Neither of us will be here forever. You knew that.'

Morrison grabbed a towel and held it to his face. His nose was bleeding like his heart.

The men shook hands with excruciating cordiality. Morrison, still wan from his nosebleed, perceived Egan to be more square-jawed and ruddy-cheeked than usual. He took some comfort from the fact that Mae had chosen to wear the bracelet he'd bought her in China.

An eager young Western man entered the dining room with a striking Japanese woman on his arm. Mae waved familiarly. The man waved back. The Japanese woman smiled and bowed.

'He's the nephew of the financier J.P. Morgan,' Mae explained. 'Our families know each other back home. I met up with him just the other day.'

Morrison and Egan looked over at the couple with interest. 'And the woman?'

'She was a geisha in Kyoto. A very famous one too, apparently. He was mad for her at first sight. Head over heels. She didn't like him at first, wouldn't even think of going with a Westerner. But he finally won her over and is marrying her later this year, here in Yokohama. But since her family won't accept the match, the two of them are going to live in France.'

'Does he speak Japanese?' Egan asked.

'No,' Mae said. 'Not more than two words. That's about the extent of her English too. And I don't think either speaks much French. The truth is that they can barely understand a word the other says.'

'That would make it a fairly typical relationship for a man and a woman,' Morrison quipped.

Although Mae insisted it wasn't that funny, Egan laughed and Morrison liked him for that.

Morrison and Egan, in truth, had many topics of common interest. To Morrison's relief the conversation proceeded more easily from then on. In his father's day, such a situation — had such a situation been conceivable — might have ended in a duel. *It really is a new century,* he thought.

However, when Egan proudly mentioned his acquaintance with the famous novelist and reporter R. Harding Davis, Morrison could not resist at least one thrust of the foil. 'Of course you would have heard the anecdote about him and Stephen Crane, the author of the Civil War novel *The Red Badge of Courage?*'

Egan admitted he had not.

'Do tell,' encouraged Mae.

'Well, I'm sure you're well aware that Davis's infinite conceit of himself is at least as well known as his books.'

'I wouldn't —'

'So the two of them, Davis and Crane, had gone out to dine. The restaurant was crowded. As there were not enough tables, the pair pressed themselves on to one already occupied by two others. Davis thanked the men whose table they were joining, adding with something of a patronising air: "Perhaps you might like to know to whom you have done this favour. I am Mr Harding Davis; this is my friend Mr Stephen Crane." With ready wit, the man replied, "You might like to know who has favoured you. I am John the Baptist and this is my friend Mr Jesus H. Christ."'

Mae laughed heartily and Egan did his best to make it seem as though the joke was not partly at his own expense. Morrison wondered if Egan knew of her imminent departure and was stabbed again by the memory of finding her ticket just hours earlier.

Egan asked about the *Haimun* and the conversation turned to the adventures various correspondents had experienced trying to get to the front.

342

Mae tipped her head to one side, observing them coolly. 'I hear both of you talk about the war all the time. You analyse the casualty figures as though discussing the score of a sporting contest and you tell amusing stories about the ways correspondents endeavour to elude the censors. But I never hear you talking about the ethics of fighting itself. Men, in my experience, seem far more tested by the morality of a woman than they do by the morality of war.' Her tone was matter-of-fact. Morrison found himself exchanging glances with Egan. Both men watched as, having spoken her piece, she tucked into her braised sweetbreads *aux petit pois* with her usual gusto.

'You know,' Egan remarked after a pause, 'the great Lord Byron hated to watch a woman eat. He liked to think of the fairer sex as too ethereal to require actual nourishment. If a woman insisted on sharing his table, he could not stand to see her consume more than the tiniest portion of lobster salad, washed down with champagne.'

Mae replaced her fork and knife on the table. 'Well, I could not stand to see Lord Byron then. Who are men to set these rules, anyway?' She turned her attention to the *terrine de foie gras.*

Egan gave Morrison a conspiratorial look. Morrison sensed his rival was on the verge of serious misstep. He was not disappointed.

'Men always set the rules,' Egan said with cheery assurance. 'It's the way of the world.'

Mae set her toast back down on her plate. 'Not of my world. And in my experience, when men prefer their women to eat like birds, it's so they can keep them in gilded cages. This is 1904 — it's the twentieth century — and I, for one, will not be kept in a cage. By anyone.' She dabbed at her lips with her napkin and smiled sweetly. 'If you two hadn't noticed. Oh, and before either of you ask me again, honestly, I don't know whose baby it was. And, yes, I'm sad. More than I can say. And it really is better that I don't marry anyone. It's not that I don't love either of you. I love you both. But I don't think I am suited to the institution of marriage. As you both know, I shall be sailing for America in a few days' time. Now, which of you would like to claim me tomorrow and which the day after? This evening I shall rest with the correspondent John Fox Jnr, whom I met the other day whilst walking at Mississippi Bay.'

The modern duel, won by a woman.

In Which Lionel James Hoists Anchor, Morrison and Miss Franklin Find Themselves Adrift in the Floating World, and We Are Told What Happens in the End to Men's Love For Women

'Mast, huts, gas engine, dynamo and some sixty pounds of dockyard fittings …' Morrison looked up from the piece of paper James handed him and shook his head. 'This is quite an inventory.'

James's hand sliced through the air. 'Sell it all.'

'And the wireless station at Wei Hai Wei?'

'To be dismantled. Dodwell's, the chartering agents in Shanghai, should be able to organise the return passage to America for the wireless operators. Please ensure they have sufficient money to get to New York. You may take it from my Shanghai bank account. I'll give up the charter of the *Haimun* myself. I cannot waste another moment. At least the Japanese have made good on their promise to give me permission to get to the front. Whilst Port Arthur's citizens will all be speaking Japanese before any correspondent witnesses what is going on there, if I leave now I'll at least be able to see the fall of Liaoyang with my own eyes.'

The men were strolling along the outer bank of the moat of Tokio's Imperial Palace. The day was overcast, the air muggy. Morrison reached for a handkerchief to wipe the sweat off his brow. He found Mae's, the one she'd given him secretly when they'd parted that first time at Mountain-Sea Pass. Its perfume had long faded. He mopped the perspiration off his face and stuffed the handkerchief back into his pocket.

'I still can't believe Bell's last telegram.'

'It was harsh,' Morrison agreed. Their editor had informed them that a Japanese contact in London had asked him if all *The Times* correspondents had died, as so little had been heard from them.

'As if he doesn't know what we've been trying to do! It puts me in a white-hot rage to be so insulted.'

'It is a wicked and brutal joke,' Morrison agreed, for he too had been stung. *Where have these months gone?*

'Will you remain here?'

'No, I will return to China. Blunt has been covering for me and deserves a holiday. I'm sure I can be more useful in Peking, anyway. When do you leave?'

'This evening. And you?'

'In two days.' The men shook hands. 'You have made a great fight of it,' said Morrison. 'And you were, indeed, ahead of your time. But as far as I can see, you have had against you the Japanese general staff, the British minister, all the press correspondents including our own Brinkley, and the foreign department of *The Times* as well. I suggest you make your peace with the Almighty because if He turns against you too, you are forever damned.'

346

That evening was Martin Egan's designated final night with Mae. Desperately eager for distraction, Morrison prowled the lobby of the Imperial in the hope of bumping into some correspondents he knew who were planning an expedition to the Yoshiwara, Tokio's red-light district. He saw them arriving but before he could join them, an attractive and modishly dressed young lady greeted him. 'Good evening, Dr Morrison.'

She looked familiar but he could not immediately place her. 'Miss …'

'Franklin. Eleanor.'

He smiled. 'Of course. Last time I saw you, you were …'

She gestured down at her skirts. 'Not trussed up.'

Morrison laughed and was about to say something when he saw Miss Franklin's eye had been caught by something. He turned to see the spectacle of Mae passing through the lobby on Egan's arm, attired in a splendid kimono, hair lacquered and shaped in the manner of a geisha. Her face and neck were powdered white, her lips dotted with colour like a plump cherry. She and Egan were on their way to a reception in the hotel ballroom.

'Funny, stunning and dreadful at the same time, don't you think?' Miss Franklin remarked. Morrison noticed an unwonted strain in her voice, though she affected nonchalance. 'For a woman of such respectable background, she *does* carry on.'

Morrison had to admit it was true.

'I understand the male fascination with the geisha,' Miss Franklin said. 'After all, the point of her is to bolster the ego of the man.' Here, she looked over again at the couple, who'd stopped to chat with some friends, and her gaze lingered on the figure of Egan. 'I'd thought,' she said ruefully, 'oh, I don't know why but I had higher expectations of him. Silly, really. Anyway, it is quite astonishing that Western women, who are just beginning to carve out some form of independence for themselves, would seek to emulate such a creature, even in fun. Did you know that a Japanese woman can be divorced simply for disobedience, jealousy, ill health or talkativeness?'

'If the same standards applied in the West,' Morrison conceded, 'there should not be too many marriages left. Certainly not many of my own acquaintance would survive.'

Miss Franklin laughed. 'I like your sense of humour, Dr Morrison. I could take a whisky right now; could you?'

One of the other correspondents approached to enquire if Morrison was still interested in visiting the Yoshiwara.

'The Yoshiwara?' Miss Franklin exclaimed. 'May I come too?'

'It is a place of courtesans,' the man said with an awkward smile.

'Oh, I know that,' she said. 'I shall run up to my room and change into my masculine attire. No one shall be the wiser. I'll be down in ten minutes.'

The correspondent looked at Morrison, who shrugged.

The group's *jinrikisha* pullers deposited them at the magnificent Sensoji Temple, on the edge of the Nightless City. They wended their way through the close, lantern-lit streets, the air full of music and the scents of jasmine and burning orange peels, the latter which the Japanese used to ward off mosquitoes. 'The world of flowers and willows, they call it,' Miss Franklin said. A sing-song girl clattered by on her *geita*, trailed by her maidservant. The melancholy notes of the *shamisen*, plucked from braided silk strings with an ivory plectrum, drifted out from one of the three-storey pleasure quarters punctuated by the shouts of men at drinking games. Their little group turned into an even narrower lane, where ladies of the night sat side by side in their barred enclosures, motionless as statues, great red lanterns throwing a pink blush on their whitened, mask-like features as the gold and silver threads in their kimonos winked at passers-by.

By 1904, though Tokio's more fashionable demimonde had drifted elsewhere, the Yoshiwara still offered an abundance of interesting restaurants and wine shops. The other men were keen to visit one of the few pleasure houses where the women were agreeable to serving men *bataa-kusai* — 'stinking of butter' — as they labelled Westerners. Morrison, not in the mood, was glad to have the excuse of keeping Miss Franklin company.

'Do you find her beautiful?'

They were seated in a small restaurant drinking sake and eating dishes chosen for them by the owner. Immediately upon asking her question, Miss Franklin poked at the mysterious blond vegetable shavings that writhed upon grilled eggplant like something alive. Morrison sensed that she was avoiding his eyes.

He did not need to ask to whom Miss Franklin was referring. 'She has an undeniable magnetism,' he answered after a moment.

Miss Franklin nodded, solemn. She pincered a small grilled fish with her chopsticks. The two of them ate in silence for a while, lost in their own thoughts.

'They call this the "floating world". Did you know that?' she asked, breaking the silence.

Morrison nodded. 'The world of pleasure-seeking and entertainment.'

'And more generally, in Buddhist terms, the earthly existence of sorrow and suffering from which we all seek release. The Buddhists say that all suffering comes from desire. Not just the desires of the flesh, but also the desires to own, to rule, to collect, to conquer, to possess, to have things go the way we want them to.'

'I've heard this. And it makes sense to me from a rational perspective. But to be honest, I'm not sure I know what life without desire would be.'

'Neither do I,' she said with a wistfulness that seemed difficult to reconcile with her normally forthright nature. 'Sometimes I wish I did.'

Morrison looked at her curiously. It was as though a shuttered window had opened a crack and then closed again. Recalling the way she had looked at Egan earlier, and remembering their first conversation on the *Haimun*, he thought that perhaps he understood.

The following day, Morrison packed, paid off his hotel bill, then took the train to Yokohoma, where Mae was waiting for him at the Grand in a subdued mood. They both knew that this parting would be the final one. He would not stay beyond the one night. There was no point.

They made love for a long time, and tenderly, after which she surprised him by laughing.

'I'm so happy,' she said.

'That we're to part?'

'No, honey. Of course not. It's just, well, you know me.'

'I'm not sure I do. After all.'

'We're going to part, and that's so sad. I have loved you dearly, more than you could know and probably more than I was prepared to. But life is funny. It gives us these beautiful, crazy experiences, it gave me you and it gave you me, and then it snatches it all away again and we're flung back out again into the mystery. And that's something to savour, too.'

'I will miss you, Maysie.'

'You'll get over me. Men's hearts are like that.'

He started to protest but she shushed him with a finger to his lips. 'I've been reading about a Japanese poetess who lived maybe a thousand years ago. She was a lady-in-waiting at the court, and the most beautiful woman in all of Japan, with hair so long it touched the floor and eyebrows like as crescent moons in a clear sky. The men were crazy about her. She usually slept alone in a room with curtains of crystal beads and decorations of tortoiseshell. She wrote in a poem that a man's love, no matter how brightly it burns, will in the end fade and fall like old petals.'

A pause, a breath. 'And a woman's?' Morrison asked.

'We keep everything here.' She patted her chest.

'What happened in the end? Did she find love?'

'She grew old. She was cast out from the court and died a crazy beggar-woman, haunted by the spirits of the men who had perished for the love of her. She was punished for her freedom and her beauty. Women usually are. You can't deny it.'

The following morning, he walked away from the hotel in a daze. Then he turned and there she was, leaning halfway out of the window of her room, waving him farewell. He fixed the picture in his mind.

In Which the Correspondent Corresponds and at Least One Love Story Ends Happily

Morrison tipped the concierge at the hotel generously to ensure that his ticket to Kobe would be for a train with both a sleeping carriage and dining car. It had neither.

The train was packed with army reservists and members of the Army Service Corps headed for the front. At every station they embarked, solemn-faced, young, flush with pride and uncertainty, their packs smelling of pickles and dried fish. Mothers and wives in dark blue 'victory colour' kimonos farewelled them from underneath banners inscribed with their names and to the bombast of military marches played by schoolchildren in brass bands. The train pulled out of each station to cries of '*Banzai! Banzai!*' Morrison took notes out of a lifetime's habit, but his heart was not with his eyes or his pencil.

At one station, the train stopped long enough for him to send a telegram: FAREWELL MY DARLING. GOD BLESS YOU AND GIVE YOU MUCH HAPPINESS. ALWAYS THINKING OF YOU. ERNEST.

At Kobe's Oriental Hotel, Morrison met up with a correspondent who had witnessed both the crossing of the Yalu and a battle at the Manchurian town of Chu Lien Cheng. 'The

Japanese fighting must be seen to be believed,' the man raved. 'They are devils unchained. Nothing can stay in their path.'

He walked out onto the beach, past fishermen laying sardines to dry on straw mats and children playing by the water's edge as their mothers squatted nearby mending nets. Overcome by unreasonable hope, he turned his steps to the Telegraph Office. He had left her his itinerary. The clerk checked. Nothing had come for him. He scribbled out a second telegram and handed it to the clerk. JUST ARRIVED. LEAVING TOMORROW. AM WRITING MUCH LOVE FROM ERNEST. ORIENTAL HOTEL. Restless, he strolled to the ancient port of Hyogo, barely taking in the fine temples and shrines. Marooned by language, he spoke to no one. Returning to the hotel, he asked the desk if anything had come for him. Nothing had. *What is she doing that she cannot find the time for a telegram?* He could guess.

The Japanese press claimed the Manchurian city of Liaoyang had fallen. *That would be good news indeed.* Morrison wondered if James had made it in time to witness the battle.

He slept poorly.

The following morning, just before ten o'clock, the hotel delivered a telegram. It had been sent from Yokohama at eight past nine. NEVER FORGET YOU AND DEEPLY GRIEVED AT PARTING. HAVE PLEASANT VOYAGE TO PEKING. SURELY LEAVING ON THE *MONGOLIA*. MUCH LOVE MAYSIE.

Morrison instantly wired back: *DORIC* LEAVING TONIGHT MIDNIGHT ARRIVES NAGASAKI SUNDAY EARLY. PROCEEDING SAME EVENING SHANGHAI ARRIVING EARLY TUESDAY. YOUR KIND TELEGRAM JUST RECEIVED GIVEN ME MUCH PLEASURE FOR I WAS WORRYING GREATLY NOT HAVING HEARD FROM YOU YESTERDAY. ALL LOVING HEARTFELT WISHES FOR YOUR HAPPINESS AND CONTENTMENT. ERNEST.

On deck, Morrison discovered in his pocket a pamphlet he'd picked up when waiting for Mae a few days earlier. Having made the acquaintance of a Japanese merchant on the same boat who was supplying canvas tents to the army, he asked him to translate it. The man read it and frowned. 'The author, Kotoku Shusui, is a famous journalist. He says that if war promotes the cause of humanity, ethics and freedom, that is good. But if it is to advance the careers of politicians and military men, and benefit speculators with the result that people's wealth is plundered and their children must die, we must firmly oppose it.'

'I see.' Morrison frowned, unexpectedly rattled by the recollection of Mae's sharp little commentary on the morality of men and war. He could have argued, of course. But that would have given Egan an advantage. It seemed so important then, the competition. It was over, all of it, and he needed to accept that. The story was finished, his last telegram the coda. He should not think of her again. He and the Japanese merchant stared into the waves.

The *Doric* stopped at Nagasaki around four o'clock on the afternoon of the twenty-sixth of June. MISS PERKINS GRAND HOTEL YOKOHAMA. JUST STARTING FOR SHANGHAI. MAY YOUR VOYAGE HOME BE ALL SUNSHINE. YOUR RETURN WHILST LEAVING MANY DESOLATE IN THE ORIENT WILL SURELY MAKE GLAD THE HEARTS OF THOSE DEAR TO YOU IN OAKLAND WHO ARE SO EAGERLY WAITING TO GIVE YOU WELCOME. I TRUST THAT AMIDST YOUR DISTRACTIONS YOU WILL SOMETIMES FIND LEISURE TO WRITE TO ME AND WILL NOT LET ME SLIP ALTOGETHER FROM YOUR MEMORY I KNOW NOT IF FATE WILL EVER PERMIT US TO COME TOGETHER AGAIN BUT WHATEVER HAPPENS I SHALL ALWAYS TREASURE YOUR MEMORY. AND GRATEFULLY RECALL THOSE HAPPY MOMENTS I HAVE SPENT WITH YOU. GOODBYE MY DEAR. ERNEST.

By the time the steamer departed on its final leg, it was four in the morning the following day. No telegram had come in reply. He was not sure why he'd expected one might. *She must have gone in the* Mongolia *after all,* he wrote in his journal. *Being always under the influence of the last-comer, she would at the time of leaving have forgotten all about me.*

Exhausted, he lay on his bunk. The cabin was airless and hot. The ship's whistle blew continuously. Sweating and tossing on the small bunk, Morrison gave up on sleep and opened his journal once more. *But what does it matter? The sooner that it ended, the better. It has been a curious episode in my career, this passionate attachment.*

He felt himself on the move again, for him a state much like home.

Breakfast consisted of a cup of terrible coffee and a greasy bologna sausage at the same table as a man who had been horribly disfigured, he explained to Morrison with disconcerting good cheer, by the blowing out of his rifle breech. It was stifling below deck and insupportable above. Trying to read on a long chair on deck, he imagined Maysie in her elegant stateroom on the *Mongolia,* singing for the other passengers in the first-class music room, playing her little food game with the fine meals in the dining saloon. He suddenly recalled her telling him that Mrs Goodnow had said that once she'd been 'kissed' by another woman she'd never look back. Mae had declared she was going to get a Japanese maid who would kiss her all the way to America. He wondered if she'd done so, and lingered a moment on that thought. Dozing off, he woke up with sore legs, a headache and sunburn, as well as the sense that beauty, comfort and pleasure had been leached from his world.

The merchant had disembarked at Nagasaki. The only remaining diversion was one Miss Florence E. Smith, tall, splendidly shaped and off to Shanghai to marry her lover in the Standard Oil Company. Morrison could have sworn he'd seen her in Yokohama in the company of Major Seeman. When the *Doric* berthed in Shanghai the next day, her lover was nowhere in sight and Miss Smith was awash in tears. Just as Morrison thought he'd worked it out — another faithless woman, another tragic tale — and considered offering to console her himself, the lover appeared and Miss Smith sprang into his arms. *What a fortunate pair. Such complete happiness. A love that is most beautiful to witness.*

Morrison's heart contracted suddenly around the thought of Maysie. It occurred to him that she might, at that very moment, be unwrapping a pile of his letters and reading them to, perhaps, the captain of the *Mongolia*. He tried to smile at the image.

In Which It Is Seen That Heat Lingers
Even as the Earth Cools

In Peking, the leafy tendrils of the willow trees whispered to the waters of the Grand Canal and the moat around the Forbidden City. Pendulous white flowers hung off the cedrela. The markets were ripe with stacks of Indian corn and melons. A racket of cicadas welcomed Morrison home. After the oppressively moist heat of Japan, Morrison revelled in the blazing aridity of Peking.

The moment his *mafoo* collected him from the station, Morrison had a premonition. 'Where's Kuan? *Kuan tsai na-li?*' He mulled over the *mafoo*'s hesitant answer, a Chinese phrase that translated as 'there is no relationship' or 'there's nothing to be concerned about', an ambiguous saying that only deepened his apprehension.

Kuan and Yu-ti had run away together. No one knew where they had gone, but there was a rumour it was to Shanghai to join the revolutionary anti-Ch'ing underground. Morrison professed himself shocked. But then he thought about it and it began to make sense. It was clear enough that Kuan and Yu-ti had been childhood sweethearts. And then there was the admiration Kuan held for Professor Ho and, more tellingly, the interest Ho and the others took in Kuan. Not surprisingly, Cook was furious and humiliated by his wife's betrayal. He had refused to speak to anyone for more than a week now. The household, Morrison learned, was much relieved at his return.

On his desk, hidden under his blotter, Morrison found a letter from Kuan, written in careful English and requesting him to destroy it after reading. Kuan apologised for not saying anything about his plans and for leaving without saying goodbye. He told Morrison he and Yu-ti would always remember his kindness. They hoped that one day they would see him again, in a China that was free of the curse of the Ch'ing, a China that was strong and sovereign. He trusted that Morrison would understand and forgive. In a postscript, couched in the politest of terms, he hoped that Morrison's faith in Japan's good intentions towards China were not misplaced.

As Morrison burned the letter, he couldn't help feeling a grudging admiration for his Boy. *He has followed his heart.*

Ten days after the battle for Liaoyang, Lionel James's report reached the paper:

A sleet of lead ... Japanese infantry is not to know failure ... mown down in hundreds ... dressing stations of the field hospital. All were filled with double their capacity ... casualties ... at the lowest computation were not less than 10,000 ... many bodies will never be found until the crops are cut ... the Japanese army, after five days of the fiercest fighting the world has seen since the American Civil War ... were in occupation of Liaoyang.

The baking heat of summer departed. The earth cooled. A sweet melancholy settled over the capital, sung into being by the plaintive cries of the grape-sellers roaming the *hutong* with the fat purple fruit stacked in leaf-lined baskets on their carrying-poles. The light grew sharp and lucid. As the Harvest Moon gave way to the Chrysanthemum Moon, wealthy Chinese donned sable-lined satin gowns and undervests of lambskin, and the poor dressed in thick jackets and trousers of cotton wadding. Fear grew in the eyes of the poorest: it would soon be the season for the mule carts to make their daily dawn rounds of the enceintes to collect the frozen bodies of the homeless. In north China now, there were more homeless than ever, thanks to the war.

Dumas came to the capital with his wife for a visit. They informed Morrison that she was expecting. Morrison congratulated them, eyes misting with joy and envy.

'Have you heard?' Mrs Dumas asked. 'That nice American correspondent Martin Egan is engaged to be married.'

'To whom?' Morrison's heart slammed in his chest.

'I believe you know her.'

Dumas hastened to clarify. 'Eleanor Franklin.'

'Miss Franklin?' Morrison thought of their conversation that night in the Yoshiwara and smiled.

'You look surprised,' Mrs Dumas remarked. 'And don't you ever think of taking a bride? They say married men live longer, you know.'

His eyes met those of Dumas, and he knew that his friend was thinking of the same quip: *Or does it just seem that way?*

'What's the secret?' Dumas's wife asked, looking from one to the other.

'I wish I knew,' Morrison replied.

When his visitors left, he opened the glass front of the rosewood curio cabinet in his parlour and wrapped his hand around the piece of imperial jade he had looted from the palace during the siege. As it warmed in his hand, he felt for the crack in its surface. It was a flaw that endeared it to him even as it confounded him, proof of the elusiveness of perfection.

In Which Morrison Dreams an Old Dream, Attempts to Account for the Unaccountable and an Illusion Vanishes

It had been a strange year, this Dragon Year, full of drama, exhilaration, optimism and risk. As for it being auspicious for marriage — sheer superstition. Mae never wrote. Morrison used a single word to express his feelings about that in his journal: *disappointed*. He remembered something else Professor Ho had told him about fox spirits that time aboard the boat to Chefoo — that they were by their nature ephemeral, transitory. 'When a fox spirit departs,' Ho said, 'the illusion gutters for a moment, then is gone. A star twinkles in the sky, a shadow flickers on the ground, wounds heal, scars disappear and life goes on.'

In the middle of December, Morrison received a parcel from his mother. In her letter, which she had written several weeks earlier, she said the mercury in Geelong had already topped one hundred degrees. She told him the house smelled of Christmas, thanks to the brandy-soaked pudding that hung wrapped in cheesecloth in the kitchen, slowly ripening. She and his father were looking forward to the break, which they would spend as usual in Queenscliff. His father anticipated good hunting of bandicoots and native bear. As he read of that and other news of home, Morrison could hear his mother's warm Yorkshire accent in his head.

The parcel included a new anthology of Australian verse. He read into the wee hours. *Heartily homesick*, he wrote in his journal before turning in. That night, he dreamed the old dream of running through the Victorian bush. He could smell the eucalyptus in the air, hear the ringing of bellbirds, the screech of cockatoos, the hum of insects and his own panting breath. In the dream he was young, and whatever he was chasing lay just around the corner.

The year's end was Morrison's time for summing up. Methodically, he squared his blotting paper, filled his inkwell and pulled on his sleeve-guards. The red leather binding of his journal, squeaky-firm at the start of the year, fell open easily to the final, faintly lined pages.

He entered the money spent on rickshas, servants and hotels, each penny fretfully counted, followed by an account of assets acquired and money saved, each pound proudly noted. Then there were snatches of gossip, remembered jokes and puns, observations about the war and politics. In his compressed, fluid hand, Morrison ordered and fixed all of these for posterity.

He stared at his ink-stained hands with their long, square-tipped fingers. The veins stood out, blue against the freckled skin, his knuckles pink and dry. The spray of freckles. *I love your opinionated, cantankerous intelligence.* Closing his eyes, he heard again her easy laugh. He felt her hot insistent breath on his ear and neck, the urgent grip of her thighs. He saw once more the flash of her eyes, a blend of seduction and defiance.

The last of the day's light, yellow as old parchment, faded behind the high latticed windows. The titles etched into the leather bindings of the books on his shelves grew indistinct and the room's lime-and-plaster walls exhaled a chilly breath. Despite the best efforts of the wheezing kettle atop the potbelly stove to introduce some humidity, the air scratched his throat, stubbornly dry. His tea grew cold. Mice scrabbled in the alleyway and a scrap collector called for bottles and rags. In the brazier, coals shifted and sighed.

From across the courtyard came the sizzle and spit of something frying in a wok; he imagined that he could smell garlic. His Boy would call him into dinner soon. Dinner for one. *Dining alone again. Much pleased with the company.* Morrison's lip curled sardonically. *At least I amuse myself.*

Turning up the flame in the spirit lamp, he snugged his scarf around his neck. He dipped his nib in ink and tapped it against the rim of the bottle. *How did I meet Maysie? War broke out … Dumas and I arrived at Mountain-Sea Pass. It was a night of perfect moonlight almost as light as day. It has done me much good to meet her. She has stimulated and rejuvenated me …* He wrote and wrote.

Blotting the ink, Morrison reread the final pages and, with a small sigh, closed the journal. *I have the presentiment that I will meet her again.* His joints ached; all the old wounds were giving him trouble.

He almost called Kuan's name, then remembered. 'Chan!'

'Yes, Master.' His new Boy, a man of forty-five, stepped smartly into the room.

'Fetch my *p'aotzu.* I'm going for a walk.'

'Very cold.'

'I know.'

Near Ch'ien-men Gate, Morrison came upon a theatre. An opera was in progress. Gongs clashed and a line of young acrobats ran on stage, each carrying a gaily painted rice-paper lantern. They twisted, tumbled and twirled to the insistent music of clappers, drums and flutes, the lanterns calligraphing strokes of light on the air like golden ink. Finally, they piled one on the other to form a fan, which opened, closed, and opened again, this time as a field of peonies, setting the scene for the opening of *Peony Pavilion*. The second piece was a popular athletic pantomime about a fight between men in a darkened inn, each unable to tell if grappling with friend or foe. The final piece brought the audience to its feet as a lithe maiden played by a young boy called Mei Lan-fang, ribbons fluttering from his costume, danced and sang the part of a celestial sent by the gods to scatter flowers over the earth, creating colour and beauty where there had been none.

After the final applause, the paper-lantern footlights were extinguished, and the rackety crowds streamed out. Unwilling to face the night so soon, and lost in thought, Morrison stared blankly at the scrolls hanging on either side of the empty stage. *Once the play is done, the tragedy, the comedy, the fallings-apart and comings-together all vanish like a dream.* Eventually he stood. Pulling his collar up and stuffing his hands deep into his pockets, he began the walk home. Fresh snow fell, creating a new landscape of jade and silver, covering up his footsteps.

In Which, By Way of Afterword, We Note That It Is True That …

With half a million combatants on either side, the Russo-Japanese War escalated into the largest-scale conflict the world had ever seen. Despite the initial efforts of the Japanese to restrict access to the front, it also become the most widely reported war in history to that point. In fact, as James once wrote to Morrison, some Japanese generals grew so fond of the coverage that they would delay the start of a battle if the correspondents had not yet arrived. Almost no one ever referred to it any more as Morrison's War.

Port Arthur fell to the Japanese on 2 January 1905. The war itself didn't conclude until September that year, with the signing of the Treaty of Portsmouth. Morrison travelled to New Hampshire for the negotiations and US President Theodore Roosevelt won a Nobel Prize for his role in mediating the peace. By then, each side had suffered hundreds of thousands of casualties. The fighting flattened more than two hundred Chinese villages and left nearly three thousand hectares of fields trampled. Thousands of Chinese perished and countless others lost their homes and livelihoods.

In 1911, a coalition of revolutionary forces overthrew the Ch'ing Dynasty and established the Republic of China. In early 1912,

Viceroy Yuan Shih-k'ai became President of the Republic and Morrison quit journalism to become Yuan's adviser. The Avenue of the Well of the Princely Mansions — Wangfujing — was for some time named Morrison Street in English in the Australian's honour.

Following several other ill-fated attachments, Morrison proposed to his winsome new secretary, the New Zealander Jenny Wark Robin, atop the Tartar Wall. He was fifty and she twenty-three when they married; he worried that he might get a nosebleed at the wedding. Morrison died of illness seven years later, in 1920, just after making his final journal entry, and she three years after that. They were survived by three children.

Martin Egan and Eleanor Franklin married in 1905 and went on to edit the *Manila Times* together. She achieved international renown for her reporting from the Mesopotamian front during World War I. When she died in 1925, her pallbearers included Herbert Hoover, General James G. Harbord and *Saturday Evening Post* editor George Horace Lorimer. Author Jack London, who travelled at least once on the *Haimun*, reportedly wanted to call his semi-autobiographical 1909 novel *Martin Egan* after his good friend but Egan objected that it was London's own story and so London titled it *Martin Eden* instead.

Lionel James retired from *The Times* in 1913 and served with the British Army in World War I, after which he managed a racing stable and stud farm, wrote books and did occasional broadcasts for the BBC before his death in 1955.

Mae Ruth Perkins married an Oakland real-estate developer about ten years after her sojourn in China and Japan. She died in her seventies in 1957, leaving no children — only the odd milliners' bill, some yellowed clippings from the Oakland social pages and a formidable collection of love letters.

In Which the Author
Gratefully Acknowledges ...

Although *A Most Immoral Woman* is first and foremost a fiction, it is inspired by real people and real events.

The idea for the novel came to me while reading Peter Thompson and Robert Macklin's 2004 biography of George Ernest Morrison, *The Man Who Died Twice* (republished in 2007 as *The Life and Adventures of Morrison of China*). Fascinated by the authors' brief discussion of Morrison's affair with Mae and wanting more information, I turned to my bookshelf and found Cyril Pearl's 1967 classic biography *Morrison of Peking*, and was then sufficiently intrigued to track down Mae's family archive with its phenomenal collection of love letters from admirers including Willie Vanderbilt Jnr and Congressman John Wesley Gaines, as well as the long-suffering, thrice-engaged George Bew. Of all the written sources I consulted, Morrison's own diaries and letters and the Pearl biography were most central to my understanding of the man himself. Another very important historical source was Peter Slattery's *Reporting the Russo-Japanese War, 1904–5: Lionel James's first wireless transmissions to* The Times (Global Oriental, Folkestone, Kent, England, 2004). I thank Dr Slattery for permission to quote from and draw on so many aspects of this fascinating book in my portrayal of Lionel James's character, work and relationship with Morrison.

I profoundly appreciate the support given to this project by the Mitchell Library, State Library of New South Wales, which granted me permission to freely and creatively rework excerpts from documents, letters and diaries in their vast and authoritative collection, the G.E. Morrison Papers. I wish especially to thank Jennifer Broomhead, Intellectual Property and Copyright Librarian of the Original Materials Branch. As I promised Ms Broomhead, although I have taken many of Morrison's own words out of their original context for use in fictional dialogue, thoughts and journal entries, I have never intentionally used them against his spirit or character.

I also wish to thank the California Historical Society, which gave me permission to use excerpts and quotations from the George C. Perkins Family Papers (MS 1676), in particular the letters of George C. Perkins. Maida Counts was the enthusiastic and diligent researcher in Oakland who combed through the George C. Perkins Family Papers and other archives on my behalf, offered thoughtful insights on Mae's character and social context, and made valuable comments on the manuscript.

The Times of London kindly gave me permission to quote extracts from reports, including those written by Lionel James on the war.

I am very grateful to the Bundanon Trust for granting me a month's residency to work on this project in the Writer's Cottage at Bundanon, the bush property on the Shoalhaven River bequeathed to Australian artists by the painter Arthur Boyd. I am also indebted to Varuna for a Retreat Fellowship of three weeks in the Writers' House in the Blue Mountains.

The Australian National University made me a Visiting Fellow at the Division of Pacific and Asian History in the Research School of Pacific and Asian Studies, giving me access to university libraries and the important work done by ANU scholars in transcribing Morrison's diaries and letters. I am most grateful to Professor Geremie R. Barmé, who encouraged this project in more ways than I can say, pointed me to sources I would not otherwise have found, and took the time to read and comment on an early draft.

I am hugely appreciative of the generosity, enthusiasm and support for my research afforded me by director Zhang Jianguo and his team at the Weihai Municipal Archives in China and local Weihai historian and photographer Yang Jichen; by China's preeminent Morrison scholar, Ms Dou Kun; Ms Li Yan, director of a documentary on Morrison for China Central Television; Tianjin historian and preservationist Fang Zhaolin; and James Yang, Director of the Executive Office of the Astor House Hotel in Tianjin.

I also thank Shiona Airlie, the biographer of Reginald Johnston and Stewart Lockhart; Lily Lynn; Janice Braun of Mills College; Jackie Ginn; Penny Mendelsohnn of the Oakland Museum; Heike Christian Bargmann; Peter French; Glenn Koch, who graciously shared his collection of 'Poodle Dog' (Le Poulet) memorabilia; N.P. Maling, Mae's first cousin three times removed and the family genealogist; Robert Thompson, then editor of *The Times* of London and now publisher and editor of the *Wall Street Journal* (as well as long-time friend and lovely landlord); and writer and historian extraordinaire Sang Ye. I appreciate that Tim Smith, Sophie Hamley of the Cameron Creswell Agency, Dr Claire Roberts and the talented young writer Anna Westbrook all took the time to read drafts of the novel and offer thoughtful comments and suggestions.

My former agent Lesley McFadzean at the Cameron Creswell Agency found *A Most Immoral Woman* its happy home at Fourth Estate with the superb publisher Linda Funnell, to whom I owe more than I can say. Jo Butler was my stellar and meticulous editor.

A Most Immoral Woman is a novel. Any blame for distortion, historical inaccuracy or simply a playful approach to chronological and other facts lies with me, the novelist, and in no way reflects upon the scholarship of the historians, archivists and others who so generously shared with me their insights and resources.